Lord

D0628482

Published by Audrey Harrison

© Copyright 2018 Audrey Harrison

Find more about the author and contact details at the end of this book.

*

This book was proof read by Joan Kelley. Read more about Joan at the end of this story, but if you need her, you may reach her at <u>oh1kelley@gmail.com</u>.

Chapter 1

Hampshire 1811

The large wooden door was flung open and slammed into the library shelving. The two occupants of the library both reacted to the sudden noise by physically jumping in their seats and looking towards the door in unified alarm.

Standing framed in the now open doorway in all his glorious fury, was Lord Livesey, Earl of Ansar, Viscount of Rothwell. His normally disinterested, slightly mocking expression had been replaced by one of exploding anger. His stance was akin to the brooding, dangerous posture of a gothic hero. His clothing only added to the overall effect of a dark and dangerous man as he always wore more dark colours than light.

"Livesey?" the elder matron asked, with a pointed look in the direction of the other occupant of the room. It would not do to have an eruption of anger in front of a guest.

"Bloody Jessica!" Livesey cursed his absent sibling between gritted teeth before managing to recall himself. "Miss Westbrook," Livesey said turning to the guest. "I apologise for my entrance and my base language, but my sister would test the patience of a saint. And I'm not that good of a person to be able to put up with her torment with grace."

Miss Phoebe Westbrook was the younger of the two women in the library. She closed her book and pushed her glasses towards the bridge of her nose, rising from her seat. She was a visitor to the home, one of the house party which was the event testing Lord Livesey so much. "Do not distress yourself, My Lord. This is your home, and you are entitled to behave in it as you will. I was seeking to escape the entertaining repartee of our fellow guests, but I can see you need some time without interruptions. If you will excuse me, I will leave you be."

Lord Livesey's scowl had not lessened at Phoebe's slightly amused tone. In fact, he seemed to glare at her more ferociously. Phoebe seemed oblivious to the animosity aimed in her direction as she smiled goodbye to the older woman, who'd been sharing the tranquillity of the library. Livesey bowed stiffly to Phoebe's curtsey and watched as she left the room. He didn't bother to close the door on her retreating form. He was too engrossed in his own anger to give himself complete privacy. He turned to face the elder woman who was watching him with open amusement now that the shock of his arrival had eased.

"What has Jessica done now?" she asked. The woman was the elderly aunt of the raging Lord. She was more than an aunt to Livesey and Jessica. When their parents died, Aunt Dickson, having no children of her own, had been the one to offer guidance, support, and an outlet for their grief. She'd mourned her sister and her brother-in-law privately, offering strength and stability to the two grieving children.

She was an independent woman in her own right with a fortune left by her husband, which gave her the freedom to live her life as she pleased. At the same time, she was never long without being in the company of either her niece or nephew, offering advice, and sometimes in Livesey's case, being the unwelcome voice of reason.

Fond of her nephew she most certainly was, but she wasn't averse to enjoying the humour in any situation, especially this one. His entrance suggested his hospitality was already wearing thin, and they were only at the start of the two-week long soiree.

"Apart from this damned house party, you mean? I detest the whole situation!" Lord Livesey ground out.

"It's no surprise you hate it, although Jessica is right: Those children of yours need a mother. You refuse to spend enough time in London to secure a match the season might offer, so Jessica has brought the party here. And you must agree with her in some respect, or you would not have consented to her using your own house to host the party."

"It was a ludicrous idea from the start," Livesey responded, refusing to acknowledge any agreement with his sister's scheme. She'd browbeaten him into submission as far as he was concerned. He was struggling already with the situation, and they were only on the third day. He had no idea how he was going to survive without either offending everyone or killing a large number of the grouping. The way he was feeling at the moment, if he chose the latter, his beloved sister would be the first in line.

"If you used it for the opportunity it is, it could turn into the best of ideas. If it secures a mother for those girls of yours, all will end well." Aunt Dickson refused to pander to Livesey's unreasonableness.

"And which of the ladies present would you suggest is my best option for finding a new wife, Aunt? The six chosen by my sister are supposed to be perfect for being a life-partner to me, in Jessica's opinion. I am certainly at a loss as to how I could bear to spend two weeks with any of them, let alone the remainder of my days," Livesey responded with derision, although there was a touch of despair in his tone that only those who knew him would hear.

Serena Dickson, smiled at her nephew. He was nearing eight and twenty but was still as headstrong as he had been as a boy. He had married young to Angelina, a fiery Italian whom he had met on his grand tour. Theirs had been a passionate but short-lived marriage, which had shocked the family. Angelina had given birth to three children in quick succession and then in one particular fit of temper had smashed too many heirlooms to count and stormed out of the house. Her drowned body had been found later in the large lake on the estate, which was ridiculously close to the house for something so terrible to happen unseen. Unfortunately for Angelina, no one had followed her outside on that fateful day.

No one could say for sure if she had meant to drown herself or if it was just an escalation of the dramatics for which she was well known. Whatever the reason, something had gone wrong, and Livesey had not pursued his wife as he usually did. He normally spent time and energy bringing her out of her dark moods. Perhaps he had reached the end of his patience with her; perhaps she had with him. No one would ever truly know. He had not sought her, and an hour later, her body had been dragged from the lake by a member of staff.

The scandal, gossip, and guilt that had been caused by Angelina's death had forced Livesey into hiding from the world for the next six years. Eventually, Lady Jessica Knowles, his younger sister, had decided that his children needed a mother whether he was ready to remarry or not.

Having daughters of eight, nine and ten, Livesey could not really argue that his girls didn't need a female influence. He had been willing to accept Aunt Dickson and Jessica supporting them. Thus, he considered the idea of Jessica's having a house party at his home with carefully selected women foolish in the extreme. He couldn't acknowledge to anyone, least of all himself, why he'd agreed to it. That reason was because of a small nugget of hope, which refused to be stamped out. He'd felt adrift since before Angelina's death, and in the dead of night on one of his many nights lying awake, he'd longed for someone who could change the way he felt. By the time dawn broke, he'd carefully packaged that longing away. He was a fool to even consider that a person could help soothe his soul and give him comfort. No. There wasn't a person alive who could do that.

"Jessica has considered the merits of each of the six ladies present. She spent months assessing who would be best suited to you," Aunt Dickson responded.

"I could have saved her the time and trouble. I could see within minutes of their arrival that none of them will do," Livesey ground out.

"You are still a handsome fellow not yet in your dotage. I'm sure one of them could be persuaded," came the slightly mocking response.

Livesey's lips twitched despite his ill mood. Only those closest to him could ever make him smile, but it was never often enough for their liking. "Thank you for the compliment. I think."

It was true. He was handsome: as dark as his wife had been with such dark eyes they were almost black when thunderous, which was more often than not. He didn't smile very often; instead he had two deep grooves on his forehead which, even when he smiled, betrayed the position of the almost constant frown he wore. Sharp featured, he was striking and considered an attractive package. He wasn't viewed as the best of catches because of his surly disposition. He was considerate of those in his care, but no one would describe him as openly loving. A handsome, rich man nonetheless could tempt many to deem him a worthwhile option by those who were looking for a husband, even if most in society would consider him an aloof and angry, cold fish.

"Jessica was able to find six young women who are all willing to consider you as a good catch. Any one of them would consider marrying you, so you cannot be completely repulsive," came the no-nonsense response.

This time Livesey did laugh, but the sound held no humour. "Are you telling me I should be flattered by the dregs of society Jessica has invited?"

"That a little harsh, Livesey! They aren't so bad." Aunt Dickson defended the young guests. She had wondered at one or two of the choices that Jessica had made but had trusted in her niece's judgement that they had something to recommend them, or Jessica wouldn't have chosen them.

"Women beyond their prime. Here because no one else will marry them, and they think because I have children I will be willing to accept one of those who other men have rejected," Livesey responded with derision. "Jessica must be as foolish as the rest of them if she thinks I'll seriously consider any of her guests."

"Miss Westbrook is pretty and intelligent to boot. She's intelligent enough not to overindulge you. You could do worse than court her," Aunt Dickson offered, having liked the young woman since being first introduced to her. She wasn't the prettiest of the group but had a pleasing face that was animated with intelligence and humour.

"Have her owlish expression facing me over the breakfast table every morning and her dull-as-dishwater conversation every time she opened her mouth? I think not," Livesey responded.

Aunt Dickson was not a cruel woman and felt pity for the expression of hurt that flickered across Phoebe's face as the unfeeling words had unintentionally hit their mark. The young woman had entered the library unseen by Livesey through the still-open door. She'd paused on entering rather than interrupt, and as a result, had overheard the callous words.

Phoebe took a steadying breath. "My Lord, your sister has asked me to let you know she requires your presence in the drawing room. She preferred to send me instead of Miss Bateson who was keen to trace your whereabouts." Phoebe's voice came from behind where Livesey stood. If it sounded a little choked, she had done her best to disguise the impact his words had had on her.

Livesey whirled around at the voice, and instead of looking remorseful at her presence, he glared at Phoebe. "And you could not keep my location secret?" he demanded.

"I'm not in the habit of lying to a direct question, My Lord. When she asked if I had seen you, I acknowledged I had," Phoebe responded, colouring a little when she realised her dull response was of the kind she had just been mocked for.

"And I suppose you wish to hear my apology for the words I uttered when you crept in?" he continued cruelly.

"Why? When you clearly would not mean any apology you gave, My Lord?" Phoebe asked with what seemed like genuine surprise at his question. "We are both here under duress, My Lord. I would argue I'm counting the days until I can make my escape as much, if not more than you." She met his gaze, and although it was not an open challenge, Livesey could see she was not cowed by his presence.

"And yet you came?" he mocked, somehow unable to stop himself from taunting the young woman. It was poor behaviour on his part, but he had been discomfited by her presence, and he was lashing out in a way that did him no credit.

"As you have obligations, My Lord, so do I. You have your children to consider. In my case it is parents and an uncle. They will accept my return home with only a tinge of regret. I came here without a fuss because they wished me to. I can assure you, I have not attended because I wanted to attend. Thankfully, they don't expect me to go as far as to try to sell my soul or to compromise myself to receive a proposal from you. I would hate to disappoint them if that were the case. Please excuse me, My Lord, Mrs Dickson. I have something to attend to." Phoebe turned and left the room, this time closing the door firmly behind her.

The silence was maintained until Aunt Dickson broke it with a shake of the head as she stood. "That was poorly done, Livesey. The chit didn't deserve a tongue-lashing from you. You're lucky she is not creating all sorts of hysterics and demanding to be taken home. I expect better from you as a gentleman and the host."

Livesey glowered at his aunt, not appreciating having his behaviour taken to task, even though he was fully aware she was correct. He'd behaved abominably, and he immediately became defensive. "She seemed unconcerned to me."

"Pah! Don't try to flummox me! We both know she was mortified at what she overheard, just as any of us would have been, including you! None of us likes to be cruelly criticised. Appreciate that she had the wherewithal to stand up to you. It's about time someone did. You have been allowed to have your own sullen way for too long. You need to become an upstanding member of society again. It's time to grow-up. Those children of yours are all that matter."

"The same ones who are like beings from another place?" Livesey responded, finally allowing a touch of uncertainty to seep through his well-practiced uninterested demeanour.

It was true. He hadn't been ready for fatherhood when it had happened when he was barely eighteen. He'd accepted the responsibility of his actions by marrying Angelina but had struggled with his increasing brood. He loved his children, but he felt at a loss around them. The enormity of having three beings completely reliant on him had rested heavily. Instead of being able to become accustomed to the new role over time, he'd had to focus his time on keeping Angelina on an even keel. Her mood swings were difficult and draining.

There'd been no time to begin to get to know his children; his whole focus had been on Angelina. She'd not been a natural mother either, visiting the nursery when she was in a good mood, which was all too rare. Once she'd died, Livesey had been racked with guilt over the circumstances of her death and the fact that he'd ultimately let his wife and children down. Such irrationality had made him withdraw from both family and society.

Now, if he ever ventured into the nursery, his children looked at him in alarm as if he were the strange, wicked ogre he very often felt he was.

"If you don't know your children, it is because you haven't made the effort to get to know them. You've hidden from the world and your own kin. Find a mother and become a real family. The girls are lacking attention and love."

"That's something I cannot give them," Livesey responded dully.

"Just because Angelina is dead does not mean you can't love another being. Humans, and especially men, are not made that way!" Aunt Dickson mocked. There was more she could say about Angelina and Livesey, but now wasn't the time. She would speak when Livesey was ready to listen.

"Let's find Jessica before she sends a search party for me," Livesey said as he crossed the room and opened the door with a lot more care than he had when he entered the library.

The pair walked out, neither willing to continue their conversation once it could be overheard by visitors and staff.

As Livesey walked into the drawing room to be greeted by the smiling faces of the women seated there, he wondered if anyone truly knew him, including those to whom he considered himself closest. Not for the first time, he felt completely alone in the world and at odds with the rest of society and those around him. It was a feeling all too familiar and all too overwhelming.

*

Miss Phoebe Westbrook collapsed against the wood of her bed-chamber door as she closed it against the world. Tears threatened, and her throat constricted with the need to cry. She gritted her teeth. She would not be weak.

Mocking seemed to be easy for those who had not the same disadvantages as the unmarried spinsters in society. She was under no illusion that Livesey would choose her as his bride, but when someone was as handsome as he, there was no need to point out the flaws of those around him. It was a sign of cruelty on his part. She had the right to detest him for such unkind behaviour. Sighing, she cursed herself for not being able to hate him but finding him attractive. Who wouldn't? He was gorgeous, she muttered angrily to herself.

At four and twenty, she had very often been reminded she was considered an oddity. It was only her connection with a maternal uncle, who was an extremely wealthy gentleman, that her family was accepted in the wider circles of society. Uncle Frederick Longton had sponsored Phoebe and her two younger sisters for their come outs. The younger ones hadn't been forced to wait until Phoebe was wed, which was fortunate for them. Susan and Georgina had both secured marriages to gentlemen, but Phoebe had remained disappointingly unmarried.

Some had acknowledged she was pretty, if you liked large hazel eyes, full lips, and a rosy complexion. Matched with mid-brown hair, Phoebe had always said that it was as if her features had been created as a complete contrast against the blonde-haired, blue-eyed, porcelain complexions that were so fashionable. Even her sisters matched society's preference, being paler, slimmer, more conforming to what was considered beautiful by the *ton*.

She had not wished to come to the house party, but once again Uncle Frederick had stepped in. Being a good friend of Lord Knowles, Lady Jessica's husband, he had been informed of the plan that was being hatched. Always one to think of his niece, he had asked for an invite on her behalf, which as a mark of the friendship, had been readily offered.

Jessica did not think for one moment her brother would seriously consider the quiet, somewhat withdrawn Miss Westbrook. It was as if she purposely kept herself on the edge of society. Jessica had met Phoebe a time or two over the years and liked the young woman, even though she was dismissed by many as a plain, uninteresting bluestocking. Jessica considered Phoebe a genuine character, both funny and intelligent in an ocean of fickleness. As Jessica was confident one of the other ladies would turn Livesey's head, it hadn't grieved her to include Phoebe in the party.

So, Phoebe had come as invited but could not involve herself in the silly games her contemporaries entered into when trying to make themselves appear to best advantage. She had no idea how to flutter a fan coyly, tease a gentleman, or flirt with an acquaintance. She would much prefer to be doing something useful, which was considered unique at best and an oddity at worse.

Add to this the glasses she needed to wear in order to see clearly, and she really was an unattractive package. She was fully aware of that. There were enough tactless people in society to point out one's flaws and more than enough perfect, beautiful people to push aside someone who did not quite fit the mould. Maybe if society were more inclined to accept those who were different, Phoebe wouldn't have withdrawn to the edges of society quite as much as she had. In a world focused on outward appearance, wealth, and connections, the theory could never be tested.

Livesey had scored a hit, but Phoebe had some pride. She would take part in this foolish endeavour. Anyone could see Livesey wished himself miles away from the lot of them, which gave her a modicum of comfort. At least she was not the only one who felt out of place. She would not return home early because of his hurtful attack.

One thing was certain: Phoebe Westbrook was not going to allow herself to be bullied by a brute.

Chapter 2

The drawing room felt oppressive even though it could fit more than double the number of people gathered. Livesey watched the grouping from his position at the mantelpiece with derision mixed with intolerance. He stood, absentmindedly fiddling with his cuffs, his annoyance being taken out on the inane cotton garment. He was actually unintentionally showing himself off to full advantage, being in front of the fire, the light reflecting off his black hair, gold waistcoat, and shining shoe buckles. His black frock coat was standing out in contrast to the white marble of the fireplace. He glowered at the room in general; the afternoon had been tedious, and it seemed the evening was going to be the same.

He always felt on the edge of society. Even now, when the party was technically for him, the men in attendance were in small groupings separate from himself. He had been gregarious when he was younger. It had been one of the characteristics to appeal to Angelina. Yet, as a result of their pairing, Livesey had withdrawn from everyone, and now it was so ingrained, he could not see a way out of his self-imposed isolation. It was laughable to feel alone in a room full of people, but he very often did. It was yet another reason he spurned society. Why place himself somewhere he didn't feel he belonged?

The all too familiar feeling of emptiness swirled at the pit of his stomach. Sometimes he longed to feel something other than anger, disillusionment, and loneliness. He glared at his guests; he hated falseness, and this was what he was surrounded by whenever he was amongst his peers.

*

Jessica had insisted the party be as society dictated with even numbers of single men and women in addition to chaperones of varying kinds. She had chosen the single men carefully, not wishing the unmarried women to fall in love with anyone other than her brother. Some of the gentlemen were much older than the women gathered; Jessica hoped their age would work against them.

Her brother was certainly the most handsome man in the room. It was a great pity his glower kept many of her guests away from him. Jessica sighed. All she wanted was for her brother to be happy, as well as her nieces getting a mother, but if he did not become at least a little reconciled to marrying again, her hopes would fail.

"George, you could at least try to smile!" Jessica whispered as she moved herself to her brother's side. She was the only person to use his given name. Even their aunt used his family name.

"What, like this?" Livesey responded gritting his teeth in a grimace.

Jessica used her fan to tap his arm. "Stop it! I do not want my reputation ruined because of you. I need to be able to show my face in society after this debacle. Not all of us want to hide as you do."

"Perhaps you should've considered that before organising this farce?" Livesey asked with a raise of an eyebrow.

"Behave! That's an order," Jessica hissed, the smile fixed firmly on her face. She was like her brother, tall and dark in looks, but the siblings were nothing alike in character. Jessica was a well-liked member of society, accepted and welcomed wherever she went. She was four years younger than Livesey but seemed older sometimes. It was probably as a consequence of losing her parents early and not having the support of her brother when he'd become embroiled with Angelina. It was down to effort on Jessica's part that the brother and sister had remained in close contact. She refused to let herself be alienated from a brother she adored, even though he was difficult to understand sometimes.

"I will try, but I'm not promising to marry anyone," Livesey said. "Especially when the best Aunt could come up with was Miss Westbrook." The comment had been made as a result of said young woman entering the room and skirting the edge of the party. She placed herself as far away from anyone else as was physically possible without it being overtly noticeable. She smiled in greeting to the person she was nearest to, but she made no effort to throw herself into the throng.

The movement had amused Livesey. He had noticed she had not looked his way, unlike most of the other women who were surreptitiously glancing at him from time to time. He wondered idly if she was sulking with him because of his earlier outburst. He hoped she was; at least that would mean there would be five women to deal with, not six.

"Did she really? That is interesting and a fortunate coincidence," Jessica said with a gleam in her eye.

"Why?" Livesey responded, all his attention suddenly focused on his sister.

"She'll be sitting next to you at supper. I thought it fair to rotate the ladies to give them all an equal chance to entertain and entice you."

"Jessica!" Livesey growled. "Change it!"

"I will not! And you will be a gentleman, or I'll have something to say about it! Bad manners are inexcusable, George. Whether you like it or not, these people are your guests, and you agreed to the party," Jessica chided.

Livesey grimaced to himself. He might not like it, but his sister was correct: He had to be polite or at least try. Underneath the scowling and derision, he was not the brute he appeared. He had wronged Phoebe and shouldn't have. But admitting he was wrong was never easy for someone as insular as Livesey.

*

Phoebe inwardly groaned when she realised where she would be spending the next few hours. She was not being mulish about the comments Livesey had made. After all, she couldn't argue against them. If one is told one is defective, it's only a short time before the cruel words are believed. The seating arrangement meant she would be on show to the rest of the party, and she'd rather have been able to blend in more than she would be able to. Her rank didn't technically allow her to sit next to her host, but she guessed, to some extent, what Jessica was doing.

Everyone was eventually seated at a table of twenty people in total. Thankfully, to Phoebe's left was a retired captain of the navy, who although nearing forty, was charming company. He was a tall, broad man, who perhaps wasn't as trim as he had been when exploring the high seas, but he was still an imposing presence. His skin was weathered as a result of spending most of his life being battered by spray and wind, but his features were still handsome with pepper pot hair crowning warm brown eyes and a wide smile. Phoebe was able to forget her angst about being seated next to the man who thought so little of her while at the same time being watched carefully by the other women in the party. Instead she listened with rapt attention at the stories Captain Hall told.

After one particularly gruesome tale, Captain Hall apologised. "I'm sorry. I am always being chided about what is appropriate language at the table. Describing losing limbs is not *de rigueur,* I believe."

"Not for the unfortunate sailor, at any rate," Phoebe said, trying to make the captain feel comfortable. His stories had been entertaining—interesting and a little shocking. It was fascinating for a young woman who was by no means squeamish but had experienced quite a sheltered life.

Captain Hall laughed in genuine appreciation. "Exactly! I must have had someone looking out for me, because believe me, I know all too well the sound of a musket ball flying passed my ear! Some of those pirates are crack-shots with guns!"

"Thankfully, you are able to enjoy your retirement in relative peace," Phoebe said with a smile.

"It must sound strange, but I admit I miss those days. The adventure is sometimes heady along with the experience of seeing the countries and civilisations I've visited. Life on shore can't always compare. There is nothing like a ship full of sailors to bring out the best and worst in people. Even the battles I've been in have had an element of excitement at their core."

"Be heartened. You could be about to see more action than you have in a while," Phoebe said.

"I don't take your meaning, Miss Westbrook," Captain Hall responded in puzzlement.

"Don't tell me you think this house party will be peaceful? I'm betting there will be more skirmishes over the coming two weeks than you've seen in a long time. There is only one prize in all of this, Captain. I think my fellow guests will be vying with each other to win," Phoebe could not resist her teasing tone. It was rude in the extreme to openly criticise both the party and the people present, but whether it was the sting from Livesey's insults or some devil within her, she pushed aside propriety for once.

"And you, Miss Westbrook? Will you be battling along with the rest of them?" Captain Hall chuckled. He appreciated such frank observations in a refined dining room.

"No, not at all. I am more appreciative of the consolation prize of spending two weeks near the Hampshire coastline than foolishly aiming for the so-called top prize. I sometimes find when you think you want something it can be very disappointing if you actually get it. I'm sure that's the case here, although I seem to be the only one of that opinion. My peers have glared daggers at me all night because I am seated next to our host when I'd swap places with any of them in an instant," Phoebe said quietly, a laugh in her voice.

"Well, my dear Miss Westbrook, I'm certainly glad you have been seated next to me. It's been a delightful evening. I hope to have the opportunity again," Captain Hall said with real appreciation in his eyes.

Phoebe smiled. Having a friend during her stay would help the evenings pass at least. She had plans to explore the area if she could escape any avoidable organised activities during the day; even though she was not usually one for travelling widely, she did not wish to waste a moment.

"So, I'm not worth fighting for, am I, Miss Westbrook?" came the deep gravelly voice of Lord Livesey.

Phoebe flushed. She thought she'd taken care so as not to be overheard, but she was not going to be cowed by a man who had such little regard for herself. "As I already pointed out to you earlier today, I do not lie to a direct question. Do you really want me to answer you, My Lord? Or shall we leave your words as a rhetorical question?"

Livesey chuckled genuinely at the answer, surprised that her response tickled him so. His intention had been to torment her for her dismissive words. "It's probably best if you do not answer. I've been indulged enough to consider myself one of the finest catches in society. I've had to cope with your shunning my conversation all evening in preference to Captain Hall. I would hate to have your low opinion of me confirmed."

"Yes. I feel it is better to remain deluded, although I'm not self-important enough to presume my opinion accounts for much," Phoebe responded. Her tone was light, but the laughter in her eyes had beguiled Captain Hall, was missing.

Livesey had seen how she had been with the older man, and the devil in him wanted to taunt her a little for not indulging him as she'd done the captain. "Perhaps if I flattered you as our good captain has done all evening, you might be persuaded to change your mind about my appeal and even be tempted to fight for me a little along with the other ladies present?"

"The captain has offered interesting, entertaining conversation, which I have enjoyed. He offered no false flattery, and if I longed for such flummery, it would make me as fickle as the utterer, don't you think, My Lord? You have enough people in this room who will pander to your conceited opinion of yourself. In reality your company is as appealing to me as my company is to you," Phoebe responded.

She had come to the house with the hope she could try to repay her uncle and parents' faith in her. A flicker of hope had whispered to her heart that there was a small possibility of gaining a husband and family in the process, but the conversation she'd overheard had put paid to those thoughts. Although she would be polite, she was not about to give false flattery to try to appease someone who clearly didn't like her. But she refused to be overawed by a man she considered cold, unfeeling, and rude, however handsome he was. And he was stunning to look at, especially as close as she was to him now. His build, raven-black hair, dark eyes, and square jaw would be enough to fall in love with, but she could not be so shallow. She needed a person she could respect and love, even if that meant she continued as an old maid.

Captain Hall laughed at the look of astonishment on Livesey's face. "Methinks you are too accustomed to being fawned over if the expression on your countenance is anything to go by, My Lord! Has Miss Westbrook given you your first-ever set-down?"

Livesey glanced at Captain Hall. "It seems I have been out of society for too long. Young ladies did not express their opinions so openly the last time I socialised."

"Perhaps it is only when faced with archaic persons that we have to stand up for ourselves and be borderline rude," Phoebe responded. "Please excuse me, My Lord, Captain Hall. Lady Knowles is withdrawing."

Livesey watched with disbelief and something akin to admiration as the woman who had just given him the most cutting put-down he had ever had left the room with the other ladies. She'd seemed such a meek miss when he had first met her—an outsider, a typical spinster—but he had to admit there was fire within her; he still stung from her words, and she had left the room.

Captain Hall chuckled as he observed Livesey's reaction to Phoebe. "A bright one you've got there, My Lord. It has been whispered she's a bluestocking, but I think she is a delight! I'm really looking forward to spending more time with her over the coming days."

Livesey shot him a glare but refrained from answering. He would certainly be speaking to Jessica later. There was little point in inviting a group of young ladies for him to consider marrying if the other guests were going to start chasing them. He had little enough to offer, especially when they got to know the cold beast behind the title; he needed no further obstacles.

He failed to acknowledge the irony of his earlier observations about the party in general and Phoebe in particular when reacting to his pride and vanity being hurt.

Chapter 3

Jessica steered the high-perch phaeton around to the front of her brother's home. It was a grand grey-stone building, updated in the last twenty years by their father and a testament to the Livesey name. A woman with a positive outlook on life, she still hoped her brother would come around to her scheme before the end of the house party.

An excursion had been the perfect plan for a sunny day, and she smiled as she viewed the scene in front of the portico. Livesey was already mounted on his black horse alongside Miss Sumner and Miss Bateson, who were on two horses borrowed from the stables. Miss Jackman and Lady Jane Bellamy were seated in the barouche with the top down, their parasols giving them shade from the sunshine.

Jessica carried Lady Bellamy's chaperone in her own equipage. Jessica's husband had persuaded the other gentlemen to join him on a fishing expedition, which suited Jessica's plans perfectly. She privately acknowledged that Livesey needed time to shine in front of the ladies. That would be achieved easier if the other gentlemen of the party were busy fishing and shooting with her husband. The fact that her brother would have preferred to be with the gentlemen was an irrelevance in her eyes. The party had to end in a marriage for him.

"Are we all ready? The ruin we are to visit is a splendid gothic structure, and it overlooks the sea. It couldn't be more dramatic," Jessica said as she pulled to a halt at the side of the barouche.

"We are two short—Miss Westbrook and Lady Sarah," Livesey said, moving his horse next to his sister's carriage.

"They have gone ahead with Captain Hall. He knew of a viewpoint the ladies decided they wished to see. He promised to meet us at the ruin," Jessica explained. She had not wished the party to separate in such a way, but when the ladies expressed their desire to explore with the captain, she could hardly refuse her consent. Lady Sarah's companion had gone with them, so it was perfectly respectable.

"I see," Livesey responded, looking none too pleased. "Ladies, if you're ready," he said before moving the party off.

It was natural the three riders would spend the first section of the excursion with each other as the horses burned off their initial burst of energy. When they calmed to a comfortable trot, Livesey was able to speak to the two women.

Within a few moments he had come to the conclusion, that although pretty and relatively well-connected, there was a reason both ladies were still unmarried. Miss Bateson was the prettiest of the pair, but her constant squeals of loud laughter and babbling conversation, which jumped from subject to subject, made the impact of the blonde-haired, blue-eyed prettiness fade very soon. She was only one and twenty, but Livesey decided he would rather see his children permanently motherless than attach himself to her.

Miss Sumner was not so exhausting, but in some ways, she was as bad. Equally as blonde and blue-eyed as Miss Bateson, she was pretty and was good at conversation, but there was one flaw: Everything Livesey said she agreed with. If he expressed that he liked something, so did she. He tried to force her into having an opinion after half an hour of compliance.

"My girls are to spend some time with us tomorrow. I think my sister wishes to have them share in some of the house party," Livesey stated.

"How wonderful it will be to meet your babies! Lady Knowles speaks very highly of her nieces," Miss Sumner responded.

"They are high spirited," Livesey acknowledged. "I sometimes do not know what to do with them. It's very difficult to know what is best. Have you any experience with children?"

"We know all about little girls, don't we, Sylvia?" Miss Bateson interrupted. "You can tell me anything that would shock me, My Lord! I was up to all sorts of tricks when I was growing! Why, I could give you a full list of the nannies I chased off. Let me see… there was Nanny Philips; she lasted six months… then there was Nanny Hall…"

Livesey had to listen to every unfortunate nanny who had suffered with Miss Bateson as a child. It was a full five minutes before he could turn the conversation back round to Miss Sumner. "If you have any advice about my daughters, I'd be keen to hear it," he prompted eventually.

"I think they are very lucky to have you as a Papa, and they must do as you dictate," Miss Sumner said with authority.

"But I am sure I don't always get it right," Livesey persisted. The reality was that he knew he spent most of the time getting it very wrong. He was a stranger to his children and they to him. His father had been a good man and a role model to copy, yet he couldn't connect to his children the way his own father had. If Livesey were honest, he would not wish his children to turn out like either of their parents; both Angelina and he were flawed.

Miss Sumner reached over and squeezed Livesey's arm. "And I am sure you do. Take comfort in knowing you are the best of fathers to those little darlings."

Livesey's cheek twitched with annoyance. He was surprised Miss Sumner was not married. There were many men who would love to have someone who agreed with everything they said. Unfortunately for Miss Sumner, he was not that type of man.

An image of Angelina came unbidden, and he moved away from the grouping a little. He did not wish to think of her while in this situation. When they had met he fell for her charms so deeply, so quickly, it had shocked him. He had been drawn to her in such a way it had almost frightened and consumed him. She was passion personified.

He had thought himself in an everlasting love, but he had been so wrong. It had been infatuation, obsession even, but not love. He had never voiced his concerns to anyone when he realised he'd made a mistake; it had been too late: Angelina was increasing, and he had dutifully married her.

Their relationship had been tempestuous although still passionate. Livesey had developed coping methods of living with a woman who was prone to fits of temper, passion, and anger in equal measure. Unlike everyone else around them, he could eventually persuade her out of her mood swings, her demands, her hysterics.

It had been exhausting.

Livesey had withdrawn from his children, too busy focusing on keeping their mother on an even keel. Then he had reached a day when he could not carry on. The temper tantrum had been extreme. She had screamed, shouted and smashed objects for over half an hour before stomping off into the grounds.

After her exit, the house had quietened, and Livesey had sunk into the nearest chair, his head in his hands, wondering if he would ever find a way out of this misery. He had no longer any idea of how to reach Angelina, how to calm her. He wished to find a way to cope with the situation they were all in. He was to get what he wished for sooner than he expected.

She had been gone only an hour. It seemed a short amount of time for such a tragic event to happen.

Relief mixed with an overwhelming amount of guilt engulfed Livesey and threatened his sanity for months after Angelina's death. He had promised to love and protect her, and although he had tried, he had failed her and their children. He had wished for relief, and as a result, his children were motherless. What kind of parent wished that on their children? How could he ever accept the love of the three people he'd let down by not following their mother when she'd stormed out?

He'd been expected to marry again, but he could not face society, let alone consider marriage. He was drained emotionally. How could he consider loving anyone else if he couldn't love someone as passionate as Angelina?

If what he'd gone through was what it meant to be in love, he wanted no more of it. His sanity could not stand another experience like that. After Angelina, he had no idea what real love was, but he sure as hell did not wish to find out.

His children not only lost a mother, they lost their father as well. He would not let himself be emotionally involved with anyone after his experience with Angelina. It was part uncertainty in his own judgement and partially self-protection.

He understood that his thoughts were unreasonable, but he could do nothing but encase himself in a shell of protection. It had saved him, although he felt empty and detached. He had to accept it was better than risking another relationship like the one he had shared with Angelina.

Only Jessica could convince him his girls needed a mother. She had tried to help but could do only so much. It was time Livesey put them first. He hadn't liked listening to his sister's words, but he had. Girls in particular needed a mother, and if nothing else, it was his responsibility to find one for them.

Livesey sighed and turned his mount towards the barouche. His sister was right; for the children not to be like their flawed parents, they would need another influence on them. They needed a suitable mother. For the first time since the party had been mentioned, he acknowledged it was time to consider his options seriously.

*

The group arrived at the ruin in good time but they had not beaten those that had set-off to explore the wider area. Lady Sarah, Phoebe and Captain Hall had climbed the hill behind the ruin and were waving at the new arrivals. Lady Jane Bellamy and Livesey decided to walk up the hill and join the threesome.

Lady Jane was the eldest lady in the grouping at thirty-one. She was rich and titled, and extremely unusual in that she'd reached the age and status of a spinster despite her advantages in society. She was handsome, rather than pretty, with dark hair and green eyes. She was almost as tall as Livesey, and in some respects, appeared a perfect match. She was one who also kept herself slightly removed from people, a little aloof.

The pair walked in silence to start with, but soon Lady Jane took the opportunity of starting the conversation. "I would like to make a suggestion to you, if I may?" she asked, breathing a little heavy with the exertion of the climb.

"Of course," Livesey responded.

"I am older than the others in the group, older than you even at one and thirty," Lady Jane started. "I presume I am here because of my dowry and title," she finished.

"I'm in no need of a fortune," Livesey said tersely. It was clear everyone knew the aim of the party. He wished the invitations could have been sent out with a little more subtlety.

"I am aware of that," Lady Jane responded. "I'm going to be honest with you, and I hope I can rely on your discretion."

"You can be assured nothing we speak of will be repeated," Livesey said, his interest piqued.

"Thank you. What I am going to say will seem outrageous but hear me out," Lady Jane said, flushing slightly. "If you marry me, I think I can offer what you need."

"And what is that?" Livesey asked with a raise of his eyebrow. It seemed everyone knew what he wanted except himself.

"A mother to your children, no pretence of love and all that nonsense, and a wife who wants a marriage in name only," Lady Jane rushed on.

"All that nonsense?" Livesey could not help querying.

"Let me explain a little further. I'm unmarried because I cannot be respectfully married or wed to the only person I want. He would not be accepted into our society," Lady Jane said. "You will give me the respectability I need while I'm with the man I care deeply about, and you get a wife and mother. I will care for your children as if they were my own."

"I see. And you would not be looking for relations with me?" Livesey asked, astounded for the second time in two days by the utterings of women.

"No. Not at all. That would be non-negotiable. I, of course, would not expect you to remain chaste. You would be free to have whatever mistresses you wished," Lady Jane continued, warming to her theme.

Livesey paused before answering. It was clear she had thought everything through. "What you say has come as a surprise. Might I have time to dwell on it, or do you require a decision now?" He hoped she didn't require a decision immediately as he was struggling with what to think.

"You can take until the last day of our stay if you wish," Lady Jane said. "I know it might seem strange, but with a marriage of convenience, I can be freer than I would be if I remained unwed."

"A married woman doesn't need a chaperone," Livesey pointed out with a wry smile.

"Exactly. Mull over what I have said. From my observations you don't seem set on a love match, or I think none of us would be here. This could give you the perfect solution without complications."

"From my experience, perfection comes with many complications, but I shall consider seriously what you have offered. Thank you for your honesty," Livesey said, taken aback but genuine in his appreciation of her directness.

"I hope we'll both benefit from my offer," Lady Jane responded.

Livesey didn't have time to answer, as they'd reached the grouping.

"Hello!" Captain Hall welcomed the new arrivals. "Come and see the view!"

"It is magnificent!" Lady Jane said with a smile. "In which direction are we looking? Are we south, or south west?" She was relieved to be able to remove herself from Livesey's side. It had taken all her courage to speak as she had done. She was not known as a simpering miss, but revealing that she was in love with someone of the lower classes could have resulted in her ruination. If marrying soon wasn't essential to retain some sort of reputation, she would never have spoken so openly, but she had no choice. She just hoped Livesey would see the advantages of her proposal. It has to work, she thought to herself before rousing from her inner turmoil to concentrate on the captain.

Captain Hall started to describe the land and sea they overlooked to Lady Jane, enabling Livesey to move across to Phoebe. She was standing on slightly higher ground facing the wind, looking out over the undulating waves of the Solent.

The wind was whipping her hair from beneath her bonnet, and her riding habit skirts were billowing out behind her. She reminded Livesey of a figure at the prow of a ship, graceful yet strong.

"You'll be whisked away if the wind increases," he shouted over the noise of the gusts.

Phoebe turned to him, a laugh on her lips. "I would let it if it promised to take me travelling far and wide!"

Livesey smiled despite his intention of tormenting her further than he had previously. Her large eyes were sparkling, and her cheeks were flushed. It was as if she were welcoming the wind's attempt to tug her off her perch. Livesey was struck by the fact that, even in such a simple scenario, she seemed so *alive* and completely opposite of how he felt inside. "Is my company so tedious?" he teased, all thoughts of torment vanished, knowing she would not be able to resist a retort.

"Do you really want me to answer that, My Lord?" Phoebe laughed, knowing he was funning with her.

"Probably not," Livesey admitted. "You clearly didn't think my company was tempting enough to wait for the larger party."

"I did not think my presence could add anything to the group, and Captain Hall gallantly offered to show us the wider area. Exploring is a treat I could not resist," Phoebe admitted, reluctantly stepping down from higher ground, so she didn't have to shout when speaking. She accepted Livesey's immediately offered hand. He might be a brute, but he knew how to be the gentleman on uneven ground.

"The captain seems to know exactly what to do to charm the ladies," Livesey responded, a tad petulantly.

"And you do not, My Lord?" Phoebe countered immediately in defence of her new friend. "I think a man of the world who is both well-travelled and well-educated would know exactly what to do to be a charming host. As long as he wanted to be of course."

"Sometimes, Miss Westbrook, I hardly know who I am, never mind how to function as a human being," Livesey said, surprising himself in his need to express some of his inner turmoil. Why he wanted her to understand him a little, he'd no idea, but the urge was too great to ignore.

"In that case I am truly saddened for you," Phoebe said seriously. "This situation can't be helping."

"No. But my sister is correct. I need to provide a mother for my children," Livesey admitted.

"One happy parent is better than two unhappy ones. My advice would be do not rush into anything you would regret later, but I'm not going to presume to expect you to take notice of my counsel," Phoebe said quietly.

Livesey looked at her sharply. The words had been said gently; he had been almost unable to hear because of the wind. "Are you one of those people who believes in love?"

"I have seen it with my own sisters. But I think I'm too practical, amongst other things, to fall in love myself," Phoebe admitted, knowing the word 'practical' covered a multitude of layers that even Livesey had referred to the previous day. She couldn't admit that she longed to be loved as others in her family were. She didn't envy them as such; she just wished she could find the same. If she'd admitted it to Livesey, she couldn't have borne the ridicule that would undoubtedly have followed her acknowledgement.

"And yet you are here," Livesey said prodding a little further.

Phoebe smiled. "I have already explained that it's because of my parents and my uncle that I'm here. I came with no real expectations and shall leave with no disappointments."

"I do not know if I'm flattered or insulted when you speak so openly, Miss Westbrook," Livesey admitted.

"Come. Let's not fool ourselves. You were clear in your opinion of me yesterday. Why should you be surprised that I'm not smitten with you?" Phoebe asked, failing to acknowledge that he was the most handsome man she had ever had the pleasure to spend time with. The fact they would never suit was helpful; she could admire, but not become foolish. Her heart could imagine but not truly believe.

"Were you smitten before my foolish words?" Livesey could not resist probing.

Phoebe laughed genuinely. "I was probably as smitten as you were with me, My Lord! No, to be fair, I think I felt a little more than you did. I can admire a handsome face along with everyone else. Luckily, I would not let myself get carried away with a pleasing appearance. There has to be substance behind the face. Come, I think it's time to rejoin our group. You have duties to attend to."

Livesey followed Phoebe away from the summit, stunned at her words. He had been unfair towards her; she was intelligent and funny, and she was sharp. He marvelled how two of the women of the group had surprised and intrigued him far more than he'd been expecting. For the first time since Jessica had mentioned the scheme, he didn't feel annoyance. It was becoming an interesting situation indeed, and with Lady Jane's offer, he certainly had something to consider. And whilst he was considering that offer, he would seek out Phoebe. He was drawn to the enigmatic young woman; she was the only female in a long time who had intrigued him, and he was determined to find out more.

His inner thoughts were interrupted when they reached the larger group. Phoebe had been slightly ahead of him, but he was able to overhear the insensitive remarks made by Miss Sumner. She'd turned to watch Phoebe's approach down the incline with a slight frown marring her pretty features.

Intercepting Phoebe, she'd immediately launched into a conversation. "Miss Westbrook! I beseech you to take a carriage home. How on earth have you arrived here on horseback without incident?" Miss Sumner asked.

Phoebe looked confused. "I don't understand your meaning, Miss Sumner," she responded.

"I would not have thought anyone needing to wear glasses would venture on such a pursuit as horse riding. Surely a carriage is safer?" Miss Sumner continued, looking quite pleased that Livesey had come to a halt at her side.

Phoebe flushed a little but smiled. "The need to wear glasses doesn't make me an invalid, Miss Sumner."

"But what if you fell? And surely, you cannot see as well as a normal person can?"

"A normal person?" Livesey was unable to stop himself uttering the words.

Phoebe shrugged slightly, as if showing him she was dismissing the remark. She was actually embarrassed as it was clear Jessica had also overheard the words as she'd turned quickly. "I've managed to survive without mishap so far," she said calmly. "Thank you for your concern, Miss Sumner, but horse riding is one of my passions, and I am loath to stop it, whether I'm normal or not."

Phoebe moved away. Miss Sumner turned to Livesey. "I'm afraid Miss Westbrook shows a distinct lack of consideration about her own safety. I feel the need to point out that she would not be suitable to look after little ones," Miss Sumner said with authority.

Livesey glowered at the young woman enough that she moved away, not quite sure how she'd managed to err. In her opinion, she was justified in pointing out the faults of the other young women, but she wasn't impressed that Livesey hadn't been as thankful as she'd expected him to be.

Jessica moved to her brother's side. "I know you aren't a fan of Miss Westbrook, but she handled that with dignity and grace. I had the urge to shake Miss Sumner at her gauche behaviour."

Livesey tried to stop gritting his teeth before he spoke to his sister. "Miss Westbrook is worth ten of the Sumner chit," he growled. "You can cross her off the list. I would not align myself with her if my life depended on it!"

"I can't criticise you for that," Jessica said quietly before moving away from her brother. No one else would suspect that anything was amiss as she moved around the group.

Livesey took a moment or two to gather his thoughts. He had also wanted to shake the foolish Miss Sumner. It was an unusual feeling for him to experience, but his ire had risen in defence of Phoebe when she was being insulted. He was beginning to suspect that she wasn't considered as real competition by the other women in the group. He felt shame at the words he'd uttered; she hadn't deserved his condemnation, just as she hadn't deserved Miss Sumner's. She'd risen above the insult, but made herself understood. Good for her, Livesey thought with something akin to admiration. Once again Phoebe had managed to surprise and intrigue him.

Chapter 4

Phoebe was comfortably ensconced in the library when the door burst open yet again. She jumped from the sudden movement and noise as she had the first time it occurred, but was further surprised when instead of the glowering face of Lord Livesey she expected to see, it was a small girl who ran into the room.

The girl faltered on seeing Phoebe but a sound from the hallway sent the child scuttling behind the wing-back chair Phoebe was seated on. A smile tickled Phoebe's lips as she waited with interest for events to unfold.

Seconds later Livesey entered the room looking thunderous. "Miss Westbrook, have you seen Sophia?" Livesey asked.

"I'm afraid I'm not acquainted with Lady Sophia, My Lord," Phoebe responded, stalling for time.

"My youngest demon of a daughter," Livesey said through gritted teeth. "We are gathering in the music room so my daughters can pretend they are talented young women instead of the brats they really are."

There was a squeak from behind Phoebe's chair, and Livesey's eyebrows drew together. In an act of interference she would blush about later, Phoebe held up her hand and shook her head at Livesey before continuing to speak. "And are your daughters thrilled with this prospect?" she asked.

"No," came a quiet, but firm voice from behind Phoebe.

Phoebe had to bite her lip to stop herself from laughing at the response; it was even harder to maintain her composure when Livesey's glower increased.

"Of course they are. I've paid a small fortune for their music teacher to instruct them on how to appear as young ladies," Livesey growled, losing patience at what seemed to be over-indulgent behaviour by his guest.

"Do they play often in front of an audience?" Phoebe persisted, her tone pleasant, but there was a challenge in her eyes.

"No. I clearly do not entertain, a fact of which you are fully aware, Miss Westbrook," Livesey ground out.

"I'd hate to perform before twenty people if I was not used to it," Phoebe said reasonably.

"I can hardly show off the talents of my brats if they will not perform, can I?" Livesey snapped.

"I'm sure the ladies of our group would love the opportunity to show just how talented they are, My Lord. Perhaps afterwards, if anyone else would want to have the opportunity to show their own accomplishments, I'd be happy to turn pages if they would like me to," Phoebe offered, closing her book and placing it on the side table in anticipation of the next few moments.

"If it would put an end to this nonsense, so be it," Livesey said ungracefully.

"Promise you will stand near to me," came a little voice from behind the chair.

"I promise," Phoebe said, smiling at the growl of frustration Livesey let out.

Sophia emerged tentatively from her hiding place, and Phoebe stood up to join the young girl. Phoebe noticed with a twinge of sadness the looks of alarm Sophia was throwing in the direction of Livesey.

"Sometimes papas want to show people how wonderful their children are," Phoebe said gently to Sophia. The looks of fear forced Phoebe to respond to the child.

"H-he shouts," Sophia responded, slipping her hand into Phoebe's in order to receive reassurance and support.

"He shouts at everyone but he doesn't mean it all the time. He talks about the three of you so much when you aren't around, we've had to tell him to stop it," Phoebe said managing to contain the laugh that threatened at the look of astonishment Livesey shot in her direction.

Sophia turned to look at Phoebe fully for the first time. Her dark eyes were wide with wonder, disbelief, and a hint of hope. "Really?"

Phoebe ached for the look of longing in the child's face. "Really," she said firmly. "Come, let's see if any of the ladies can play as well as you do. I'm sure they will all want to take turns at the lovely instrument I have seen in the music room." She moved towards the door bringing Sophia with her.

"I cannot play very well, but Mr Reece our music teacher says Eliza is a natural," Sophia said.

"In that case, I hope she wants to play for us," Phoebe responded. Her hand was dropped as Sophia saw her sisters waiting as if summoned to an execution in the hallway. Sophia babbled quickly what Phoebe had promised, and the air around the girls lifted as they began to chatter and look towards Phoebe with shy, grateful smiles.

Phoebe was touched by the picture. They could have passed for triplets, they were so similar with their jet hair and dark eyes. They would be the hit of each season when they eventually had their come outs. Even though she was convinced Livesey would never consider herself a match, she hoped to goodness he would marry someone who could love his children as they deserved.

"I thought you said you never lied," Livesey growled quietly as she passed him. Her actions had stirred emotions inside him he had not expected to feel. She had angered him with her playing of games, impressed him with her handling of the situation, and most surprising of all, the feelings he'd experienced made him envious when Sophia had gone to her for reassurance.

"I did not lie. When she burst in, I had no idea who she was," Phoebe defended herself.

"You said I never stop talking about them," Livesey pointed out, trying to find fault in her interference.

"I admit that was a twist of the truth," Phoebe acknowledged. "But for someone who is considering marrying a total stranger just so his children can have a mother, you must think the world of them. You just did not put it eloquently. It doesn't mean the sentiment wasn't there."

Livesey smiled slightly. "If you continue in this vein, Miss Westbrook, you will have me portrayed as an upstanding member of society."

"Now, now, let's not expect miracles, My Lord," Phoebe said, leaving Livesey chuckling in her wake.

*

Lady Jane soon had Eliza playing a duet with herself. They played and sang together in perfect harmony. Jenny the middle child was too shy to perform anything. Livesey had learned a valuable lesson from Phoebe, and instead of glowering at Jenny, he smiled and was rewarded when she ran to his open arms and remained on his knee while Sophia performed with Phoebe's assistance.

Miss Bateson had tried to persuade Jenny to join her, but the child had almost burrowed her way into her father's frock coat in an effort to get away from the young woman's entreaties. Livesey was rewarded with a happy sigh when he intervened and informed Miss Bateson that Jenny would not be performing.

When the children had been paraded for long enough, the nanny was rung for, and the three said their goodnights. Phoebe and Livesey were to receive a hug from Sophia and Jenny respectively, which made Miss Sumner request the children be allowed to spend more time in their company.

"It seems Lady Jane and Miss Westbrook have hogged their attention tonight," Miss Sumner said mulishly.

"My great-nieces are not toys to be shared around," Aunt Dickson responded sharply.

"I realise that, but..." Miss Sumner tried to recover.

"There are no buts about it. When my nephew decides they will join us, they will. Don't try to use them to score points; it will not work," came the brusque response.

Lady Jane continued to play the pianoforte when the girls had been removed, and everyone settled into little groupings around the room. It was a more relaxed night than the previous two evenings had been, and Livesey was grateful for it. He moved over to his aunt.

"I thought you said we had to be nice to our guests?" Livesey teased the older woman about her outburst.

"I won't stand for furtively gaining favour. Never have, never will," came the short response. "But in some respects the Sumner chit has a point. If you are to marry for the benefit of the children, you need to make sure the one you pick has some empathy towards them. The more time they spend with the girls the more any pretence by the gathering will be found out. Children aren't fools."

Livesey was immediately reminded of the episode in the library and how well Phoebe had dealt with it. He knew if she hadn't intervened, the situation wouldn't have ended well. There would have been tears and tantrums and not necessarily from his children.

He looked at his aunt. "It gets better and better. I now have to try to control my children while being an entertaining host," Livesey responded through gritted teeth. One evening had gone well. He couldn't rely on his girls to behave for two weeks.

"It will be worth it in the end."

"So Jessica keeps telling me," Livesey said, unconvinced.

*

The following day was bright and sunny, and Livesey, knowing the advice of his aunt was true, arranged to have the girls join them on a picnic. The guests walked to the folly on the hill about half a mile from the house. The children had been accompanied by their nanny and were quite happy to run alongside the other guests. Miss Bateson insisted on running with them, and although the girls were wary of her at first, she was soon accepted into their grouping.

The men of the party had joined the group for this event with Lady Jessica promising them a card party later in the evening.

Mr Flynn, a young man of five and thirty walked alongside Phoebe, who was quick to pick up on the young man's opinions of the gathering.

"It's all well and good being invited for a house party, but to know you are just here to make up numbers is a little rum!" he said with feeling.

"I'd have thought two weeks with a number of single ladies and plenty of entertainments would appeal to most men," Phoebe said reasonably.

"But everyone is mooning over Livesey. Hardly seems worth making the effort. I have money enough, but I can't compete to this level!"

"Oh, I think not everyone is as smitten as you suggest," Phoebe said, fairly sure she spoke only for herself. Although Lady Jane wasn't acting like a smitten idiot either.

"Do you not think?" Mr Flynn asked, hopeful.

"Do you have a favourite?" Phoebe asked.

"Well, if I can be assured of your confidence..." Mr Flynn started.

"Of course," Phoebe assured him.

"Miss Sumner is very amenable and so pretty!" Mr Flynn added with feeling.

"She is," Phoebe admitted, watching the young woman chattering to Lady Jane. She didn't mention the characteristics of inappropriate and interfering behaviour, silently cursing herself for her ungenerous thoughts. "If I could give you a piece of advice?"

"Anything!"

"I would pretend Lord Livesey wasn't looking for a wife and go-ahead with pursuing Miss Sumner. She might give the impression of preferring Lord Livesey, but that could be as a result of being polite to Lady Knowles," Phoebe pointed out.

"Do you think so?" Mr Flynn asked, ever hopeful.

"You have over a week to spend every moment trying to get to know Miss Sumner. I would not waste that time. At the end of the party, who knows what affections might have developed in the bosom of a young woman," Phoebe said.

"You could be right, Miss Westbrook! I've the perfect opportunity and did not see it for what it was! By Jove! I'll woo her like she's never been wooed before!"

Phoebe was left alone as Mr Flynn sped off to start his pursuit of Miss Sumner. She smiled at his retreating form. He was a nice, pleasant man. Miss Sumner could do a lot worse.

"If it were anyone but yourself giving the encouragement, I would swear you were trying to lower the odds for yourself!" came the clear voice of Aunt Dickson.

Phoebe flushed, but a laugh escaped her lips as she turned to the woman who had been walking close behind Phoebe and Mr Flynn. "I thought hearing was one of the senses to fade as one gets older?" she asked with a smile.

"Impudent chit!" Aunt Dickson responded with appreciation. "So, that's one less for my nephew to consider. I could not see him with her anyway."

"She might not choose Mr Flynn," Phoebe pointed out.

"She'd be a fool if she didn't," Aunt Dickson said, voicing Phoebe's inner thoughts.

"They'd make a good couple," Phoebe admitted, watching how Miss Sumner's face was lighting up at Mr Flynn's words.

"Yes. Both as silly as each other," Aunt Dickson said with a humph. "Now, who else are you going to pair up?"

Phoebe laughed. "No one! I'm here to make as little impact as I can."

"I think it's too late for that," Aunt Dickson said, as Sophia headed towards Phoebe with her father close behind.

Chapter 5

"We are to have a kite-flying competition, Miss Westbrook! Will you help me?" Sophia, Livesey's youngest child asked, arriving breathless and flushed.

"Of course!" Phoebe said with pleasure.

"There are to be groups of three," Lord Livesey explained, arriving a few steps behind his eager daughter. "Eliza wants to know if you're taking part, Aunt Dickson?" he asked with a grin.

Phoebe had to swallow at the effect the grin had on Livesey's face. He looked younger, as if he was more likely to get up to mischief, but above the appealing effect on his face, it made his eyes sparkle. Phoebe suddenly realised why some women were prone to swooning, her heartrate had increased as a result of seeing him in such a way.

"I'm the oldest here! I'll be sitting out, away from the wind," Aunt Dickson said.

"You will not be able to hear as much there though," Phoebe pointed out with an arch look.

"You're not too old to receive a box around the ears!" Aunt Dickson said, trying to glare at Phoebe, but the twitch of her lips gave her away.

Sophia looked alarmed.

Phoebe immediately responded to the child's distress. "Lady Sophia, sometimes adults say things they do not mean because they are just funning. Let's go and find who is to be our third!"

Sophia grabbed Phoebe's hand, and they walked away.

"What was that about?" Livesey asked.

"Nothing. She's got spark that one. Don't let the glasses and the demure look deceive you!" Aunt Dickson said with appreciation. "Now, who are you going to partner?"

"I suppose I should stay away from the children?" Livesey asked.

"Yes. Good idea. You're learning. Stay away from the Sumner chit as well; something I overheard makes me think she's not for you."

"I found that out yesterday!" Livesey said with feeling. "Miss Bateson hasn't a chance in hell either," he said with feeling.

"This is reducing the choices," Aunt Dickson pointed out.

"Lady Jane is an interesting prospect, but for this afternoon, I'll team up with Miss Jackman and Lady Sarah."

Livesey approached his chosen ones like a man going to the gallows. Aunt Dickson walked over to where Jessica was making herself comfortable on some chairs which had been brought out of the folly.

"We are down to four possibilities," Aunt Dickson said without preamble.

"I had thought two didn't come up to scratch yesterday. He had a more pained expression than usual when we arrived at the ruin," Jessica said.

"He seems interested in Lady Jane, which surprises me," Aunt Dickson said, curious as to why her nephew would be drawn to the one, who along with Phoebe, had fawned over him the least. She could be considered on the edge of the grouping, which was no different than Phoebe, but Aunt

Dickson hadn't seen the same spark of life, humour, and affection she'd detected in Phoebe. Lady Jane seemed removed and distant.

"Really? He could do worse than Lady Jane," Jessica admitted. "She comes from a fine family."

"Yes, but she hasn't got a spark about her. There is something not quite right. I can't put my finger on it, but she's a puzzle at the moment and not necessarily in a good way," Aunt Dickson mused as they watched the grouping.

Each person moved into their allocated threesome. Two held the strings of the kite, and the other held and ran with the kite until it caught the wind. There were squeals and shouts as kites hit the ground, tangled into each other and people—who were concentrating on what was in the air—crashed into other people.

Phoebe ended being in a trio with Sophia and Mr Kersey. He was a gentleman of fashion, who insisted he could not run around, so Phoebe had the harder task of running with the kite whilst Mr Kersey instructed Sophia about flying it once it was in the air.

Phoebe noticed that she was the only female running across the field in the most indecorous way, becoming hotter as each minute passed. Sophia wasn't very good at flying the thing once it was in the air, so Phoebe was the one working the hardest. Her cheeks were very soon burning, and she had to push her glasses up her nose more often than normal due to the perspiration forming on her face.

Captain Hall finally stepped in and stopped Phoebe from running any further. He shouted up to Mr Kersey. "Kersey! Call yourself a gentleman! You're wearing Miss Westbrook out!"

"It doesn't matter," Phoebe said, trying to catch her breath and burning an even deeper red than the exertion caused in reaction to the number of eyes now looking in her direction.

"It does indeed!" Captain Hall said with feeling. "Kersey! Get yourself down here and take Miss Westbrook's place!"

"Aw dash it all! I don't want to get hot and bothered!" Mr Kersey responded mulishly.

"Honestly! It isn't a problem!" Phoebe insisted to the captain. "Please leave us!" she appealed to him.

The captain looked annoyed but honoured Phoebe's appeal by walking away, returning to his own trio. Everyone soon returned to their own kites, and Phoebe was able to breathe a sigh of relief, although it would be hours before her cheeks stopped burning.

When everyone was fully engrossed once more, Livesey left his group and motioned to a servant, who hurried down the hill with a drink to Phoebe. The servant and Livesey arrived at Phoebe's position at the same time.

"Miss Westbrook, please have this drink and allow me to take over your position while you join my Aunt," Livesey said, in his usual gruff way.

"Oh no! Please! There's too much fuss being made!" Phoebe said, mortified.

"If there is, it's because of ungentlemanlike behaviour, rather than anything on your part," Livesey assured her, his tone slightly more gentle than his usual brusque manner. "I insist."

Phoebe's shoulders sagged in defeat. She took the drink with gratitude and followed the servant to the seating area.

When she arrived, Jessica apologised to her. "I'm sorry. Mr Kersey acted very poorly. You must be exhausted."

"I am, I think," Phoebe said, almost collapsing on the ground. Now that she was able to stop, she realised how tiring the activity was. She didn't think she'd ever cool down again.

"Kersey is now regretting his choice of position," Aunt Dickson chuckled. "Livesey is glaring at him with menace!"

"Good!" Jessica said with feeling.

Phoebe wanted to sink into the ground with mortification.

*

At the end of the afternoon, when everyone was readying themselves to walk back to the house, Livesey was approached by Jenny.

"Papa, I am so very tired," she said, looking rather pale.

"We'll soon be back at the house, and you can go to bed," Livesey responded.

"My legs feel a little wobbly," Jenny said with a sob and sank onto the grass.

Livesey frowned, but having noted the paleness of his daughter, he didn't growl at her as he might have previously. "How about if I lift you onto my shoulders for the walk home? You will be the tallest in the group."

"I will not need to walk?" Jenny asked pitifully.

"Not a step," Livesey said.

"Oh, thank you!" the young girl said with feeling.

Livesey smiled and bent, lifting the light weight onto his shoulders. He seated Jenny comfortably, asked her to carry his stovepipe hat, and started down the hill.

He passed Phoebe as he strode ahead. "I should have offered to carry you, Miss Westbrook. I think you ran about more than any of us."

"Don't remind me!" Phoebe groaned. "I shall ache for days!"

"You should have stopped the fool," Livesey ground out.

"We were perfectly grouped. It would have put Lady Sophia to disadvantage, and I say that without any wish to gain favour with yourself," Phoebe said with feeling. "My motivation was to give Lady Sophia an enjoyable afternoon. I think I achieved that."

"I know you well enough not to suspect you of artifice," Livesey admitted. "And I thank you on my daughter's behalf."

Captain Hall approached the pair. "Miss Westbrook, let me offer you the support of my arm on our walk back. You must be fit to drop."

"Thank you, you are very kind," Phoebe said demurely, accepting the escort.

The couple moved off ahead of Livesey and enabled him to glower at their figures as they all headed indoors. Yet again, Captain Hall had taken the attention of the one he wanted to speak to. He cursed the easy manners of the older man.

Once inside the house, the guests and children separated to prepare themselves for the evening. Phoebe flopped on her bed, exhausted. The last thing she wanted to do was to spend hours exchanging polite conversation and then attend a card party.

Reluctantly, she forced herself to prepare for the evening, choosing a lavender gown, which suited her colouring perfectly. As she looked at herself in the mirror, she touched her cheeks. They were still heightened in colour from the exercise of the day. Usually, her propensity to hide in libraries helped to control her naturally rosy complexion; there would be no such regulation tonight: She glowed. At least no one would know if she were blushing; she smiled wryly at herself, as if there was any worry of that!

*

Phoebe was seated between a Lord Fletcher and Captain Rosworth. They were both polite gentlemen, who were clearly disappointed with her as a partner, each preferring the partner on their opposite sides. Instead of being insulted, Phoebe was forced to suppress a smile and enjoy the meal more than she had anticipated. She could remain quiet and recover a little of her energy from the day's exertions.

It was clear the gentlemen were not being put off, as Mr Flynn had been, by Lord Livesey's task of finding a wife. The other ladies were being flirted with to the best of the ability of the gentleman seated nearest each of them. Further round the table, Captain Hall seemed to be enjoying Lady Jane's company immensely. Phoebe puzzled about Lady Jane once more; there was something unusual in the woman, as if she was removed slightly from the rest of them. Phoebe wondered idly if the others thought the same about herself;

she certainly felt as if she were removed from the wider grouping. She smiled slightly, she was too insignificant to even be noticed by the others. The thought gave her comfort rather than upsetting her.

After the ladies had retired to the large square drawing room, they each took their cups and saucers and seated themselves around the room. The gentlemen eventually re-joined the ladies, and Lady Jane took advantage of the disruption to approach Phoebe.

"Miss Westbrook, have you recovered from your unexpected exercise of the day?" Lady Jane asked, sitting herself comfortably next to Phoebe.

"I have, thank you," Phoebe responded.

"I think you are of the same mind as me in thinking there are a few here who would not be suitable as a wife for Lord Livesey," Lady Jane said.

Phoebe smiled, disguising her surprise at being asked such a direct question. "As I include myself in that grouping, I can hardly disagree."

"Really? You seem to get along well with our host," Lady Jane persisted.

"You think so? I'm surprised you've come to that conclusion!" Phoebe responded honestly.

"Forgive my bluntness. You seem very comfortable in his company," Lady Jane said.

Phoebe paused. "Perhaps if I felt more for him, I would be uncomfortable, but I'm under no illusion. He regards me as little as I regard him."

"I see. That does make some sense."

"I do not play games, Lady Jane. I have not the wiles to do so," Phoebe said honestly.

"Neither do I. I'm purely sorting out who is the competition and who is not," Lady Jane said with a smile.

"Is that not very calculated?" Phoebe asked in surprise.

"If it means I win and become the next Lady Livesey, so be it," Lady Jane responded.

"You seem very focused."

"I think determined is the most appropriate term," Lady Jane responded.

"Although, I suppose others in our group are equally determined," Phoebe acknowledged.

"I think I can offer the most appealing arrangement," Lady Jane said. It was perhaps time to let them see just how focused she was on becoming Livesey's bride. Phoebe could spread the word to the others.

"I see," Phoebe responded, not really understanding what Jane meant, but it sounded too calculated in her opinion.

"I'm glad we understand each other," Lady Jane said, moving away from Phoebe. She had received the information she needed: There was no threat from Phoebe. Jane admitted to herself she would never have considered the bluestocking as serious competition; most of the women had more to offer than Phoebe. There was a companionable air about her whenever she'd been near Livesey, and that made it worth trying to find out what was going on. She didn't want to waste time on someone if it didn't work out. She needed to be with Stuart more than she could be at the moment, and Livesey was her best option to achieve that aim.

Aunt Dickson put down her cup silently. The frown on her face was the only sign of what she'd overheard. It was information she wouldn't be forgetting in a hurry.

*

The card party was set-up in what was normally used as the morning room. Four small square tables had already been arranged, ensuring that sixteen of the party would be entertained with cards, for the next few hours at least.

Captain Hall indicated that Phoebe should join his table, but she smiled and shook her head. "No thank you. I'm no card player."

Miss Bateson quickly offered her support. "Miss Westbrook, I can loan you some pennies if that is your hesitation. Do not let lack of funds stop you from joining our table."

Phoebe flushed at the insensitive way of pointing out that money might be a problem. She tried to stop the glare she wanted to give to Miss Bateson, but she wasn't convinced she'd achieved her aim. "Please don't worry. It's more to do with lack of inclination than lack of funds that prevents me joining in tonight. I had much rather seek out a book from the library and sit near the fire."

"It takes all sorts, I suppose!" Miss Bateson said, turning her back to Phoebe. "I've never met anyone who preferred books to cards before! Come, Captain Hall, you should deal the cards."

Gripping her fists, Phoebe left the room.

Chapter 6

Almost stomping across the hallway to the library, Phoebe came to an abrupt halt at the bottom of the stairs. She'd stopped in surprise when noticing the small figure crouched half-way up the stairs.

"Lady Eliza!" Phoebe stated, holding her hand to her chest. "My goodness! You startled me!"

Eliza sniffed, but didn't make any other communication.

Phoebe climbed slowly up the stairs. After her shock had passed, she noticed that Eliza was clearly upset and so she joined the young girl. Sitting on the stairs on a step which was slightly lower than Eliza so she could be on eye level with the child, Phoebe smiled gently.

"What's upset you so much? Have we not all had a lovely day?" Phoebe asked.

"Y-yes," the child sobbed.

"In that case, what can have distressed you so?" Phoebe asked, gently taking hold of Eliza's hand and rubbing it in a soothing motion.

"N-n-nanny, says we'll all end up in the pond like our mother. She says she'll take Sophia there herself if she does not behave," Eliza confessed. "I ran out of the room to try to stop her bringing Sophia down the stairs. But nanny is so big! If she comes, I don't know what I'll do!"

Phoebe had stiffened at the words. Everyone knew the way Lady Livesey had died, but to threaten young children with the same fate was inexcusable.

"I promise you this, Eliza: Nanny will not be bringing Sophia or anyone else down these stairs," Phoebe said through gritted teeth, dispensing with the formality of the children's titles in the circumstances. "Does she say this often?"

"Quite often," Eliza admitted. "Tonight, she brought in a spare shoe and says she is going to make us behave, or we'll get the shoe before she takes us to the lake."

"Oh, she did, did she?" Phoebe said ominously. "Come, I need to have words of my own with nanny."

"Oh! No!" Eliza wailed. "She will tell me off for telling tales!"

"No she won't," Phoebe said grimly. "If you all have to sleep in my chamber, you will not be left alone with nanny until I inform your father about her."

"He will say nanny knows best. He's said it in the past," Eliza said, still looking terrified.

"I'm going to convince him that she does not," Phoebe said.

She should have gone to Livesey and explained the upset and her concerns. She was going to until Eliza said he'd supported the nanny in the past. It might be his house and his children, but Phoebe couldn't stand by and let cruelty against three young children take place. No. If it meant she was going to get thrown out of the house tomorrow, so be it. At least she would've tried to stop such cruelty.

Holding out her hand she took Eliza's small one and started up the stairs.

Livesey had come out of the card room, mainly to see if Phoebe was suffering because of the insult Miss Bateson had offered her. It was ironic that he'd been quite happy to insult her, but hadn't liked it when someone else had done it. He had glared at Miss Bateson and had received satisfaction when the chit had seen his expression and had shrunk into herself. Turning away from his other guests, he hadn't cared who had observed him leaving the room.

On entering the hallway he'd heard Phoebe's voice and he'd hung back. Not sure why, he stood and watched her with Eliza. He hadn't heard the whole of the conversation, but it was enough to make his blood boil. As they rose and started up the stairs, Livesey moved forward and then paused. He should intervene on his daughter's behalf but for some reason he hesitated. He decided to follow and listen to what happened. If need be he could dish out his own punishment to the nanny later. For the moment he would let Phoebe react to the situation.

Phoebe had no idea she was to have an audience, but by the time they reached the children's attics, she was angrier than she'd ever been.

Walking in without announcing herself she saw the nanny shake Jenny and throw her onto the bed. Sophia was already in hers, crying loudly. Phoebe pulled Eliza to her side in a movement of unconscious protection.

"I suggest you move away from the children. Now," Phoebe said fiercely.

"Oh! I did not see you there, Miss! I'm just sorting out these rascals," Nanny said, her demeanour undergoing a change into the smiling nanny any parent would want for their children.

"I don't like your way of 'sorting out' children. I suggest you leave these rooms and wait in the kitchen until Lord Livesey speaks to you."

"I beg your pardon?" Nanny asked, her smile slipping. "And who do you think you are giving me orders?"

"I'm the person who won't stand to watch, or hear about, children being treated appallingly," Phoebe responded.

"Lady Eliza has an over-active imagination!"

"What is that shoe doing on the end of Lady Sophia's bed?" Phoebe asked, her tone menacing for one substantially smaller than the woman in charge of the children.

"What? Oh! I left my shoe there earlier!" came the quick response.

"And if I examine Lady Sophia and Lady Jenny I won't find any evidence the shoe has been used against them?" Phoebe asked.

"Listen here, Miss. Lord Livesey trusts me to look after his daughters. If he was concerned perhaps he'd come up more! He never visits because he is happy with the way I look after *his* children!" the nanny responded tartly. "When I tell him what impertinence I've been expected to put up with, he will take hold of the shoe himself! These children need a firm hand."

"If you don't leave this room soon, I will need a firm hand when I slap you senseless!" Phoebe ground out.

"Mind your own business, young lady, and leave me to do my job! Lord Livesey lets me administer punishment in a suitable manner!"

"Does he indeed? So he approves of you threatening his children to suffer the same fate as their mother? And that you'll carry them down to the lake yourself if they don't do as you ask?"

"WHAT?" came the roar from behind Phoebe, startling everyone in the room.

Livesey had found it quite amusing at first. He'd almost burst out laughing when Phoebe had threatened violence against a woman who was easily twice her size. But when Phoebe had uttered what the nanny had been torturing his children with, he'd gone cold and could remain silent no longer.

"My Lord, it's all lies!" Nanny responded first.

"Hardly something children would make up," Phoebe said, swallowing at seeing the fire in Livesey's eyes, but determined to protect the children.

"You haven't got a clue what these three are like!" Nanny spat at Phoebe.

"They could be the worst children in the world, and they wouldn't deserve that. My Lord, I beg you to remove this woman from her post. I do not think the girls are safe under her care," Phoebe said quickly but firmly. She hoped Livesey would not turn on her, but from the look of him, she didn't think he would support the nanny as he had in previous altercations if what Eliza had said was true.

"You have exactly thirty minutes to leave my home," Livesey ground out, glaring at his nanny. "How dare you threaten my daughters with such a fate?"

"It's all been blown out of proportion, My Lord," Nanny said, flustered.

"I doubt very much that is the case. You now have twenty-nine minutes," Livesey said with a snarl. "Now go before I throw you out myself!"

Nanny sobbed and ran out of the room. Phoebe sighed with relief. She looked at Livesey and felt sorry for him; he looked horrified.

"I can stay with the children tonight, if it would help," she said quietly.

"No. Thank you. One of the junior maids will stay with them until a new nanny can be found," Livesey said. "I need to speak to my daughters."

"Of course! Please excuse me," Phoebe said, glad she'd spoken out, but Livesey could still want her out of his household. She had interfered when she should have trusted him to do the right thing.

She left the girls alone with their father.

Livesey didn't really know what to do. He'd hardly ever been in his children's nursery rooms. Running his hand through his hair, he sat on the corner of Sophia's bed. He pulled Eliza to him and indicated that Sophia and Jenny should come to him. They each approached, a little reluctant, but soon clambered onto their father's lap.

"Did nanny hurt you?" he asked.

"Not very," Sophia said with a sniff.

"A little," Jenny admitted.

"I'm so sorry," Livesey said.

"It's not your fault, Papa," Eliza said, looking concerned for her father. "Nanny tells us it is because we are bad like our Mama was. She says it's in the blood."

Livesey gritted his teeth, but took a deep steadying breath before he spoke. "Your Mama was full of life, but she was not bad," he stated. They didn't need to know the reality of their parents' marriage or know the faults of Angelina's personality. "She was not a lady who would sit quietly in a room. She would laugh a lot, dance, and sing until everyone else was exhausted."

"She sounds nice," Jenny said quietly.

"She was. Many people loved her," Livesey admitted. "What happened in the lake was an accident. A terrible accident. She never wanted to leave her girls."

"Do we look like her?" Sophia asked.

"Yes. You all do in your different ways. You are all so beautiful," Livesey admitted, not knowing where the words were coming from, but at the more relaxed, happier faces of his children, he was grateful to be so unusually eloquent.

"We wish she was still here," Eliza admitted.

"I know, but one day hopefully I'll find someone else to marry and then you'll have another mother to love," Livesey said.

"Aunt Jessica says that is what all the ladies are here for," Jenny said with a mischievous smile. "We hope you don't marry Miss Sumner!"

Livesey chuckled. "I'll be having words with Aunt Jessica for telling you about the party, but I can promise you I will not be marrying Miss Sumner."

"Good," Sophia said with feeling.

"Now. Come, back to bed all of you. I will go and sort out Meg to stay with you tonight. She'll be with you until you get a new nanny."

"If Meg cannot stay, Miss Westbrook said we could all stay in her bed chamber. She made nanny not seem quite so scary," Eliza said. "I like Miss Westbrook."

"Yes. So do I," Lord Livesey said.

Chapter 7

Re-entering the temporary games room, Livesey was accosted by Miss Sumner.

"My Lord! We have missed you this past hour! Where have you been?"

"I've had a slight problem with my nanny. I had to arrange for there to be some changes. Not the best time for it to happen, but it needed my immediate attention. I'm sorry for my absence," Livesey admitted.

Jessica paused in her card game. "Is everything well, brother?"

"It is now," Livesey admitted, not wishing to go into details of what had happened.

"We thought you were on an assignation with the bookish Miss Westbrook!" Miss Bateson pealed with giggles. "You were both gone so long."

"Is Miss Westbrook not here?" Livesey asked, for the first time taking a good look around the room. He'd presumed she had returned as he had done.

"As you see we are pining for her company," Miss Bateson said. "Come and see, My Lord. I am doing so well!"

The card games finished earlier than was usually the case. Aunt Dickson contrived that she was the one to break-up the party and encourage everyone to retire. Only Jessica, Aunt Dickson, and Livesey were eventually left in the card room. Upon questioning Livesey, Aunt Dickson nodded in approval at his actions.

"Those poor children!" Jessica said. "They can come for a visit with me after this house party has finished until you appoint someone new. They would enjoy the adventure and deserve one after this evening."

"Thank you. I think it would be helpful to them to spend some time away from here," Livesey admitted. "The irony is, they are about as different from their mother as it is possible to be, apart from in looks of course."

"They are like you when you were little," Aunt Dickson said to Jessica. "They're no fools, but they are good girls."

"So they aren't like me then?" Livesey asked with a raised eyebrow.

"Ruled by their emotions and not thinking through the consequences of anything? No. They are not like you," Aunt Dickson replied.

"I wish I'd not asked!"

Jessica smiled. "They are like you. Stop teasing him aunt! He's going through enough torture with this house party."

"Ah, so you admit it do you?" Livesey asked with a gleam in his eye.

"Only now, when even I'm tiring of one or two of the young women!" Jessica admitted with a smile. "I hope there is one worthy of you, brother."

"There is, but I don't think he will see it," Aunt Dickson said with feeling.

"I am considering someone," Livesey said, sending daggers to his aunt.

"Hurmph" came the disparaging response.

"Who? Who? Pray tell!" Jessica said eagerly.

"That wouldn't be fair, and I've not completely decided," Livesey admitted. It would be the perfect solution he thought to himself, a way he could remain cold and aloof for the rest of his days. If it were so perfect though, why hadn't he already accepted? He could end the house party early and be done with it. He inwardly shook himself; he was a fool not to announce his engagement, but something was holding him back.

"I want to know as soon as you've made a decision," Jessica said with feeling. "I'm glad you are going to marry again, brother. You deserve some happiness," she said gently.

Livesey stood. "As long as the chit cares for the children, genuinely, and I can bear to face her every day, that is all the criteria I have. Let's not start any foolish talk about love and happiness!"

The two women watched with varying levels of despair as Livesey's back disappeared through the door.

Aunt Dickson was the first to break the silence. "The fool has started to fall in love, but he has no idea what is happening to him. If he doesn't realise in time, he could be about to make yet another huge mistake because I'm sure he's not thinking of marrying the right girl. And yet the perfect one is under this roof."

"I could not bear it if he chooses the wrong one and isn't happy, Aunt. I really could not," Jessica said sadly.

*

Livesey walked into the library. He'd known she'd be here as soon as it was pointed out that she was missing from the card room. He could have roared at Miss Bateson's impertinence, but like a simpering miss, he'd held himself back. There was no point revealing there was any favouritism on his part towards Phoebe.

He paused when he saw her. She was asleep on one of the wing-backed chairs near the fire. She held her glasses loosely in her hand, her book still on her lap. Livesey leaned on the now closed door. Of all the people gathered in his home, Phoebe was the one who was surprising him the most.

He smiled as he thought of the evening. The way she had stood up to his nanny. There had been no hesitation in her defending his children. She had not been cowed or faltered in the slightest.

She looked to be in a deep sleep. Livesey should wake her or leave her be, but he did neither. He moved to a chair and sat opposite her, watching her. She seemed so peaceful and relaxed in her sleeping state. In reality, she always seemed controlled, not in a repressed way as he knew full well he was, but in a more content way. She seemed at peace with her lot in life, or was it at peace with herself? For someone who was constantly haunted by past actions or the responsibilities he faced, he envied someone who was sure where they fitted into the world. He wondered if he'd ever feel that way.

He had seen passion and fire in her. He doubted she could ever be cold to those who deserved kindness or whom she cared for. It warmed him that she had defended his children, who until this party he'd hardly been able to look at, never mind love. At least the situation was changing where his children were concerned. He seemed to be making progress with getting to know them and making them less wary of him. They'd all given him kisses before he'd left the nursery. It had warmed his heart and terrified him at the same time.

He sighed, and it must have been louder than he thought because Phoebe moved slightly. Livesey remained still until it seemed as if her glasses would slip out of her hands. He moved quickly to catch them, but the movement woke her.

Phoebe blinked in surprise. "My Lord, what are you doing in my chamber?" she asked without hysterics. Stretching deliciously, she smiled slightly at him.

Livesey smiled in return. "Miss Westbrook, you are in my library." He handed her the glasses.

"Oh, really? Dear me! I must have dozed off! I do apologise!" Phoebe said with a laugh in her voice and a blush on her cheeks as she placed the glasses back on her nose.

Livesey's insides warmed to think he'd seen her without her glasses. He continued to smile at her. "After the service you did my children this evening, you could sleep anywhere you wished."

Phoebe flushed further as an unbidden thought of sleeping in the master bed chamber flitted through her mind. She pulled herself together quickly. "I half expected to be thrown from the house," she admitted.

"Yes. You know enough of my harshness to fear I would not defend my children," Livesey said in a self-mocking tone.

"I've never doubted your affection for your girls!" Phoebe said quickly. "I was thinking more along the lines of criticising a member of your staff. Especially when I realised you had been in the background, listening!"

Livesey laughed slightly. "It was amusing at first to see the quiet Miss Westbrook take nanny to task. When you threatened to slap her senseless I nearly gave myself away, but then of course you revealed what that woman had been threatening them with. I wanted to kill her."

"I think I might have done if you had not intervened. I've never felt so angry before. I didn't know I could feel such fury," Phoebe said with a rueful smile.

"I owe you a great debt," Livesey admitted.

"No you don't," Phoebe responded, standing up. "It was pure luck that I passed the bottom of the stairs when Lady Eliza was there. None of us would have left her alone in such a state."

Livesey wasn't so sure, but he also stood and walked with Phoebe to the door. "I'm sorry Miss Bateson offered you an insult earlier."

"It's of no concern. Those who have much can behave as they see fit. She is not unusual in that respect, and I'm sure she meant well," Phoebe said.

Livesey smiled gently. "You are a wonder," he said before stepping closer and bending towards Phoebe. Her eyes opened wider as he placed a gentle kiss on her lips. Moving his arm around her waist, he moved to pull her closer, but Phoebe placed a hand on his chest to stay him.

"My Lord, do not do this," Phoebe said quietly, so close to Livesey she could feel the warmth of his breath tickling her skin and feel his heartbeat under her hand.

"Why not?" Livesey asked, looking into the enlarged pupils, which gave away the fact she would welcome another kiss if he pressed it on her.

Phoebe sighed. She would curse herself later, but her pride made her speak out. "You feel obliged to me because of tonight. I'm vain enough to want someone to kiss me because they like me above anyone else. We both know that not to be the case here."

"You were magnificent, and I'm looking for a mother for my children," Livesey said with feeling.

Phoebe sighed. "I know, and it is laudable that you are preparing to marry for such a reason. You know why I'm here. My parents and my uncle wish for me to have every opportunity I can. I would not argue against them; their motives are created because of affection, but I cannot be married to someone who does not love me."

"I like you. Isn't that a start?" Livesey asked, his frown reappearing. He hadn't meant to speak words of matrimony, but at the moment she was going to leave the room, he'd been compelled to stop her. He wanted to try to explain in his inelegant way how much he'd been affected by her.

Phoebe reached up, and in a brazen act, rubbed her fingers gently across the all-too-present frown. It deepened at her touch as he tried to understand what she was saying. "As I make you do this above anything else, I do not think it's a good enough start for marriage," she said gently. "You're a good catch, My Lord, but while you cannot love me, I cannot be your wife." Phoebe kissed him gently, once more not restraining herself with the need to touch him before she forced herself to move away.

Livesey stood rooted to the spot. "This might be the best offer you receive," he said a little tartly.

"It might," Phoebe said, reaching for the door.

"You would be an old maid rather than accept me? God! You must really dislike me!" he said incredulously.

Phoebe smiled slightly. "I would not be so harsh on yourself. There are women of our group who are keen to marry you."

"I wonder if Captain Hall would receive the same refusal if he asked you to marry him!" Livesey spat, reacting badly to being rejected. He'd never received rejection before, and it stung. The fact that it was given with tact and consideration meant nothing to him.

Phoebe paused from her exit through the door and looked back at Livesey. "You are better than that comment, My Lord. I bid you goodnight."

Livesey was left dumbfounded. He'd offered marriage, and she'd turned him down! Of all the nonsensical, befuddled chits! Well, let her marry the aging captain and see what marriage was like to a man past his prime! She would end up nothing more than a nursemaid!

He turned into the room, approaching the brandy decanter in two strides. It was going to be a long night.

*

Phoebe dismissed her maid as soon as was practicable. He had insulted her and now he'd proposed to her! This was certainly not how she'd expected her visit to develop. She rested her head in her hands; she couldn't marry him, but oh! how she wanted to!

She had developed feelings for Livesey in such a short time, but they were there, and they were strong. It was those same feelings that had caused her to reject him. Squeezing her eyes closed, she breathed slowly. She was half-way to loving a man and yet had turned him down, but she could not have married him. Was she so foolish, as he certainly thought, to turn him down because he didn't love her? He had admitted he liked her.

Phoebe stood and walked over to the window. Opening the wooden shutter slightly, she looked out onto the night. The lake in the distance glittered in the moonlight. She'd listened to the idle chatter when none of the family had been present. Livesey's marriage had been one of love and passion. But it had gone horribly wrong. There'd been some speculation at the time of the accident that there'd been foul play, but it had been idle gossip, nothing more. There was evidence that the marriage hadn't been a happy one after the first flush of love had eased.

If a passionate love with Livesey hadn't survived, what he could offer her wouldn't stand a chance of growing into something deeper and long-lasting. How could she enter into a marriage where love was one-sided and expect to be happy?

She could marry for the sake of the children; she already cared for them, but that would be as foolish as Livesey offering for her purely based on the needs of his children. No. She'd made the right choice; it would just be a long time before her heart agreed with her head.

Chapter 8

If Phoebe worried about how Livesey might be with her after their kiss and conversation, she needn't have. He was on top form in being the glowering host the morning afterwards. If she had been so inclined she could have convinced herself that he was downhearted that she had refused him. She could have spent a happy day feeling smug towards the others. She was certain she was the only one he'd proposed to, but it wasn't in her character to be so top-lofty. Instead, she accepted that this was who he was and got on with her stay, looking forward to any light relief she could find.

During a walk through the gardens, only Lady Jane and Miss Jackman were brave enough to face up to the glowers and join either side of Livesey. He offered his arms to the ladies, but it was done with little grace. Phoebe idly wondered if Lady Jane would have a conversation with Miss Jackman as she had with herself.

Phoebe was grateful to be walking with Captain Hall. Whatever Livesey had accused her of, Captain Hall was the only visitor who had shown Phoebe pleasure when in her company. He was a gregarious man, so Phoebe didn't let herself get carried away but enjoyed his company for what it was.

"This house party seems to be a hotbed of romance, Miss Westbrook!" Captain Hall said with a laugh at Mr Flynn mooning over Miss Sumner.

Phoebe smiled. "One budding romance is hardly a hotbed, Captain!"

"Oh, I think there's more going on," Captain Hall said. "A few of the ladies are still holding out for our host, but once he makes an announcement, they will settle for the others they like."

"It sounds very cold and contrived," Phoebe admitted.

"Come! It is the way of our world!" Captain Hall chuckled. "I thought you, above anyone else, enjoyed the ludicrousness of our situation. You are not going missish on me, are you, Miss Westbrook?"

Phoebe shook herself. "Me? No! I'd be ashamed to do such a thing! I admit to finding it a little tedious to being confined so much in a group though."

"When you're used to a ship full of sailors, many of whom are characters you would not spend much time with on land, you get used to filtering out a lot of what goes on," Captain Hall admitted.

"I need to learn that skill!" Phoebe said with feeling.

"I'll tell you what; let me speak to Rosworth and see if he's up for a horse ride, shall I? A good gallop across the fields will blow away that hemmed in feeling," Captain Hall offered.

Phoebe paused. She shouldn't really; it could be seen as impolite, but how she wanted to escape! All she wanted to do was watch Livesey when in his company, and it was clear he wanted nothing to do with her after their exchange last night. She smiled. Why make herself suffer?

"Why not, Captain?" she said with a smile. "I will need a groom to accompany us, but I'm ready to let the wind clear my head!"

"Capital! I'll return in a moment," Captain Hall said, walking with purpose to Captain Rosworth. The two men had a swift chat, in which Captain Rosworth shot her a curious look, but he agreed, and the three excused themselves from the walk. They spoke only to Jessica, not wishing to turn it into a large outing.

Walking away from the larger group, Phoebe felt exhilarated and daring, completely unaware of the looks of equal measures of longing and annoyance Livesey was aiming at her retreating form.

*

The horses pounded over the rolling countryside. She was free and let her mount gallop as fast as he wanted. The two captains kept pace with her, as comfortable on horses as they were on a rolling ship. The thud of the hooves felt, as if with easy forward movement, she was escaping from the oppression she felt inside the house.

Laughing as Captain Hall indicated they should aim for the folly on the hill, Phoebe kicked her steed and increased her pace. Hair streaming behind her unchecked, she galloped on; for once she wasn't going to be the mild Miss Westbrook.

They reached the top of the hill, everyone breathing heavily at the exertion. Letting the horses catch their breath, Captain Hall smiled at Phoebe. "Better?" he asked.

"Oh, much, thank you! It feels good to escape," Phoebe said, her skin glowing and her eyes shining with the exercise.

"My escape is going to be of the more permanent kind," Captain Rosworth stated.

"Why is that?" Captain Hall asked.

"I've had enough of being on the fringes of the entertainment," Captain Rosworth admitted. "It sounded like a good idea when Lady Knowles invited me. I didn't realise at the time that the gentlemen were being asked purely to make up the numbers! I know Flynn has complained bitterly about it, but he is right. It's not good *ton*."

Phoebe thought it prudent to remain quiet. Captain Rosworth hadn't been very gentlemanly when seated next to her, and he'd been quite cutting of some of the other ladies in the group. She'd never really warmed to him.

"Didn't think you would be one to run at the start of the battle!" Captain Hall said, but his tone wasn't condemning.

"It's not really, though, is it?" Captain Rosworth asked. "I am not waiting around to pick up someone else's cast-offs!"

"With ladies as fine as those Livesey's invited, I'm more than happy to mop up the tears when the announcement is finally made!" Captain Hall said with a grin.

"Not I!" Captain Rosworth said. "I'll be calling for my carriage as soon as we return."

"Perhaps we should return and let Captain Rosworth make use of whatever daylight is left?" Phoebe suggested.

"Are you not going to try to persuade him to stay, Miss Westbrook?" Captain Hall teased. "One less gentleman to entertain you will be a sad loss, will it not?"

"As I have already admitted I'd rather hide for most of my visit. I think any words I utter would hint at falsehoods," Phoebe said with a small smile.

"Ah! Here's one who is not repining your loss, Rosworth! Never mind. I'm sure when you get back to town your bruised ego will soon be soothed," Captain Hall said.

"Soothed, as is every sailor with a girl in every port," Captain Rosworth said with a smug look.

Phoebe didn't like condemning people but she was glad he'd be leaving. She didn't like to think of him chasing any of the ladies in the party. His conversation had convinced her further that he wasn't a gentleman in the truest sense of the word.

They turned back to the house, preventing further conversation by galloping at a thrilling speed.

*

Phoebe had been delayed in the stables. She always liked to help brush the horse she'd been riding; it was her way of saying thank you to the beast. The two captains had left her to her ministrations, so she was alone as she entered the house.

Taking off her riding hat, she touched her hair and smiled. Her hair was a tangled mess; she'd cause her maid untold angst to sort it for the evening.

Livesey walked out of his study as Phoebe was crossing the hallway. He paused for a second, seeing her as if for the first time. Jessica followed him out of the room, and she looked in the direction her brother was staring. Phoebe continued to the stairs and made her way to her bed chamber without noticing she was being watched.

"I was a little deflated when I was obliged to invite Miss Westbrook," Jessica admitted. "But she has turned out to be quite a surprise."

"Oh?" Livesey asked, trying to focus on what his sister had said, having been affected by the flushed cheeks, sparkling eyes, and enigmatic smile on her lips.

"Next to her sisters and others, she looks the plain miss, but she is pretty in a quiet, surprise-you kind of way and is intelligent and witty to boot. I'm glad her uncle asked for the invitation. I have enjoyed getting to know her," Jessica admitted, as Phoebe disappeared out of sight at the top of the stairs.

"She's too clever for her own good! She doesn't know how to agree to something that is the best offer she will ever have," Livesey grumbled.

"Whatever do you mean?" Jessica laughed at her brother.

"She turned me down last night, saying I don't love her!" Livesey ground out. He wouldn't normally confide in his sister; he'd never done so with Angelina, but for some reason, Phoebe's refusal had eaten at him like nothing else, and he had to voice his frustration.

"You did what?" Jessica asked, moving to face her brother.

"Yes. I asked one of your chosen few to be my wife, and she turned me down!" Livesey ground out.

"Well, I never!" Jessica said in surprise and shock. "What made you chose Miss Westbrook?"

"She was perfect with the girls," Livesey admitted.

"And?" Jessica probed.

"And? That's it," Livesey shrugged, noticing the expression on his sister's face and started to regret speaking.

"That's it? You expressed no other feelings for her?" Jessica asked.

"I have told you before Jessica: I'm not opening myself to anyone! After what happened with Angelina, I refuse to go through that again," Livesey said. "And I have had an offer I'm considering. So Miss Westbrook's refusal is hardly going to prevent me marrying anyone else."

"*You* have had an offer of marriage? Goodness me! Tell me more!" Jessica said in astonishment.

"Lady Jane has offered me a marriage of convenience, but she has assured me she'll love the children as her own." Livesey took a little enjoyment at his sister looking so astounded.

"A marriage of convenience!" Jessica reached over and touched her brother's chest gently with her hand. "We can fall in love more than once, my dear. If you are open to it, perhaps it will happen…"

"Jessica, you have no idea about me, my previous marriage, or any future marriages I might have. Don't try to understand. You'll be wasting your time!" Livesey walked around his sister and into the library, slamming the door behind him, leaving Jessica staring open-mouthed at a closed wooden door.

Chapter 9

Captain Rosworth's departure caused a stir in the household. It spurred Mr Flynn to make his declaration to Miss Sumner, which surprisingly enough, was accepted, the young lady coming to the conclusion that Lord Livesey was not the catch she had presumed he would be.

Jessica had spent the afternoon in the nursery, and when she joined the guests in the drawing room, she could not prevent a frown from marring her usual relaxed features.

Aunt Dickson approached her niece. "What is ailing you, child?" she asked.

"Eliza isn't well," Jessica confided in her aunt. "She's got a temperature and is quite restless. I have separated her from the others. I don't want them coming down with whatever it is she's suffering from, but I am worried."

"Does my nephew know?"

"Yes. He says I'm not to go to Eliza in my condition, and I know Knowles feels the same. He wants to protect his unborn child; I understand that, but poor Eliza! How can I leave her to her maid?" Jessica said with a wail.

"I will attend her, of course," Aunt Dickson said immediately.

"If I might interrupt?" came Phoebe's quiet voice.

The two ladies turned towards Phoebe who'd been sitting on the sofa a little away from the main group.

"I'd like to offer my services, if I can be of use," Phoebe continued, flushing a little.

"The sick room can be an unpleasant place to be if you aren't used to it," Aunt Dickson said.

"I've nursed my younger sisters," Phoebe said. "I cannot claim all the credit, as my mother was usually there, but being the eldest, I helped. Nothing can be worse than sisters in crotchety moods!"

"Are you doing this to gain favour?" Aunt Dickson asked, her eyes narrowing.

"No!" Phoebe said heatedly. "I would never use children to gain favour from anyone, no matter who they were!"

"I thought not, but I also thought it prudent to check," Aunt Dickson said pleasantly. "I can look after her until you've eaten. You would not want to miss supper?"

"If I could have a tray sent up to Lady Eliza's room, I'd be happy to go immediately," Phoebe admitted.

"Thank you, Miss Westbrook. I know Eliza likes you. It will comfort her to have someone there whom she trusts," Jessica said with feeling.

"I'll call in on you later," Aunt Dickson said with a nod.

Phoebe rose and left the room, unnoticed by most of the people there.

Aunt Dickson watched Phoebe leave. "I've liked her from the start. He could do a lot worse."

Jessica sighed, knowing Livesey would take her to task for the words she was about to utter. "He has already proposed, and she's turned him down," Jessica said quietly.

"What on earth is the chit thinking?" Aunt Dickson asked dumbfounded.

"Apparently, wanting a mother for his children was not enough to tempt her," Jessica said with a smile.

"That's all he offered? Sometimes I think my nephew is a complete blockhead!" Aunt Dickson said with feeling. "Although, did you see the way he watched her as she left the room?"

"Do not see something that isn't there, Aunt. He tore a strip off me for mentioning love to him," Jessica advised.

"No man knows when he's in love," Aunt Dickson poo-pooed.

"Lady Jane has offered him a marriage of convenience, and he's considering it. I doubt he'll ask Miss Westbrook a second time," Jessica said.

"Oh, she has, has she? And why is a young woman, who admittedly is a spinster, but who has title and fortune, offering a marriage of convenience?" Aunt Dickson asked her eyes narrowing in on the unsuspecting Lady Jane.

"I have no idea, but it's something I would never do, no matter how desperate I was!"

"If he marries her, I'll disinherit him!"

"If he marries her, anything you leave him will be nothing more than pin money!" Jessica said with feeling.

*

Phoebe had been taken to Eliza and found the girl feeling very sorry for herself in one of the guest rooms. She had kindly dismissed the maid who'd been assigned to attend to Eliza. Phoebe had promised she would call for anything she needed.

Climbing onto the large canopied bed, Phoebe had pulled Eliza onto her lap, covering them both with a blanket and had stroked the child's hair and sung to her gently. Eventually, Eliza's distress had eased, and she'd fallen into a fitful sleep.

Phoebe was no expert but remembered feeling comfort whenever she was ill and her mother held her like a baby, so she cuddled the child in the same way.

When Eliza was sleeping, Phoebe leaned her head against the large wooden structure of the canopied bed and sighed. What was she doing? She had turned Livesey down and yet every night he was the last thing she thought of before falling asleep and the first thought that entered her head upon waking. She could have said yes so easily.

Her stubbornness insisted she needed more though. She needed to be loved and couldn't accept 'liked' even if the utterance came from the enigmatic Lord Livesey. She sighed. Perhaps she was being cruel, establishing a relationship with his children, but she couldn't stand back and let them be cared for without love by a maid just doing her job. Phoebe found them so easy to love.

Eliza became disturbed, time and again complaining of a sore throat. She would wince and struggle to speak, becoming distressed until Phoebe's soothing words calmed her. Then she would fall asleep until her breathing caused the dryness of her throat to build up once more, and the agitation would start again.

Phoebe was glad when Aunt Dickson entered the room. "I think Lady Eliza would benefit from a hot concoction my father always made us when we suffered from sore throats," she said to the woman.

"We can have a maid prepare it."

"No. I would like to do it myself, if you don't mind comforting Lady Eliza for a few moments," Phoebe said.

"Tired of the sick room already?" Aunt Dickson asked.

"Not at all! I do wish you'd stop trying to find fault with my methods! I've told you previously that I'm not one for playing games," Phoebe said tartly. "I want to make sure it is prepared correctly then I'll return and spend however long I'm needed."

Aunt Dickson smiled. "I do hope you marry my nephew. I would enjoy you being a part of this family. Those other chits are too frightened to challenge me. You'd make a good wife for someone as irritable and troubled as my nephew."

Phoebe flushed furiously. "That will not happen."

"A pity. For both of you," Aunt Dickson responded. "Go and make your medicine. I'll stay with the child."

Phoebe busied herself in the kitchen once the staff had got over their shock of seeing one of the ladies below stairs. She obtained everything she needed except for a tot of whisky. She decided to obtain that on the way back to the sick room.

Entering the library, which she knew contained the spirit she needed, she was surprised to see Livesey and his sister. It was late, and she'd supposed most people were above stairs.

"Please excuse my interruption. I've just come to use a small amount of whisky," Phoebe explained.

"Have my children turned you to drink so soon?" Livesey asked wryly.

Phoebe smiled. "No. I'm giving some to Lady Eliza. She is complaining of a sore throat."

"And whisky is your solution?" Livesey asked, his smile slipping.

"A small amount, yes. Along with honey, lemon, hot water and sugar. It will coat the throat, ease the pain and allow her to rest undisturbed. My father used to make it for us, and we all swore that it made us feel better. To be fair, it could have been the whisky we were fond of, but I don't think so," Phoebe said, mixing the whisky to the cup of liquid she held.

"It smells delicious!" Jessica said with an appreciative sniff.

"It tastes good, which is an advantage when feeling under the weather," Phoebe said. "I should get back to Lady Eliza. Please excuse my intrusion."

Phoebe left the room, leaving brother and sister looking at each other.

"You chose the right one to propose to," Jessica admitted.

"She probably chose the right one to refuse," Livesey said dryly, finally admitting to himself that Phoebe deserved more than he had to offer.

"You could try to woo her," Jessica offered.

"No. I'm going to marry Lady Jane," Livesey said darkly.

"Have you decided to accept such a cold proposal?"

"It is a convenient proposal," Livesey shrugged. "I will not have to try to be someone I'm not, which is an added bonus.

I can go on with my life; she can get on with hers, and the children have a mother."

"I'm sorry you're agreeing to such a marriage," Jessica said sadly.

"It was your idea to arrange this party," Livesey pointed out.

"But I wanted you to fall in love!" Jessica said heatedly.

"You have to have a heart for that to be achieved," Livesey said, standing. "I should check on Eliza. See if Miss Westbrook hasn't turned her into a raging drunk."

Jessica watched her brother as he approached the door. "George?" she said, stopping his exit from the room. "I know she turned you down, but you smile more when she is near or when you speak about her. Please think carefully," Jessica said quietly.

"You are imagining things," Livesey ground out before leaving the room.

Chapter 10

Livesey did not immediately approach the sick room. It was out of character for him, but he made his way to the nursery to check on Jenny and Sophia. They were both asleep in their beds, their cheeks rosy and hair ruffled.

He felt a tug towards them that he had only allowed freedom since the party had commenced. He was almost afraid to love them, but he knew he was fighting a losing battle in trying to maintain his hardened heart, where they were concerned at least. He wanted to do the best for them, and Lady Jane would be it. If he pushed aside the nagging at his inner thoughts, insisting that Miss Westbrook would be the perfect mother, so be it.

He approached the window in the nursery and looked out onto the clear night. The reflection of the pond where Angelina had died mocked him. If he couldn't love someone as beautiful and vibrant as she had been, there was no hope for anyone else to capture his heart.

He wondered at Phoebe's decision. She was on the way to being considered an old maid. Yet she'd turned down a proposal she didn't favour, even though it would have made her secure for the remainder of her days. Not many would do that. He couldn't decide whether it was brave of her or foolish. Probably a little of both he sighed.

He shook himself. He had mocked her and meant every word he'd uttered. Then he had been shown, yet again, he was the fool, not her. She was no great beauty, although Jessica had been correct; once he'd condemned her looks, but he had started to see prettiness in her features and elegance in her deportment. She also had intelligence, wit, and something else. She appealed to him on a level he could not afford to examine. He couldn't open himself up to feel, no matter what. He had tried that once, and he'd made a terrible mistake. No. Lady Jane would be perfect and safe.

Leaving the nursery, he closed the door quietly. His children would have a mother soon; his duty would be complete.

Sighing to himself at the thought, he walked downstairs to the room in which Eliza and Phoebe were ensconced. Opening the door quietly, he saw Phoebe cuddling Eliza, a quilt covering them both. Phoebe was watching Eliza, gently stroking the child's hair. The action caused Livesey's gut to constrict, and he wished to withdraw unnoticed.

Phoebe looked at the door and smiled slightly. "She sleeps," she whispered.

The time for Livesey to exit had passed, and he entered the room. "You need to rest."

"One disturbed night won't put me out of sorts, and she'll be comforted if someone is here if she wakes," Phoebe said.

Livesey approached the bed, looking down at the unnaturally flushed face of his daughter. "You seem to know what to do to offer comfort."

"I'm the eldest, and although it does not have many benefits, it's easy to watch how a family works," Phoebe said with a smile.

"If the family works in the first place," Livesey ground out. "I doubt my offspring have learned any valuable lessons so far."

"We grow-up despite our parents' foibles," Phoebe said with a smile. "That is what my father says anyway."

"It sounds like he knows what he's talking about." Livesey sat on the edge at the bottom of the bed.

"I think it was my father's way of absolving himself from any responsibility for our faults," Phoebe responded fondly.

"Angelina wasn't a natural mother," Livesey admitted quietly.

"It must be a difficult task to take on," Phoebe said gently. She wondered at the complicated man revealing something so damning about his late wife.

"You seem to be able to do it. From the start, they took to you," Livesey pointed out.

"Easy, when it is not a requirement every day. None of us knows what type of parent we'll be until we actually perform the role."

"I wasn't a good father, either," Livesey admitted. He was speaking to Phoebe, but he never took his eyes off Eliza.

Phoebe remained quiet.

"No reassurance, Miss Westbrook?" Livesey asked with a small smile, glancing at her.

"I would not insult you by uttering false platitudes when I've no idea what kind of father you are. You seem to be making amends now, if you were lacking."

Livesey couldn't help grin at her response. "Thank you for a back-handed compliment."

"You're welcome," Phoebe responded with an answering grin.

"I spent most of my time trying to maintain Angelina's good mood," Livesey admitted for the first time to anyone.

"Have you any idea what it's like to live with someone whose mood can change by the minute?"

"No," Phoebe said quietly.

"It is absolutely exhausting," Livesey admitted. "I had no time for anything or anyone else."

"You must have loved her very much," Phoebe said. She tried to push aside the stab of jealousy at the thought. It was an unreasonable emotion that she wouldn't waste time on.

Livesey looked at Phoebe. "I've never said this to anyone else, Miss Westbrook. I did not love Angelina. Oh, I thought I did, but I realised it was only a youthful lust when it was too late. When she died, I was relieved. Can you believe that? Relieved that my wife had died! What kind of man does that make me?"

Phoebe paused before speaking. "A foolish one for not realising quickly enough that your wife was not the one for you. Many couples are joined because of compromising situations. I've been out in society long enough to have seen that on many occasions. But you stood by your family when others would have abandoned them. It would have been easy to abandon your wife and unborn child whilst you were still abroad. It's to your credit, you didn't."

"You're more forgiving than I would be if our roles were reversed. I feel like a monster most of the time. I doubt I'll ever be able to look at myself without condemning my actions from the moment I met her," Livesey admitted.

"You are too hard on yourself. You need to accept what has passed and stop regretting your actions. It's your history now, it doesn't have to influence your future," Phoebe smiled slightly.

"I doubt my regrets will ever go away." Livesey stood, pausing. He had seemed to be leaving the room, but he turned to Phoebe, this time meeting her gaze. "I wanted you to understand why I could never give you what you needed, Miss Westbrook. I scorn you and anyone else who wants to marry for love because I am unable to love."

Phoebe smiled sadly. "I'm sure that if you met the right person, you would be able to take the leap of faith that we all have to take when loving someone."

"I will not be waiting for that to happen. I'm going to marry Lady Jane. I wanted you to know, bearing in mind our previous conversation," Livesey said, moving to the door. He could see she was shocked and disappointed at his words, and he needed to be away from her. Why she affected him so much left him puzzled, but he couldn't cope with seeing disappointment in her expression. He wanted to have her laugh and tease him, but then he would want to crawl onto the bed and beg her to love him enough for the both of them.

"I see," Phoebe said. Her voice croaked. "I wish you happy. I truly do."

"And that is exactly why you made the right choice in turning down my proposal," Livesey said. "You deserve better than me, Miss Westbrook."

As Livesey left Phoebe alone with Eliza, she knew without doubt that the only person she had ever loved and who she would ever want was going to marry someone else. And she'd missed her chance to be joined to him. There was a fool in the house, and it was she.

She leaned her head against the structure of the bed. She had never felt so desolate in her life.

Livesey spoke to Lady Jane during the morning. "I've decided to accept your proposal," he said, after inviting her to join him in his study. He'd come straight to the point. There was no benefit in dallying now he'd made up his mind.

"Really? I thought your favour lay in another direction," Lady Jane responded.

"No. What you have offered seems to be the best option. We neither of us are under any illusion. It is the safest outcome for finding someone suitable for the upbringing of my children." His tone was as dead as his insides.

"We need to sign a legal document. I have one prepared," Lady Jane said, matter-of-factly.

Livesey raised an eyebrow. "You were clearly confident of the outcome of this party."

"Not at all. I needed to be prepared, just in case," Lady Jane responded. "It covers the practical side of things. I need to reiterate that I refuse to enter into any sort of physical relationship with you, Livesey."

"You've already made that clear. You don't need to worry on that score." It didn't concern Livesey that he wouldn't be sharing a bed with his future wife. He had no attraction towards her, and knowing there was someone else, he wasn't about to try to seek marital relations.

"There are a number of issues the contract covers. Shall I give it to you, and we can discuss any concerns you might have before we make an announcement?" Lady Jane asked.

"No. I will look over it tomorrow. We can announce our engagement tonight when we're gathered in the drawing room. If nothing else, I hope it will bring the party to a close," Livesey said with feeling.

"It will be better once we are married," Lady Jane soothed. "Neither of us will want to socialise much. You will be able to do exactly as you wish."

"No, I don't suppose we will be seeking to be in the public much," Livesey acknowledged.

"I'd also like you to consider us being married by special licence," Lady Jane said. Once more she was nervous. If he disagreed, the reason she needed to marry quickly would become obvious very soon.

"What's the hurry?" Livesey asked. "Would your parents not wish to invite half of London to a grand spectacle?"

"They would. But it would benefit me—us—if the marriage took place sooner rather than later," Lady Jane said, for the first time looking shamefaced.

Livesey frowned at her for a second. "So the affair has already begun?"

"For some time, but it is the first time I've been in this position. Let's just say, a timely wedding would cause less questions needing difficult answers," Lady Jane responded.

"Ah, I see. I'll read the contract tomorrow, and we can decide how to proceed for a special licence," Livesey said.

"I'll retrieve the contract now, so you can start to peruse it," Lady Jane said. She left the study half-hopeful, half-fearful. A marriage to Livesey would solve much of the angst she'd been suffering since before the house party started. She just hoped Livesey would agree to her terms. It was a lot to ask of anyone, and she hoped he would appreciate the benefits a union between them could have. There was too much at stake now for it to fail.

Livesey waited in his study for Lady Jane to return. He'd felt empty long before agreeing to marry her, and he was under no illusion that he would ever feel better. The decision had been made, and he would at least have the reassurance that his girls would have a mother who had promised to care for them as her own. That aspect would clearly be put to the test early in their marriage. It appeared she was already with child.

He rubbed his hands over his face, moving from the despairing position only when Lady Jane returned.

"Here you are. Please read it this afternoon," Lady Jane urged.

Livesey accepted the document and nodded. He should by rights have his solicitor look over the document, but if she wanted a quick wedding, there would be no time for such delays. He was happy to trust his own judgement; it was his life after all, but for now he couldn't face it.

Glancing over the parchment, he pushed it to one side. It was time to seek out his sister and aunt and let them know what he'd decided.

*

Livesey found Jessica and Aunt Dickson in the library. Thankfully, they were alone.

Jessica looked crestfallen when Livesey told her the news.

"Don't look so down, Jessica. It is what you wanted after all," Livesey said with a growl.

"I wanted you to fall in love," Jessica almost whined.

Livesey smiled. "And be like you and Knowles? One besotted pair in the family is quite enough!"

Jessica smiled slightly. "Don't fun with me! I saw how you were with Angelina; I wanted you to experience that again."

Livesey rolled his eyes and shook his head. There was no benefit in trying to convince his sister that his marriage was anything other than what she presumed.

Livesey turned to his aunt. "No comment, Aunt?" he asked.

"None that you would listen to, so I'll save my breath to do something useful with," Aunt Dickson said, without her usual fire.

"I'm astounded!" Livesey responded. "It is almost worth getting married if it renders you speechless!"

Jessica rose. "I'll leave you. I want to tell Knowles. Your news will upset a few in the party, I fear."

"I doubt that," Livesey said dryly.

Before Jessica left the room, she approached her brother, giving him a kiss on the cheek. "I just want you and the children to be happy. I hope you will find that with Lady Jane, even though it is not a love match."

Livesey smiled slightly at his sister. "You worry too much," he said gently.

Jessica left the room, and Livesey watched his aunt. She seemed in deep thought, and it puzzled him. "Is my news so shocking?" he asked.

"What? No. Not at all. It's just the type of buffleheaded behaviour I have come to expect of you!" Aunt Dickson responded.

Livesey smiled. "I'm glad to have acted true to form for your entertainment, if nothing else."

"Just because you couldn't love the chit who fooled you into marrying her, doesn't mean you have to keep making foolish errors. You are a lot older now than when you met Angelina," Aunt Dickson said.

Livesey looked in surprised shock at his aunt. She'd never uttered anything previously that would suggest she had any inclination about how he truly felt about Angelina.

"It was obvious you were in above your head within the first year of marriage. An unfortunate consequence of not using your brain to think before your body responded to a beautiful face!" Aunt Dickson said tartly.

"I'm not sure this is the type of conversation one should be having with their widowed aunt!" Livesey said with feeling.

"Nonetheless, it is the truth."

"You're the only person to have suggested my marriage was a farce," Livesey admitted.

"I might be older but I'm not blind or deaf. Everyone saw Angelina's beauty and excused her temperament due to her foreign birth. I saw the reality of the effects of an unstable woman on a foolish boy. For that is what you were," Aunt Dickson said.

"I was old enough to produce children," Livesey said.

"Yes. Some fourteen year-olds are capable of producing children but not of raising them. Those girls are the best things to come out of your union," Aunt Dickson admitted.

"I'm beginning to feel that at last." Livesey did feel as if he had come to be less of a stranger to his girls. He realized that it was mainly due to Phoebe's actions, a thought he tried to push from the forefront of his mind.

"And so you should. A pity you cannot trust your feelings in your choice of wife."

"I'm not going to discuss anyone who I have not chosen. I've made my decision for the right reasons," Livesey defended his decision.

"You've made the safe choice. The one that will keep you in the little bubble you exist in, afraid to leave because you are terrified of being hurt," Aunt Dickson said.

"Aunt, you should be writing poetry, uttering such prose!" Livesey responded derisively. "You've mistaken my motives and the reason I have made my choice," he lied.

"I've tired of this party. I'll be leaving tomorrow. I need a trip to London to convince myself that the world has not gone completely mad! At least if it is just my family who are the fools, I've no need to see them again!" Aunt Dickson said with disgust. She stood and moved towards the door. "I'll eat in my room tonight, I do not wish to be in your company at the moment. I curse you to the devil for what you have done! You're a complete buffoon!"

"There is no need to separate yourself from us," Livesey said in an effort to pacify his aunt. It was unlike her to be so cutting towards him. She usually spoke her mind, but indulged and forgave his misdemeanours in equal measure.

"There is every need! I cannot bear to be near you! You're throwing away the one chance of happiness you have, and you're not listening to yourself or anyone else. I know you do not believe this is the right course of action, but while you won't admit it before it's too late, I have done with you!" Aunt Dickson snapped before leaving the room.

Livesey was stunned by his aunt's words. She was always acerbic, but her outburst had been different. She'd never cursed him in such a way, more often than not siding with him.

He was surprised at her insight. She'd never approached him whilst he was married to say what she'd seen. No. He'd been alone with his struggles then, so it was frustrating that she chose to interfere at this point in his life. He might have been comforted when he was suffering with Angelina to know someone else had seen his difficulties. Instead she'd held her counsel, and he'd battled on alone.

He gritted his teeth. He'd made his decision and was sticking to it.

Chapter 11

Phoebe had joined the party for their evening meal. She would have preferred to have stayed with Eliza, but the child was feeling a lot better, bouncing back to health far quicker than was expected. Phoebe wondered if she'd been overwhelmed by the incident with her nanny and had felt ill, rather than actually being ill. After a quiet day Eliza was now keen to join her sisters in the nursery. Phoebe almost cursed the effectiveness of her father's tonic, but she could not be sorry that Eliza was feeling better just because of her own discomfort.

She had been on edge throughout the meal, waiting for an announcement to be made. Lady Jane had been seated next to Livesey, and although they'd chatted during the meal, there didn't seem to be much affection between the pair. Phoebe was hardly surprised at this, but to her shame, she was glad of the fact. It was an irrational thought which she cursed herself for, but she couldn't shake that particular thought.

When the gentlemen rejoined the ladies in the drawing room, Livesey immediately approached Lady Jane and took her by the hand. She stood next to him in front of the fireplace, and Livesey coughed to draw the attention of the guests. They looked fine, him in his usual black frock coat and contrasting cream breeches, she in a deep red taffeta dress. They were a handsome pair, both confident with their position in the world.

"I'd like to make an announcement. Lady Jane has done me the honour in agreeing to be my wife," Livesey said with a small smile, not quite meeting anyone's gaze and certainly not looking at his wife- to-be.

There were a few shocked expressions as the room became uncomfortably silent. Jessica moved across to the couple standing in front of the fire.

"Let me be the first to congratulate you both," Jessica said, giving them each a kiss.

Jessica's words seemed to stir everyone into action. Some approached the couple to chat and congratulate, some spoke in hushed whispers between themselves.

Captain Hall approached Phoebe. "A curious choice," he stated without preamble.

"Not really," Phoebe said. "They are both rich, titled and intelligent."

"Yes, from the outside one can see the advantages, but I would never align myself with a woman like that," Captain Hall said.

"Oh?" Phoebe couldn't help asking. It was impolite to speak in such a way, but her own mixed-up feelings caused her to encourage the Captain.

"There is something about Lady Jane I couldn't take to," Captain Hall admitted. "There is a cold heart underneath that calm exterior."

Phoebe couldn't disagree. She'd seen how Lady Jane had been business-like in identifying her opposition. She ached that Livesey would enter into a marriage without love, but she acknowledged that he was a man and perfectly capable of doing as he wished.

"I do not really know her," Phoebe said diplomatically.

"I would not want too," Captain Hall admitted. "I'm looking for a wife who will be on my level in every regard.

You've helped me put things into perspective, Miss Westbrook."

"Me?" Phoebe asked in surprise. "I've done nothing."

"Two people have stood out for me at this house party. Yourself and Lady Sarah. You're both intelligent, sensible and have warm hearts. With the fawning some of the others have done, it would have been enough to set my teeth on edge, if it hadn't been for you two."

"You are very kind," Phoebe said.

"It's made me decide what I truly want in life."

Phoebe's heart-rate started to increase. She looked in alarm at the captain. She didn't want to ask the question, but knew it would be impolite not too. Bracing herself, she tried to smile. "And what is that, Captain?"

"A wife," Captain Hall said. "Now Livesey has chosen, it leaves the way open for me to declare myself. I'd like to thank you for your friendship, Miss Westbrook. It has been a pleasure getting to know you."

"I've enjoyed your company," Phoebe admitted.

"If you will excuse me, I'm going to see if I can have a private word with Lady Sarah. I'd like to make her an offer. There is no point in delaying further," Captain Hall said, looking over at his chosen one.

"Lady Sarah?" Phoebe asked in surprised relief.

"Yes. From the first moment I saw her, I knew she would be the one for me," Captain Hall admitted. "I might be an old fool, falling so deeply, but I could not help it."

"That's wonderful!" Phoebe said with genuine pleasure. "Lady Sarah is lovely, and I sincerely wish you all the happiness in the world."

"Thank you, Miss Westbrook. Now, wish me luck as once more I go into the fray!" Captain Hall said with a laugh.

Phoebe couldn't help smiling at him as he crossed the drawing room and seated himself next to Lady Sarah, who smiled in welcome to him. Phoebe had never noticed any spark between the pair, but looking at them now, it seemed Captain Hall wouldn't be receiving discouragement from Lady Sarah, large age gap or not.

Phoebe failed to notice Jessica approach her. "Captain Hall looks happy. I thought his favours lay in that particular direction," Jessica said quietly.

Phoebe smiled. "For one scary moment just then, I thought they lay in another. Fortunately, my presumption was unfounded, and I've learned a prudent lesson about being too arrogant."

"I would never accuse you of being arrogant!" Jessica smiled. "Would you have accepted the captain if he'd asked?"

Phoebe looked in surprise at Jessica. It was an impertinent question to ask. "No," she responded.

"Forgive me," Jessica said with a rueful smile. "I know you've turned down my brother. I suppose I was testing you…unfairly."

Phoebe had flushed at the words. She had no idea that Livesey would have told anyone about his proposal. "I hope you would keep that knowledge to yourself. I know my parents and uncle would not understand my reasoning, and I would hate to cause them upset."

"But you could not say yes, even for your family's happiness," Jessica pointed out.

"No. Ultimately, I needed to consider my own peace of mind," Phoebe admitted. She did not mention love; that would be giving too much away, and there was no benefit of that at this point.

"A shame," Jessica said with feeling.

Phoebe decided that it was time to take control of her life. "Lady Knowles, please could I use a carriage tomorrow? I know it's a presumption, but I would like to return home if you've no objections."

Jessica sighed. "Livesey said the announcement would be the break-up of the party."

"In that case, he will be pleased with my request," Phoebe said with a slight smile.

"Are you sure you don't want to stay? Your uncle is to collect you at the end of the two weeks," Jessica said.

"No. I'd rather return sooner. I've enjoyed my stay here, but it is time I seriously looked to the future instead of relying on my uncle to secure invitations for me," Phoebe said.

"I have enjoyed having you here," Jessica responded.

"Oh! I didn't mean to sound ungrateful in the slightest. I just want to change a few things about my future. I'm past the age of marrying," Phoebe admitted. At least she would have loved once in her lifetime, and that would have to be enough.

Jessica sighed. "I should have evened the numbers more fairly. I was determined Livesey was going to find a bride, not considering the young ladies who would not be chosen."

"It's a perfectly reasonable aim to have," Phoebe said. "It has been a pleasant change to experience the delights of this part of Hampshire. I'd never been so far south before, and I like what I've seen."

"You really are a sweet girl. I will be sad to see you go, but I will arrange for a carriage to be available. Your maid and a footman will travel with you."

"There's no need to waste the time of a footman!" Phoebe said.

"Of course there's a need!" Jessica chided. "You will be returned safe and sound to your family. I'll not change my mind, so you will have to accept escort!"

"Thank you. You are very kind."

*

The marriage announcement was certainly the catalyst that broke up the party. There would be three weddings as a result of the gathering, Captain Hall being accepted by his chosen one. Overall Jessica thought it was a huge success, although she would have preferred to know her brother was smitten with his bride.

Livesey had watched Phoebe's carriage leave from his study window. Apart from wishing her a safe journey home, he'd not spoken to her. He had wanted to go with her when she visited the nursery to say her goodbyes to his children.

Part of him hoped they would beg her to stay, and they would convince her of something he could never voice.

He felt empty as the carriage trundled down the drive of his home. He knew he would never see her again, except in his dreams, which occurred more than he would ever admit.

Once the carriage was out of sight, Livesey returned to his desk. He needed to read through the contract and sign the damn thing and then his marriage could go ahead.

Sighing, he started to read.

*

Storming out of his study, half an hour later, Livesey nearly collided with his sister.

"Where is my so-called future wife?" he growled.

"She's gone into town for the day," Jessica said in surprise at the look on her brother's face. "Whatever is the matter?"

"I'm being taken for a fool, that's what!"

"I think we had better return to your study," Jessica said, taking hold of Livesey's arm and steering him back into the room he'd just left. "We do not want this conversation in the hallway."

Livesey followed, remaining mute until the door was closed. Walking over to the decanter of brandy he poured himself a large one and drank it in one gulp. "Damn it!" he muttered to himself.

"What is it?" Jessica urged. "What can Lady Jane have done to upset you so much?"

"She has a lover who isn't of our class, which was the reason she wants a marriage in name only," Livesey stated.

"No!" Jessica said, shocked.

"I could live with that," Livesey admitted. "It makes life easier in some respects. But she's asking for too much."

"What else could she possibly be asking for? What she's already asked for is outrageous!" Jessica asked in disbelief. She was stunned to find out the slightly aloof Lady Jane had made the initial proposal for a convenient marriage, but now to find out she had a lover was too much.

"Oh yes! He is to have a house on the estate, so they can be together as much as possible. I'd be the laughing stock of my staff and the locality within a month if that were to happen!" Livesey ground out.

"She cannot expect you to agree to that! Her lover living on your estate! How could anyone tolerate such a situation?" Jessica responded.

"That's not everything. I know she is already with child. She asked that we marry on a special licence, but what I didn't realise was she would expect me to accept her children as my own," Livesey said with a whoosh. He sat down as if all his energy had evaporated.

"She's increasing?"

"Yes. Another complication."

"You would take on another's by-blows?" Jessica asked shocked.

"That is what she wants me to do," Livesey said, running a hand through his usually impeccable hair. "She points out she would be taking my children on as her own, so she wants me to do the same."

"It's completely different!" Jessica said indignantly.

"It is. I doubt she would be willing to try to be a mother if Angelina was still alive," Livesey said. "Not only would she be visiting her lover, but she would be taking his children to visit him. It's yet another point she specifies: that the father of the children have a relationship with his offspring."

"No! This is too much!" Jessica was shocked beyond words. No woman of her acquaintance would behave in such a mercenary way.

"She is trying to protect her future, which I'd applaud if it did not have such a damned effect on my own life and family!"

"Bringing up someone else's children in such a way can only lead to disaster," Jessica said.

"It's the cuckoo putting his eggs in someone else's nest."

"How can she think those terms are acceptable?"

"There's another implication you haven't realised," Livesey said grimly.

"What?"

"If they have a son, he would inherit all this," Livesey said, opening his arms to encompass the house.

"No!" Jessica gasped.

"The property and title are entailed. I have not produced a son and won't in a marriage to Jane. But she might."

"This is too much!" Jessica said with feeling.

"Isn't it just," Livesey said wryly.

"What are you going to do?"

"Try to speak to her, I suppose. I'm not entering into a marriage with such a contract hanging over me. I'm certainly not seeing my own children dependent on a by-blow for their future!"

"If you refused to marry her, she could sue for breach of promise," Jessica said quietly.

"I know. I will need to seek legal advice," Livesey said grimly. "I'm going to speak to Jane and hope to goodness she is reasonable."

Chapter 12

Phoebe's journey home was uneventful. The north of Basingstoke was only two days travel from Lord Livesey's home, which was located a little way from Portsmouth. She'd been received with pleasure on her arrival, no one asking the outcome of the trip. Everyone had seen the announcement about Lord Livesey's engagement in the Times; the announcement had been sent to the newspaper before Livesey had read the contract.

It was a few days before Georgina came to visit her sister. Using an excuse to retrieve a bonnet which had been borrowed by Phoebe they seated themselves in Phoebe's bed chamber for a private chat.

"What was it like?" Georgina asked, as soon as the door had closed.

"I was definitely the one least likely to walk away with the prize that was Lord Livesey," Phoebe smiled at her sister. "I wonder at some of the ladies being there. They had titles, or fortunes; one would have guessed they wouldn't need such an experience to secure a husband."

"Titles and fortunes don't always compensate for personality defects," Georgina said with a grin. "Although the glowering Lord Livesey would be a lot to put up with."

Phoebe internally pushed away the lump of longing in her chest at Georgina's words. She had made her choice; she could not repine over it now. "He did not always glower," she said with a smile.

"He's very handsome. I've seen him a time or two at the few entertainments he has attended. He doesn't socialise much. But I've never spoken with him," Georgina said.

"He is handsome," Phoebe admitted. "I thought him an ogre at first, but he's not, really."

"I suppose we all hide behind personality traits. Like you pretend to be meek and yet you are anything but," Georgina teased.

"I'm your elder sister, and I warn you to mind your impertinence!" Phoebe said tartly.

"And I'm the married woman, so I now outrank you!" Georgina responded. "What other schemes can we devise to get a husband for you?"

Phoebe groaned. "Please have mercy! I had nothing in common with most of the ladies there and none of the gentlemen. I was seen as an oddity—the one to be constantly in the library."

"You will never find a husband in a library. Most men don't want a bluestocking, Phoebe. Your intelligence frightens them. Let the men you meet feel superior for at least as long as it takes to receive a proposal," Georgina pointed out reasonably.

"You and Susan married for love," Phoebe started. "I wanted that too, but it seems we are unusual in that respect. Some of the ladies there seemed to be happy to marry a man they did not know just because he had a title and was desperate for a wife. I could never do that even if it means I'm in disagreement with most of society," she continued.

"I do not think we are that unusual in wishing for love. There are many who marry for affection now. You were at the wrong gathering, that's all," Georgina said with conviction.

"I think it's time I accepted I am to be a spinster," Phoebe said.

"No! You're only four and twenty!"

"Your loyalty is touching, but I must consider what I'm to do in the future. I know I cannot remain in a library for the rest of my days!" Phoebe said with a laugh.

"I'll force Albert to build a huge library in our home, and you can come and live in it," Georgina said.

"Now that is an idea I like!" Phoebe smiled.

She was glad Georgina had visited. Having the weight of her parents' hopes on her shoulders was sometimes difficult for Phoebe. They would never openly show how disappointed they were in her not finding a husband, but it was the only thing that would secure her future, so it was natural as parents to be concerned. It was this that spurred Phoebe on to consider other options. They weren't a wealthy family, and she couldn't face becoming a burden on her sisters when her parents died. It was time for Phoebe to take control of her future as much as a poor, unmarried woman could do within the constraints of society.

Over the next two weeks she poured over advertisements in the newspaper to try and give her an idea of what she should apply for. The options were governess or companion and for some reason, she couldn't settle on either. She was not destitute, having a small dowry settled on her and an annual allowance which kept her in fripperies if she was careful, but she was not rich either. If she kept her dowry, it would only give her fifty pounds a year, which was not enough to live on. She would have to earn a living, but for some reason her heart wasn't in finding a position.

It could have something to do with the troubled dreams she experienced every night. No matter how tired she was when she went to bed, she dreamt of him. Her brain seemed to insist on reminding her every moment of every look, every expression he had. It was obviously colluding with her heart, which ached to see him again.

Into the third week, she was disturbed from reading her book in her bed chamber by the maid.

"Miss, Mrs Westbrook requires your attendance in the morning room. There is a visitor wishing to see you."

"A visitor? At this early hour?" Phoebe asked in surprise. She immediately arose from her seat, straightened her hair quickly in her looking glass, rubbed her hands down her slightly crumpled cotton day dress, and made for the stairs. It was too early for morning calls. She was curious to see who was breeching protocol.

She entered the small morning room, positioned at one of the rear corners of the house to benefit from the morning sunshine when the day was bright. Sitting opposite her mother was Aunt Dickson. The older woman turned when she heard Phoebe's entrance.

"Thought you were going to keep us waiting all day, child!" Aunt Dickson said.

"And good morning to you, Mrs Dickson," Phoebe said with a smile and a curtsey.

"Phoebe!" Mrs Westbrook chastised her daughter.

Aunt Dickson chuckled in response to Phoebe's greeting. "I've missed you."

Phoebe was touched by the sentiment. She knew the older woman didn't utter false praise. "And I have missed you. I hope Lady Knowles is well?"

"Yes, increasing every day it seems. She's hiding herself more from society now, more's the pity. There are few people in public I like, which makes it harder when those I do tolerate disappear. You did not say goodbye!"

"No. I'm sorry. I had the sudden urge to return home," Phoebe admitted, a flush stinging her cheeks.

"I can't blame you. My nephew is a fool. I told him exactly what I thought of him."

"Then he deserves our pity!" Phoebe smiled.

"The buffoon lives to be idiotic for another day; don't you worry!" Aunt Dickson responded. "I left only an hour after you, I was also keen to leave once that foolish announcement had been made."

"Was the party so bad?" Mrs Westbrook asked in surprise. She was astounded her daughter had not mentioned any of the problems there seemed to have been.

"No, Mother," Phoebe said with a smile. "Everything was kept in order by Mrs Dickson. We were all too frightened to step out of line."

Aunt Dickson chuckled. "You were not afraid of anything. Which was to your credit."

"Thank you."

"I needed to spend some time in London," Aunt Dickson stated, becoming more serious. "I had some business to attend to and needed to consult with my doctor."

"I hope you are not ailing?" Phoebe asked.

"The fool says I need to take life a little easier," Aunt Dickson said with derision. "If everyone did as they should, my life would be completely uneventful!"

"And you'd be bored," Phoebe said with a smile.

"Exactly! There is no point in living if life is to be peaceful and tedious," Aunt Dickson replied. "Nevertheless, I've decided to take the waters in Bath for six weeks or so, and I've come to ask if you will join me."

"Me?" Phoebe asked.

"As I've never previously met your mother, I'd hardly be inviting her, would I?" came the brusque response.

"N-no," Phoebe stuttered. "I'm just surprised you have chosen me."

"You're one of the few people I know who can talk sense. I'll pay you as my companion."

"There is no need for that!" Phoebe said quickly.

"Why? Have you suddenly come into an inheritance?"

"Well, no," Phoebe admitted. "But I am no charity case, either."

"Phoebe! For goodness sake! Mind your manners," Mrs Westbrook chided her daughter, horrified in the way her daughter was speaking to a woman of rank.

"The girl has spirit. There's nothing wrong with that. Reminds me of myself at her age," Aunt Dickson defended Phoebe. She smiled at Phoebe's expression. "Yes, that has given you a fright, hasn't it? If you carry on the way you are, you will be like me when you're older, surrounded by fools!"

"I cannot see how I can change. It looks like my future is mapped out before me if what you say is true," Phoebe said eventually.

"You can find a husband who deserves you and challenges you," Aunt Dickson said with a shrug. "It's only since my Samuel died that I've been at the mercy of family and friends and have been crotchety as a result. When he was alive, we rarely left Herefordshire, and I had rarely a bad word to say about anyone."

Phoebe narrowed her eyes. She wasn't sure she believed everything Aunt Dickson claimed. "This is not some convoluted scheme to find me a husband is it?"

"No, child. That chance disappeared when my foolish nephew made his announcement. This is purely a restorative trip to Bath," Aunt Dickson admitted. "There will not be any matchmaking on my part."

"So, no other members of your family will be in attendance?" Phoebe had to ask the question. She knew her mother would be curious to know the reason behind such an utterance, but that was preferable to meeting Livesey and his new wife in Bath.

"None. Of that you can be sure," came the firm reply.

"Good. In that case, I'd love to come to Bath with you. I've never been before," Phoebe said with pleasure.

"Don't get over excited. It is full of invalids and the elderly. You will be wishing yourself a million miles away before the six weeks are up. When can you leave?"

"Mama?" Phoebe asked.

"Whenever you like, my dear. I wouldn't keep you here for selfish reasons. I travelled to Bath in my youth and enjoyed it immensely," Mrs Westbrook said.

"Those were its glory days. Before that buffoon who is Regent decided Brighton was better. Thankfully, my doctor recommended the waters, and not the sea," Aunt Dickson said with feeling. She turned to Phoebe. "If you have no objection, we'll start out tomorrow, and we'll have no more twattle about not being my official companion. I will be paying for your company, so I expect to be entertained!"

"Why am I suddenly afraid?" Phoebe asked with a smile.

Chapter 13

Livesey waited impatiently while his solicitor took his time to read the contract Lady Jane had presented him a week ago. Most of the guests had left on the day after his marriage announcement—something he regretted in hindsight. A few of the gentlemen had remained keen to take the opportunity for sport on his land. With his blessing they went on shooting or hunting parties. It left Livesey free to try to negotiate with Lady Jane.

"You cannot have believed I would accept all your terms without question," Livesey had said when they were alone in his study.

"You raised no objections to it yesterday," Lady Jane responded.

"I did not bloody read it until today!" Livesey growled, not apologising for his use of language.

"I told you to read it as soon as I'd given it to you," Lady Jane said sharply.

"Whether I read it last night or this morning, there wasn't the opportunity to speak to you. I had a house full of guests."

"Who would have understood if we'd separated ourselves from them," Lady Jane insisted.

"This is ridiculous!" Livesey snapped. "We are arguing about the wrong thing! It's the terms which are the issue, not when the thing was read!"

"I cannot give way on the terms," Lady Jane said forcefully. "You're getting a wife who will care for your children. That's all you really want."

"Is it? Is it really?" Livesey argued. He glared at Jane, his brow almost meeting in the middle of his forehead. His glower was not only aimed at Jane; he was annoyed with himself. Hearing his needs on her tongue made him seem cold and empty, and for first time in many years, he realised he wasn't cold. He actually had a heart, and he no longer wished to feel the desolate emptiness he carried within him.

"Do not tell me you want a love match! I'm not that person! You knew I was in love with Stuart!" Jane said, her usual confident, almost arrogant self looking slightly panicked.

"I don't want a love match," Livesey spat. "I've about as much attraction to you as you have to me. But I refuse to be played the fool. Not only having to bring up someone else's by-blows but having him live on my own estate! You ask too much madam!"

"It's the most discreet way of going about things," Jane insisted.

"Not from my point of view," Livesey said. "And there is another issue with regards to the children."

"What?"

"This estate is entailed. I refuse to allow my title and estate to go to a child I've had no part in creating," Livesey ground out.

Jane faltered for a moment. "I would not expect that to happen. I did not realise your estate was so encumbered."

"It is," Livesey responded darkly.

"I don't mind if you find a mistress and bring more children into the family," Jane said in a rush, trying to overcome a problem she hadn't foreseen.

"And what if the child you carry now is a boy?" Livesey asked. "For all intents and purposes, the child will be seen as mine."

"We will arrange some agreement with your solicitor. There will be something we can do," Jane said. She needed to marry soon. Once any sign of her pregnancy was visible, she'd be ruined.

"No. There won't. Or other estates would have found the loophole. I'm afraid I cannot go ahead with this. I will not pretend to bring up someone else's offspring when the man is alive and able to care for them himself," Livesey said firmly.

"Are you asking me to give up any children I might have?" Jane asked aghast.

"The choice is yours, but this engagement goes no further if you cannot," Livesey said, standing.

"I'll sue for breach of promise!" Jane responded in desperation. "We need to marry!"

"You can sue all you like. I'm leaving for London soon to speak to my solicitor about the contract and breach of promise. I doubt there will be any case to answer to when it is proved how far the pregnancy is and the realisation that I could not possibly be the father," Livesey said.

Jane dissolved in tears.

Livesey groaned. "I'll leave you be while you compose yourself. It was a foolish plan which neither of us should have ever entered into." He walked out of his study, closing the door behind him. He wanted to leave the house as soon as possible. Everything was a complete shambles.

Jane had tried to control herself through the argument; she wasn't one for crying. The problem was that she was in a predicament that she could see no way out of. The relief she'd felt when Livesey had agreed to marry her was monumental, but she should have realised he wouldn't agree to her terms. She was no fool. They were excessive, but she needed his agreement.

A quiet knock came on the door, and she wiped her eyes, quickly trying to pull herself together. Her shoulders slumped when Jessica walked into the room, a sympathetic expression on her face.

"My brother told me you might wish for some company," Jessica said gently.

"At this moment in time, I have no idea what I want," Jessica wailed, starting to cry again.

"Oh, dear me!" Jessica said, closing the door and hurrying to Jane's side. "Don't upset yourself so! Come now, it cannot be as bad as this."

"It's worse," Jane said grimly.

"He told me what was in the contract," Jessica admitted.

"Then you know why I need to be married," Jane responded.

"Yes. But I do not think you've thought this through," Jessica reasoned. "I doubt anyone would risk their estate being given to an illegitimate child."

"I never considered to check if the estate was entailed," Jane admitted. "I was so desperate to cover all eventualities from my point of view, I never thought of the danger of having a son."

"So, you'll release Livesey?" Jessica asked.

"I cannot. I need to marry, and he's announced the engagement," Jane said mulishly.

Jessica tried to school her features into a passive expression, hiding the annoyance she felt at what she considered was Jane's unreasonableness. "Can you not marry the father of your child? You have a fortune in your own right."

"I would never be a part of society if I did," Jane admitted.

Jessica felt riled. "You cannot love him as much as you think you do," she said with authority.

"I do!"

"No. You see, if my darling Knowles was an undergardener, I would have to follow him. Whatever he did and wherever he was, I would need to be beside him. It's a physical need as well as an emotional one," Jessica explained.

"That's easy for you to say with your titled husband!" Jane responded tartly.

Jessica shrugged. "That may be so, but it's how I feel. I live in London for half the year because he loves it. I don't particularly, and if it were up to me, we would leave our estate only to visit my brother and aunt. I have little desire to spend any time in the filthy, crowded, dangerous place that is the capital, but if Knowles is there, then so am I."

"I'd never see my family again. I would be disowned," Jane acknowledged.

"That would be hard to bear, but if my family were against my happiness to such an extent, I would still choose my husband. Even with regards to my brother," Jessica said with a smile.

"I can't do it," Jane said.

Jessica stood. "That is a pity. To have three unhappy people."

"I didn't coerce your brother into agreeing to marry me!" Jane said defensively.

"I know," Jessica admitted. "He is as foolish as you are in his own way. I wish there was something I could offer that would see you all being happy, but I'm afraid however much I think of it, someone is going to be hurt."

"Probably me," Jane admitted, looking crestfallen.

"One thing's for sure. You are not going to get the quick marriage you were hoping for. From the sounds in the hallway, it appears my brother is ready to leave for London," Jessica said moving to the door. "Please excuse me. I need to wish him a safe journey."

Jane put her head in her hands once she was left alone in the room. Her gamble had not paid off. It had seemed like the perfect solution, but she should have known that a man like Livesey wouldn't be a meek and mild husband. She had lost. His trip to London would enable him to break off their engagement, and she would be ruined. She longed for Stuart, but he was waiting for her in Northamptonshire.

*

Livesey impatiently waited for his solicitor to sit back in his chair and meet his gaze for the first time since he'd handed over the contract to him.

The older gentleman was rotund and looked as if a six-week visit to Bath on a diet of Bath Oliver biscuits and water would do him the world of good. His small eyes peeped over ruddy cheeks.

"Well?" Livesey asked, finally losing patience.

"A strange state of affairs, My Lord, but quite straightforward," the solicitor responded with a benevolent smile.

"Really? You mean I can get out of this damned engagement?" Livesey asked, for the first time in days feeling a sense of relief.

"Yes. We could state that there was both false representation and with regards to the pregnancy, false concealment," the solicitor said confidently.

"She did give me the contract before I announced the engagement," Livesey said fairly.

"She wasn't clear enough about being with child. She only hinted at it. You should have seen me before announcing anything, but no one will go to court while we have this document in our possession," the solicitor said.

"I feel sorry for the woman, but not sorry enough to do what she asks," Livesey ground out.

"There is an arrogance to the contract which is hard to stomach," the solicitor said. "I should never have advised a client of mine to proceed along these lines."

"She probably did not seek advice, as I did not," Livesey acknowledged. "I'll send a missive to her explaining the outcome of my meeting with you."

"She clearly has intelligence. She probably knows what the outcome will be," the solicitor said.

"Then she could have saved me embarking on this wild goose chase!" Livesey said with feeling. "I'll bid you good day."

Leaving the building, he immediately directed his carriage to his home on Jermyn Street. It was a bachelor set of rooms, consisting of a drawing room, dining room, bedroom and small study. It was perfect for himself and his valet and was cleaned daily by a maid. Now that there was no imminent chance of him being married, he looked forward to keeping the rooms for some time to come.

Sitting in his study he took out a piece of paper and dipped his pen in the ink. A decent man, if not a loving one, he was uncomfortable with inflicting pain on anyone. That being said, he was not prepared to sacrifice himself for another.

He started to write.

My Lady,

I have sought advice from my solicitor, and I'm sure you will be fully aware that we have grounds to refute any claim for breach of promise.

I've no desire to see our personal business laid bare before a court, as I am sure you are not, but be aware that any claim against me will be fought wholeheartedly. As I cannot agree to the terms set-out in your contract, I am therefore, ending the engagement we have thus far entered into. I will not discuss the matter with anyone else, hopefully preventing you from being the object of speculation. My only proviso to my silence would be if there is any suggestion that I am the father of your unborn child. I don't wish to cause distress, but I will not take responsibility for something that is not my own, so I will speak out if I hear of rumours to my detriment.

I sincerely regret raising any hopes you may have experienced because of my agreement to your proposal, and I wish you all the best in the future. I feel there is little else to say apart from I am sorry it has come to this.

With best wishes for your future and that of your child.

Livesey.

Sitting back once the letter had been given to his valet to arrange for posting, Livesey felt relief and anger. He shouldn't have acted so foolhardily. He had almost tied himself into a situation that would have been hellish for all those involved. He was convinced now that the relationship could have impacted his children and not for their good. Bringing up children in such a complicated household would never have worked. Too many lies would have to be told, and he'd already gone through that with Angelina. No. He could not live such a falsehood again. A pity he hadn't realised it sooner.

He'd had a lucky escape. Now all he had to do was learn how to put a pair of large hazel eyes out of his mind, and he could be content.

If he thought getting out of an engagement was going to be hard, it was going to be easy in comparison to trying to forget Phoebe.

Chapter 14

Northamptonshire

Jane rested her head on the plush inside of her father's carriage. Seeming to watch, but actually not seeing the scenery pass her by, she returned home for what would probably be the last time.

She'd stayed at Livesey's home until the coach had arrived as planned, at what should have been the end of the party. That she was the last guest to leave, her parents had no idea, nor would they be anticipating the conversation she would be forced to have with them on her return home.

Her chaperone, an older cousin, had tried to find out what was amiss, for there clearly was something wrong, but Jane had refused to confide in the woman. She knew without doubt an express would have been sent home if she had uttered the truth, and Jane had to rely on the hope she could speak to her father without her mother present.

Jane had set out with such high hopes. Everything had seemed so straightforward and sensible. It was only now she was questioning the reality of her plan. She had tried to force Livesey's hand in declaring she'd sue him. She felt some shame for threatening that. It would have been worse if she'd thought he cared for her. Thankfully, they were equally indifferent to each other.

She sighed. Everyone at home thought she was engaged. Her mother would be delighted because Jane had been considered a failure by not securing a marriage, but she knew her father would be pleased for her sake. She hated to hurt him, but it was inevitable.

Four days later, Jane stepped down from the carriage, looking up at the red-brick Georgian mansion that had been her home. She wasn't sure what the next few days would bring, but this could be the final time she saw this building and her heart ached for all the memories the bricks and mortar stirred. Setting her shoulders she stepped inside.

Lord Bellamy walked out of his library to meet his daughter. He was a tall, slim man, who liked to laugh and was popular with his peers. "Jane! It is good to have you home! I've missed you!" came the booming voice of the man.

"I've missed you too, Papa," Jane said, crossing to hug her parent. Squeezing her eyes to prevent the tears which pricked the back of her eyelids, she clung to her father.

"We have a lot to talk about. I think your mother has already half-organised your wedding!" Lord Bellamy said, holding his daughter at arm's length. "You look tired, my dear. Do you need to rest?"

"Yes, Papa," Jane said gratefully. She needed to speak to Stuart, who'd been in the hallway since she'd arrived. She'd longed to run to him, but could not.

"Go and have a lie-down. Your mother is out visiting. We'll talk later," Lord Bellamy soothed.

"Papa, can I please speak to you without Mama in the first instance?" Jane said, suddenly not being able to face her mother's wrath.

Lord Bellamy frowned. "Is there something amiss?"

Jane sighed. She couldn't lie to him, not anymore. "Yes. There is. But I need to rest in my chamber first. I do not feel at all well. Rogers, I need your arm up the stairs," Jane said, turning to the man she'd been in love with for nigh on ten years. He'd immediately approached her side.

"Yes, My Lady," Stuart Rogers responded.

Walking slowly up the stairs, Jane knew her father was looking at her with concern, but she couldn't face the conversation now. Since realising she was increasing she'd never felt as tired in her life, and the journey had been a drain on her resources. Any other time she would have taken the opportunity to speak to her father while her mother was absent, but she felt nauseated she was so exhausted and overwhelmed.

Leaning on Stuart's arm, she felt some comfort. The love of her life would catch her if she should faint.

Closing the bed chamber door, which was against all propriety, Stuart took Jane into his arms. "What is it? You're not well," he whispered urgently, holding her and running his hands up and down her back as if he would be able to feel the problem.

Jane sagged into him. "Livesey broke off the engagement as soon as he saw my contract," Jane said with a sob.

"Good!" Stuart said fiercely. "I do not want another man bringing up my children!"

Jane pulled away from Stuart slightly, annoyed at his words. "It's not as simple as that, though, is it?" she snapped.

"You keep telling me it is not!" Stuart snapped back. "I'm beginning to think only one of us wants this to work out."

"We will be cast out!" Jane sobbed, the tears finally spilling over.

Stuart immediately held her close. Her head rested on his shoulder. They were perfectly matched in height. His size making the tall Jane feel small and protected. "Your father would not leave you destitute. He might not give you any funds, but he will not be cruel enough to turn me out without a reference. That's all we need, Jane. I'll provide the rest."

"I have been saving every penny I could," Jane said, finally realising there had only ever been one course of action they could take. "I asked Papa for extra money for clothes before I went to the party, but I didn't spend a penny of it. It will give us a start."

"Jane, I want you to be my wife. I have hated this idea ever since you came up with it. Now will you let me see your father with you? We are in this together, until death us do part," Stuart said gently. He'd known she had to work things out for herself. She was going to lose everything she'd ever known, and he would always feel guilty about that, but he loved her and couldn't face life without her.

They sprang apart as the door opened, and Jane's portmanteau was carried in. Jane's maid tsked as she entered the room. "Come, My Lady, you need to lie-down."

Jane squared her shoulders. "No. I think it is best I speak to my father now. Rogers, I still feel feeble, can I make use of your arm once more?"

"Should you not be resting, My Lady?" Stuart asked.

"Probably. But let's get this over and done with first," Jane said with a sigh.

"Of course, My Lady," Stuart said with a bow before offering his arm.

Jane leaned her head against Stuart's shoulder as they walked. It was time for honesty.

*

"By God man! I'll beat you black and blue for this!" Lord Bellamy exploded at Stuart when Jane had finished speaking.

"And what will that achieve, Papa?" Jane asked wearily.

"It'll make me feel better and send out a clear message! My daughter is not to be treated like a one-shilling doxy!"

"My Lord, I love her!" Stuart responded, trying to keep calm.

"Of course you do! She's a Lady! I expect every servant falls in love at some point or other with their betters, but most have the decency to know their station in life. You have abused our trust," Lord Bellamy roared.

"You're talking about me as if I had no part in it!" Jane said heatedly. "I was a willing participant!"

Lord Bellamy winced at Jane's words. "We need to keep this within ourselves. You," he said pointing at Stuart, "are to leave this house within the hour. Try to contact my daughter again, and I'll have you shot on sight."

Stuart looked to retort, but Jane placed her hand on his arm. She looked at her father. "Papa, it's too late for that. I'm with child."

"Dear God!" Lord Bellamy gasped, his face losing colour. "But your engagement?" he asked Jane.

"Lord Livesey did not want a wife in the traditional sense, so I proposed a marriage of convenience. At first, he agreed to it, but then he realised any child I had with Stuart could inherit his estate. I had failed to realise his property was entailed," Jane explained.

Lord Bellamy rubbed his hands over his face. "So he knows you're soiled goods. No doubt the whole of society will know soon."

Jane was distraught to be hurting her beloved father in such a way, and only the strongest love for Stuart would make her do such a thing. "Lord Livesey won't speak about what has gone on," she said.

"How the hell are we to hide this? You will have to go away until the bastard is born. We will have it adopted," Lord Bellamy said, his mind racing.

"No!" Jane and Stuart said together.

"What do you mean, no?" Lord Bellamy said fiercely.

"This is my child, and I am going to provide for it," Stuart said.

"And how will you do that without a reference?" Lord Bellamy snarled.

"Papa! You cannot do that to us!" Jane appealed.

"To us? You are not going anywhere, young lady!"

"I'm one and thirty, Papa! I'm a spinster and have been for years. It doesn't matter what anyone else thinks. I've found someone to love and who loves me. I do not want anything else," Jane said with feeling.

"Easy to say now. Wait until the money runs out!" Lord Bellamy snapped.

"If you cast off Stuart without a reference, then we are doomed for a slow death, probably of starvation," Jane said.

"If he has a reference and can find work, then all I need is a home, food and his love."

"Your head is in the clouds," Lord Bellamy insisted.

"Maybe. But which would you choose, Papa? A life of wealth and absolutely no love whatsoever if married to Lord Livesey? Or the chance to be poor but loved?" Jane asked.

"It easy to talk as you are now but you have never experienced poverty," Lord Bellamy said, gentler than he had previously.

"I have not," Jane admitted. "But I've experienced uncertainty, loneliness and now love. I do not want to give up that love, Papa. The child I carry was made with love and will be adored, just as I was by you. I have to give this a chance."

Lord Bellamy no longer looked angry, but distraught. "I wanted the best for you."

"And you gave it to me," Jane said gently. "All we need is a reference for Stuart. I'm not asking for anything else. I know mother will be furious when she finds out, but please promise us a reference."

"He will abandon you when times are tough," Lord Bellamy said, shooting a glare in Stuart's direction.

"Then I will have misjudged his character, but I don't think I have," Jane responded.

"You haven't. I would never desert you," Stuart said firmly.

"I need to think," Lord Bellamy said finally. "Leave me."

"Papa, please give Stuart a reference," Jane pleaded, knowing once her mother knew, the house would be in an uproar.

"I'll not force you into destitution, but I do not want to ever see your face again," Lord Bellamy said to Stuart. "You have abused your position in my household, and I don't take kindly to that. I still want you off the premises."

"Papa! No!" Jane said.

It was Stuart's turn to calm Jane. "We can ask no more, Jane," he said gently. "I will be waiting for you in the village. Thank you, My Lord. I will only understand the hurt I've unintentionally caused you when I have daughters of my own. I did not mean to cause upset."

"Even then you will not understand. How will you possibly understand that your daughter is not only throwing away her future but her family and her society as well?" Lord Bellamy asked.

Stuart left the room. Jane had wanted to follow, but she held back. Turning to her father, she started to speak. "I know Mama will hate me until her dying day because of this," Jane said. "She has always set a lot by appearances, and this will hurt her deeply. I'm sorry for that. But, Papa, if you can find it in your heart to see me occasionally in the future, it would mean so much to me."

"I don't know, Jane," Lord Bellamy answered honestly.

"I know I don't deserve your forgiveness, but believe me, none of this was entered into with the intention to hurt you. The only reason I proposed to Lord Livesey was because it would keep me in your social sphere. I do not care about leaving society on my own account, but I do care about losing you. I know I have lost your good opinion, and I truly regret that, but I love him, and I love the child we have created," Jane said, unable to stop the tears rolling down her cheeks.

"Jane..." Lord Bellamy started.

Jane stood. "I do not expect you to answer now," she interrupted. "Think about what I've said. You don't need to give me an answer before I leave, but please consider it."

"You are leaving?"

"My place is with Stuart. I'll be staying with him in the village for a few days. If we have not heard from you by then, we'll get on the stage and never return," Jane said, leaving the room. Just as she was about to exit through the doorway, she turned back. "Thank you for everything, Papa. I could not have wished for a better life. You gave me all I could have needed and more."

Chapter 15

Bath

Aunt Dickson almost flopped on one of the sofas in the drawing room in number 23 Gay Street. She had rented the whole house for her six-week visit to Bath. Gay Street wasn't in the most fashionable part of Bath; that was to be found in the streets beyond Pulteney Bridge, one of the bridges which had led to the further development of the City. The rent in Gay Street had reflected the change in desirability, and Aunt Dickson had taken advantage of the lower prices.

"Well, my dear, this diet of Bath biscuits and water is doing me the world of good! It's my first week, and I feel better already!" Aunt Dickson said.

"I have no idea how. I'm sure the doctor intended you to stick to his recommendation for more than one day," Phoebe retorted with a smile.

"It's disgusting stuff! I would rather die early than put up with that! I think we will have Bath buns for lunch instead of some unappealing healthy mush."

"Your doctor will not be happy," Phoebe pointed out.

"I'll just have to find a new doctor." Aunt Dickson shrugged. She laughed at Phoebe's expression. "Don't go all missish on me! I know there is a devil under that educated exterior."

Phoebe smiled. "I knew spending so much time in your company would reveal my darkest secret."

"Rather that than be bored with you after a day," Aunt Dickson said.

"We have still got five weeks to go. You might think differently at the end of it," Phoebe pointed out. She had thoroughly enjoyed her first week in Bath. Alone in her room at night, her heart and mind wandered to Livesey, but during the day she was able to put her longing for him to one side because of the woman she was companion to. Aunt Dickson kept her so busy it was almost as if the woman was purposely trying to distract Phoebe.

"Thankfully, there are some entertaining people in Bath. Who'd have thought a city full of invalids would be so amusing?" Aunt Dickson asked rhetorically.

"Not everyone is an invalid," Phoebe pointed out fairly.

"No. I wonder why gentlemen who have little to recommend them waste their time on the season in London? They should just come to Bath. The women outnumber the men greatly."

"I suppose the richest and prettiest women frequent the balls of London. That is probably the attraction."

"Prettiness fades, and riches won't make a Friday face more attractive over the breakfast table after years of marriage. There's a lot more to marriage once the wedding trip is over," Aunt Dickson said with authority.

Phoebe smiled. She loved the bluntness of her companion. She spoke a lot of sense; there was no false flattery with Aunt Dickson. Phoebe thought she'd want to be like that when she aged, although she wouldn't have the money to do as she wished, as the older woman did.

"What shall we plan to do today?" Aunt Dickson asked.

"I would like to return my book to the circulating library while you rest," Phoebe said.

"Pah! I can rest when I'm dead!"

"I think your family would like that to be a long way off."

"When one has bequests to make in a will, one always outlives the hopes of the family!" Aunt Dickson said with a smile.

"Lady Knowles would be horrified to hear you speak in such a way!" Phoebe chastised. She couldn't mention Livesey; her voice or expression would give herself away.

"Yes. Jessica is a good girl. A pity about my buffoon of a nephew," Aunt Dickson retorted tartly. She visibly shook herself before continuing. "I refuse to allow myself to get annoyed. We shall take a stroll in Sydney Gardens."

Phoebe rolled her eyes. She was sure so much exercise couldn't be good for the older woman, but there was no stopping her when she set her mind to something.

They walked at a slow but steady pace along Great Pulteney Street. Aunt Dickson had poo-pooed the idea of taking a sedan chair to the gates of Sydney Gardens. Phoebe didn't mind the more sedate stroll; it enabled her to take in the City.

The sandstone glinted in the sunshine; the area where they were staying was a lot darker than the newer buildings, having had more time to weather. Great Pulteney Street had wide paved pathways, giving the area the feeling of being an area along which to promenade. The road itself was wide, enabling carriages to make easy turns.

The area was busy and vibrant, but the population was older than London's, and Aunt Dickson had been correct: There were far more women than men. As Phoebe had no interest whatsoever in looking for any kind of romance, it didn't matter to her who made up the population. Her heart was firmly wherever Livesey was.

They stopped quite a few times along the street while Aunt Dickson spoke to acquaintances and old friends. Aunt Dickson chuckled after yet another delay.

"One advantage in getting old is that you know more people," she said when she'd wished her friends good-bye. "Although it can be a mixed blessing sometimes."

"I have not travelled much, so my acquaintance is limited to my small town," Phoebe admitted.

"Yes. Money allows one freedom, whether you're man or woman," Aunt Dickson said.

Phoebe laughed. "I was not complaining! I'm happy with my lot." In the main, she thought to herself.

They walked only a short way through the greenery of the parkland before returning to the hotel on the edge of the gardens to take refreshments.

Aunt Dickson started when she saw a captain of the Navy walking through the hotel. "Captain Chester? Well, I never!"

The captain paused and smiled warmly at Aunt Dickson. "Mrs Dickson! How the devil are you?" He was what could be considered a typical captain of the Navy: tall, broad, weathered features, sun kissed hair, and a wide smile.

"I'm all the better for seeing you." Aunt Dickson smiled. "Join us."

"With pleasure," the captain said with a smile. "I have not seen you these last ten years."

"No. We've not met since your father passed. Your father's death was a blow to us all," Aunt Dickson said.

"I still miss him," Captain Chester admitted.

"I understand why." Aunt Dickson turned to Phoebe. "This rogue is the son of a dear friend of mine. He is as handsome as his father but hasn't the same charm!"

Captain Chester laughed. "That is not what you used to tell father. I was always preferable to him, you said."

"It's best to keep one's close friends on their toes. Patrick was big-headed enough without my adoration," Aunt Dickson said with a grin. "This is a friend of the family, Miss Phoebe Westbrook. She has to put up with me, so if you are staying in Bath, I expect you to dance with her at every opportunity!"

Phoebe glared at Aunt Dickson before turning to Captain Chester. "I am Mrs Dickson's companion, so I have no desire to dance, thank you."

Captain Chester grinned in appreciation at both ladies. "Still interfering in everyone's lives, Mrs Dickson?" he asked.

"Maybe. When they have the sense to listen to me," Aunt Dickson said with a sigh.

Captain Chester turned to Phoebe. "My father told me he would curse her to the devil when she tried to matchmake when they were younger."

"Yes, but eventually he listened and married Agatha and had a long and happy marriage!" Aunt Dickson retorted.

"He did," Captain Chester acknowledged with a smile. "But not everyone needs or wants your help. I am an engaged man, so you can stop planning my future before you start."

"Really? I hope she is worthy of you."

"She is, although she's suffering from a sort of malady, so we're here to take the waters," the captain acknowledged, a frown marring his good looks.

Phoebe turned to Aunt Dickson. "You'd have met her if you had stuck to your doctor's orders and taken the waters each morning."

"We can meet her by you bringing her for a visit tomorrow. Here is my card with my address on it. I expect to see you at the end of visiting hours, so you can stay for some time," Aunt Dickson instructed. "Come child," she said to Phoebe. "It's time for us to meander back."

"I really think you should employ a sedan chair on our return journey," Phoebe said.

"I agree," Captain Chester said. "It is a long way back to Gay Street and almost all uphill."

"I'm surrounded by fusspots!" Aunt Dickson grumbled, but she allowed Captain Chester to secure a chair for her.

Phoebe thanked him as she climbed in her own chair.

Captain Chester smiled. "I know what she's like. You will not have an easy time of it."

"Thankfully, I realised that before joining her," Phoebe said with feeling.

*

After having had a busy day, Aunt Dickson rose late the following morning, although she was in time to be ready for visits. She'd refused to go to the Pump Rooms to take the water. As she looked a little pale, Phoebe had not pushed the issue.

As directed, Captain Chester brought his lady around at the requested time. They were introduced and then seated in the large drawing room on the first floor of the building.

"This is a lovely house," Martha said. She was a fragile-looking woman but very pretty. Her dark hair framed her pale complexion, making her look like a delicate doll. From the moment they arrived it was clear that the captain doted on her.

"It suits me," Aunt Dickson acknowledged. "I can watch the comings and goings. Lots of people pass on their way to promenade around the Crescent. And it is quite central except when one wishes to visit Sydney Gardens, of course."

"I love the labyrinth," Martha said. "We've walked around it on a number of occasions."

"Have you been in Bath long?" Phoebe asked.

"This last month. My parents are here as well. They are using the opportunity to see all that Bath has to offer," Martha said. "By now I was hoping for better results from the waters than I'm actually feeling. My slow improvement means I will be staying for some time longer."

"There is no hurry, my dear," Captain Chester said gently. "You can take as much time as you need. We're all prepared to stay for as long as it takes. It will be worth it in the end."

"We haven't been to many of the evening entertainments. My trips to the hot baths in the morning are very early, and I'm finding I tire easily," Martha explained.

"It is a ridiculously early time to be carried to the baths," Aunt Dickson agreed. "Invalids should be allowed to wake later in the day."

"My instructions are that I return to bed for a few hours, wrapped tightly in blankets. It isn't very pleasant. I always feel overheated after bathing," Martha admitted.

"We have to do as the doctor instructs," Captain Chester said gently.

"You aren't missing much by not attending the evening entertainments," Aunt Dickson assured the woman. "There are not enough gentlemen, so the ladies have to double up, and one doesn't know who is supposed to be a gentleman or lady!"

"At least they're dancing," Phoebe pointed out.

"Yes. Such an arrangement would never be allowed in London, but at least here more ladies dance. Not sure I would appreciate taking on the male part though. It doesn't seem right somehow," Aunt Dickson said.

"I shall have to dance with you at one of the assemblies, and we can show them how it's done," Captain Chester laughed.

"Away with you, impertinent scamp!" Aunt Dickson chastised good-naturedly. "My dancing days are long gone."

"How are Livesey and Jessica these days? I've not seen either of them for years," Captain Chester asked, changing the subject.

"Jessica is increasing. Her first child, so she's full of wonder at every new stage," Aunt Dickson said. "She will not be so awed when it's her tenth!"

Captain Chester laughed. "I can imagine her with a brood of children. Jessica was always one who cared about everyone's comfort. The last time I saw her she wasn't even married and now she is expecting her first child. Time passes too quickly."

"Yes. She married late; we were all presuming she would remain single. Fortunately for Jessica, she listened to no one who tried to advise to marry some of the fools who offered for her. She chose wisely with Knowles. He's a good man and adores his wife, so I cannot criticise her for waiting longer than normal," Aunt Dickson acknowledged. "As for my nephew, that is a whole other story!"

"I heard about the death of his wife. It being such an unfortunate accident, it was reported widely in the newspapers. It must have hit him hard," Captain Chester sympathised.

"It probably gave him the first moments of relief he'd had in years!" Aunt Dickson said with feeling.

"Mrs Dickson!" Phoebe scolded, shocked at the harsh words that reflected badly on both her nephew and his wife.

"It is true!" Aunt Dickson defended herself. "The chit was as unsuitable for Livesey as could be. Too highly strung and demanding. He needed a bride who would be a challenge for him but not in dramatics. Jessica once told me of how many ornaments were destroyed when Angelina flew into one of her rages. Things which had been passed down through generations were broken beyond repair because of someone who acted like a spoiled child. It was a horrible way to die, but Livesey has been better off without her."

Phoebe was silenced by the words. It related closely to what Livesey had said when Eliza had been ill. All of a sudden, he was someone who stirred sympathy within her—as well as everything else.

"It is a shame he had such a rough time of it," Captain Chester said. "He's obviously faring better now. I saw an announcement of his engagement in the Times."

"Don't even get me started on this latest farce!" Aunt Dickson almost spat. "Although Jessica has to take some responsibility for that hare-brained scheme."

Captain Chester laughed. "It seems your niece and nephew keep you entertained. Come, my dear Martha. Let us say our goodbyes before Mrs Dickson turns her attention to us! We would not stand up to her scrutiny, and I've not got a strong constitution to withstand her scoldings!"

Martha laughed at Aunt Dickson's tsk before standing, and with warm goodbyes, the couple left the room.

Aunt Dickson was quiet until she'd heard the thud of the front door closing. "I pity Chester. He will suffer when he loses her."

"Do you think she'll not recover?" Phoebe asked.

"Not at all! My guess is she was a sickly girl for most of her life. I just hope for his sake she doesn't last until she bares a child. I cannot imagine either would survive. It's not good for the child when the mother is sickly."

"Oh dear. How very sad."

"Chester was always a gentle soul. It's no wonder he has been attracted to a slight girl. He'd be better off choosing a sturdy wife," Aunt Dickson said with feeling.

"One cannot choose who one falls in love with," Phoebe said with feeling and a slight blush.

"No, I suppose not. But chances are sometimes missed by foolish notions," Aunt Dickson responded with a raised eyebrow.

Phoebe flushed deeper, guessing she was the one being chastised, but not quite sure what Aunt Dickson knew. She decided the best course of action was to remain silent on the matter.

Chapter 16

London

Livesey should be feeling relieved. He'd escaped a cold marriage that would have threatened the future of his daughters, but all he felt was frustration. For the first time in his life, he was unsettled, and he had no clue as to why. He was having disturbed nights as well. All he dreamt of was Phoebe, which was ridiculous as he'd never noticed her except to scorn her until the damned party.

No one wanted a wife who was a bluestocking. One would probably feel inferior, even though he considered himself reasonably educated. No. She wasn't attractive in the conventional sense. She wasn't beautiful enough to tempt him. Yet, all he could think about were her laughing eyes and her smile, which when bestowed on him, could make his heart flutter as if he were a youth just out of the schoolroom. There was no reason why he should be thinking of Phoebe, but yet he couldn't stop himself.

He'd also never confided in anyone as much as he had in her. What was it about her that drew him to her? He hated to admit it, but he was actually missing her. She had rejected him, and it still hurt. He would not be so foolish as to chase her across country to try to persuade her to change her mind. No. She would remain a spinster, and he would force himself to forget her.

Jessica had travelled to London in a more sedate way than her brother, so it was over a week before they met once more. Jessica visited Livesey at his home on Jermyn Street.

"I take it from the scowl on your face you have to pay Lady Jane a substantial amount for breach of promise?" she asked, kissing her brother lightly on his cheek.

"No. Not at all. I'm free from that fiasco," Livesey responded.

"So, why the dark looks?" Jessica asked in surprise.

"I am perfectly happy," Livesey shrugged.

"Good grief! If that's your expression when you're perfectly happy, God help us when you are upset!"

Livesey smiled at Jessica. "I'm considering returning to Hampshire. I did not like leaving the girls this time," he admitted.

"That's good. Have you been out in society much since you've been in London?"

"No. I thought it prudent to allow Lady Jane to spread the news about her change in status," Livesey responded.

"I had hoped for better for you. I'm sorry it did not work out," Jessica said.

"I'm surprised you ever thought it would," Livesey replied. "The chits you invited were a strange choice."

"And yet you asked one of them to marry you," Jessica pointed out.

"Because I thought she would be a good mother," Livesey admitted.

"I saw the way you were around her, George. You liked her."

"I do wish you would not revert to my given name only when you're starting on a lecture!" Livesey said with a growl.

Jessica smiled. "Well, stop acting like a bufflehead and chase Miss Westbrook now you are free."

"She was quite clear in her rejection. I have nothing to offer her other than a marriage of convenience," Livesey insisted.

"I wish you could see what I see. I think you'd be able to persuade her if you revealed your true feelings," Jessica said gently.

"Stop it, Jess. I cannot reveal what I don't feel. I will not be chasing Miss Westbrook to her home," Livesey responded sharply.

"That's a good thing as she's in Bath with Aunt Dickson," Jessica said with a smile.

"In Bath? What the devil is Aunt Dickson thinking of?" Livesey said.

"She likes Miss Westbrook," Jessica said with a shrug.

"What mischief is she planning?" Livesey growled.

"Nothing! If she needs a companion, why should she not choose Miss Westbrook?" Jessica asked in all innocence.

"I know how our Aunt works. She does nothing without a reason," Livesey responded with authority.

"She took to Miss Westbrook. Although she was annoyed at your choosing Lady Jane and was threatening to disinherit you, I don't think she had any motives in choosing Miss Westbrook other than because she liked her. Even Aunt Dickson would not meddle between an engaged couple,"

Jessica said. "You have to admit, Miss Westbrook would be a good companion."

"Hmm," Livesey responded noncommittally. "So, she's threatening to disinherit me, is she?"

"I told her you would not be concerned with that when you were going to receive Lady Jane's wealth, but now, you'll have to hope she didn't mean it," Jessica said with a smile.

"I would rather not inherit if she thinks she can dictate who I marry. I want your assurance that you will not write to Aunt Dickson and let her know of what happened," Livesey said.

"How can I not mention it?" Jessica asked.

"It's nobody's business but mine and Lady Jane's," Livesey insisted.

"Which will seep out into society, if it has not already," Jessica pointed out. "Aunt will be furious if one of us doesn't tell her and she finds out from someone else."

"She's in Bath. It will take an age for it to reach there," Livesey said with a shrug.

"They do send the newspapers to Bath," Jessica said with a smile. "And the gossip columns will love this particular piece of gossip."

"Do *not* tell her, Jessica. I do not want her getting any fanciful notions," Livesey ground out.

"Fine! But I'll make sure it's you who gets the roasting when she eventually finds out!" Jessica said tartly.

"I am shaking with fear," Livesey responded with derision.

"You will be. Now, I want you to escort me to the Thornley's ball tonight," Jessica said, changing the subject.

"Where is Knowles?" Livesey asked.

"He's feeling under the weather, so I have excused him," Jessica said.

"I don't want to attend a ball. Too many questions will be asked," Livesey said.

"But you will never find a wife hiding away in your gentlemen's clubs."

"I've decided it's too much trouble," Livesey said with feeling.

Jessica stood up, and putting her hands on her hips, she glared at the amused expression on Livesey's face. "Lady Jane has had ample time to let everyone know she is no longer engaged. I've got only a short period of time before I have to confine myself to home, so I'm certainly not wasting the opportunity to visit a ball with my brother! I expect you to collect me in good time this evening!"

"Yes, Jessica," Livesey responded with a smile.

"That's better. I'll leave you to prepare. I expect you to look your finest," Jessica instructed before giving her brother a farewell kiss.

Livesey smiled when Jessica left the room. His sister was such a considerate, gentle creature that he enjoyed it when she lost her temper. He would have preferred to spend the evening in some bawdy house, trying to subdue images of hazel eyes, but perhaps this would be better. He could prove to himself once and for all he'd only felt a pull towards Miss Phoebe Westbrook because she was the best of a bad bunch. Once in wider society, her attributes would pale into insignificance.

*

It had been soon whispered around the room that the rumour was correct: Lady Jane Bellamy had broken off her engagement to Lord Livesey. Questions were asked as to why, but as no one was brave enough to approach the glowering Livesey and ask the impertinent question, speculation would have to suffice.

Lady Jane had not been seen since the announcement of the engagement, but people had found out that she'd broken off with Livesey. A word here or there had soon passed through society. It was hard to tell if Livesey was upset or not; he more often than not stood at the edge of the dance floor glowering at everyone who considered approaching him.

Jessica approached her brother once she'd circulated the room saying her hellos and confirming that the engagement was indeed off.

"Now that I've done all the hard work spreading your news, the least you can do is dance with me," Jessica said with a huff. "Allowing me to face everyone alone is a poor show."

"You were desperate to come here. Do not expect me to open myself up to unwanted conversations," Livesey shrugged.

"It's for the best this way," Jessica said. "Now I need to dance."

"In your condition? I don't think so!" Livesey responded.

"Oh, please!" Jessica almost wailed, which brought a smile to Livesey's lips.

"I'm not having Knowles call me out for putting his future heir at risk. No. You may stand with me, and we can both watch proceedings."

Jessica glowered at her bother but didn't argue. She knew her husband wouldn't have agreed to her dancing but had hoped to convince Livesey that she could still take part.

"Mrs Belshaw! How are you?" Jessica asked, as an acquaintance moved into their small area.

"I'm very well, Lady Knowles!" Mrs Belshaw responded. "I have not seen you for these last few weeks."

"No. I was at my brother's house. We just returned to London a few days ago," Jessica responded.

Mrs Belshaw glanced at Livesey, clearly having heard about his broken engagement. "Of course. Your Aunt seems to be enjoying Bath."

"Oh?" Jessica asked.

"My sister wrote to me. Her daughter, Martha, is taking the waters and has come across your aunt. It appears she is enjoying life to the full with her new companion. My sister says your aunt is all over town, attending as much as she can," Mrs Belshaw said with a smile.

"That sounds like Aunt Dickson," Livesey couldn't help uttering.

"A friend of yours is often in their company," Mrs Belshaw said to Livesey. "Captain Chester has renewed his acquaintance with your aunt and is enjoying spending time with his newly extended circle."

Livesey didn't respond to the piece of news.

Mrs Belshaw continued unperturbed. "My sister, says he's accompanied them to more than one ball at your aunt's insistence. She certainly does not allow for refusal, does she?"

"She certainly does not," Jessica said cheerfully.

"Martha says Captain Chester always dances first with your aunt's companion. She is a delightful young lady, according to Martha."

"Miss Westbrook is lovely," Jessica admitted.

The ladies chatted for a few minutes more before Mrs Belshaw left to move further into the room. Jessica wafted her fan. "My goodness, the heat has built quickly tonight!" she said.

"Neither of us should be here," Livesey ground out.

"Where should we be?" Jessica said. "In Bath, protecting Miss Westbrook from the gallant Captain Chester?" she asked with an arch expression.

Livesey shot Jessica a look. "What do you know?"

"Nothing other than what Mrs Belshaw reported, but I'm assuming aunt will be playing matchmaker, if I know her!" Jessica smiled.

"I'm taking you home!" Livesey ground out. "I will not have you unwell on my account."

He failed to notice the smile Jessica sent to her friend, Mrs Belshaw, and the nod the woman gave Jessica in return. It would not hurt her brother to think Phoebe was being courted by another, Jessica thought smugly as she followed her brother out to the hallway to call for his carriage. No. From the way he reacted, it had been worth entering an overly hot ballroom.

Chapter 17

Northamptonshire

Jane awoke with a smile. She was wrapped in Stuart's arms on their first complete night together. It didn't matter that they weren't married; she knew they would be at some point. All that was important at the moment was that they were together and could be open with their affection.

She snuggled deeper into Stuart's embrace and was rewarded with a kiss on her hair.

"Morning, my lovely," Stuart whispered.

"Good morning," Jane replied.

"It certainly is a good morning. I never thought this would happen," Stuart said with feeling.

"No regrets?" Jane asked.

"Not now. I hated the thought of you sacrificing yourself to another," Stuart responded.

"I would never have betrayed you," Jane said quietly.

"You could not have made that promise," Stuart said. "But I refuse to think of that now. You are here in my arms, and I couldn't be happier."

"Nor could I," Jane said.

Before either could respond further they were disturbed by an insistent knocking on the bed chamber door. It was not the type of knock that could be ignored. Stuart scrambled out of the bed, pulling on his breeches whilst pulling a shirt over his head. Jane sat-up, pulling the sheet under her chin.

Stuart unlocked the door. Immediately he put his hand on the handle, the door was pushed open, forcing him to leap out of the way.

"What the devil…" he started to utter, before realising that Lady Bellamy stood before him, looking angrier than he'd ever seen her.

"Mother!" Jane exclaimed in shock.

Lady Bellamy stormed into the room followed closely by Lord Bellamy.

"How dare you shame us in this way!" Lady Bellamy snapped at her daughter.

"Mother! Keep your voice down!" Jane appealed to her parent as Stuart closed the door, trying to contain the argument within the room.

"I will do nothing of the sort!" Lady Bellamy snapped. "You will get yourself dressed and prepare to leave. You are going to visit your Aunt in Northumberland."

"I am going nowhere!" Jane responded, getting out of bed.

Lady Bellamy glowered at the slight bulge of Jane's stomach, visible through a clinging nightdress. "You will do as you are told!"

"I am beyond the age that you can force me to do anything I do not wish to do. Well beyond the age!" Jane snapped in return. She had never been close to her mother; she was the aloof parent whilst Lord Bellamy had been a warm and encouraging parent.

"You do not care that you have brought shame on this family! I told your father you had been overindulged, but he never listened! Always the one to give in to you! If you think we will stand aside whilst you ruin the Bellamy name, you have underestimated me!"

"We are in love," Stuart said quietly, moving around Lord and Lady Bellamy to stand next to Jane.

"Poppycock! You have spied a chance and played on a spinster who was completely on the shelf! Of course she was charmed by you. Anybody would be who had no decent prospects!" Lady Bellamy spat at Stuart, looking him up and down as if it were the first time she'd ever seen him. In reality, it probably was. Servants were there to do a job not to be noticed, in Lady Bellamy's view.

"Mother! How dare you!" Jane responded. She knew her mother would be upset at her news and decision, but her words were vindictive.

"I dare when you try and besmirch the Bellamy name by bringing a by-blow into our midst! It will never be accepted," Lady Bellamy responded. "The sooner it is dealt with the better for all involved. I will not have it anywhere near our home."

Jane put her hands on her stomach in a protective gesture. "I would not want you anywhere near any child of mine. You are poison, Mother."

"How dare you!" Lady Bellamy launched herself at her daughter in an attempt to strike her, but Stuart reached the woman first. He was over six feet in height and broad-shouldered, so he easily restrained the smaller, older woman.

"Enough!" Lord Bellamy roared at his wife, finally speaking. "There is no excuse for violence, especially in Jane's condition."

"There is every need," Lady Bellamy responded, extracting herself from Stuart's grip. He let her go but moved to Jane and wrapped his arm around her waist.

"Jane is carrying my child. I will not allow anyone to hurt her," Stuart said quietly. "No matter what title and wealth you have."

"Ha! You have hurt her more than anyone!" Lady Bellamy spat. "She will never be able to appear in public again! It would be better if she lost the child and returned home."

"Mother, I would never return home even if I weren't with child or if Stuart abandoned me," Jane said firmly.

"Then you are happy to bring shame on us!"

"I never set-out to hurt anyone," Jane said, refusing to use the level of voice her mother was using as she shouted out each sentence. Jane had enough control to speak in a reasonable tone. "I fell in love. Everything else is irrelevant. I tried to do the decent thing and marry someone from within society, who would never care for me. It would have been an acceptable marriage in the eyes of the world but not to me."

"Lord Livesey will never accept you now!" Lady Bellamy said.

"He knew I was with child before you did," Jane said simply. "He was not willing to bring up another man's child."

"And who can blame him? If you have the thing adopted, he would consider you," Lady Bellamy said with authority.

"The thing? The thing?" Jane asked in disbelief. "I have always known you to be a cold, uncaring parent, but referring to my child as a thing is unforgiveable!"

"What else is it? A mistake? A burden? An inconvenience?" Lady Bellamy snapped.

"It is a new life. *Our* child," Stuart said, glaring at the peeress.

"It is a mistake at best and a bloody disaster at worst!" Lady Bellamy snapped again, hating that one of her servants was answering her back.

"You can tell society you cast your wicked daughter out. I am sure you will relish the opportunity to explain how disrespectful and inconsiderate I have been," Jane said derisively. "That should gain you the sympathy vote."

"Do not think when you are homeless and starving, we will have you back. Because we will not. However much you beg. Once you have gone that is it," Lady Bellamy said.

"I would not dream of darkening your door ever again," Jane said with feeling.

"At least we can agree on something!" Lady Bellamy said. "You have one last chance, before I disown you as my daughter. Come back home, and we will pack. You can visit your aunt and come back into society when the...child...is adopted."

"If I ended up destitute and on the streets, I would not give up my child or Stuart," Jane said firmly.

"Then you are a fool, and I want nothing more to do with you!" Lady Bellamy said, before turning her back on her daughter. "Alfred, I shall wait in the carriage. We are going to write new wills immediately. She will receive nothing!"

Without looking back, Lady Bellamy left the room, slamming the door behind her. Lord Bellamy looked torn but turned towards his daughter. "I wish you would come home with us."

Jane's eyes filled with tears. "I cannot, Papa. Stuart would never be accepted, nor would our child. She would force me to abandon them, and I cannot do it."

"No," Lord Bellamy said. He'd been angry yesterday, but now the reality of losing his only daughter was sinking in.

"Can I write to you?" Jane asked. She'd always been closer to her father, and it was breaking her heart to think she might never see him again.

"Yes," Lord Bellamy said. He turned to Stuart. "If you do not take the best of care of her, I will hunt you down and give you a beating."

"And I would not fight back because I would deserve it, My Lord," Stuart said seriously. "I will do my best by her."

"Aye. Well. I need to go. We are not going to change our wills. You will still inherit," Lord Bellamy said to Jane.

"If it makes your life easier with mother, do as she wishes," Jane said.

"No. I have never let her interfere with my business, and I do not intend starting now," the usually amiable man said firmly.

"Papa, I am going to miss you," Jane said, moving across to her father and embracing him.

"I am going to miss you too," Lord Bellamy said. He returned his daughter's embrace then reached inside his hat, which he'd carried since his arrival. "Here, take this."

"What is it?" Jane asked.

"A reference," Lord Bellamy said, glancing at Stuart before kissing Jane's cheek. "Take care, my love, and let me know when you are settled."

"I will," Jane said softly, wrapping her arms around her waist.

Stuart stood behind Jane, enfolding her in his arms in an act of support. They waited until Lord Bellamy had left the room, glancing back at his daughter with a look of regret and sadness.

"I didn't expect him to give me a reference once Lady Bellamy made her disgust clear," Stuart admitted, kissing Jane's head gently.

"Nor did I. But he's a fair man, and although he'll support mother, he would not see us destitute."

"We have what we need. I think we should leave today," Stuart said gently.

"Yes," Jane responded without enthusiasm.

"Are you having second thoughts?" Stuart asked, turning Jane so he could look into her eyes. "You need to speak now if you are. If you have any doubts, go back to your family. I do not want you to regret your decision to leave with me."

Jane smiled a watery smile at her beloved. "No. I've never doubted being with you. I only tried my foolish scheme in order to not cause problems with my parents, but you were right. It would never have worked. By your side is where I want to be and where I will be."

Stuart kissed her. "I'm glad. Shall we see what the reference says?"

"I think we had better," Jane said, rousing herself. She frowned as she opened the envelope. It felt very thick but she was astounded by what was inside. "There's so much money! Papa has given us more than we asked for, more than he should."

"We can return it," Stuart said. "I meant what I said. I'm going to provide for you."

Jane smiled at him. "Good. But this, along with my own money, will give us a good start. He has given us five hundred pounds and a cheque for two thousand pounds!"

"A cheque?" Stuart asked in shock.

"Yes. Papa was determined to be one of the first with a personalised cheque when they were issued. This is the first he's written to my knowledge and for so much!" Jane said. "We can set-up a small house with this. You will not need to rush to go into service."

"It is what I know," Stuart pointed out, looking slightly uncomfortable.

Jane reached up and kissed his lips gently. "I know, but we now have nearly a thousand pounds in cash and a two-thousand-pound cheque. We can choose carefully where we live and what we do. This removes any pressure. After all, our first job is to get married."

"Yes, it is. I can't wait until you are Mrs Rogers," Stuart said with a smile.

"Neither can I, Mr Rogers," Jane said, before deepening her kisses.

Chapter 18

Bath

Phoebe was worried. Aunt Dickson wasn't well and was in full denial of the fact.

She had rushed hither and thither for three weeks, and it was taking its toll on the older woman. Even Phoebe felt the effects of non-stop walking, theatre trips, card parties, dances, and public breakfasts and suppers.

Last night, they'd watched fireworks in Sydney Gardens until late and then had planned a shopping excursion to Milsom Street the following day. Putting on her bonnet in the hallway of 23 Gay Street, Phoebe had been on hand when Aunt Dickson had stumbled slightly and almost collapsed onto the floor. Phoebe had supported her employer until a servant had brought a chair for her to sit on.

"Let me call a doctor. You're very pale," Phoebe said.

"You will do no such thing!" Aunt Dickson said with feeling, although her voice was without its usual strong tone. "There's no need to make a fuss. He will only say I've indulged too much and should rest."

"And he'll be right," Phoebe said.

"I'll have no insolence from you, young lady," Aunt Dickson glared at Phoebe.

"And I refuse to accept any stupidity from you," Phoebe glared back.

"Don't you dare speak to me in such a way! I deserve your respect!"

"And you'll get it once you stop this fool's errand of yours. For days you've been pushing yourself too hard. I have no idea why," Phoebe finally admitted.

"I've wanted to find you a husband to make up for that bumbling nephew of mine using you ill," Aunt Dickson shrugged.

Phoebe looked horrified. "You've been wearing yourself out to try to find me a husband? How will I ever explain that to your family?" she asked, mortified.

"You'll not need to do any explaining to anyone," Aunt Dickson responded.

"They need to know you are unwell," Phoebe insisted.

Aunt Dickson stood up from where she'd been seated. "I want your firm promise that you'll not contact either my niece or nephew and tell them I'm ill."

Phoebe paused. She was convinced Livesey or Jessica needed to know, but if she promised, she could not then, in all conscience, break that promise. She sighed. "I give you my word if you promise to rest for the next few days."

"I'll be fine," Aunt Dickson said. "It was a moment's weakness and has passed now."

Phoebe shrugged. "No resting, no promise. I won't have your death on my conscience."

Aunt Dickson glared at her companion. She valued the girl a great deal, partly because she stood up to the older woman. "I did not have you down as one for dramatics. It appears I was wrong. I will rest for three days and no more," she said loftily before walking into the drawing room.

Phoebe smiled. "If you agree to spend today in your chamber, I shall agree to the three days and not push for the week that I think you need."

"Don't antagonise me, or I'll send you home!" Aunt Dickson snapped.

"Don't torment me by trying to find me a husband!" Phoebe retorted. "Bath has suddenly lost its appeal if that is your aim!"

*

Three days later, although Aunt Dickson was still refusing to see a doctor, she hadn't left her bed chamber. Phoebe read to her in an effort to relieve the boredom, but she could see how frustrated the vibrant woman was. Phoebe also had a suspicion that Aunt Dickson was a little afraid to seek help.

She was in a dilemma. If the weakness had just been overexertion, surely it would have started to be relieved after three days complete rest. There was still a sickly pallor and complete lack of energy which concerned Phoebe. She needed to send a letter to let someone know Aunt Dickson was unwell in the hope they would support her in seeking medical advice, but she'd given her word.

On the fourth day, Phoebe decided to take matters into her own hands and sent out a missive. She waited in the drawing room, pacing up and down the bright room, hoping for a speedy response.

Pausing only when she heard the knocker on the front door, she almost sagged with relief when Captain Chester was announced.

"Miss Westbrook, I came as soon as I could. What's amiss, and how can I be of service?" Captain Chester asked with his usual smile.

"Oh, Captain Chester! How relieved I am to hear your offer of assistance!" Phoebe said with feeling.

She went on to explain what had happened over the last few days and how she had promised her employer not to inform on her.

"So, you see my predicament?" Phoebe asked.

"I certainly do!" Captain Chester laughed. "She's a wily one, is Mrs Dickson. You have to admire her!"

"I could admire her more if she were less stubborn!" Phoebe said, but there was no malice in her words.

"So, I'm to write to Lady Knowles and tell her everything?" Captain Chester asked.

"Yes, please! I think it would be best sending it to Lady Knowles. Lord Livesey is recently engaged and probably not up to racing across the country," Phoebe said, willing her cheeks not to blush at the mention of Livesey's name. "Lady Knowles is increasing, which makes her position difficult, but I hope Lord Knowles would respond to your letter."

"I'll suggest that someone needs to be here," Captain Chester said. "It' is not for us to dictate who it should be."

"No," Phoebe acknowledged. "I'll just be glad when one of her family attends. She should be seeking the counsel of a doctor."

"Would you like me to speak to her?" Captain Chester offered.

"No. I'm sure she would guess the motive of your visit if she knew you were here," Phoebe said hurriedly.

"Good point. I shall leave you and send a letter immediately," Captain Chester stood.

"I thank you for your assistance. I know you could do without my troubles adding to your own worries," Phoebe said gratefully.

A look of sadness flitted across Captain Chester's face. "Yes. I was hoping for better results when we came to Bath. I'm trying to be positive for Martha's sake, but she is not improving, and I'm beginning to think she will not. Her parents seem to be coming to the same realisation. They aren't talking so much of recovery anymore. I think they're losing hope."

"Oh no! I'm so sorry! You both seem to be trying so hard to enjoy yourselves and make the best of things," Phoebe said with real sadness.

"We're both facing the fact that there might not be a wedding, or if there is, Martha will not survive much beyond it. I honestly don't know what to do for the best," Captain Chester admitted.

Phoebe wanted to wrap the kind Captain in an embrace purely to offer comfort. Instead she took hold of his hands. "Do whatever she wants to do. Give her as much happiness as you can. If there is anything I can do, you need only to ask."

Captain Chester smiled slightly and squeezed Phoebe's hands in return. "Thank you, Miss Westbrook. I appreciate your offer of help. The last few days have been the most worrying we've ever experienced. We have been forced to have conversations no engaged couple should ever have to speak of."

"And I've added to your burden!" Phoebe said with feeling.

"Not at all! It has given me something else to think about. It can get quite insular when dealing with your own concerns. I'll return to Martha and send off the letter at the earliest opportunity," Captain Chester said.

"Thank you, and please, let me know if there is anything I can help with," Phoebe said, leading the way out.

"I will. Good day," the captain said with a bow before leaving Phoebe once more.

Phoebe returned to Aunt Dickson's bed chamber to find the woman awake, but still looking pale. "Are you still refusing to let me send for the doctor?" she asked.

"Yes," came the terse reply.

Phoebe sighed. "So be it. What shall I read to you today?"

"No arguments?" Aunt Dickson asked.

"There is no point in making you feel worse by arguing with you," Phoebe said with a shrug. "I'm finally admitting defeat."

"What sort of companion are you?" Aunt Dickson asked. "Capitulating immediately!" she continued with the ghost of a smile.

"One who refuses to be the conscience of a foolish old woman!" Phoebe retorted.

"If you were not so useful to have nearby, I'd send you home with a flea in your ear!" Aunt Dickson scolded.

"I think my position is safe. You'd never be able to employ a nurse who would put up with your demands!" Phoebe said with a smile.

"Whereas you are a delight to be with!" Aunt Dickson responded tartly.

"I've learned from a master," Phoebe said with a laugh.

Aunt Dickson smiled with appreciation before laying her head against her pillow. "Read to me, child. I tire too easily for my liking."

"And mine," Phoebe said quietly but did as she was bid. She hoped Lord Knowles would leave his home immediately when he received the captain's letter.

Chapter 19

London

Livesey responded quickly to Jessica's missive requiring his attendance at their home in Portland Street. Entering the marble hallway, he shed his hat, gloves, and cane before walking into the drawing room.

"Jessica! Are you unwell?" Livesey asked, crossing the room to place a kiss on his sister's cheek, before looking at her closely.

"Apart from looking more grotesque every day, I'm fine!" Jessica responded.

"You are positively glowing," Livesey said with a smile.

"That's because I no longer feel the cold! It is very strange!" Jessica said with a grimace.

"So, if you're not ailing, what is the urgency?" Livesey asked.

"One of the family is unwell," Jessica stated. "I have heard Aunt Dickson isn't faring too well."

Jessica watched as a range of emotions raced across her brother's face but made no comment.

"And how do you know this?" Livesey asked.

"Captain Chester has written me a letter, expressing his concern," Jessica explained.

"And why is it his concern to inform us of this when Aunt Dickson has a companion who could do the job of advising us herself?" Livesey asked with annoyance.

"I have no idea why Miss Westbrook hasn't written, but I know there must be a good reason. Thankfully, Captain Chester has taken it upon himself to inform us, and you need to go to Bath with me," Jessica said.

"You shouldn't be travelling such a distance," Livesey said.

"Knowles said the same, but I need to go to my aunt," Jessica insisted.

"No. You do not," Livesey said firmly. "I'll go."

"And barge in like a tyrannical father? I don't think so!" Jessica responded.

"I would not."

"This is your sister you're talking to!" Jessica said with a scowl. "I know what you'll do, Livesey! You will ride roughshod over Captain Chester and Miss Westbrook and make Aunt feel worse."

Livesey paused, realising that Jessica had quite a poor opinion of him. "You haven't much faith in me."

"I know you are either confused or in denial, which will make you act irrationally," Jessica insisted.

Livesey sighed. "If I promise to be reasonable? Will that keep you at home?"

Jessica smiled a little. "As long as you stick to your promise!"

"I'll try my best to," Livesey responded.

"That will have to do, I suppose," Jessica said. "Please let me know how Aunt is. I want her to be well when her great niece or nephew is born."

"She's made of hardy stuff. I am sure this is a temporary set-back," Livesey assured his sister. "I'll set-off today. I'll travel by horse, and my carriage can follow. I think speed is needed whilst we do not know exactly what is going on."

"I hoped you'd say that," Jessica admitted. "I am worried about Aunt. She's never ill."

"Miss Westbrook isn't, or she would have contacted us," Livesey ground out. His emotions muddled through worry at seeing his aunt indisposed but mixed with anticipation of seeing Phoebe.

"George! You promised!" Jessica scolded.

"Yes. But it doesn't mean I can't think there is something amiss with Miss Westbrook's silence."

"As long as you only think it, George!" Jessica chastised, watching her brother leave the room. She hoped he would think before making unsubstantiated accusations towards Phoebe. This was an unlooked-for opportunity for her brother to come into contact with the woman Jessica was sure would make him happy.

*

Bath

It was a full seven days before Aunt Dickson felt well enough to be helped downstairs into the drawing room. Phoebe had helped her, alongside a maid, each trying to take the weight of the older woman. It was a slow descent, but eventually she was seated on the most comfortable sofa, surrounded by cushions and covered in blankets.

Phoebe poured tea with a dash of brandy. She smiled as she placed the drink on a small side-table next to Aunt

Dickson. "There. Hopefully that will give your cheeks a little colour."

"You worry too much," Aunt Dickson responded, but she drank the tea.

"It's a good thing one of us does," Phoebe responded, but her tone was gentle.

They were interrupted by the arrival of Captain Chester.

"Good afternoon!" the captain said as he walked into the large, square room. "I'm glad to see you below stairs!"

"Rumours of my demise have been grossly exaggerated," Aunt Dickson responded, but she looked pleased to see the captain. "Tell me all of your news. I've been sadly lacking in gossip this last week!"

"I have little to entertain you with I'm afraid," Captain Chester stated, his face clouding. "Martha's taken a turn for the worse, so we have been housebound like yourselves. She isn't going to improve. In fact, there is only one possible outcome." The Captain choked on his words but managed to gather himself. "I had another errand to run, so I thought it prudent to call in to see how you were faring."

"Ah. I'm sorry to hear that," Aunt Dickson said. "Is there no hope?"

Captain Chester glanced at Phoebe before continuing. "No. The doctors have said it is only a matter of time."

"I'm sorry about that, Captain Chester," Phoebe said with real sadness. "Is there anything we can do?"

"I was hoping you would be able to come to our wedding. That's why I've left Martha. I have finally convinced her we should get married, and tomorrow, in one of the side chapels in the Abbey, we will be joined. We chose the Abbey as it's not far from our lodgings, and we can transport Martha in a sedan chair. If you could join us, it would mean a lot to us both," Captain Chester said. He was trying to mask the pain he was going through, but his eyes revealed his inner emotions.

"We'll be there," Aunt Dickson said firmly.

"But, you are not well," Phoebe said, not wishing to miss the event but not wanting to put Aunt Dickson at risk either.

"I'll take a sedan chair. The girl needs her friends around her on her wedding day," Aunt Dickson said, all her usual acerbic tone gone.

"I should persuade you to stay at home because of your health, but I'm selfish enough to want you to be present. It would mean a lot," Captain Chester said. "The service will be at eleven. I'm afraid there will not be a wedding breakfast; Martha just isn't up to it."

"It does not matter. We'll be there for the service," Aunt Dickson said.

"Does she have everything she needs for the day?" Phoebe asked.

"There has been no time to organise the wedding as we'd like. We're all so busy caring for her and spending time with her that there has been little time for anything else. It is to be a very quiet affair," Captain Chester admitted.

"I'd like to make her a posy to hold, and I could make flowers for her hair, if that would be acceptable?" Phoebe asked. "I could visit Bath market early in the morning."

"I'm sure Martha would be delighted!" Captain Chester said with appreciation. "Thank you, Miss Westbrook. It's a very kind offer."

"It would be my pleasure," Phoebe responded.

The conversation was interrupted by the arrival of another visitor. When the housekeeper announced that Lord Livesey had arrived, Phoebe sent a panicked look to Captain Chester, who shrugged. Phoebe flushed, and Aunt Dickson glared at Phoebe, all whilst Lord Livesey stood in the doorway of the room, taking in the scene before him.

"Good afternoon, Aunt," Livesey said, finally crossing the room and kissing his aunt on the cheek. "You all look very cosy."

"What the devil are you doing here?" Aunt Dickson asked roughly. "Or, need I ask? Have you betrayed me, child?" she asked, glaring at Phoebe.

"I contacted Lady Knowles a few days ago," Captain Chester interjected before Phoebe could answer.

"And why did you do that, bearing in mind I haven't seen you for this past se'nnight?" Aunt Dickson demanded.

Captain Chester smiled but stood. "Just because you are not in the thick of society doesn't mean that it ceases to function. Your presence was missed. I made enquiries and thought your family would want to know you were unwell."

"A trifle presumptuous on your part!" Aunt Dickson snapped.

"Maybe so, but I can't face going to two funerals in quick succession," Captain Chester responded seriously.

"You cad!" Aunt Dickson responded. "You know full well, I can't curse you with those sentiments!"

Captain Chester smiled. "I might not be my usual self at the moment, but I'm not stupid! I will leave you be now. My Lord, it's good to see you again. Good day, Mrs Dickson, Miss Westbrook. I'll look forward to seeing you tomorrow morning. Thank you for your assistance, Miss Westbrook. It is very generous of you."

"I will see you out, Captain," Phoebe said quickly. She wanted a little time to gather her inner turmoil at the sudden arrival of the man who haunted her dreams and thoughts.

Livesey and Aunt Dickson were left alone. "What's this about you being ill and not seeking the advice of a doctor? You look pale. You are obviously not well. Hiding from the doctor is foolish and bloody-minded."

"It's a fuss about nothing," Aunt Dickson insisted.

"Chester thought it was enough to write to Jessica," Livesey ground out.

"He shouldn't have interfered," Aunt Dickson insisted. "We were doing perfectly well on our own!"

"I'm here now and I do not care what you say. I'll be inviting a doctor to pay a visit!" Livesey said.

"Oh, go back to your betrothed!" Aunt Dickson snapped. "She might tolerate your moods for the need of a respectful marriage, but I certainly don't have to put up with you!"

Livesey gritted his teeth. He was clearly angering his aunt, and he recognised that it probably wasn't good for her health. The problem was that he was angrier than he'd been in ages. Interrupting the intimate scene had shaken him. He'd arrogantly presumed that Phoebe had regretted turning down his proposal, but it seemed she hadn't given him a second thought.

He tried to relax his features and took a few steadying breaths. "I'd rather be here with you, Aunt," he said, his tone more conciliatory. "Jessica and I are worried about you. We care about you. Please seek the counsel of a doctor."

"Ah, emotional blackmail is always the hardest to ignore," Aunt Dickson responded, sounding annoyed.

Livesey smiled. "Does that mean you'll see a doctor?"

"I suppose so. Whatever is ailing me does not seem willing to leave on its own. Send for the most expensive quack. There are a lot to choose from in Bath. Let's see what they have to say," Aunt Dickson said resignedly.

"I'll send for the most recommended doctor I can find. Only the best for you, Aunt," Livesey said with a smile.

"I have reduced the inheritance you'll receive when I die, you know," Aunt Dickson said.

"Really? Jessica said you'd threatened to disinherit me completely if I married Lady Jane," Livesey couldn't help the smile showing.

"The chit is wrong for you," Aunt Dickson said with feeling.

"Aunt," Livesey said warningly. Now was not the time to start telling her about what had happened. He was more concerned about her health.

"That isn't the whole reason though. I decided for once in my life to do something that will really benefit the recipients of my wealth. Phoebe is to receive a substantial amount of money at my demise," Aunt Dickson continued.

"Really? That is a surprise," Livesey admitted.

"Are you angry?" Aunt Dickson asked.

"It's your money. Even if you do not leave it to me, I won't end in debtor's prison. I know that might come as a surprise. Why not give it to a spinster?"

"She isn't going to end her days as a spinster," Aunt Dickson said confidently. "Be gone. Leave me to rest," Aunt Dickson commanded. "You can employ a sedan chair to take me to the Abbey at nine of the clock tomorrow morning. We are meeting Chester there."

"I don't think that is a good idea," Livesey said.

"I'm seeing those two marry, if it's the last thing I do!" Aunt Dickson said. "You can call on any doctors you wish, but I shall be at the Abbey in the morning."

Livesey's colour drained. So Phoebe was to marry? It made sense he supposed. Just because he couldn't love anyone didn't mean to say that no one could love her. He was sure she'd felt something towards him. It proved he was right in guarding his heart if she could swap affections so easily. Her fickleness would make it easier when he tried to find out what her motivation was because she hadn't sought the assistance of a doctor or contacted the family when his aunt had started to deteriorate.

Livesey recalled himself. "Aunt, I'll leave you to rest. I intend seeking out the best doctor in Bath despite its reputation of being full of quacks and cheaters. I'll bring someone back as soon as I can."

"There is no hurry. I'm not going anywhere," Aunt Dickson said, closing her eyes.

Chapter 20

Livesey knocked on Phoebe's bed chamber door. Not waiting for a reply, he turned the handle and entered the room.

Phoebe had been writing a list of what she would need from the market, but Livesey's sudden entrance had her rising from her chair in surprise.

"My Lord! Is anything amiss?" she asked, flushing red.

"You tell me, Miss Westbrook," Livesey snarled.

Phoebe stiffened. "I don't take your meaning, My Lord."

"I want to know why you felt it acceptable to keep my aunt's illness a secret, and worse than that, did not seek the help of a doctor," Livesey snapped.

"I carried out your aunt's wishes to the best of my ability, whether I agreed with her decisions or not," Phoebe said stiffly.

"Potentially putting her life at risk, if the look of her is anything to go by!" Livesey snapped. "Why did it take someone else to contact my sister about my aunt's condition? You are supposed to be her companion! She is ill, for God's sake! You have betrayed her trust in you in the worst possible way!"

"Is that what you think?" Phoebe asked, trying to blink away the hurt.

"Tell me that is not the case," Livesey growled.

"I have done nothing that your aunt could reprimand me for," Phoebe said quietly.

"But that's just it, Miss Westbrook. You did nothing! Except to look out for your own interests, obviously!" Livesey spat. "I hope the wedding is everything you hoped for!" He should have kept to lambasting her about his aunt, but he could not. He was hurt and angry and feeling desperate, and he didn't know what to do with such a range of feelings. True to form he reacted in the worst way possible.

"The wedding?" Phoebe asked in confusion.

"The one my aunt is desperate to attend tomorrow, no matter what it does to her health! Yet another way in which you've failed her. Were you going to abandon her afterwards?" Livesey asked with derision.

Phoebe frowned. "I refuse to continue this nonsensical conversation. Your aunt has a mind of her own, and although I might disagree with some of her decisions, they are *her* decisions, My Lord. It is not my place as companion to ride roughshod over your aunt even if she'd allow me to do that. She'd more likely cast me out if I tried to act above my station!" she said with feeling.

"In normal circumstances, I'd agree with you, but she is ill," Livesey said, his tone not quite as aggressive. "You should've acted. We had a right to know how she was faring. But perhaps it was in your interests not to act?"

Phoebe stiffened once more. "I do not know what you're insinuating, My Lord."

"That you are to inherit a substantial amount of money when my aunt dies," Livesey started. "Most would agree it could be motivation for neglect," he finished.

Phoebe faltered. "You think I've purposely neglected your aunt for my own benefit? The person who has been nothing but kind and decent towards me?"

"She has been beyond kind, although some would say foolish if this is the thanks she receives from you."

"I don't want her money! I didn't know she was intending to do such a thing!" Phoebe said in her defence.

"Easy to say now, Miss Westbrook," Livesey said.

Phoebe paused before grabbing her bonnet and pelisse from her wardrobe. She hurriedly put on her outerwear. Livesey watched her movements through eyes that were almost slits. Phoebe turned to him when she was buttoned up and glared at Livesey.

"With such a high regard for my personality defects, I'm surprised you let me within feet of your daughters, let alone your aunt. I'm glad you are here, as I've been worried sick about her, but that is irrelevant. I'll take my leave of you and remain out of doors today. I'm afraid I shall have to return to my bed chambers tonight, but I shall arrange my permanent removal tomorrow after the wedding has taken place," Phoebe said, her chin tilted in defiance.

She walked past Livesey, not waiting to see if he was going to respond. As she reached for the door, Livesey's words made her falter.

"It seems my girls and I had a lucky escape," he said with venom.

Tears in her eyes, Phoebe left the room.

*

Phoebe wasn't sure in which direction she walked, she just walked. Heading first uphill past the New Assembly Rooms and out of the centre of Bath, she tried to avoid places that held many people. She couldn't have held the tears back if she'd tried and didn't want to make a public spectacle of herself on top of everything else.

His words were ringing in her ears, as if he were walking alongside her, hurling the condemnation over and over again.

This was worse than the very first insult he'd aimed in her direction. Although that had been hurtful enough, it was based on presumption and arrogance. But now he knew her; he had asked her to marry him! And yet, he had said things that had been so wounding, she wouldn't have been surprised to have found actual injuries on her being after they'd hit their marks.

What had made him be so cruel? She couldn't understand it. It was as if she'd been the one inflicting pain on him, the way he'd reacted. It didn't make sense, but whatever had been his motivation, it was unforgiveable. He had lashed out at her in the most painful way possible, and she would never be able to overlook it.

Making a large circular walk, she returned to the centre of Bath, walking more calmly, her cheeks dry of the tears that had soaked them for the first hour of her journey. She was flagging when she reached the front of the Abbey, deciding to enter for some respite.

She walked to one of the side chapels and sat on a wooden bench. There were a few people inside the building, but no one was bothered about disturbing a lone young woman seated with her head down as if in an act of prayer.

Phoebe's breathing calmed, and she was eventually able to look up at the statue on the altar of the chapel. The silence in the Abbey had calmed the usually controlled young woman enough that she stood. She needed some refreshments. Luckily, she'd had the wherewithal to grab her reticule, which had some pennies inside.

Making her way to the Abbey entrance, she stopped when she saw Captain Chester finishing a conversation with a clergyman.

The captain spotted Phoebe and waved at her to stay her exit. Catching up with Phoebe he smiled.

"Miss Westbrook! I didn't expect to see you here."

"It was best I had some time away from Gay Street," Phoebe said, trying to sound brighter than she felt.

Captain Chester frowned slightly. "Is something amiss?"

"Yes. No. Mrs Dickson has not deteriorated further," Phoebe said hurriedly.

"I was asking about yourself, actually," Captain Chester said gently. "Have you been crying, Miss Westbrook?"

Phoebe blushed a beet red. "A while ago," she admitted, cursing the fact that her eyes filled with tears at Captain Chester's question. It was a sign of weakness that she didn't want to show, added to which she was amazed that she had any tears left.

"Come," Captain Chester said. "Let's go and have some refreshments. It's only round the corner to a lovely tea shop."

"Oh no!" Phoebe said quickly. "You must have much to do!"

"I have only to purchase a ring and then my duties are complete. Martha is resting; she sleeps most of the time now," Captain Chester said.

"I am sorry," Phoebe said. "My troubles are nothing in compared to yours. Please, there is no need to join me."

"There's every need, for my sake and yours," Captain Chester said. "I need a little normality, Miss Westbrook. If I do not keep seeing that the world is continuing to spin and that people are still going about their daily lives, I'm afraid I might just disappear into the dark hole that seems to hover over my shoulder for most of the time. I promise you I have no need to be anywhere else other than enjoying a warm drink with you."

"In that case, I thank you for your company," Phoebe said, accepting the offered arm, walking out of the Abbey. She was grateful for his presence. She'd felt so alone walking through the streets. In a large place like Bath, it was very easy to feel lost and inconsequential. Captain Chester's concern had meant a great deal to Phoebe.

They talked about inconsequential things until they were settled in the bay window of the popular Bath shop, enjoying a variety of cakes and a refreshing pot of tea.

After a few moments, Captain Chester started the conversation they'd both been edging around. "Now, what is amiss? It's not Mrs Dickson, is it?"

Phoebe sighed "No. Although I am worried about her."

"But no different than your worries for the last week?"

"No," Phoebe said with a small smile. She sagged. "Lord Livesey thinks I have not been the companion I should've been," she said trying to be diplomatic.

"That's ridiculous. You have done everything you can to make Mrs Dickson comfortable," Captain Chester said. "The woman thinks the world of you, and she's no fool."

Phoebe smiled slightly. "After the conversation I had with Lord Livesey, I do not want to be in his company. I've said I will return home after I attend your wedding tomorrow. I do not want to miss it."

"I appreciate your staying for that, but I wouldn't demand it if it means you are distressed," Captain Chester said.

Phoebe smiled. "Lord Livesey and I—we have just spent some time together in his home at a house party. Let's just say I thought he had a high opinion of me, but I was mistaken. It's complicated."

"Because?"

"You will ridicule me. I think I'm a fool myself, but I have feelings for him," Phoebe admitted.

"I see. Yet from what you hinted at, he unfairly took you to task this morning," Captain Chester surmised.

"Yes."

"Am I guessing correctly when I say he berated you strongly?"

"Yes."

"And yet this is the man you have feelings for?"

Phoebe smiled a little. "I did have, although this morning has shown him in a different light. I could excuse the arrogance he has displayed previously because of his wealth and title, but today he was hurtful and vicious."

"I can't say I know Livesey well. I've not spent any time in his company for years," Captain Chester admitted. "But you are somebody's daughter, somebody's sister, and I would hate to think a relation of mine was being ill-treated in such a fashion. Bad manners and poor behaviour is inexcusable, Miss Westbrook, by whoever issues it."

"I know. My sensible side agrees with you completely," Phoebe admitted.

"I'm no expert on life, but all this with Martha has shown me that you need to be with someone who truly values and loves you. Anything else, is accepting second best. I can treasure the time I have had with Martha. It has not been long enough, and I'm arranging to go to sea for a long time after she's gone. I won't be able to face life on land without her," Captain Chester confessed. "But I do not regret meeting her or falling in love with her. She's made me a better person and enriched my life in ways I could not have foreseen, and I love her all the more for it. Do not waste tears on someone who doesn't deserve them, Miss Westbrook. I know only too well that life is too short."

"You are perfectly correct," Phoebe said. "I will return home tomorrow and forget I ever met Lord Livesey. Someone who hurts you can't be worth crying over."

"Certainly not! Now, if you have had your fill, please, will you accompany me to the jewellers on Milsom Street where I'm to collect Martha's ring? I would like to buy us each a locket, and I'd value a female opinion on the matter."

"Of course," Phoebe said, smiling at her friend. She considered him one of the bravest people she knew. He was determined to enjoy his wedding even if his wife was dying. His intention to give his wife a special day showed him to best advantage. It was a stark contrast to Livesey.

"Excellent! Come, Miss Westbrook, we have some money to spend!" Captain Chester said with a flourish, leading Phoebe out of the shop.

They walked together, arm in arm, laughing at some comment of the captain's when Phoebe spotted Livesey on the opposite pavement. She stiffened, but Captain Chester raised his hat slightly at Livesey, smiled, and continued to walk.

"Don't worry, Miss Westbrook. From the look on our foe's face, he is also out of sorts," Captain Chester said cheerfully as he opened the door of the jewellers. "That does not mean you are to feel sorry for him, mind you! Let him suffer a little. It'll be character building!"

"After this morning, I want nothing more to do with him!" Phoebe said with feeling, the sickened expression on Livesey's face going unnoticed as she entered the retail premises.

Chapter 21

Phoebe entered Aunt Dickson's bed chamber during the early evening. She was relieved to see the woman was alone, and although she had her eyes closed, she had a little more colour.

"You wished to see me?" Phoebe asked quietly.

"You weren't with me when the doctor visited," Aunt Dickson responded, her eyes opening and pinning Phoebe to where she stood.

"No. I'm sorry. I needed to be out of doors," Phoebe responded.

"That can only mean that nephew of mine is still being a bloody fool, but it's of no matter," Aunt Dickson stated. "The doctor says nothing ails me apart from over-exertion. I could have saved my money. You told me that a week ago!"

Phoebe smiled. "But will you listen to him?"

"He seemed sensible enough, and he never mentioned taking that disgusting water once or being submerged in one of those horrifying baths, so he obviously was a decent sort," Aunt Dickson explained.

"What has he prescribed?"

"A concoction of his own making. Calls it his pick-me-up tonic. It will probably be nothing more than water, but it tastes fine, and I've promised to take it."

"That's a start at least," Phoebe said. "Did he advise you to stay indoors tomorrow?"

"I failed to mention my little trip out," Aunt Dickson said with a mischievous grin. "So, he could not prevent me from going, could he? I want to see that wedding. They haven't many friends in Bath. Let the chit have a lovely ceremony. She's not fit for anything else."

"No, I do not believe she is."

"Livesey will escort me. I expect you will be wanting to go early to give her the flowers you're making?"

"Yes, please."

"It's settled then," Aunt Dickson said.

"There is one other thing," Phoebe stated.

"Oh?"

"I will be leaving you tomorrow after the wedding has taken place," Phoebe said, not quite meeting Aunt Dickson's eyes.

"You'll be doing what?" Aunt Dickson almost shouted, sitting upright in bed.

"Please don't move! I don't wish you to have a relapse at my doing. I'm sorry, but I cannot stay here any longer."

"Why ever not? What's got into you, child?"

"Your family think I have used you ill. That I have neglected you and put you at risk. I cannot act as your companion if their opinion is such," Phoebe explained.

"And don't I have a say with who I keep at my side?"

"Not when I've been accused of neglecting you to receive my inheritance, which I had no idea about and do not want!" Phoebe said, finally raising her voice a little.

"Now don't you be foolish. The inheritance I am leaving you will set you up in your dotage. Don't underestimate how uncertainty and insecurity can age a person. I know you do not wish to be a burden to your family, but you cannot work forever," Aunt Dickson said firmly. "I'm not intending to die anytime soon, so you will not get it for a while. But it will be useful if you don't marry and an unlooked-for advantage if you do."

"It's a kind gesture, but I did not become your companion in the hope of getting recompense in such a way," Phoebe said.

"I know, and it's to your credit," Aunt Dickson said. "I would never have employed you if I'd even had a hint of your being mercenary."

"Good," Phoebe said with feeling. At least one person didn't think ill of her. "I am afraid I still have to leave tomorrow. I've had some accusations thrown at me today that I just cannot forget. So, unfortunately, I wish to return home. I'm sorry my departure is when you are still unwell."

"That blasted nephew of mine!" Aunt Dickson cursed. "I'll box his ears for this!"

"Please do not on my account," Phoebe said.

"He needs to know he can't go around lording it over everyone!"

"He can, and he does. I haven't the inclination to battle with him. He has settled on his opinion of me, and it's so completely opposite of who I am, I cannot bear to be here any longer," Phoebe said, finally showing the hurt Livesey had inflicted on her.

Aunt Dickson sighed. "I'm sorry child. You have not been treated fairly by my nephew from the start. I thought he would come to value you, but it appears his poor judgement is still clouding his reason. I'm suspecting jealousy is the motivation behind whatever words he uttered today."

"Jealousy? What on earth could I have done for him to be jealous of?" Phoebe laughed bitterly.

"He's made some stupid decisions over the years, and he's made another idiotic one recently. I am sorry he's the cause of you leaving. I will miss you," Aunt Dickson said with feeling.

"And I will miss you," Phoebe said, before leaving the room.

*

Livesey had hardly slept. He might have ranted and raged at Phoebe, but it was all bluster when it came down to it. He thought she'd let him down, and he'd reacted badly. He was fully aware she wouldn't neglect his aunt, but he wasn't ready to admit that. Neither was he ready to admit to being jealous of her romance with Captain Chester.

The thought of Phoebe marrying the smiling, handsome captain had filled the long hours of the night as he'd stared at the ceiling in his chamber. He knew he was being a hypocrite. He didn't want her, so why shouldn't anyone else have her? It was just that he couldn't stand the thought of someone else receiving the looks and laughter he'd had the pleasure of receiving when they'd shared moments at his home.

He sighed as he was helped to dress. Why hadn't he been able to pretend to offer her love? Then she would have agreed to marry him, and she would have been his. He gritted his teeth. No. She'd let him down with regards to

Aunt Dickson's care. She would have let him down as a wife as well.

Entering the drawing room, he walked to where his aunt was seated, waiting for him.

"Are you sure this is wise?" he asked.

"Of course. Is the sedan here?"

"Yes," Livesey said.

"We shall be speaking after the wedding has taken place of how you've managed to upset my companion," Aunt Dickson said stiffly. She allowed Livesey to help her out of her seat and used his arm to support herself when exiting the house.

"You would have lost her anyway. She at least knows what the wider family thinks of her before she sets out on the rest of her life," Livesey responded.

Aunt Dickson glared at her nephew before being helped into the sedan chair. He set-off down Gay Street in the direction of the Abbey at a quick pace. The chair bearers would overtake him, but he was determined to remain close to his aunt until the ceremony was over; then she would have to return home alone. He felt the need of finding the nearest den of ill-repute. Surely that would help clear his mind as nothing else so far had.

*

Phoebe had risen promptly and made her way to Bath's market. It opened early so the staff of the large houses could purchase all they needed to keep their residents well-supplied.

Expecting it to be busy, Phoebe had smiled to herself at the unanticipated hustle and bustle that filled the area. Shouting and calls filled the air as people advertised their wares and responded to the calls of people purchasing goods. It seemed as if the place was filled with constant movement in which Phoebe had to join if she was to secure the flowers she needed.

Choosing carnations, sweet William, roses, and foliage, she made her purchase. Walking to Martha's place of residence, she was admitted.

Phoebe had been shown into the drawing room, and a maid had helped her arrange the flowers into a beautiful, but delicate bouquet. When finished, she was invited to carry the results of her labour to Martha's bed chamber.

On entering, Phoebe smiled at the young woman. It was hard not to react to the change in Martha since Phoebe had seen her last, but Phoebe smiled warmly at the young woman, who was already dressed in a pale blue, silk gown.

"Good morning!" Phoebe said, crossing the room. "How are you?"

"I'm happier than I've ever been," Martha said with a smile. "The flowers are beautiful!"

"Thank you," Phoebe said, handing over the bouquet. "I should have asked what colour you were wearing, so I decided to err on the side of caution and go with white. It contrasts against your dress perfectly."

"It smells divine! Miss Westbrook, I haven't got any of my friends with me today. Would you act as my bridesmaid?" Martha asked.

"I would be honoured," Phoebe answered.

"Good," Martha said. "We are returning here after the ceremony. I'd hoped to return home, but the doctors have advised against it."

"I'm so sorry," Phoebe said, unable to offer words that would encourage hope when there was none.

"As am I. I wanted to see my home for one last time, but it isn't to be. At least I will be with my darling husband when my time comes. I do not deserve his devotion," Martha said, touching the locket around her neck.

Phoebe noticed the movement and smiled that the piece of jewellery the captain had picked had been well received. "I'm sure you do," she said gently. "The captain is smitten with you, which is lovely to see."

Martha turned more towards Phoebe and reached out her hands. Phoebe took them gently, noticing how translucent the skin was and cold to the touch. "Please help him when I've gone," Martha said with tears in her eyes.

Phoebe blinked away moisture in her own eyes at the heartfelt plea. "I've only known Captain Chester a short while, but I have seen how well regarded he is. Everyone will rally round him, I'm sure."

"I hope he remarries in time," Martha said, quietly. "I'd hate to think of him being alone."

"I think it will be a long time before he could consider something such as marrying anyone else," Phoebe said gently. "When you fall in love with someone, it is hard for anyone else to match the ideal of the one you love."

"I could never have loved anyone but him," Martha admitted. "And I am selfish enough to want him to miss me.

Eventually though, he needs to find someone new. He's not good on his own."

"I think none of us are, if we are truthful," Phoebe said with a smile. "But come. As your bridesmaid, I implore you not to have such thoughts, today of all days! It's a time to be happy!"

Martha smiled. "I am so very happy."

Chapter 22

Livesey stood next to his aunt in the side chapel, taking in the scene whilst gritting his teeth. There were few people in the chapel, and it had more of a feeling of a funeral than a wedding. People were speaking in hushed voices, some of the ladies present wiping away a tear or two.

Captain Chester had approached them when he'd entered the chapel.

"Mrs Dickson, I'm so glad you could make it. It means a lot to us that you are here," Captain Chester said with a smile.

"I would not have missed it for the world," Aunt Dickson said gently.

"I appreciate the effort it's taken for you to be here. I hope you'll be feeling better soon."

"I'm already feeling a little brighter. This doctor my nephew found seems to know his business, so I will be around to create mayhem for a little longer," Aunt Dickson admitted.

"Good. I hope you can forgive me writing to your niece. Miss Westbrook explained to me about the promise you'd prised out of her, and she wouldn't break it even though she was worried sick about you," Captain Chester said.

"Ah, so that's how I was betrayed," Aunt Dickson said, but there was no chastisement in her voice. "I suspected as much. I knew she would not have broken a promise."

"We can't get much past you," Captain Chester smiled. "Time to take my place, I think," he said, leaving the pair to greet others in the chapel before seating himself next to his best man at the front of the chapel.

"What promise?" Livesey growled.

"Now is not the time to explain," Aunt Dickson responded sharply.

Eventually, one or two turned to the rear of the chapel, and the guests stood. Livesey had spent most of his time convincing himself that he wouldn't watch the bride's entrance, but along with everyone else, he turned.

Struggling to comprehend what faced him, Livesey paled slightly. Aunt Dickson smiled at her nephew's reaction.

"Been jumping to conclusions, boy?" she whispered before turning her attention to Martha.

The young woman was being pushed into the chapel on a Bath chair which had been covered in cream silk. She wore the pale blue dress, which gave her a little more colour. Flowers had been intertwined with her hair, replacing a bonnet. Martha looked happy as her eyes sought out her beloved at the front of the altar. Holding her bouquet firmly she rested one hand on her father's arm as he walked at her side, looking both proud and emotional.

Phoebe was pushing the Bath chair. Her hair had also been decorated with flowers to match Martha's. Although her dress was not of silk, as Martha's was, the cream muslin complimented the bride's attire as if they'd planned it.

Phoebe concentrated on Martha, ignoring anyone else in the room. When they reached the altar, Martha stepped out of the chair and leaned heavily on her father for support. She was determined to marry Captain Chester as a wife should, standing by his side.

Phoebe had seated herself on the left of the chapel, accepting Martha's flowers. She watched the ceremony without once turning to glance at Livesey. He'd hurt her, and she couldn't bear to see his continued dislike of her reflected in his eyes on such a loving occasion. Instead she watched with pleasure as two people committed to each other fully and with open love. It was both uplifting and emotional.

Livesey was in turmoil.

She wasn't marrying Chester.

His mind raced. At what point had he come to that conclusion? What had been said that had given him the impression she was betrothed to the captain? He'd seen them together, and they'd been very comfortable in each other's company. He'd even seen them entering a jewellers together. Surely, it wasn't too far of a stretch to presume they were shopping for their own wedding? Why would the captain have taken Phoebe instead of his betrothed?

Livesey sighed. The reason the Captain hadn't taken his betrothed was as clear as the nose on his face. His new wife was in very poor health.

Hurting his jaw with the force with which he was gritting his teeth, Livesey realised something: Once more he'd been a complete idiot.

From the comments of his aunt, it appeared she'd already come to the same conclusion.

He'd misjudged everything in the most spectacular fashion.

*

Martha's father pushed the Bath chair out of the chapel and out of the Abbey while Captain Chester held his wife's hand, bending down to kiss it at every opportunity. The couple could barely take their eyes off each other as they progressed through the grand building.

Phoebe was in the middle of a small group of people as she made her way over to the newlyweds. She'd purposely positioned herself in such a way so as to avoid coming into contact with Livesey.

Each guest gave their best wishes to the newly married couple before leaving them. Aunt Dickson and Livesey were one of the last to wish the couple well.

"Look after her," Aunt Dickson said gruffly to the captain.

"I will," Captain Chester responded, looking with adoration at his wife.

"You look beautiful, child. Now go home and rest," Aunt Dickson ordered.

"Today, I feel I could do anything!" Martha said, smiling at her husband.

"You've got a good man there," Aunt Dickson said.

"I know," Martha responded. "Goodbye, Mrs Dickson, Phoebe, My Lord. Thank you for making today special and for your friendship. I hope to see you again, but if I do not, I wish you all the best for the future." Martha seemed calm when uttering the words, as if she'd completely accepted her fate.

Not one for showing her emotions, Aunt Dickson bent forward and embraced Martha in a hug. "You're a good, brave girl," she said before walking away towards where a sedan chair was waiting.

Phoebe said her goodbyes to the new Captain and Mrs Chester, before heading towards where the sedan chair had travelled.

It was time to return to Gay Street and arrange her removal.

She knew Lord Livesey hadn't followed his aunt immediately, but she did not look in his direction, instead setting off at a brisk pace.

She wasn't surprised when she heard the heavy footsteps of Lord Livesey behind her.

"Miss Westbrook!" he said, reaching out to catch her arm in an effort to halt her progress.

Phoebe turned slightly, and although she slowed her pace, she didn't stop. "Please excuse me, My Lord. I have a lot to arrange."

"Miss Westbrook. Please!" Lord Livesey said, coming to a halt in front of Phoebe.

She sighed. Trying to walk around him would only bring attention to them both, and she didn't wish to cause a scene in the middle of the shopping area of Bath. "We have nothing further to say to each other, My Lord. You've already said all I could possibly want to hear."

Livesey didn't know how to start. He faltered at the expression on Phoebe's face. There was none of the humour or mischief that he'd seen previously. She was cold and shuttered, and he had no one else to blame for her reaction.

"I thought you were marrying Captain Chester," he said eventually.

Phoebe frowned. "Why on earth did you think that?"

"I don't know. Words that were said. The fact that he was the one who contacted Jessica," Livesey tried to explain.

"He was acting as a friend to your aunt," Phoebe responded in confusion. "How could you make such a presumption from Lady Knowles receiving a letter expressing concern for your aunt's health?"

"I'm not sure. Things you spoke about. Words my aunt uttered," Livesey tried to defend himself.

Phoebe paused. He'd thought she was marrying someone else, a decent man. She looked at Livesey. She had wanted to belong to him so much, had wanted him to feel for her what she had so quickly felt for him, and still did, much to her chagrin. She'd presumed she'd seen the real person behind the title when they'd shared what they had in Hampshire, but now she had to reassess what she'd thought she'd known.

"You were vicious and vindictive towards me because you thought I was marrying another?" Phoebe asked.

"No. Yes. Possibly."

"I see. In Hampshire I gave you credit for being a decent person underneath the unwelcoming exterior, but I was wrong," Phoebe said, finally having the courage to utter the words which had been choking her since he'd arrived in Bath. "Because I would not agree to marry you, but you thought I'd accepted someone else, you have accused me of neglect, ingratiating myself with your aunt for monetary benefit, and being some sort of monster who you'd wish a thousand miles from yourself and your family."

Livesey visibly winced at her words.

"It seems I was the one who had a lucky escape, My Lord," she started. "What sort of verbal abuse would I have faced on a daily basis if I'd done something you disagreed with? What sort of man would think the worst of someone he had spent so much time with? I thought you knew me. Did my actions not give you any hint of my true character?" Phoebe continued. "I've told you before that I do not lie. My motives and behaviour since I met you have been consistent and open."

"They have," Livesey admitted.

"How could you then accuse me of what you did?" Phoebe asked, but quickly raised her hand when it seemed Livesey was about to speak. "No. I don't want to hear excuses, for that is all they'll be. You've said your piece; now I've said mine. I would appreciate it if you didn't return immediately to your aunt's home. I'd like to take my leave of her without you present. My belongings will be packed by now, so I will not remain there for long."

"I will leave you be," Livesey said. "I'm sorry."

"Not as sorry as I am," Phoebe said, looking at Livesey for the last time. It gave her no feeling of pleasure that he looked at her in despair. For once in her life, she could not offer comfort to someone who was hurting.

She sighed quietly and turned away from Livesey, walking up the hill towards Gay Street.

Chapter 23

Aunt Dickson waited in the drawing room. She'd given instructions that Phoebe should join her before doing anything else. She heard the front door open and muted voices as her instructions were given. Before too long, Phoebe walked into the drawing room.

"I wouldn't have gone without saying goodbye," Phoebe said with a small smile.

"I was hoping to persuade you to stay," Aunt Dickson admitted.

"I'm afraid I cannot. Too much has been said that can't be unsaid," Phoebe admitted. "I shall miss you, but I need to return home."

Aunt Dickson scowled. "That damned nephew of mine!" she muttered.

Phoebe smiled sadly. "Yes."

"I'll order my carriage, and you're to take Violet with you," Aunt Dickson said, accepting defeat.

"No! I can easily catch the stage," Phoebe said hurriedly.

"You will certainly not travel in such a way!" Aunt Dickson snapped in return. "You would be travelling unprotected, and I will not accept that. You will use my carriage and maid. Because you're getting a late start, I will tell Violet where to stay, and I shall bear the cost. If you are to return to your family, you will travel safely. I'll not have you put at risk because of one of my relations."

"Thank you," Phoebe said, acknowledging defeat. "I'll admit, I was not looking forward to travelling by stage. I knew I wouldn't be able to complete the journey in a day, which was a little concerning."

"And yet you'd have gone ahead and done it," Aunt Dickson said with a shake of her head.

"We shouldn't avoid what we're frightened of. It makes life too limiting," Phoebe said with a half-smile. "I had better go and check that everything is packed."

Aunt Dickson rang the bell as Phoebe left the room. There was little point in making Phoebe's good bye more difficult than it was already. She ordered her carriage and instructed her maid in what to do.

Only moving when Phoebe re-entered the room, she stood and moved towards Phoebe. "Is everything ready?" she asked.

"Yes. My portmanteau is being loaded onto the carriage now. There's no point in delaying my departure any further," Phoebe said. "Thank you for allowing me to become your companion. You have been very kind to me."

"Don't say that too loudly. It will ruin my reputation!" Aunt Dickson said with a smile.

"I won't." Phoebe smiled weakly. "I hope you continue to improve," Phoebe said, feeling guilty at leaving Aunt Dickson when she was still not fully recovered, although she looked better than she had done.

"I'm sure I will. I think I will leave Bath soon. It won't be the same without you here. Being surrounded by invalids is no fun if they can't be ridiculed with my sharp-tongued cohort by my side!" Aunt Dickson said.

Phoebe laughed. "I object to that! You are the one with the sharp tongue! I'm too afraid that someone will overhear a cutting remark if I should make one!"

"You would have changed if you'd spent enough time with me," Aunt Dickson assured her. "I had high hopes you'd be even sharper than me! You are definitely more intelligent. Just imagine, me with more intelligence. You would have been incorrigible!"

"Oh my goodness! What a fate!" Phoebe couldn't help laughing.

"I suppose you've had a lucky escape," Aunt Dickson said becoming serious.

"I need to ask you something before I leave," Phoebe stated. "Please change your will as soon as you can to disinherit me. I would be happier knowing your family couldn't reproach me about receiving money from you."

"It has nothing to do with my family!" Aunt Dickson said.

"Unfortunately it does, and their poor opinion could potentially affect me. I will have to work in the future, and I'd hate my reputation to be besmirched."

"I will consider it," Aunt Dickson said, having no intention of changing her will for the second time. But she would be speaking to Livesey and Jessica about it.

"Thank you," Phoebe said.

A footman knocked quietly on the door and announced that the carriage and Violet were ready. Phoebe pulled on the gloves she'd been holding in her hands and fixed her bonnet slightly.

"Goodbye. Thank you for everything," Phoebe said, her eyes glistening.

"Be gone before I try to guilt you into staying!" Aunt Dickson responded, looking upset.

Phoebe crossed the room quickly and kissed the old woman on the cheek. "Please take care."

Phoebe walked out of the room and left the house with a heavy heart.

*

Livesey had stayed away for two hours but then had returned to his Aunt's abode. He'd been drawn to the house, wanting to burst in and try to explain himself to her once more, but he had forced himself to stay away; he owed Phoebe that.

Entering the hallway, he was met by his aunt, coming downstairs.

"Ah, the prodigal nephew has returned," she said wryly. "Join me in the dining room. I've ordered luncheon."

Livesey followed mutely. There was no advantage in delaying the inevitable cursing he was about to receive.

Aunt Dickson busied herself with helping herself to food, before nodding to the footman in attendance that he should leave the room. Pausing before taking her first bite of a thick piece of ham, she looked at her nephew.

"Whatever you said to that child was unfair and unreasonable," she said, biting the meat.

"Yet you have little idea of what I said," Livesey said dryly.

"She's not the type to make a fuss over nothing. And she would have been within her rights to have a bout of hysterics after yet another of your dressing downs, but she did nothing but behave with grace."

"I was misinformed," Livesey defended his actions.

"You jumped to conclusions," Aunt Dickson said with derision. "Shall we go through each of your accusations?"

"I would rather not," Livesey admitted.

"I'm afraid I must insist," Aunt Dickson said. "After all, you have a low opinion of our Miss Westbrook, and that's something I cannot tolerate."

"I haven't got a low opinion of her," Livesey admitted.

"Then you're a bigger fool than I thought," Aunt Dickson said.

"Possibly," Livesey acknowledged. "I thought she had neglected you by not sending for myself or Jessica when you became ill."

"I am not ill!" Aunt Dickson responded tartly. "I over-exerted myself! It was my own fault, and I was taken to task enough times by my companion. I didn't want you and Jessica interfering as well!"

Livesey half-smiled. It was typical of his aunt. "She should have sent word."

"She did, the minx, in the only way she could. From what Chester said today, she clearly colluded with him to write to you."

"He wrote to Jessica."

"Ah, and you wondered what motivation he had in avoiding you, the head of the family," Aunt Dickson guessed correctly. "He was hardly likely to write to you when you would be in the middle of planning the wedding of the year!"

Livesey sighed. There'd been no mention as such of his engagement, but now was the time to break the news. "I am no longer engaged," he said simply.

"Really?" Aunt Dickson said, putting down her knife and fork. "Why did she cry off?"

"I'm letting society think Lady Jane broke off the engagement, but it was I who cancelled the agreement," Livesey admitted.

"Realised you had made a mistake?"

"Something like that." Livesey went on to explain what had gone on between himself and Lady Jane.

Aunt Dickson leaned back in her chair after Livesey had finished his story. All idea of eating had been forgotten. "Well, I never!" she said. "What a conniving chit!"

"She was desperate. I understand why she did it," Livesey admitted. "I just was not prepared to accept someone else's children above my own."

"Certainly not!" Aunt Dickson said with feeling. "You were lucky not to have a claim made against you for breach of promise."

"I had to be as calculating as she was to prevent that. I was prepared to make her secret public, which is not very gentlemanly of me, but I was not going to agree to the terms in her contract. Life would have been worse than it is now," Livesey admitted.

"A pity you didn't speak about this sooner. I still say Miss Westbrook would be perfect for you," Aunt Dickson acknowledged.

Livesey put his head in his hands.

"What is it?" Aunt Dickson asked. Her tone was gentle.

"What does it feel like, Aunt?" Livesey asked, his voice choked.

"Love?"

"Yes. What does a healthy, reciprocal love feel like?" Livesey asked. He looked at his aunt with eyes that were troubled.

"It feels all-encompassing but not exhausting. It is warmth, excitement, and pleasure all rolled into one. And desperation when it feels as if it's being lost," Aunt Dickson replied quietly, her sympathy stirred by his obvious distress.

"When Jessica read me the letter, I couldn't think straight. I jumped to conclusions—wrong ones. I thought I had been as wrong about her as I was with Angelina. To think I hadn't known her after all, to presume she'd wronged my family and I had been replaced in her affections ripped at my insides as nothing else has ever done. Not even Angelina's death," Livesey admitted.

"You thought she was to marry Chester."

"Yes."

"And what did you feel today when you realised you were wrong?"

"I had been vicious with her when I arrived. I thought she'd met him, persuaded you to leave her an inheritance, and then was neglecting you. I was an idiot of the highest order," Livesey said.

"I won't argue against that," Aunt Dickson said. "How could you think that of her?"

"It says more about me than it does about her," Livesey admitted. "Travelling to Bath, I just got myself into such a rage, I couldn't hold it in. I had to think of her as if she had betrayed me—us. I couldn't face the simple truth that she had found someone else to love when my feelings were still as strong."

"I hope you apologised after you realised your mistake at the wedding this morning."

"Quite rightly, she didn't give me the opportunity. She pointed out that I had become angry when I'd thought she was marrying someone else when I had already told her I couldn't offer what she wanted from a marriage," Livesey said. "It was unfeeling on my part, and I am ashamed of how I reacted."

"She wanted love," Aunt Dickson responded.

"Yes. And I couldn't give her that."

"Yet you've been in love with her since the first few days of your house party," Aunt Dickson pointed out.

Livesey groaned. "Yes, I suppose I have, but if you could see it, why couldn't I?"

"You mistrusted your feelings because of Angelina. I understand that, but you should have thought it through. Miss Westbrook was perfect for you from the start."

"As you pointed out, and I offered nothing but insults, which she overheard," Livesey admitted.

"Yes. You seem to have a habit of that," Aunt Dickson said. "What are you going to do to make things right?"

"I have no idea."

"You are going to follow that girl and not leave her be until she listens to you. When you've finished lying prostrate at her feet, begging her forgiveness, I suggest you then start to beg for her hand in marriage. She is one who feels sorry for lost causes. Let's just hope she takes pity on you," Aunt Dickson instructed.

Livesey smiled a little. "I suppose it's an idea."

"It is the best there is. If you go on horseback, you'll easily catch my carriage, especially as I advised Violet to stop at the inn in Avebury. You will be able to speak to her there."

"I'd have pressed on further," Livesey said.

"Yes, but I knew you would want to catch her before you lost the light, so I didn't want her travelling too far away," Aunt Dickson said.

"I should be worried you know my mind better than I do," Livesey said, but he stood in preparation for leaving.

"I observed the way you watched her in Hampshire. Lady Jane saw it, which is why she questioned Miss Westbrook over her intentions. She wanted to find out who she was in competition with. I knew there was something not quite right with Lady Jane, but I couldn't put my finger on it."

"Jane needed me to marry her quickly, but she was playing a risky game," Livesey said bitterly. "After offering Miss Westbrook an insult, I suddenly realised she was the one I could speak to about anything meaningful. There was never any pretence. Nothing but honesty and a lot of funning."

"So follow her and persuade her that you are not the ogre you act," Aunt Dickson instructed. "There's just one more thing."

"Oh?"

"She asked me to change my will when she left. She doesn't want to be a beneficiary of it because of the trouble it will cause," Aunt Dickson said sternly. "I said I would consider it, but I have no intention of changing the details. If you or Jessica give that girl one ounce of trouble about her inheritance when I'm gone, I promise I will come back and haunt you!"

"What a thought!" Livesey shuddered. "I give you my word. I'll never accuse her of misdeeds and will ensure she receives the amount she is due."

"That's more like the nephew I love not the buffoon who has been existing in his body these last few years. Now go and get her!"

Chapter 24

Phoebe accepted the early stop. She felt drained after the last few days' events and would be glad of an early bed. Violet had done all the arranging of the room, and Phoebe was soon ensconced within a clean but basic bed chamber with seating area and small dining table.

Violet had ordered a light meal of soup and bread and had left Phoebe to enjoy the food in the peace of her own room. Phoebe was glad to have a few moments to herself. She felt emotionally empty.

Sitting on the window seat when she'd finished her meal, she rested her head against the cool glass. The window overlooked the village green. It was quieter than if she'd been to the rear of the inn, where people came into the yard to change horses, purchase sustenance, or seek accommodation.

Phoebe felt disappointment above anything else. She was returning home, once again having failed. She'd never expected to be the one marrying Livesey, even though it would have been so easy to say yes to his proposal, but being a companion had been a way of being less of a burden on her family. She would have to look for another position, but she was certain she wouldn't find anyone she liked as much as she'd liked Aunt Dickson.

A knock on her door interrupted her reverie, and she moved quickly to open it. She stepped back when faced with Livesey at the door. He had come straight from the stables, not even shedding his greatcoat. He looked magnificent, but his expression betrayed uncertainty, not the usual confident Lord.

"Is your Aunt well?" Phoebe asked, trying to mask the shock of seeing him.

"Yes. She was the one who suggested I follow you. Could I have a word, Miss Westbrook?" Livesey asked.

"Have you not said all that needs to be said?" Phoebe asked.

"I think I have not even started," Livesey responded with a small smile.

Phoebe rested her head against the wood of the door. "I can't do this," she said quietly.

"Do what?"

"Be emotionally battered by you," Phoebe admitted.

Livesey paused, trying to maintain a neutral expression at her words. "Is that how you feel?"

Phoebe sighed. "If I'm being honest, yes. Since our first day together you have caused such highs and lows for me, I hardly know who I am anymore."

Livesey was stunned. He took a moment to reply. "I say this not to gain sympathy from you, just as an example to show I understand. That's exactly how I felt with Angelina. Life with her was wearying because of the ups and downs. I hated living like that, and I sincerely apologise for making you feel in such a way. Perhaps I'm more like my deceased wife than I would like to admit."

Phoebe looked into Livesey's eyes. She'd always thought they were his best feature, even when he was glaring daggers at her. She'd heard the saying that eyes were the windows to the soul, and with Livesey, she could finally understand those words.

"I do not wish to give you pain," she said, admitting to herself that she could see pain in his depths. It gave her no pleasure to see it reflected there.

"No. But you give me honesty, which I should have appreciated more. I won't bother you further, Miss Westbrook. I genuinely wish you all the best for your future and my only regret is that I did not value you from the moment I met you, as I do now," Livesey said. He stepped forward and kissed Phoebe on her forehead. "I wish you every happiness for the future. I truly do."

"I wish you well for your upcoming marriage. I hope you and your girls are happy," Phoebe said quietly.

Livesey paused. "I am not marrying Lady Jane. We decided we wouldn't match after all."

Phoebe could curse the surge of relief that flooded her body at his words. Why did she feel such exhilaration when she'd just admitted he drained her? Did she honestly think he was chasing her to replace Lady Jane? No. He'd been quite clear in Hampshire: He couldn't give her what she wanted.

Livesey noticed Phoebe's surprise, but there was nothing else he could do or say to make things better. He'd treated her in just the same way he'd been treated, and he refused to inflict that on anyone, especially her. He turned away and walked down the hallway which led to the stairs that would take him downstairs and out of her life forever.

Phoebe stood watching him walk away. She wanted to stop him, tell him all would be well, but she couldn't. She couldn't risk being hurt more than she had been already. She didn't step away from the doorway until Livesey had disappeared from sight. Then closing the door, she pushed aside any niggling feeling of remorse at refusing to hear what he had to say.

No. It was better this way.

*

Livesey arrived in Gay Street late in the evening. He should have stopped riding when he lost the light, but he wanted to return to someone to whom he could voice at least some of his pain.

Walking into the drawing room, he flopped into a chair which was nearest the door. Still wearing his hat and greatcoat, he closed his eyes briefly.

"You are back earlier than I expected," Aunt Dickson said, knowing without Livesey uttering a word that he'd failed to persuade Phoebe that he loved her.

"She pointed something out to me that made me realise just what a beast I've been," Livesey said, all fight gone, his eyes dulled with pain.

"You admitted as much before you left. What could she say that you hadn't already acknowledged?"

"Do you know who I sounded like when she was describing how it felt to be with me? Angelina. The woman who made my life hell, and Miss Westbrook compared me to her! It was not done with malice; she would not be so cruel. She didn't know how I felt about Angelina, after all. But she described the emotional turmoil that knowing me had caused her. It seems the reality is that I'm more like Angelina than I would like," Livesey acknowledged.

"It was perhaps too soon to chase her," Aunt Dickson said, changing tack.

"No. I followed her, and she rejected me, and I can't blame her for it. I am going to return to Hampshire. I've been away from the girls for too long."

"You have been trying to get a mother for them."

"Yes, and what a bloody mess I've made of it!" Livesey said with feeling. "The poor devils will have to accept me as their only parent. They have everything they need in money and security, yet they haven't got even a half decent parent to help them through life. It's pitiful."

"Don't go all maudlin and feeling sorry for yourself!" Aunt Dickson chastised.

"I'm not. I will just continue to live as I was. They will lose out; I won't. Even if I try to be the best father I can be, I'm too flawed to achieve greatness."

"Well, I would not be beaten so easily. Miss Westbrook is the perfect wife for you; now all we have to do is figure out a way for her to see it. At least you're no longer in denial of the fact," Aunt Dickson said, already starting to mull over possibilities.

"I am afraid I'm not going to subscribe to any more schemes that you or Jessica think up," Livesey said darkly. "I'll take the girls to stay with Jessica for a while; I promised them a trip before I left for London."

"I'll join you," Aunt Dickson said. "There is nothing keeping me in Bath now."

"You are not well enough to travel so far," Livesey said quickly.

"I'm not quite ready for my grave yet," Aunt Dickson said. "I am coming with you."

Chapter 25

Surrey

Livesey was relieved to arrive at his sister's home. Three days of travel with three young girls and an aging aunt did not translate into a quiet, relaxed journey. Even though it was two weeks since he'd travelled home from Bath, it felt as if he'd been constantly on the move, and he was glad to finally step onto firm ground. He'd taken the journey especially slowly to maintain his aunt's improving health.

Lord and Lady Knowles lived in a house on the outskirts of Godalming, close to the larger town of Guildford. The house was a medieval manor house, which sprawled across a large area. Jessica had turned a draughty, crumbling pile into an inviting home. Lord Knowles teased that his wife had bankrupted him, but everyone who visited the house appreciated the improvements which had been made.

Three bundles of excitement almost fell out of the carriage and into the arms of their aunt and uncle. Livesey followed, helping Aunt Dickson out.

"George, Aunt, it's so good to have you here!" Jessica said, giving each a kiss when she was able to extract herself from her nieces. "We have so many outings planned for the girls: picnics, horse riding, shopping and swimming in our lake."

Livesey had told Jessica what the nanny had been threatening the girls with, and it was decided they should spend time in water, gaining confidence, but in a lake far away from the one their mother died in.

"It's enough to send me racing back to Hampshire," Livesey said with a wry smile. "What say you, Aunt? Shall we make our escape?"

"The hunting is fine at the moment," Lord Knowles said with a smile at his brother-in-law.

"Yes. Long days hunting, away from my brats, sounds perfect to me," Livesey responded.

Jessica tutted at her brother before leading the party into the house. She spent some time settling the girls into their rooms in the nursery. As well as having the company of the maid who'd replaced the nanny, she'd allocated one of her own maids, who had lots of younger siblings. She was determined that the girls would spend their time with her playing and having fun.

Returning downstairs, she joined her brother, husband, and aunt in the morning room. The room which had windows opening onto a wide stone-paved terrace was her favourite place on bright sunny days.

"It's lovely to have children in the nursery rooms before their cousin eventually arrives," Jessica said, sitting down with a sigh.

"Not far to go now?" Livesey asked.

"No, thankfully. Another couple of months," Jessica said with feeling.

"You need to make time to rest. Do not plan too much while we're here," Aunt Dickson said.

"Oh, I will rest; don't worry. Everything is ready for when the day comes. I will show you the renovations we have made upstairs later on," Jessica said.

"When she says 'we', you know I had very little to do with it don't you?" Knowles asked with a raised eyebrow.

"You provided the money, so you did have some part in it," Jessica pointed out. "I found some of Knowles' baby clothes in the attics. I can't wait to show them to you, Aunt."

"If the talk is going to be about babies, I have a new whiskey in my study I can recommend, if you would like to join me, Livesey?"

"Certainly. Drinking whiskey beats baby talk any day," Livesey responded, standing to follow his brother-in-law out of the room.

"You will have to spend some time with our child when it arrives!" Jessica said with mock-seriousness as her husband and brother left the room.

"Leave him be," Aunt Dickson said.

"The funny thing is that he will be completely besotted when he or she does make an appearance," Jessica said with confidence.

"As he should be. I'm glad they left us. I want to seek your opinion on a matter I cannot solve on my own," Aunt Dickson said, before going on to explain what had gone on in Bath.

Jessica listened, a frown deepening as the story unfolded. "Oh dear. He has finally realised he has feelings for her. I never thought he'd be open to love again."

"You have done the same as everyone else," Aunt Dickson chastised. "He didn't love Angelina. It was a young man's infatuation that went too far. I doubt Angelina felt anymore for him than he did for her. She never seemed to care about him when I was in their company."

"No, that is true. I noticed her indifference. It was all about herself. She seemed so very self-absorbed, but I did presume he was deeply in love with her," Jessica admitted. "I wonder what type of man he would have been if he hadn't met her?"

"There is no point wasting time about puzzles we can never know the answer to. We need to work out a way of getting Miss Westbrook and Livesey together once more. I don't think it would take much of a push for them both to give in to their feelings," Aunt Dickson said.

"There's absolutely no point in trying to arrange a meeting. He would immediately know what we were trying to do and leave," Jessica said. "My ears are still ringing from the scoldings I received for my interference last time."

"Eventually you will be able to crow over him because he actually met the woman he's going to love for the rest of his days at the party you insisted on," Aunt Dickson said with confidence.

"That's all well and good, but how do we get her here?" Jessica asked. "I cannot write to her. She'd be as suspicious as George would be."

"Yes. Thankfully, I've thought of a way around that, but I will need to speak to your husband," Aunt Dickson said with a mischievous smile.

*

Hampshire

Phoebe was annoyed. In fact, she was absolutely fuming. Silently she cursed and stomped around the lanes around her home every single day.

She was the female version of a chawbacon—a country bumpkin who should know better. That had to be the case. She was supposed to be intelligent, so how could she be so idiotish at the same time?

He had mistreated her on more than one occasion. Any self-respecting person would've condemned him as a cad, a monster, a cursed rum touch. Yet, despite his poor behaviour towards her, she was still thinking of him for most of the day and dreaming of him at night.

While she couldn't forgive some of the things he'd said to her, she clung to the Livesey she'd seen whilst at his home. The man who was prepared to marry for the sake of his daughters, the man who'd seemed as out of step with the rest of the world as she was. It was that image of Livesey she clung to as a drowning man would cling to a piece of wood. He'd been so funny, vulnerable, sincere, and handsome, all rolled into one. It made it impossible to push that Livesey to one side.

What made it worse, was the fact that she'd had her chance. He'd asked her to marry him, and her response had been laughable. Who the heck did she think she was, presuming a man like Livesey would fall in love with an old maid like herself? She'd accused him of all sorts of personality defects, but in reality, she was the one who was arrogant. How high and mighty must she have sounded spouting that she could marry only for love? She'd been a fool and now she was a lonely fool.

She was returned home for a second time with no future and little to suggest her situation would change any time soon.

Entering the gentleman's country residence she called home, she took off her bonnet and gloves. Placing them on a side table, she heard two male voices and smiled to herself. Crossing to the morning room, she peeped her head around the door. Seated opposite each other were her father and uncle. They were brothers-in-law but had been best friends before becoming related. Although relatively poor in comparison to his friend, the match hadn't been forbidden when Phoebe's father had fallen in love with the sister of his best friend. Frederick Longton had supported the family over the years, partially through family obligation and partially because of his high opinion of Charles Westbrook.

"Uncle Fred! How lovely to see you!" Phoebe exclaimed. "This is a nice surprise."

Frederick rose from his seat. He was a tall man who'd never married, although he was considered handsome. He'd never met anyone he'd wished to spend his days with, but he was comfortable with his life and had no regrets that marriage and a family hadn't been for him.

He smiled at Phoebe, holding out his arms to give his niece an embrace. "I'm going to visit an old friend and decided to call in on my way. I haven't been over these parts for too long," he explained.

"I'm glad you made the detour," Phoebe responded. "How long are you staying?"

"Actually only until tomorrow," Frederick responded.

"That's a shame. It would've been nice to have seen you for longer," Phoebe admitted.

Frederick looked at Mr Westbrook who gave a slight nod, before he turned once more to Phoebe. "I was going to wait until later, but I might as well mention it now. I was actually hoping you'd accompany me."

"Me? Would I not be an encumbrance?"

"Certainly not! If I'm honest, you'd be a real help," Frederick admitted. "I'm visiting Lord Knowles. I know you'll know him after the house party at Lord Livesey's house."

Phoebe tried not to react to the words her uncle was saying.

"In earlier correspondence, Knowles mentioned his wife thought a lot of you, and so I was wondering if you could join me? You can spend time with Lady Knowles while I discuss business with Lord Knowles. He's promised me a few days shooting as well, and it would certainly help if you could be with Lady Knowles. I know she's increasing and is more restricted these days. I think Knowles is looking to you to entertain his wife," Frederick explained with an endearing smile.

"I don't think it would be appropriate for me to join you," Phoebe said quickly.

"Why not? It's not as if it's another party. It would be only the four of us. A husband feels less guilt when spending time away from his wife when she has a companion to entertain her," Frederick said quickly.

"Go, Phoebe. You've been restless since returning from Bath," Mr Westbrook said. "And you said yourself you liked Lady Knowles."

"I do, but I don't know if it's a good idea," Phoebe said doubtfully. It seemed almost like fate was laughing at her, constantly putting Livesey's family in her life, as if she was to never be allowed to forget him.

"Please. You know you're my favourite niece, and we can have a real catch-up on our journey," Frederick argued.

Phoebe smiled. "It's a good thing Susan and Georgina aren't here. They'd have something to say about your preference!"

"I would appreciate your company. It's always more enjoyable when travelling to be with someone who offers good company," Frederick said.

Phoebe could never resist responding to an appeal by anyone she cared about. She couldn't refuse her uncle. "If you're sure it will be just the four of us."

"Yes, it will. Does this mean you'll come?"

"Why not?" Phoebe responded. "Lady Knowles is a lovely person to spend time with." And she might tell me about her brother, so I'd better understand him, she thought silently to herself. If nothing else, it might ease her troubled mind.

"Excellent!" Frederick responded with an unnoticed triumphant smile at his brother-in-law.

Chapter 26

Surrey

Phoebe had spent a pleasant few days in her uncle's carriage. He was very good company and had kept her entertained the whole time. Uncle and niece had always been close to each other, sharing a passion for books and learning. Phoebe had always felt that her uncle understood her more than anyone else did. He would never use a derogatory term like bluestocking, which was used in the most hurtful way by society. Instead, he'd encouraged his niece from an early age to push herself and learn as much as she could.

When finally riding down the drive at the Knowles' abode, Phoebe looked out of the window with interest. "It's an impressive house," she commented as the carriage turned a corner, bringing the house into view.

"Yes. There is a large fortune in the Knowles estate. And Knowles is a shrewd businessman, so his wealth isn't going to lessen any time soon," Frederick explained.

"A lord of the realm doing business? Whatever next?" Phoebe smiled.

"It's the future, if the old money is to survive," Frederick responded. "Here we are!"

The carriage came to a stop outside the large, wooden, open door. A footman sprang into action, opening the carriage door and lowering the steps.

As Phoebe and Frederick stepped down, Lord Knowles came out of the house. "Longton! How the devil are you?"

"I am very well, my friend!" Frederick responded.

"Miss Westbrook, it's good to see you again," Lord Knowles said in welcome. "My wife has been counting the hours until your appearance. She is struggling a little these days with having her activities curbed!"

"I'm looking forward to seeing her again," Phoebe admitted.

"Come in! Come in! We'll soon have you settled," Lord Knowles instructed, leading the way inside.

They entered a large, square hallway which had dark wooden panelling on its walls. It was quite a dark room, but a roaring fire and furniture covered in light fabric helped give it a welcome feel.

The group paused when the voices of children could be heard before three young girls burst out of the drawing room, followed closely by a laughing Jessica.

"Miss Westbrook! The girls have been looking forward to your arrival almost as much as I have!" Jessica said, reaching over the heads of her nieces who had fallen into Phoebe's arms en masse.

Phoebe had been stunned when the three girls had run out of the room. Unable to react to her shock, she'd been forced to say hellos to three constantly moving beings.

"Miss Westbrook, we've had picnics!" Sophia gabbled.

"We're learning to swim, but Jenny doesn't like it!" Eliza said.

"I've got a pony here for my own self!" Jenny said.

Phoebe laughed, unable to react in anything but a positive way to the children. "Really? It all sounds very exciting!"

Jessica smiled at Phoebe. "I promised Livesey the girls could have a holiday here after the house party. We've been keeping very busy."

"It must be a real treat for you all," Phoebe said, looking at the girls.

"Yes. A time to run and play without worrying about lessons," Jessica said.

"And misbehave when your Papa isn't here!" Phoebe laughed.

"I am sorry to disappoint you, Miss Westbrook, but their Papa is here," came the deep voice of Lord Livesey.

Phoebe spun around to see Livesey entering the hallway. He had a gun cocked over his arm and looked a slight challenge at Phoebe, but his expression was fairly neutral.

Instead of responding to Livesey, Phoebe turned back to Jessica. "I was told you were alone and in need of company, which is why I agreed to visit." Her tone was stiff. "It appears I was misinformed."

"I am sorry," Jessica said. "I'd forgotten until this morning that your uncle had offered to bring you with him. It's all happened very fast."

Livesey walked past the group and into the rear of the house, where the gun room was located. He'd been almost overwhelmed to see Phoebe in the hallway, standing there in her grey pelisse and straw bonnet. He could recognise her in a room filled with hundreds, he was so attuned to her appearance. Jessica had given no hint of her visiting. He was convinced Phoebe was as shocked as he was, but he didn't believe Jessica's excuse that their visits had clashed. Jessica was far too organised for an oversight like that to occur.

He wasn't sure what he was going to do. If he was a gentleman, he should probably arrange his removal at the earliest opportunity after the last conversation he'd shared with Phoebe. But yet—perhaps it was the chance of showing her he was better than she thought. Better than *he* considered himself.

He pondered as he cleaned his gun. This could be his last chance with her, and he couldn't walk away from it. His mouth set in a grim line. He was going to stay whether Miss Westbrook liked it or not.

Back in the hallway, Sophia, Jenny and Eliza had started speaking again once their father had left the room. Phoebe was talked into the morning room, where she came to a stop once more.

"Mrs Dickson!" she said in surprise.

"I thought I would stay in here until your carriage moved off. I didn't want you fleeing," Aunt Dickson said with a smile.

"Are you well?" Phoebe asked.

"I am perfectly well, thank you."

"Miss Westbrook, please take a seat," Jessica implored, sitting herself on a sofa.

Phoebe sat on the edge of a chair. She wasn't relaxed, especially as she could feel the eyes of the two other women in the room observing her.

"I'm sorry. You are not happy to be here," Jessica said, for the first time having doubts about her and her aunt's scheme.

"I admit I feel a little as if this visit has been orchestrated," Phoebe admitted.

"My brother didn't know you were coming," Jessica said hurriedly. "There has been no scheming on his part."

"But there has been on yours?" Phoebe smiled.

"Maybe a little," Jessica admitted.

"And Lord Livesey could think I had something to do with it, if previous experience is anything to go by," Phoebe said.

"No. He will not. Not from the expression you're betraying at the moment anyhow," Aunt Dickson said.

"Please stay," Jessica appealed. "From the look on your face, I'm half expecting you to run away. We don't see my brother during the day if it is any consolation."

"You can't go!" Sophia appealed. "We are going kite-flying tomorrow!"

"Don't say that!" Jessica responded with a smile at Phoebe. "Miss Westbrook was exhausted after your last attempt at kite flying!"

"Papa has promised to run," Sophia said.

Phoebe looked at Jessica with her eyebrows raised. "You do not see him during the day?" she asked wryly.

"Well maybe once or twice," Jessica admitted with flushed cheeks.

*

Jessica was interrupted by a quiet knock on her bed chamber door while putting on the last touches while dressing for the evening meal. Livesey entered when the maid opened the door.

"Have you a moment?" he asked.

"For you always, as long as it isn't a scolding," Jessica said with a smile, nodding to her maid to leave them alone.

"For once it's not," Livesey acknowledged with a small smile.

"You have my rapt attention then!" Jessica said with glee.

Livesey shook his head slightly in amusement at his sister. "You're incorrigible!"

"I know. Knowles despairs of me sometimes," Jessica admitted.

"I can understand why," Livesey acknowledged. "I am presuming Miss Westbrook was genuine in her surprise and shock to see me here?"

"Yes. She had no idea you or the girls were here, or even Aunt Dickson," Jessica admitted.

"We left on poor terms when in Bath," Livesey admitted.

"Aunt said as much."

"Oh! To have some secrets from my interfering family!" Livesey said in desperation.

Jessica grinned at her brother.

"Anyway, I'm glad you've arranged for her to be here," Livesey admitted. "I'm going to use this time to persuade Miss Westbrook that I am not as bad as I appear, or act for that matter."

"My first reaction is to fling my arms around you, but I shan't just yet," Jessica said. "I have played with Miss Westbrook's life a little in luring her here under false pretences, but I need you to see something before you gain my utmost support."

"What is that?" Livesey said warily.

"She needs someone who can love her. I know that sounds ridiculous from a girl with no dowry and of the age she is, but it's to her credit that she has been steadfast," Jessica stated. "You couldn't offer that the last time you asked her to marry you. If you still cannot, please be friendly towards her but don't make her fall in love with you anymore than she already is."

"You think she loves me still?" Livesey asked in surprise. He was afraid to acknowledge the surge of hope that pulsed through his being at Jessica's words.

"If she didn't, she would have never agreed to travel here," Jessica pointed out. "It is not me that's attracted her to visit; it is the fact that I'm a link to you."

"It sounds a little far-fetched to me," Livesey admitted.

"Trust me. I'm a woman. I wanted to be near everything and everyone connected with Knowles when we first met," Jessica said. "Doing that meant I felt close to him, even when he wasn't there."

"I cannot say I understand," Livesey said with a scratch of his head. "But I suppose it sounds plausible. Don't worry about my mistreating her. I will not."

"Does this mean you're admitting to being in love with her?" Jessica asked.

Livesey smiled slightly. "You're making lots of leaps with only the minimal amount of information!"

"I'm not. I have already said that I saw the way you watched her when we were in Hampshire," Jessica admitted. "You would be happy with her; I'm sure of it. She would not indulge you but would worship you at the same time. You need that. If you married someone who completely worshipped you just because of your title, it would make you even more arrogant than you already can be."

"How can you assassinate my character while seeming to have my best interests at heart?" Livesey asked.

"Easily, when I have you as a brother!"

Chapter 27

Phoebe dressed after spending a restless night. The previous evening had been trying to say the least. She had been sat between her uncle and Lord Knowles, but she'd felt on show, as if everyone was waiting to see what she would do or say.

Livesey had been quiet throughout the meal, being perfectly polite and pleasant.

It had made Phoebe extremely wary.

Now she was to spend a few hours flying kites with her uncle, Lord Knowles and Livesey while Jessica and Aunt Dickson looked on. It was going to be a long day.

The grouping walked across the formal lawn to the side of the house and up to the top of a slight incline. It was high enough to feel a little exposed and ensure there was wind enough to fly three small kites.

Phoebe was paired with Lord Knowles, and Eliza and the three of them made a more successful team than the others, who had only two people. Livesey started to torment Phoebe and Lord Knowles, cursing them for cheating and having the advantage.

Eliza had started to look a little disconcerted, so Phoebe stepped in.

"I didn't have you down for a poor loser, My Lord," she shouted across to Livesey as he stomped to the kite which was once more crashed into the ground.

"Another pair of hands would make all the difference," Livesey grumbled.

"Just accept your skills are not at the level of ours!" Phoebe retorted.

"Swap places?" Livesey asked.

"Not a chance!" Phoebe said gleefully.

Livesey laughed. "Coward!" he retorted.

Phoebe grinned in return, which warmed Livesey's insides. Watching Phoebe, rather than concentrating on what he was doing he stumbled and fell heavily onto the ground.

His yelp of pain, brought activities to a stop as everyone ran over to him. Sophia, Eliza, and Jenny were all concerned for their father. Jessica hurried down the hill from where she'd been seated.

"Let me look!" she said, pushing through to her brother.

"It's nothing. I have just twisted my ankle," Livesey said through gritted teeth.

Jessica touched the injured joint, and Livesey groaned. He looked at his brother-in-law. "I think I'll not be going on many hunting excursions for a while."

"Let's get you back to the house," Jessica said briskly. "You need to keep that foot raised, or it will swell."

Jenny started to cry, feeling guilty because it had been her kite that had caused the tumble.

Phoebe moved to embrace the girl. "Don't cry. It was an accident. Your Papa will be well."

"But it was my kite!" Jenny sobbed.

"The ground was uneven, and I was laughing at your Papa, so it was more my fault," Phoebe acknowledged with a smile and glance at where Livesey was being helped to his feet.

"He will be very angry he can't go hunting," Jenny whispered.

"We can think of things he can do whilst his foot is resting," Phoebe whispered in return.

"Really?" Jenny asked.

"Yes. Let's go back to the house, and we will plan what we will do," Phoebe encouraged.

Jenny wiped her eyes and ran to her sisters, to tell them of their next task. Sophia and Eliza seemed to welcome their sister's news as they all started to babble.

Livesey looked at Phoebe as he walked past, using Lord Knowles and Phoebe's uncle as crutches. "What have you got my children planning now, Miss Westbrook?"

"Ways of preventing you from being bored," Phoebe said with a smile.

"Oh, God. Knowles, you'd better shoot me now," Livesey groaned darkly.

The party returned to the house, and Livesey was ensconced in his bed chamber with ice from the ice storage wrapped in a towel around his raised foot.

Eventually left alone, he was able to curse his foolishness. He'd been concentrating on Phoebe not on where his feet were going. He was lucky to have not broken his ankle. It would mean the next few days would be boring while the swelling reduced, but more than that, he wouldn't be spending any time with Phoebe. He could hardly show her he wasn't the beast she thought he was when he was confined to his bed.

*

A knock on Livesey's door during late afternoon, roused him from a nap.

"Come in!" he shouted, glad for contact with anyone.

Three faces looked around the wood of the door frame as Phoebe opened the door.

"What are you scamps up to?" Livesey asked.

"We've been making a hunting game for you!" Eliza said. "Do you want to play?"

"Of course!" Livesey said quickly, pleased that Phoebe was also coming into the room, admittedly behind his children, but at least she was here.

"The girls were concerned that you would not be able to hunt while you were injured, so we've made a game ourselves," Phoebe explained.

"Excellent!" Livesey said, looking at his children. He was touched they were so worried about him and would go to so much effort.

Phoebe returned to the door and carried into the room a piece of wood that had paper ducks fastened along very thin pieces of doweling. She looked at Livesey with a faint blush on her cheeks. "Lord Knowles' gardener was quite surprised at my request for help."

Eliza held a bag which she gave to her father. "These are instead of a gun to aim at the ducks."

"We drew the ducks!" Sophia said.

"They're very good," Livesey said. Out of the bag he took small, smooth wooden blocks.

"You aim at the ducks and see if you can hit them. The ones at the front are worth three points. The ones at the back are worth five points," Eliza explained.

"I thought you could have a competition between the four of you, and I could keep score," Phoebe suggested.

"Frightened you'd lose?" Livesey asked.

"Not at all. I do not want you to hurt yourself further in trying to push yourself too hard," Phoebe responded. She couldn't help the smile touching her lips. She was wary around Livesey, but the teasing man he was at the moment was extremely hard to resist.

There commenced a noisy game of kill the paper duck in which the room was constantly peppered with the wooden blocks. At least they were light enough not to cause any damage, although Phoebe had moved two vases away from on top of a chest of drawers—just in case.

Two hours later, Livesey thought he'd never want to see a paper duck again. The ducks were looking decidedly the worse for wear after the barrage, but the children were overjoyed that their game had worked so well.

Responding to Livesey's pained looks, Phoebe called a halt to the game. "I think it's time your Papa had a rest. He should not have too much excitement in one day."

Livesey raised his eyes at Phoebe but she was doing an excellent job of ignoring his efforts to interact with her. It wasn't being done nastily; he had the distinct impression that she felt uncomfortable in his bed chamber, even with three young girls clambering over the bed and him.

Each child gave their father a kiss good-bye before they followed Phoebe to the door.

"Miss Westbrook," Livesey said.

"Yes, My Lord."

"Could you ask for some refreshments and fresh ice to be sent to me, please?"

"Of course," Phoebe responded before leaving the room.

She took the children to the nursery. They'd had a lot of excitement, and it was now appropriate for them to have some quiet time before they started their bedtime routine. She left them with the two maids, who were trying to concentrate on three voices all speaking at once.

Phoebe ordered the tea and ice for Livesey and started to make her way downstairs to seek out Jessica or Aunt Dickson. Halfway down the stairs, she faltered before continuing downstairs and heading into the library.

Exiting a few moments later, she returned upstairs, once more knocking on Livesey's chamber door.

Livesey couldn't help the smile forming on his lips when he saw Phoebe on the threshold of his bed chamber for the second time that day.

"Come in, Miss Westbrook," he said.

"I've just brought you these books. I thought you would appreciate a quiet night's reading after the day you've had," Phoebe explained, suddenly feeling very vulnerable, even though Livesey was incapacitated on his bed.

"Thank you. You're very kind," Livesey said, touched at the gesture. "Could you bring them to me please? I really cannot take them off you any other way."

Phoebe smiled and flushed at her silliness. She had to enter the room, but she left the door fully open. "Here you are," she said, placing the two books on the bed.

"Are they gothic novels or sweet romances?" Livesey asked with a cocked eyebrow.

"Neither. They're books of improvement," Phoebe responded archly.

"They'll be wasted on me then!" Livesey responded with feeling. Recalling himself, he looked at Phoebe seriously. "Thank you for distracting Jenny away from worrying about her causing my accident."

"It's no problem. She is a sensitive little thing," Phoebe responded. She didn't move towards the doorway, when every rule of etiquette screamed that she shouldn't be in a man's bed chamber alone, whether he was incapacitated or not.

"She is. I've come to realise how much these last few weeks. I actually feel as if I am getting to know them for the first time," Livesey admitted.

They were interrupted by the arrival of tea, brandy and cake and two blocks of ice, wrapped in towels.

"I'll leave you be," Phoebe said quickly when the servants entered the room.

"Please don't," Livesey said quickly. "I have something else I would like to say."

They both waited until the room was empty before continuing their conversation. Phoebe busied herself with pouring tea for Livesey.

"I have an apology to make," Livesey said seriously. "I'm ashamed of my behaviour in Bath."

Phoebe flushed. "I would never do anything to harm your aunt. I think very highly of her."

"I know. I was a buffoon and nasty to boot. I'm truly sorry," Livesey said.

"Thank you for apologising. I did not know you were going to be here, or I never would have come," Phoebe said quickly.

"You despise me so much?" Livesey asked.

"No! It wasn't that," Phoebe said with feeling. "I did not want you to think I was hounding you."

"Oh, if only!" Livesey said quietly. He smiled at Phoebe's blush. Her reaction gave him the slightest bit of hope.

"You don't mean that," Phoebe said hotly. "I overheard your opinion of me at the start of our acquaintance, remember?"

Livesey could have cursed. "That was a fool speaking. These last few weeks have been the most revealing, the most changing I have ever experienced in my life."

"For us both in some ways," Phoebe acknowledged. "Please excuse me, My Lord. I should return downstairs."

"I wish you'd stay and talk with me," Livesey said.

"I'm afraid I cannot. I've stayed too long already," Phoebe said, making her way to the door. "Goodnight My Lord."

"Goodnight," Livesey said. He could roar with frustration. How could he prove he was worthy of her, if he couldn't spend any time alone with her?

Chapter 28

She loved him.

It didn't matter that he'd been a brute. Her feelings were strong and could forgive the way he was sometimes. He'd apologised for being a beast which meant a lot to her. He was rich and powerful enough to never need to apologise for anything if he didn't wish to. That was one of the many advantages of belonging to the aristocracy.

So, she not only loved him, she'd forgiven him.

It was pure torture that he was in the same house.

Entering the breakfast room, she was greeted by Aunt Dickson and Jessica. When good mornings had been exchanged, she seated herself at the table, taking a warmed scone.

"Is Lord Livesey well this morning?" Phoebe asked.

"He's not too bad. More bruised ego than damaged ankle I think," Jessica said. "He is desperate to move, but I've told him if he tries to walk on it too soon, he could be crippled for longer than is necessary. He cursed me to the devil."

"It's unlike him to be bloody minded," Aunt Dickson said wryly.

"It's all bluster," Jessica said easily. "He's not used to listening to anyone else's opinion. Although he is beginning to realise that being a father is about compromise and negotiation."

"Better late than never," Aunt Dickson muttered.

"I think I need a quiet day today," Jessica said. "There was a little too much exertion for me yesterday, something I will not be admitting to Knowles if I want to do anything for the next couple of months!"

"Are you feeling unwell? You should've had breakfast in your chamber. We can look after ourselves," Aunt Dickson said, scanning her niece's face for signs of exhaustion.

"I will be fine. I'm increasing, not ill. I just need to take things a little easy today. The girls are spending some time with Livesey this morning then they are going for a picnic with Mary and Rose. They'll be well entertained," Jessica said.

"I'd like to spend a day resting myself," Aunt Dickson said. "I have some letters to write, so I'll do those and then perhaps have a quiet afternoon. What are your plans for today?" she asked turning to Phoebe.

"I could join the picnic?" she offered.

"Don't do that!" Jessica said quickly. "Spend some time away from the children. I think yesterday was exhausting for everyone."

Phoebe didn't think she needed to rest. If she did nothing, she would think of Livesey all the time, and that wasn't good for her. She nodded and smiled slightly, remaining quiet while the other two ladies chatted about people in the region with whom both were acquainted.

Eventually Phoebe excused herself from the table and left the room. Silence descended on the pair for a few moments.

"I hope this plan works," Jessica whispered. "Livesey being injured has put an unforeseen problem in our scheme!"

"It will work. If she's alone, she will go into the library," Aunt Dickson said confidently. "Let's just hope Livesey uses the situation to his advantage."

"Don't say that! If we are relying on my brother, it will never work!" Jessica said, as only a long-suffering sibling could do.

*

Phoebe had tried to see if her uncle was free, but he'd already left the house with Lord Knowles for a day's fishing. No one knew exactly where they were aiming to go, so she couldn't catch-up with them.

She'd spent the morning walking outside through the grounds of the Knowles' household and returned before luncheon. It had been an aimless meander, which made Phoebe feel restless.

Deciding to go to the library before seeking out sustenance, she was startled out of her reverie at the sight of Livesey seated in a wing-backed chair, his foot raised on a footstool in front of him, with a table to his side. He was dressed in just his breeches and shirt, the neckline open, revealing a light-dusting of chest hair. Phoebe swallowed.

"Miss Westbrook!" Livesey said with feeling. "You have to rescue me!"

Phoebe smiled slightly, not able to withdraw at such an appeal. "And from what am I to rescue you?"

"Complete and utter boredom!" Livesey said with his usual frown.

"It must be even more frustrating to know my uncle and Lord Knowles are out. They've gone for a full day of fishing while the weather is fine."

"Yes. That's it. Rub salt into the wound! I did not have you down as the cruel type," Livesey said grumbling.

Phoebe smiled. "Don't worry. I'll be out of your way soon enough."

"Oh?" Livesey asked, becoming serious.

"My uncle received news yesterday, which requires him to return home earlier than we both expected. We are to leave tomorrow," Phoebe said. She'd felt desolate when her uncle had told her his news, but she'd tried to convince herself it was for the best.

Livesey put his head in his hands. Phoebe was alarmed at the action and was concerned he was being taken ill.

"Are you sure you should be downstairs? Shouldn't you be resting in your chamber?" Phoebe asked.

"I promised I would not move from this seat, but if I don't have some company, I might have to take matters into my own hands and make my escape from this room, whatever the cost to my foot!" Livesey said. He had to act quickly if she was to leave so soon. He wasn't sure when he'd finally admitted he was in love with Phoebe, but the thought of losing her once more without her knowing how he truly felt, made him panic. He had to delay her.

"I am not sure I'm the one who can relieve your boredom," Phoebe said honestly.

"You're just the person. Please. I beg of you. Do not abandon me!" Livesey appealed.

Smiling, Phoebe sat down. Pushing her glasses up her nose, she looked at Livesey. "What do you wish to talk about?"

Livesey groaned. "Do you not think when someone asks you a question like that, your mind goes immediately blank?"

"Yes. And when you're asked to sit near a stranger at a dinner or party, panic makes you seem the most prim and proper miss there ever was."

"You always seem quietly confident. As if you're comfortable in your own skin. No one would guess you are anything but happy with the situation," Livesey admitted.

Phoebe paused. "I would not say I'm a confident person, but there is no point being dissatisfied with oneself. We can't change our features. I learned a long time ago it was no use longing to be someone else."

"Who would you want to be if you had a choice in the matter?" Livesey was intrigued with who she would say. Having admitted to himself that he loved her, it was easier for him to acknowledge that he'd found her looks appealing far sooner than he'd realised. It had occurred almost as soon as he'd offered her the first insult, and he'd deserved to be tortured by a change of heart.

Phoebe laughed self-consciously. "Either one of my sisters. They are pretty, younger, and neither have the curse of having to wear glasses," she admitted.

Livesey sat and studied Phoebe for a moment. He would have to pick his words carefully. "When I first met you, I easily dismissed you," he stated.

"I remember," Phoebe said quietly. Her cheeks flushed at the memory of being so openly mocked.

Livesey sat forward. "But don't you see? That was more about me than you," he said earnestly. "Within a very short period of time, I realised just how wrong I'd been."

"Please don't flatter me falsely. I have a looking glass. I know how I appear," Phoebe appealed.

"Miss Westbrook, I know you never lie to a direct question, and you know enough of me to know I don't care who I upset in my brutish way," Livesey said. "I am not saying shallow meaningless words. I'm just a man talking truthfully to a woman."

Phoebe inclined her head. She had no words to say to an impassioned speech.

"You weren't the prettiest of women in the house party," Livesey admitted. He smiled widely when Phoebe looked at him with a raised eyebrow. Her silent look expressed more than a hundred words could have done. "See? That's exactly what I mean! You are a delight! You've taken me to task without uttering a word! You are also funny and empathetic without being patronizing and fawning. I could've killed Captain Hall for taking up so much of your time during my house party."

"It wouldn't have made any difference in the end," Phoebe said quietly, though she wasn't unaffected by his words.

"And again, that was down to myself rather than having anything to do with you," Livesey pointed out. "I thought I couldn't love. I was afraid to open myself to a possibility of anything that could hurt me. Angelina did hurt me in a way. I was disappointed, wounded by the constant ups and downs and tortured by the fact that I had made a mistake when I'd thought I was infallible."

Phoebe tried to steady her breath. She had no idea where this conversation was leading and why it had become so serious so soon. "You were honest when you offered me marriage. I would have never believed it if you had professed love." Even though, by that point, she'd already loved him.

"No. I wasn't honest. I said what I thought was right, but these last weeks..." Livesey paused. "I have realised so much about what I want for myself and my children. Existing and future children. Aunt Dickson has been the only person who saw my marriage and lifestyle as it really was. A complete disaster which was as lonely as hell."

"I'm sorry to hear that," Phoebe said quietly.

"I was drawn to you above everyone else," Livesey admitted, "But I didn't see it for what it was. When you refused me, instead of trying to convince you to give me a chance, I panicked. Running from what would have been a true love match, eventually, if not at the start, I ran towards a match that would have destroyed me and probably everyone around me."

"Why would a marriage with Lady Jane have been so bad?" Phoebe asked. She had to focus on something else other than the words 'true love match'. Those words had the ability to bounce around the inside of her head like an ever-increasing echo.

"I'll tell you the full story another time, but believe me, there are some things that should not be asked of another," Livesey said with feeling. "After I released myself from that situation, all I could think about was you. You haunted my every thought. No. That's wrong. You'd haunted my thoughts long before then. I just wasn't ready to acknowledge it."

"Please! Stop funning!" Phoebe appealed. She stood as if to leave but paused when Livesey started to stand. "Do not get up! You'll hurt yourself."

Livesey gritted his teeth as his ankle caught the edge of the footrest. "I can't let you leave without hearing what I have to say. If you decide to leave then, so be it. I'll hurt myself by following you; I will follow you wherever you go, so on behalf of my injured foot, please stay."

Phoebe closed her eyes as if in pain. "Please don't lie. You were vicious in Bath. Those were not the words of someone who cared."

"I was despicable. But do you know why?" Livesey asked. "I was frightened you were going to marry another. I thought you'd let me down with keeping Aunt Dickson's illness a secret. In fact, I wanted to believe you had because, one way or another, I had to make myself dislike you. I couldn't allow myself to feel what I did and know you were married to someone else."

"It certainly sounded as if you hated me with a vengeance," Phoebe said with feeling. They were both still standing. She wasn't sure she should stay, but she was like a moth, and he was her flame. She was unable to move away from him whilst he was speaking such words. She wanted his words to be sincere; she almost ached with the need.

"I am so ashamed of how I behaved. When you described how I'd made you feel, I could have wept with sorrow and remorse, and I'm a man who does not cry," Livesey admitted. "That it will take you a long time to forgive me, I know. All I can promise is that I'm a different man than the person who reluctantly agreed to a house party. I'm different than how I was with Angelina. With her, I never looked to the future, it was all about surviving each day, nothing else. It's because of you that I have finally been able to feel. You've changed me for the better, and I need you in my life to continue that."

"I don't understand how I can have altered you as much as you claim. And even if I have caused a change, what do you want from me?" Phoebe asked, needing clarity.

"I'm asking you to marry me. Will you please marry me?" Livesey asked quietly. He was terrified of rejection, but he had to take the risk and speak. He knew without doubt he would never have another chance. "Before you answer, I've just got one more thing to say, then I will shut-up," he smiled gently at Phoebe. "I thought I was afraid to love, but I started loving you so much that it scared me, and I denied it. But now I know the truth, and I can speak honestly. I love you Phoebe. Not because you're a wonder with my children, although you are, but because I want to spend every day with a woman who can make me someone I will like when I gaze in the looking glass every morning. Before you came along, I couldn't bear to see my reflection. With you by my side, I know I will be fulfilled. I'll be happy, and I hope you can forgive me enough to love me back. I promise you that I will spend every day trying to make you content."

Phoebe noticed the heightened moisture in Livesey's eyes, and her own eyes filled with tears in response. This was what it was meant to be, she realised: Loving someone so much that when they hurt, you hurt, as if it were a physical thing. Her instinct was to reach out to him, but she forced herself to hold back. She needed to be sure of him before she took the step of faith.

"Why do you think I don't love you?" Phoebe asked.

"If you had treated me as poorly as I have treated you, I don't think love would be my uppermost emotion towards you," Livesey admitted. "Phoebe, I want you to marry me on any terms. The thought of you leaving tomorrow is terrifying me at the moment. If you need time to think about it…"

"I don't need time to think about your proposal," Phoebe said quietly. She took a deep breath and set her shoulders, looking Livesey in the eye.

Livesey paled. "I've lost you, haven't I?" he choked out. "Oh my God, Phoebe! I can't be without you. I really cannot!"

Phoebe watched, stunned as two large tears rolled down Livesey's face. He closed his eyes as if in pain; the movement caused more tears to squeeze out onto his cheeks.

Phoebe took the step to reach Livesey and stretched out her hands to wipe away the tears with her fingers. "Don't cry," she whispered gently. "Please don't cry." If she had needed any further reassurance of how he felt, his reaction was it. Her heart lifted, while at the same time, it ached to offer him comfort.

Livesey opened his eyes, the two orbs so quick to glare at those who antagonised him, were bleak with loss. "I'm sorry I hurt you. I am so very sorry."

Phoebe continued to stroke his cheeks between her hands. "Sshh. It is fine. Don't fret. I've forgiven you already. I could not do anything else but forgive you."

"You have?" Livesey asked in a whisper, hardly able to believe she could do something as monumental as forgive him. "Is it because you pity me now I've shown my weakness?" Livesey asked his voice choked with emotion.

"Of course," Phoebe said with a smile.

"I would accept you as my wife even if you could feel only pity," Livesey acknowledged. "I would take you on any grounds."

"There's no need for you to do that," Phoebe said with a smile.

"Will you consider my offer? Please?" Livesey asked once more.

"I don't need to," Phoebe said. Livesey looked alarmed, and instinctively, she reached up and touched her lips gently to his. Pulling back, she was warmed by the expression of hope on his face. "I love you, can't you tell? I have almost from the very beginning, and if you still want to marry a foolish chit of a woman, I am not going to refuse you this time. I need a husband who is silly enough to want to marry me even when I refused him the first time, when I shouldn't have."

Livesey's expression turned serious. "Don't ever put yourself down in my company again. You are worth ten of me. I know I'll need to work damned hard to be worthy of you, but I'm prepared to do it if it means you will be my wife."

Phoebe smiled archly. "I'll remind you of that when you're being mulish and annoying over the years to come."

"So, that's a yes, then?"

"Yes. It's a firm yes," Phoebe said, enfolding Livesey into an embrace as he broke down once more.

Livesey had never felt anything like the release he did when Phoebe said yes. How he remained standing, he'd never know; it was probably because of Phoebe's support, and he knew without doubt, he would be able to achieve anything with her by his side.

Eventually, Livesey pulled away slightly and took Phoebe's face between his hands. "I love you, Miss Westbrook."

"I love you, My Lord," Phoebe responded. She felt good to be able to actually voice the words. She smiled at Livesey. He seemed different; his eyes were still moist with tears, but they sparkled at her and were warm. She touched the place where the frown grooves usually were. "I'm going to try my best to keep your frowns at bay," she said quietly.

Livesey kissed her, gently at first before he deepened the kiss, pulling Phoebe firmly against his body. She was deliciously responsive, yet another thing to surprise him. He pulled gently at her hair, tugging it so it came loose from its clips. He'd wanted to run his fingers through her locks since he'd seen her walking into the hallway after she'd been on the horse ride and returned dishevelled.

Livesey moaned as Phoebe wrapped her arms around his neck, plunging her fingers into his own hair. Pulling her close he was desperate to take things further, but he restrained himself. She was too precious to be treated to anything but utter respect, and they had the rest of their lives to explore each other.

Eventually, they parted slightly, Livesey running his fingers along the edge of Phoebe's neckline, smiling as she shivered when his fingers gently touched her skin. Her sharp intake of breath was enough to make him smile, pleased she responded to him.

Kissing Phoebe gently, he rested his forehead against hers. "I've a promise I need you to give me before this goes any further," Livesey said.

"Oh?" Phoebe's eyes were delightfully dilated. Livesey wasn't convinced she'd registered his words at all.

"You have to promise me that no one will ever know I've cried. My credibility would never survive such a slur," Livesey said with a slight flush and a bashful smile.

Phoebe laughed, pulling Livesey closer. "I can promise you that, my complicated Lord," she whispered before being kissed once more.

Epilogue

Much to Livesey's chagrin, he was to cry a number of times in the future. In fact, most of his family were to see what he considered a weakness, but they deemed it as yet another indication of how much he loved his wife.

He cried on his wedding day when exchanging his vows with his blushing bride as his three children stood alongside them. Phoebe had reached up and gently wiped the tears away before shocking those who'd come to the wedding by stretching up and kissing her husband before the ceremony was complete. Both Jessica and Aunt Dickson had reached for their handkerchiefs in response to seeing Livesey so emotional, but they'd looked at each other with smiles, happy that he'd finally come to appreciate what they'd known almost from the start.

He cried when his first child with Phoebe was born. Even when Phoebe gave birth to child number eight, he couldn't stop the tears when he was told mother and baby were both well. It was once more a release of pent up emotion at the fear his wife might not survive childbirth, as so many didn't. Usually Jessica or Aunt Dickson were on hand to offer him a modicum of comfort until he was able to see his wife. He would climb on the bed and hold Phoebe and his new offspring until Phoebe fell asleep. He could do nothing during the birth, but afterwards he was the main caregiver for his beloved much to the chagrin of the midwives involved.

He cried on each day one of his children married, proud and saddened in equal measure as another one flew the nest. Walking each of his many daughters down the aisle, he would smile at Phoebe as, silently, they were able to celebrate each match. He cried at his sons' marriages as well.

Watching with pleasure as they married the women they'd chosen.

Mostly, though, he cried with laughter when Phoebe and his children amused him as they did every day of his new life. Each day he was able to build a stronger relationship with his three girls, who were delighted with their new mother. As far as Phoebe was concerned, she might not have given birth to them, but they were hers in every other sense of the word. As each new brother and sister was born the Livesey household became noisier, happier, and a little more crowded.

Jessica and Aunt Dickson were regular visitors at the Livesey house, unable to stay away for long because of the change in Livesey. He was a pleasure to be around. Both agreed, that on the day he married Phoebe, it was as if the ghosts of the past had been finally put to rest. Both congratulated each other on seeing the potential of Phoebe before their brother had.

Jane and Stuart stayed together, setting up as a gentleman farmer and his wife. Lord Bellamy saw his daughter and her family on a regular basis. Lady Bellamy never forgave her daughter's betrayal. Jane never missed society. She had Stuart and her children. Being able to see her father was all that she needed to be completely happy. Lord Bellamy visited as often as he could, fully aware that the poorer home his daughter lived in was a far happier, more welcoming place than his own cold home. Lady Bellamy's bitterness made the place less like a home as each year passed. Having his grandchildren cry out with joy when their grandpa arrived was enough to make living at home bearable. He was true to his word in that his will stayed the same and eventually Jane and Stuart inherited a large home and an even larger income. It still wasn't enough for Jane to rejoin society, but that was of no loss to her.

Captain Chester was to be widowed a few days after he married his darling wife. He went to sea for years, before returning home for good. He never remarried but was a regular welcome visitor to the Livesey household.

And Phoebe? She no longer wished to be anyone else. She no longer envied even her more beautiful sisters. She had the man she loved and who worshipped her in return. She had the family she'd longed for, eleven children in total, including her adored step-daughters. They had regular visitors in Jessica's children as well as Susan's and Georgina's growing families, and life was always busy but fun. Her uncle had admitted he'd been contacted by Lord Knowles and told of the plan to get her in the same place as Livesey, so he could plead his case, and Phoebe was always thankful her uncle had agreed to the scheme. She was content beyond all she'd dreamed of.

Most of all she loved being wrapped in Livesey's arms when the house was quiet at night as they ended every day. At those times they would speak about their day, always needing to be in physical contact with each other. Their teasing would often lead to lovemaking, both completely content. If visitors sometimes commented on how large the main guest room was, they would be told quietly that it had once been the master suite, but the master always slept in Lady Livesey's room, as they never spent a day, or night apart. They were two people completely in love.

The End.

About this book

I wanted to write a story that focused on the struggles some of the men of the Regency period would face. Childbirth was a dangerous occupation and many wives were lost as a result. The mother in my story had a more gruesome end because I needed Livesey to be wracked with a number of emotions which would muddy his future.

I also wanted to explore a man's feeling of love and affection, as well as terror at being left with young children. How many times have we met men who have scorned deep love, as Livesey did at the start? Those tend to be the ones who fall the hardest and I wanted that for my hero.

I also wanted a heroine who could be easily overlooked. In this world of fickleness – just like the Regency world – many of us are easily dismissed. I wanted Phoebe's strengths to become more obvious as the story developed.

I love Phoebe and Livesey and hope you do too!

About the Author

I have had the fortune to live a dream. I've always wanted to write, but life got in the way as it so often does until a few years ago. Then a change in circumstance enabled me to do what I loved: sit down to write. Now writing has taken over my life, holidays being based around research, so much so that no matter where we go, my long-suffering husband says 'And what connection to the Regency period has this building/town/garden got?'

I do appreciate it when readers get in touch, especially if they love the characters as much as I do. Those first few weeks after release is a trying time; I desperately want everyone to love my characters that take months and months of work to bring to life.

If you enjoy the books please would you take the time to write a review on Amazon? Reviews are vital for an author who is just starting out, although I admit to bad ones being crushing. Selfishly I want readers to love my stories!

I can be contacted for any comments you may have, via my website:

www.audreyharrison.co.uk

or

www.facebook.com/AudreyHarrisonAuthor

Please sign-up for email/newsletter – only sent out when there is something to say!

www.audreyharrison.co.uk

You'll receive a free copy of The Unwilling Earl in mobi format for signing-up as a thank you!

Novels by Audrey Harrison

Regency Romances:
Return to the Regency – A Regency Time-travel novel

My Foundlings:
The Foundling Duke – The Foundlings Book 1
The Foundling Lady – The Foundlings Book 2

Mr Bailey's Lady

The Spy Series:
My Lord the Spy
My Earl the Spy

The Captain's Wallflower

The Four Sisters' Series:
Rosalind – Book 1
Annabelle – Book 2

Grace – Book 3
Eleanor – Book 4

The Inconvenient Trilogy:-
The Inconvenient Ward – Book 1
The Inconvenient Wife – Book 2
The Inconvenient Companion – Book 3

The Complicated Earl
The Unwilling Earl (Novella)

Other Eras:
A Very Modern Lord
Years Apart

About the Proofreader

Joan Kelley fell in love with words at about 8 months of age and has been using them and correcting them ever since. She's had a 20-year career in U.S. Army public affairs spent mostly writing: speeches for Army generals, safety publications and videos, and has had one awesome book published, *Every Day a New Adventure: Caregivers Look at Alzheimer's Disease*, a really riveting and compelling look at five patients, including her own mother. It is available through Publishamerica.com. She also edits books because she loves correcting other people's use of language. What's to say? She's good at it. She lives in a small town near Atlanta, Georgia, in the American South with one long-haired cat to whom she is allergic and her grandson to whom she is not. If you need her, you may reach her at oh1kelley@gmail.com.

31293680R00149

The advent of interactive telecommunication and mass air travel ʼ
enabled people to move far across the world and yet remain ҁ
homes and people they have left behind. *Oceans Apart* is ҁ
wise book that address these issues. I look forward to sʼ
my clients and encouraging them as well as their faʳ
work to maintain and strengthen their relationshʲ
distance.

Joy Epstein holds an M.S.W. and has cʲ
family therapy. In 1998, she moved
children. In 2005, she joined thҁ
Supervisor of the Departmenʻ

Introduction

From the time our older son, Josh, was fifteen, he knew he wanted to live in Israel. When he graduated from high school, he decided to defer admission to Princeton University for a year so that he could study at a religious academy in Israel. This was a common path followed by seniors at his school, so we went along with his decision. After a year, when most of his classmates returned to enter college in the States, Josh wrote us requesting permission once again to defer college so that he could take advantage of the rare opportunity to study in Israel for an additional year. We were reluctant, but since Princeton agreed to the deferral, we gave our consent as well. He ultimately did return home to complete his undergraduate education, but immediately following graduation, he fulfilled his dream of making *aliyah*— the term used to refer to Jewish immigration to the land of Israel.

Even though Josh chose to study in Israel, I had always hoped that he would marry an American girl and settle in this country. He did marry an American girl—one whom he met in Israel and who shared his conviction that the Holy Land should be their permanent home.

In the twenty years that they have lived in Israel, we, as parents have been supportive of their conviction and their choice. But at the same time we have been torn by the separation and the inability to enjoy them as a frequent visible presence in our lives. I recall receiving the long-distance phone call that they were expecting their first child.

The phone call came early one Sunday morning. It was my son to tell us that his wife of four months was pregnant. I expressed my excitement and we chatted briefly about when the baby would be born and how his wife was feeling. When I hung up, I was struck with an undefined melancholy.

I had not seen the young couple since their wedding in Jerusalem. The news that they would soon be parents made me yearn for a glimpse at their life as a married couple. I longed to see how they arranged their new apartment, and how the china we gave them as a wedding gift looked on their dining room table. And now there would be a baby—my first grandchild—whose life I would encounter only intermittently and for brief periods, surely missing many significant milestones. The distance between us became my personal enemy.

My need to connect in some concrete way led me to dig out the knitting needles, buried deep in a drawer, unused for many years. I perked up considerably at the thought of knitting a sweater and hat for the baby's homecoming. As I knitted and the garment emerged, I continuously related it to the new life taking shape seven thousand miles away. The sweater and hat arrived shortly before the baby's birth and were received with great excitement and much appreciation.

My grandson wore my hand-knit sweater and hat for his trip home from the hospital and again eight days later for his ritual circumcision. Though I was not there in person, the labor of my hands enveloped the baby on the first two major events of his life. I was thrilled.

Now a decade and a half later, we have made many trips across the ocean and the baby for whom I knit the sweater and hat is a strapping teenager standing six feet tall. He has been joined by three additional siblings, two brothers and a little sister, all born and living in Israel. Sitting on my desk is an e-mailed photograph of the four of them dressed in orange and black Princeton T-shirts I bought for them on a recent trip to their father's alma mater. I look up from my work often to visually caress each of their bright, happy faces. But, alas, you can't hug a JPEG.

Living in two worlds was part of my growing-up years. My parents, who were immigrants, longed their entire adult lives for the extended families they left behind in Russia. Letters and photos were few and far between Those that did arrive were savored, read and reread dozens of times. Sepia-colored photographs of men, women, and children, all dressed in what looked like their best clothes, dotted our living room.

"Who are these people?"

"Your grandparents, uncles, aunts, and cousins," I was told. The worn, faded photographs are the only memory that remains of these family members. They were never to be seen again. Those who did not die of natural causes were ultimately victims of the Nazis' cruel and relentless war against the Jews.

Immigration continues to separate families. The foreign-born population in the United States is growing, with an increasing number of people living oceans apart from those who nurtured them. Similarly, record numbers of Americans have moved abroad to conduct business, to serve their country, or to further a cause or ideology. Surprisingly little has been written about these families . . . or for them.

Oceans Apart: A Guide to Maintaining Family Ties at a Distance is about these families, the challenges they face in maintaining their relationships, and their courageous and creative responses to those challenges. It includes the thoughts and feelings of seventy people from twenty-five countries—grandparents, parents, adult children, grandchildren, and brothers and sisters. I have learned so much from their compassionate and touching stories. Their experiences provide a helpful guide to sustaining our bonds with loved ones living far away.

My social work training stood me in good stead as I began identifying people to interview. I first talked with friends who, like me, have one or more children living in Israel. I then began to look for people from different countries and diverse cultures. I did not have to look very far—they were everywhere! Before long, I had interviewed neighbors from Sweden and India, a young Romanian woman who worked in our local pharmacy, a Colombian physician's assistant in my doctor's office, a Venezuelan personal trainer at the gym, a Brazilian massage therapist at the beauty salon, and a Bangladeshi family I met in a doctor's waiting room.

Trips to Israel, New York, and Princeton to visit family and friends yielded additional interviews with people from far-flung places. A family who has a daughter doing missionary work in Madagascar and another who have three children who are Chabad emissaries in various parts of the world provided insights into those who move to distant lands to fulfill religious callings.

I conducted interviews in person or on the telephone that generally lasted for about two hours. Even though I had no prior personal connection with most of the interviewees, they were all anxious to share their stories and to suggest others to whom I might wish to speak. Each interview was like a painting whose brushstrokes depicted the interviewee's most personal and private thoughts. It has been my task to frame these paintings, extracting useful techniques and placing them in a larger context.

The collage of voices culled from these narratives sheds light on the issues that make up the fabric of life for those living long distances from family. Throughout the book, their stories are woven into the text as they provide insights and solutions to the various topics discussed. At the end of each chapter, I have included "Lessons from Life," which highlight practical applications for maintaining family ties at a distance.

The inaugural chapter, "Why People Move Far Away," pinpoints why people choose to move, and how they deal with the pangs of separation and the stresses of adjusting to new environments. Chapter 2, "Keeping in Touch" tells us how parents and children maintain contact on the phone, via e-mail, letters, photographs, and Internet video communication; how they resolve conflict; how they deal with the financial issues of travel as well as how they cope with the trauma of fifteen- to thirty-hour travel schedules. The dynamics involved in preparing for and experiencing a successful visit and the long-term effect of distance on family relationships are also discussed. "Grandparenting at a Distance," Chapter 3, explores the feelings of both generations and offers ways in which resourceful grandparents can deftly knit together the strands of long-distance relationships with grandchildren of all ages.

Perhaps the most prevalent fear of those living oceans apart is "How will I cope at a distance with the illness, frailty, and death of a loved one?" Chapter 4, "Getting Through the Rough Times," features accounts of loving children who have mounted heroic efforts and exhibited incredible devotion, courage, and strength in these times of crisis. For those of us yet to face this predicament, they provide stunning role models to emulate.

Chapter 5, "Maintaining Ties with the Rest of the Family," reveals the special challenges adult siblings face in attempting to preserve their relationship with distant brothers, sisters, nieces, and nephews. Also discussed in this chapter is the growing paradigm of husbands and wives who spend part of each month or each year separated by an ocean.

The ways in which family ties are maintained are culturally defined. Émigrés continue to feel deeply attached to the language and traditions that shaped their formative years. The ways in which these can be passed on to children born in new lands are discussed. Similarly, holidays, festivals, life-cycle events, and family milestones are imbued with long-held traditions that are difficult to replicate in new environments. Those that are shared with loved ones are exhilarating and joyful. Those that are missed because of the distance separating some family members from others are circumscribed with profound longing for the sense of love and support that only family provides. Chapter 6, "What's Happening to My Traditions?" addresses these concerns and suggests compromises and adjustments to alleviate the loss.

Oceans Apart concludes with Chapter 7, "Creative Uses of Technology," presenting ways in which families have successfully used e-mail, video communications, voice over Internet phone (VOIP), family websites, family blogs, and online photo albums to maintain ties.

This book provides those living oceans apart with a guide that helps them maintain connections with loved ones who live far away. It also assures them that they are not alone in their struggle to maintain the ties that bind. I hope, too, that the experiences and insights shared here will raise awareness and increase understanding of these issues among the general population. The wrenching choices, the gritty determination, and the joyful successes chronicled here should encourage all of us to sustain the solidarity and security of our families.

1

WHY PEOPLE MOVE FAR AWAY

The hardest thing of all is not being close to my family. I miss my mother more than anybody else.
—Vicky, a young Romanian woman who moved to the United States

Like many others, when Vicky uprooted herself from her country of origin, leaving behind family, close friends, and all that was familiar, she was faced with many challenges. Often, moves like this entail becoming accustomed to another culture and require learning a new language. Everyone involved, including those left behind, experiences some pangs of separation and the loss of intimacy that family provides.

Whether voluntary or involuntary, migration leaves families in a fractured state. The decision to leave home and relocate thousands of miles away to another country creates a paradox of devastation and hope. It is fraught with uncertainty and simultaneously imbued with prospects of a more fulfilling life.[1]

In this chapter, people from a variety of backgrounds and countries share their motivations for moving. Through their voices we gain greater understanding of the complex emotions that accompany their choices and the adjustments they have made. Many of them reappear in subsequent chapters as they resolve issues created by distance. A number of different reasons for moving are explored:

- Looking for a better life
- Forced migration
- Educational and career opportunities

- Changes in marital status
- Pursing an ideology

While some of these individuals have made a more successful adjustment than others, the theme of "Yes, I can!" resounds throughout most of the narratives.

Looking for a Better Life

A desire to live in an environment with greater freedom and more opportunities prompted Vicky and Ecaterina, both from Romania, to migrate to the United States. They describe their struggles with issues of language, the loss of day-to-day contact with their parents. and questions about whether or not they had made the right decisions. We then read about Maria from Brazil and Satyen from India, whose incentives to relocate were to improve their economic situations. While both succeeded in making more money than they would have in their native lands, they both long to become reunited with family left behind. All four stories underscore the importance of perseverance in adjusting to new environments.

Anthropologist Jacob Climo, who researched the issue of long-distance relationships in *Distant Parents,* said, "The overriding conclusion is that although distance certainly diminishes the frequency of contacts, the quality of affection and feeling of parents and children remain the same regardless of distance."[2]

I met Vicky, a woman in her thirties, while I was picking up a prescription at my local pharmacy. Her accent prompted me to ask about her place of birth and the family she had left behind. We met several days later and talked over coffee. She came to this country three years ago from Romania with her husband and two young children. She is a graduate pharmacist with several years' experience. Because she is not licensed here, she works as a pharmacy intern. Throughout the interview, Vicky was tearful as she shared the sadness of separating from her family and the challenges she has faced in the United States:

We left Moldova, Romania because the Russian government was unfriendly toward us. I was very close to my family and it was very hard for me to say good-bye to my parents and my sister.

The first year I was here, I didn't understand English and I didn't have a job. At the beginning, the children didn't want to go to school, but they got used to it and learned very quickly. Every evening I did homework with the children and I, too, soon began to pick up the language.

In my country I had much more respect. It's hard here because I don't have the right papers for my profession. When you can't work at your profession, you don't feel good about yourself. When I talk to my mother, she always asks me when I am going to get the papers for my pharmacy license. I graduated from school ten years ago and the program is very different here. I don't want to her to worry so I don't tell her that I would have to go back to school and I can't afford it right now.

For Vicky, and many other immigrants, the loss of professional status is dispiriting, crushing their self-esteem and diminishing their personal identity. It also represents an enormous disappointment to their families back home. Most of these young people are among the first generation in their family to go to college and achieve professional status. Their inability to practice their profession robs parents of the pride they felt at their children's accomplishments. This setback is difficult for parents to understand and fills them with regret. Vicky concludes:

The hardest thing of all is not being close to my family. I miss my mother more than anybody else. I'm going to wait two more years. If our lives don't improve, I'm going to move back.

Sadly, Vicky's inability to come to grips with these challenges has been an obstacle to her adjustment to her adopted country. It is, however, to her credit that she has decided to give herself more time before making a decision to return to her family in Romania.

***

Ecaterina is an optimistic, determined woman who grew up in a rural section of Romania. At age twenty, she and her husband and their young daughter came to the United States. She describes their decision to make the move and to stay the course despite initial hardships.

I used to work for the Romanian Treasury Bank and I saw in the newspaper an announcement for a United States Green Card lottery. I applied, along with at least three or four thousand other people. I was shocked when I found out that I was one of four people who won. In order to come to the United States, we also needed a sponsor. The family of one of my husband's friends, who lived in South Florida, said that they would be our sponsors and that we could stay with them for two weeks when we arrived.

We wanted to move because we felt that in the United States we would have more freedom and more choices that would ultimately offer us a better life. Our daughter was three and a half years old and we hoped that she would have a better education and a brighter future. It was a very hard decision for us and even harder for our parents. Both my husband and I are only children. Our parents cried and were very sad. They felt abandoned because they didn't have anybody else. In Romania we lived with my in-laws in a house that had been in the family for generations. They were very supportive and especially helpful in caring for our daughter. But we felt we did not have a future there.

When we came to the United States, neither of us could speak a word of English. My husband was so unhappy that after two weeks he wanted to go back. It was extremely hard. Suddenly you come to a country where you can't speak the language and you have to find a job in order to survive. Our friends, who had been through this hardship, told us not to give up, and that little by little we would adjust. When my husband talked about going back, I encouraged him to continue to try. Within two weeks we managed to find a small apartment to rent and began to look for work that didn't require too much English.

As we can see, the strength of at least one partner is required to get the family through the rough spots. Ecaterina and her husband did manage to find jobs. Within a year they had saved enough money to pay for the travel expenses of one member of their Romanian family to visit them in their new home—a custom that has become an annual event.

***

Dissatisfaction with one's native country is a common motivation for migrating. People who feel economically or politically disadvantaged, like Ecaterina, leave to seek greater opportunity. Once they get jobs and have their basic expenses covered, their first thoughts are to send money to family back home, even in cases where there is family discord.

Maria is a forty-eight-year-old Brazilian woman who worked as a teacher in her native country. She followed her three adult daughters to the United States in hopes of earning more money. She left behind her husband, who is ten years her senior, her father, and two brothers. In the United States she works as a cleaning woman.

> I came from Brazil six years ago. I was an elementary school teacher and I didn't make enough money. I went to college for two years but couldn't continue because I couldn't afford it. I loved my work with the children and was sorry to leave it.

> I was able to obtain a visa, but my husband was not. He felt bad about my leaving, but we had no money. He is an educated man, but could not get a job. He lives in our house alone. I send him about $500 or $600 every month and sometimes more. He doesn't ask for money, but I know the situation so I send him money. I feel responsible for him.

My husband is a difficult, angry man. My children did not like that. When he got excited he would shout and sometimes hit us. That's partly why I left. He didn't treat me right. If he came here or I went back, I would tell him he would have to change the way he acts. I don't want to be yelled at anymore.

I don't want a divorce because we lived together for twenty-three years. If he got sick, I think I would go back and take care of him. I wish my family could be together—me and my husband, the children, and the grandchildren.

Respect for the male authority figure is the norm in Maria's world. Despite instances of domestic abuse, she continues to be committed to the marriage and to her husband's well-being. She is even hopeful that the situation will improve and that the family will be reunited.

***

Satyen is an engaging sixty-year-old man who came to the United States from India forty years ago. During this time, he has maintained close ties with his native country and continues to uphold Indian customs and traditions. Over the years, his entrepreneurial spirit has enabled him to start and expand several commercial enterprises. He currently owns businesses and property both in the United States and in India and enjoys a very comfortable lifestyle. He speaks about his humble beginnings and his subsequent achievements with pride:

I was born and raised in a small rural village in India that had no telephone and no electricity. At age twenty, I got married in India and decided to leave my wife with my family and come to the United States to seek my fortune. I arrived at John F. Kennedy Airport with $8 in my pocket.

At the beginning I lived with my brother-in-law in the Washington area. Through an ad in the newspaper, I got my first job in a synagogue, straightening out prayer books and assisting with weddings. I felt very comfortable doing this because many of the Jewish customs reminded me of the Indian ones. I was paid $100 per month. I immediately began sending money to my father and continued to do so until he died.

Contrary to Western child-rearing practices, which place a priority on parental custody, in India, leaving a wife and even children to be cared for by extended family is an accepted practice.

I went back to India after two years and was reunited with my wife. When our first baby was born, we decided to return to the United States. At that point, we determined that it would be best for our son to remain with my family so that he could be reared in the ways and customs of the Indian culture. After four years he came to live with us in the United States and was educated in this country. When he reached maturity, he asked me to go to India and arrange a marriage for him. The wedding took place on the grounds of my father's home with one thousand guests in attendance.

Even though Satyen made his fortune in the United States, he is still very much rooted in the Indian culture, which continues to define his personal identity. It was not surprising to hear him reveal: "When I retire, I plan to return to India to spend my final years among my large extended family."

Forced Migration

Those fleeing political or religious persecution usually cannot return to their homelands. They have different family issues to confront than those who come seeking economic opportunity. Contact with family members in their homeland may expose them to danger. Camilla, a young Colombian woman and the Faminis, an Iranian couple, are examples of people who had to migrate, suffering the loss of family as well as the rupture of historical and cultural continuity.[3]

Camilla has thick black hair and piercing dark eyes. She is a petite forty-year-old woman who was a physician in her native Colombia. Because she is not licensed in this country, she works as an assistant in a doctor's office. She recalled the harrowing circumstances that led to her departure ten years ago from Colombia, along with her husband and small children.

> I come from the city of Cali in Colombia. My father was a very wealthy man who owned mines. He had a fleet of privately owned airplanes, and several homes throughout the country that were cared for by many servants. There had been a regime change in Colombia that was not friendly to our family. One day when I came home from my office, I felt very apprehensive. I feared that my children and I would be kidnapped. My husband was on a business trip in Bogotá, where we also had a home. My son was only three months old and my daughter was a little over a year old. I decided to take the children and go to Bogotá.
>
> I arrived there late in the evening and went to our apartment. My father called from Cali and told us not to leave the house and to keep the windows covered. We stayed in the apartment for three more days with bodyguards until we could make arrangements to come to the United States. On the evening of the third day we left in a bulletproof car for the airport. Eight of us left together. In addition to my husband, me, and our children, there was my father, my stepmother, one of my brothers, and our chef.
>
> We arrived in the United States, having left everything we owned behind. My father was very unhappy here. He was concerned about his business and he heard that the authorities were looking for him. He was afraid that if they found him it might endanger those of us who came with him. He went back to Colombia, turned himself in, and was imprisoned for ten years. This is something I have not shared with anybody.

Repressing important facts about one's life increases vulnerability. "The effects of this hidden history may be all the more powerful for being hidden."[4] Camilla felt that revealing the fact that her father was in prison would not be well understood and would be a sign of disloyalty to him. She found herself in an unexpected situation in which she had to confront her secret. She recalls:

> One day I was having lunch with my colleagues in the office. One woman said that the government spends too much money on people who are in jail. I said that not all the people in jail are criminals. She seemed to have ignored my comment and said that if it was up to her she would just put a match to the jails. I got up from the table, ran into another room, and burst into tears. Of course, no one in the office knew my father's story.

***

The Faminis are a middle-aged Iranian couple. They left Iran with their two teenage children because life for Jews in Iran is very difficult. They still have a large extended family there. They would not permit me to tape-record the interview because they fear that there might be repercussions for their remaining family. They also would not reveal the circumstances surrounding their flight from Iran. They hold only an Iranian passport, so they cannot leave the United States to visit siblings who live in Israel. In order for the sister in Israel to have a phone conversation with the one in Iran, a conference call must be arranged by Mr. Famini in the United States so as to avoid detection in Iran.

The children adapted to their new surroundings far more easily than their parents and did not experience the losses with the same degree of intensity. Now they have learned both English and Hebrew and have a wide circle of friends. This is a great source of comfort and pride to their parents.

At the end of our visit, Mr. Famini walked me to my car. With tears welling up in his eyes, he told me that in leaving Iran to escape rampant anti-Semitism, he is experiencing not only the loss of family, but the loss of a rich and cherished Jewish tradition that dates back 2,500 years. This leaves him with a sense of cultural homelessness because his heritage is not understood or acknowledged in his new environment.[5]

Educational and Career Opportunities

Pursuing higher education or career advancement prompts many to move oceans apart from their families. These motivations for leaving are usually supported by families because it is their hope—not always realized—that the young people will return home after a few years. The responses of two different generations are shared in these accounts, which demonstrate the different issues each faces. First, we hear from Rajan, a young Indian physicist who left his homeland to study abroad with the enthusiastic encouragement of his parents. Next, Janice, who lives in London, provides a mother's perspective on her eldest son, who pursued an academic career in the United States.

Rajan is a well-spoken research physicist from India who teaches at an Ivy League university. He and his wife, also Indian, have two preschool-age daughters. Rajan came to the United States in 1984 as a twenty-one-year-old graduate student. He shared his initial impressions and adjustment:

> When I came to the United States, I was single. I left behind my parents and my younger brother. Both my parents had studied in England for many years. They are part of a social class in India that thought it was important for people to study in the West in order to be well-educated and in touch with modernity.
>
> My father had a dual career. He was a professor of international relations and a member of Parliament. Ours was a very close-knit nuclear family and I missed the day-to-day contact. My father's public life was very interesting and our household revolved around his activities. He often shared the things that were happening in his political life in the evening over dinner. We would discuss tactical issues and the conversation would sometimes continue for an hour or two after dinner. This was suddenly all gone, as was my whole association with Indian political and social life.

I experienced a major adjustment when I came to the United States. It was a bit of culture shock. My first day in Manhattan I saw a young couple kissing in the street. This is something one would never see in my country. It was a definite reminder that I was not in India anymore.

Rajan spoke about how fortunate he felt to be assigned an American host family with whom he could spend time on a regular basis.

The thing that is most alienating about being a foreign student is that you see other students and you see faculty only in their professional roles. You never see a family and you don't know what people are like when they are not working. When you go to someone's home, you see husbands and wives interacting with each other and with their children. It humanizes them. My host family provided this for me.

It is a common practice for educational institutions to provide surrogate families for young people studying from abroad. This is a less formal setting, which enables the student to relax and re-create some of the intimacy he experienced with his family back home.

***

Janice is a woman in her mid-sixties who lives in London. She is a writer and a translator. Of her four married sons, only one still lives in London. The others all live abroad with their wives and children. When her oldest son, Donald, a computer scientist, was in his early twenties, he decided he wanted to live in the United States. Janice expresses the dismay she felt at first and the welcome relief she experienced when she met Donald's future wife:

When I heard that Donald was planning to move to the United States, I was very upset. I felt terrible and cried just thinking about his being alone in a strange country. I thought at first that he would go for only a year or so. Over the years, whenever he came home to visit, I found it very hard to say good-bye again. This all changed when he came home with Carol, a young American woman he planned to marry. After their first visit, I recall watching them leave at the airport and go through the departure gate together. From then on, I felt entirely different. I felt, "He's got somebody. He's not alone." They were married in New York with the whole family present. He now lives in Boston where he is a tenured professor at a prestigious university.

Janice is realistic about her expectations and finds comfort where she can. She says that she is thankful that they don't live farther than they do and also that this is not the nineteenth century, when children who left their families for distant lands were never seen again.

Changes in Marital Status

Marriage and divorce often lead people to move long distances from their families. Some do this with enthusiasm, others with trepidation and sometimes regret. We read the accounts of two women, Toby, an Australian woman who married an American, and Kim, a Malaysian who married a man from Switzerland. Both of these women were very young and inexperienced when they married and moved to locations that were so distant from their families that frequent visits were impossible. Their stories reflect their struggles in maintaining family ties and in adjusting to lifestyles to which they were not accustomed. By contrast, Rashida, who was in her thirties when she left India, viewed her marriage to an American with a remarkable sense of adventure. She continues to maintain very close contact with her family abroad and at the same time speaks openly and happily about how the move has improved her life. Finally, we hear from Laura, a young college student from Jamaica, who moved with her mother to the United States when her parents were divorced.

Toby, who was born and raised in Australia, moved to the United States twelve years ago when she married Bruce, an American. They have two young children. Toby talked bout her conflicting feelings:

I met my future husband when we were both studying in an overseas program. Following the program, we spent six months in New York before we became engaged. I was only twenty-one, and I knew that marriage to Bruce would mean relocating to America. At the time I was young and in love and I would have moved to Mars if I had to. My family has deep roots in Australia, having lived there for many generations. I have one married sister who continues to live there with her family.

From the outset, my American in-laws, who have three sons, were eager to embrace a daughter. Their intentions were admirable. However, with all the changes—new husband, new country, new culture—I was unable to accept their embrace at the time. I told them that I fell in love with their son and that with time my relationship with them will surely grow.

In the beginning, I also felt I'd betrayed my parents by moving. I felt especially guilty when I had children. My parents never once said anything to me, but those were my own feelings. Now, twelve years later, I'm not sure about whether or not I have regrets. I love my husband and my children and I have a good life here. I have become integrated into my husband's family, where there is a great deal of mutual love and respect. However, I miss the contact and comfort of being among people I grew up with and the Australian lifestyle.

Toby's ambivalence was so troubling at first that she decided to seek counseling to help resolve the issues that were plaguing her. Following our interview, she wrote me a note in which she said, "The time we spent together was a chance to do some valuable soul-searching and a great opportunity for me to look back and see how far I have come."

***

Kim is a lively Malaysian-born woman who administers a large department of engineering at a major university. At sixty, she is youthful and spry. She talks about the unusual circumstances surrounding her marriage, more than four decades ago, to her first husband, from whom she is now divorced:

> I grew up on a family-managed rubber plantation in Malaysia. I have one sister who is fourteen years older than I am. In 1963, after high school I got a job as a bookkeeper and receptionist in the city at a hotel. It was a hotel where many expatriates stayed while they worked on projects throughout the country. One of these was a Swiss engineer who came to Malaysia to oversee the building of a power plant. We dated, and when his job in Malaysia was finished, we got married. I was seventeen years old. He had suggested that I visit Switzerland before we were married to see if I liked it. But my mother would not allow me to travel with a man to whom I was not married.

Kim was totally unprepared for the events that followed and overwhelmed by the ensuing radical changes in her life. She describes the sense of alienation and abandonment she experienced:

> We were married on the plantation among all our family and friends. His family did not come. I don't know why. I was too inexperienced to know that I should have asked. After a year, we moved to Switzerland to live with his family. On the plane I cried the entire time.

Shortly after Kim and her husband arrived in Switzerland, their son was born. Her husband then went to England on a project, leaving Kim and her newborn with his family. Her in-laws did not speak English—only German and French—and Kim's German was not very good at first. They were lovely people, but she felt like a stranger in their home.

***

Rashida, a young woman who emigrated from India to the United States to join her fiancé, whom she subsequently married, is thrilled with her decision to do so. She is currently awaiting the birth of her first child and eagerly anticipating the arrival of her mother, who, according to Indian custom, will help her care for her newborn for several months.

> When I relocated five years ago, I left behind my mother and a sister in India and another sister who lives in Dubai. I see her much less now. When I lived in India, she used to visit us often.

> I came here to join my fiancé, now husband. I did not choose to come; it was his decision. He was based in the United States. It was his choice to live here, at least for some time. Even though it was his decision, it was something I also wanted. I have not regretted, even for one day, that I relocated. My life has improved in many, many ways—the number of things that I've learned, the things I keep learning every single day. I have completely changed as a person since moving to the United States.

Rashida's adventurous spirit allows her to learn from and enjoy her new environment. In subsequent chapters we see that she does so while continuing to embrace her family members still living abroad.

***

Divorce is both a major life change for parents and a disruptive element for children. This is further exacerbated when one parent then moves to a distant country.

Laura is a college senior with a deep voice and a winning personality. She immigrated to the United States from Jamaica as an adolescent after her parents were divorced.

> I came to the United States when I was thirteen years old. My parents split and I came with my mother and two sisters. Two older sisters stayed behind in Jamaica, as did my dad. We also left my grandparents behind.

> At the time I wasn't happy about the decision because I was "Daddy's little girl." My mother had full custody, but I would spend every other

weekend with him. Sometimes he'd pick us up at school in the evening or he would just drop by at lunchtime and bring us lunch. I saw him practically every day. It was really hard. I didn't want to go.

Laura was an innocent victim in this dispute, which was further complicated by deception. Her mother did not inform her former husband that she was taking the children and moving to the United States. This led to mistrust and devastation for both the father and the children.

He didn't even know we were leaving. He didn't find out where we were until a couple of months later. But he couldn't travel because he didn't have a passport. For a couple of years we couldn't travel either until we established our residency. At first my dad wasn't happy. He said my mom stole his kids. But he got over that. Now he's pleased that we're having better opportunities and that we are going to college.

The move also created disruption for the extended family. Laura's mother provided the primary support for her parents and the relocation necessitated a change of roles for other family members. Ultimately, her mother did assume some of her previous responsibility from a distance.

My mom's family was not happy about the move because she used to help out a lot with my grandparents. It meant that her sisters would have to pitch in a little bit more. It was a big change.

Now they are better adjusted to it because they realize that my mom didn't stop helping altogether. She sends money and barrels of stuff twice a year. She also sends my grandmother red lipstick and clothes and things for the house.

Pursuing an Ideology

A commitment to going global with God's word inspires Christian missionaries to move to remote parts of the world in response to their calling to serve. Rev. Patricia McGregor, who serves with the Episcopal World

Mission in Madagascar, spoke with me about her decision to become a missionary while she was in the United States on home leave:

> At first I felt it was my husband's calling and I felt that it was my role as his wife to help him fulfill his calling. Over the past seventeen years, our callings have evolved. I have become ordained and now I personally also have a calling. We chose Madagascar because we wanted a place that didn't have many missionaries working there and a place that had a great need. Madagascar is the ninth poorest country in the world and there are not many Christians. We focus on providing spiritual, educational, and economic development.
>
> I was thirty-two and the mother of two young children when we left. I was willing to go and I was sure that it was there that we needed to be. I knew it was going to be a life of sacrifice and one filled with suffering and hardship. As a Western woman who grew up in America, I knew it was going to be hard. I was certainly not going there with rose-colored glasses. I knew that I was going into a life of uncertainty.

Patsy talked about her parents' understandable concerns. However, following a discussion with their priest, her parents very quickly became supportive and their children's best cheerleaders. When Patsy comes to the United States to share word about her mission, her parents take her to her speaking engagements and man the table where her book is sold.

A similar commitment infuses the lives of the Chabad-Lubavitch emissaries who serve all over the world in order to spread the teachings of the Torah to Jews in countries where there are few or no Jewish communal supports. Masha Lipskar, a young woman with a growing family, who moved to Johannesburg, South Africa to take up this cause wrote the following in a resource handbook for emissaries:[6]

> What inspired us to take this massive step of leaving family, friends, and a society that we understood, to travel to the other side of the

globe? Primarily it was a total devotion to the idea and ideal of being an emissary . . . to go out and spread the teachings of Torah.

It wasn't always easy. Vast geographic distance and separation caused moments of loneliness and uncertainty. Although the South African Jewish community is a particularly warm and hospitable one, the physical absence of family . . . was keenly felt.

Young couples who undertake this work in the Chabad movement are not only supported, but commended for their efforts by their families and communities back home. Devorah, a sixty-four-year-old mother and grandmother, has three grown children who serve as Chabad emissaries abroad—one in Argentina, one in Israel, and one in China. She talked about her enormous pride in their accomplishments. She feels that the importance of what they are doing transcends the devastating distance that separates them as a family:

Our family has been committed to *shlichus* (emissary work) for generations. It is an honor for parents to have children that make this choice in life. In helping others, there is a real power to your existence. It is just an awesome feeling to be chosen to do this and then to do it.

***

Since the Israeli War of Independence in 1948, there has been a continuous stream of Jews from all over the world who have moved to Israel, motivated by religious, ethnic, and nationalistic ideals. Despite the ideological incentives, these moves represent challenges for parents and for the younger generations. Ben, an Australian who moved to Israel in 1996 with his wife and children, describes his decision and the effect of that decision on his aging mother. Following this account, we hear from Miriam, the seventy-two-year-old mother of two sons who also pursued their dreams, based on an ideological commitment. Ben recounts:

I had always longed to live in Israel. My wife and I wanted a more intensive Jewish environment for ourselves and we felt that it would be a better place to raise our children. It's now twelve years that we have been here and we have no regrets. Our children are flourishing!

When they left Australia, Ben's mother, a Holocaust survivor, was heartbroken, but supportive. She had dreamed of coming to Israel after the war, but circumstances led her to emigrate to Australia instead. This feeling of ambivalence is shared by other parents of children who have moved to Israel to make *aliyah*.

Miriam is a tall, statuesque woman who lives in Florida with her husband, a retired dentist, in a comfortable home filled with family memorabilia. She has four married sons, two of whom live in the United States and two in Israel—one moved fourteen years ago and the other seven years ago. Both of these sons are physicians. She talks about her eldest son's decision to move to Israel.

Mark was an established physician with a private practice and a part-time teaching position at a medical school. His wife was a systems analyst who was also working at the time. Their four children were between the ages of four and nine. When they shared the news with us that they had decided to move to Israel, we were in a state of shock. There had never been any indication on their part that they had any interest in moving to Israel.

They decided to move because they wanted their children to grow up in a Jewish environment. They wanted them to be brought up living the principles they were being taught in the Hebrew day school they attended. In the Bible we read about the sages who lived, learned, and died in Israel. There are many references in our sources to the obligation of Jews to live in the Holy Land.

Nevertheless, I was amazed that they would be prepared to walk away from the lucrative and comfortable lifestyle they enjoyed. I was also concerned about the distance because we were accustomed to seeing them once a week or once every other week. We certainly didn't let more time pass between visits. We are a very close-knit family and I was devastated that we would not be able to see them so often.

Now that they have been in Israel for fourteen years, I think the decision for them to move was wonderful. They are very happy and we are happy for them. We did not lay a guilt trip on them. I have known parents who have said, "You can't do this to us. How can you move so far away?" We taught them the importance of Zionism and Israel, so when they finally decided to move, how could we possibly tell them not to?

Miriam and her husband visit Israel twice a year. She thinks that if they ever get to the point where they cannot travel as frequently as they do now, they might consider moving to Israel and spending the end of their days there. Since both of their sons who live there are physicians, she feels that they would be in the best position to adequately care for them.

It is interesting to note that Miriam and her husband are part of an American parents' group whose children live in the same settlement as their son. The group holds an annual dinner meeting in South Florida, where many of them spend the winter. They add $5 on to each person's dinner check, which goes to support youth groups in the settlement. Via e-mail, they let each other know when they will be visiting their Israeli children. This enables others to send small packages to their children or to get together with other parents while they are in Israel. One parent in the group said, "For our children, the parents' group is like another flower in the vase—another layer of security."

***

As we move toward a global society, characterized by frequent migrations, there is increasing optimism that families can handle these stresses. For example, in "Changing Families in a Changing World," Froma Walsh, cofounder and codirector of the Chicago Center for Family Health, says, "We have the ability to create new psychological, social and family configurations, exploring new options and transforming our lives many times over."[7] In the following chapters, those we hear from demonstrate that families are resilient, ever-changing constellations, capable of adapting to geographic dispersal. Because families represent the basic source of life happiness, people search for ways to bridge the gap that distance creates.

Lessons from Life: Why People Move Far Away

- Family members left behind who are accustomed to frequent visits with their children and grandchildren will miss the day-to-day contact. Keep a diary or blog, and share as much as you can as often as you can about everyday life in your new environment. They will be delighted to hear about how things look, the weather, your neighborhood, people you have met, shopping experiences, new foods you have tried, and surprises you have come across.

- Create photo albums of distant grandparents, uncles, aunts, and cousins. Look at them with your young children and reminisce about special occasions they participated in together. It's a good idea to keep these albums current and to review them prior to visits. As a result, when family members come to visit, youngsters will more easily recognize and remember them.

- Maintaining family customs and traditions will help you feel connected to your loved ones, even though you are oceans apart. Favorite foods, for example, are a powerful and very tangible reminder of the people who cooked them for you and those with whom this food was shared.

- Try to locate other families from your country of origin. Community centers, churches, synagogues, temples, and mosques are a good place to start. Whether they immigrated long ago or recently, these families will be a source of support and connection to your roots.

- Find or found an organization of people from your native country or town. It will provide a source of mutual support, and give you an opportunity to speak your native language and socialize with people who are in similar life situations. People who travel back and forth can take packages for your oceans apart relatives or simply call to give regards. The folks back home will be thrilled that you still care to be part of the life you left behind.

- Students from foreign countries should inquire at their colleges and universities about special services, such as host families, that are available to help ease the transition. For a young student, the home of a host family is a place to relax, eat a home-cooked meal, and be in the company of caring and interested adults with whom the student can share experiences and concerns about being in an unfamiliar environment.

- Some ambivalence about having moved far away from family may linger on for years. If so, you may wish to seek professional counseling in order to resolve these feelings.

- Children of divorce are especially vulnerable. Parents must ensure that the children's best interests are considered in terms of long-distance contact and visitation with the parent left behind. Prior to leaving, children should be reassured that they will continue to be involved with both parents despite the distance.

- Parental acceptance and support of decisions made by adult children to move to distant countries is a crucial ingredient to maintaining family ties. Parents who engage in self-pity only make their children feel guilty about their choice. This invariably results in less frequent contact and creates a barrier to an ongoing healthy and open relationship. Concentrate on maintaining your relationships with your far-off children and their growing families.

Chapter 1 Notes

1. Sharon McGuire & Kate Martin, "Fractured Migrant Families," in *Community Health* 30, no.#3 (2007): page 178
2. Jacob Climo, *Distant Parents* (New Brunswick, N.J.: Rutgers University Press, 1992), p. 12.
3. Monica McGoldrick, "Culture: A Challenge to Concepts of Normality," in Froma Walsh, ed., *Normal Family Processes: Growing Diversity & Complexity,* 3rd ed. (New York: Guilford Press, 2002).
4. Ibid., page 237
5. Ibid.
6. Masha Lipskar, *Shlichus: Meeting the Outreach Challenge, A Resource Handbook for Schluchim,* (North Bergen, N.J.: Bookmark Press, 1990)
7. Froma Walsh, "Changing Families in a Changing World," in Froma Walsh, ed., *Normal Family Processes*, p. 21.

2

KEEPING IN TOUCH:
PROBLEMS AND OPPORTUNITIES

*There are many families who live next door to each other who don't have the
relationship we do. Mom, we will always be close despite the distance.*
—A son to his mother following her yearly visit

Twenty years ago, when our son first moved to Israel, he was living in a
dormitory with twenty other students. There was one phone in the dining
hall, which was about ten minutes away from his dorm room. Although
we tried to call him weekly at an appointed time, we often missed him and
would have to wait while someone went to fetch him. Before we had even
said "Hello," we might have incurred a $10 phone bill. At that time, the
lack of availability of phone service in foreign countries, plus the inordinate
expense, made frequent calls a luxury.

Rajan, who came to study in the United States from India in 1984 recalls the
difficulties of keeping in touch with his family and the ways his mother tried
to overcome her concerns:

> I kept in touch with my parents mostly via phone. It was very expensive
> then, so I only called once a month at that point. My mother was
> concerned about my eating so she would send me some simple Indian
> recipes. She also felt I didn't write often enough, so she had some
> preprinted postcards made for me with a choice of three options for me
> to check: "I'm fine"; "I'm not fine"; and "I'm very busy." In the end, I
> never did use them because letters took about three weeks to arrive. By
> then the information on the card might very well have been obsolete.

Most mothers, like Rajan's, find it difficult to surrender their traditional roles, looking for ways to extend them to their children living in far-off foreign countries. Hence, "If I can't cook traditional Indian food for you, I'll send you my easy recipes." Similarly, the preprinted postcards were an affirmation that "I need to hear from you because you are still very much part of my life."

Perhaps the most daunting challenges to keeping in touch were faced by the family who moved to Madagascar to do missionary work. Rev. Patricia McGregor recalls that in 1991, when she and her family first arrived in Africa, the American Embassy was sending nonessential personnel back to the States because of political unrest. There were very few possibilities for communication. For example, if the electricity was off, the phones didn't ring. The first letters they received from home took six months to arrive!

Fortunately, continuing advances in technology have made a significant difference in our ease of communication. The multitude of options are discussed in detail in Chapter 7, "Creative Uses of Technology." Of all the choices available, the most popular by far is e-mail. One person said,"If something comes up that I want to share with my overseas family, I can e-mail them anytime of the day or night. It helps overcome the problems created as a result of time zone differences. I don't feel the distance as much as I did in the past."

Electronic mail and instant messaging enable us to share information quickly, but are often devoid of feelings. They tend to be episodic, not reflective. I truly treasure the occasions when my son or daughter-in-law takes the time to describe in writing the changes in their cultural environment, what they are doing personally and professionally, how it affects their lives and the lives of their children. Between visits, these are communications that are savored, read and reread, and eventually become keepsakes.

This chapter will primarily explore issues between parents and children. Subsequent chapters will deal with distant relationships among grandparents, siblings, and other family members. Topics in this chapter include:

- Keeping in touch between visits
- Things to think about in advance of a visit
- The importance of visiting
- One-on-one visits
- Tension and conflict
- Fear of facing illness at a distance
- When parents are separated from young children
- How distance affects relationships

Keeping in Touch Between Visits

While e-mail and instant messaging have become very popular, there is still nothing quite like hearing the voices of your loved ones on the other end of the phone line. Calls to other countries are no longer prohibitively expensive and you can talk without keeping an eye on the clock and worrying about the dreaded phone bill at the end of the month. One mother who was accustomed to dropping in to chat with her daughter over a cup of coffee, now calls her overseas daughter several times a week during her morning coffee break, which turns out to be her daughter's afternoon break as a result of the time difference.

Mothers place phone calls far more frequently than fathers and speak mostly to their biological children, with an occasional "hello" to their spouses. Weekly phone calls, lasting for about a half hour, include conversations about grandchildren, work, health and household issues, family, friends, and neighbors.

Simon moved from the Middle East in his late twenties to start his own construction business in the United States. His conversations with his mother reflect a common pattern:

> My parents are not computer-literate so we only communicate on the
> phone. I talk mostly to my mother. My father misses me, but due to the

time difference, he is usually at work when I call. Sometimes three, four, even five months can pass without our speaking to each other.

I talk to my mother about everything—my work, my daily life, I tell her about estimates I gave, the work I do, and about customers that are giving me a hard time. Sometimes I ask her how my brother is doing and she tells me that she has not heard from him in two weeks and that she hears from me more often. She very rarely talks to my wife, except to wish her "Happy Birthday" or to wish her well before a holiday.

In talking to Simon about his relationship with his parents before he left home, it was very clear that he was his father's "favorite." His father keenly feels that the absence of his son has created a void in his life. The time difference does present obstacles, but it would be wise to set up a telephone appointment once a month exclusively for the two of them to speak so that this important tie can be preserved. Generally, when fathers do speak to their distant children, they center their conversation around specific issues, rather than simple chitchat. Politics, current events, and finances are usually discussed with fathers rather than with mothers.

Shared interests form the basis for phone conversations and e-mail exchanges and can create and strengthen bonds. My son, Josh, and I are both currently writing books. Even though our fields of writing are different, we often share ideas about titles, book design, and ways of promoting and marketing our work. It makes each of us feel very invested in the other's life and is another dimension of our lives that we are able to share, even at a distance. At our son's request, my husband reviews his book manuscripts, sent via e-mail. This willing assistance prompted Josh to insert the following line in the "Acknowledgments" of one of his books: "My father instilled in me a zest for learning and for writing, and lovingly copyedited the manuscript, a process that reminds me of how much more I have to learn from him."

Mothers verbalize their concerns about the safety of their loved ones living in countries where there is unrest more easily than do other family members.

Miriam, the mother of two sons who moved to Israel, whom we first met in Chapter 1, says, "I worry all the time. The first question I ask when I call is, "Is everybody okay?" She has a grandson who is currently studying in Sderot, a town in the south of Israel that is under frequent rocket attack from Gaza. Given the threat of terrorist attacks, she is amazed that her grandchildren are given so much freedom to travel around the country.

Over the years, Miriam has learned to respect her children's convictions, even when she feels terribly uneasy regarding their safety. She observes, she listens, she is sympathetic, but she never questions the basis for their decisions to live in Israel.

The general rule when it comes to giving parental advice to adult children is this: "Don't, unless you're asked." Young people living far away from their parents often don't have anyone else to turn to for help and are grateful for the input. However, if it's advice they don't want, it's easier to ignore at a distance. Jason, an academic teaching at a large university abroad, frequently turns to his father for advice on handling difficult political situations at work and on how to negotiate a promotion or a raise. He says, "The advice is never wrong. It's authoritative and it makes me feel secure and loved." Angela, a single parent, is a successful massage therapist from Brazil now living in the United States. She accepts the advice her mother gives her about being supportive of her son, yet she largely ignores her mother's suggestions on how she should spend her money.

In some cases, parental concerns center around religious obligations and cultural identity, which are different in America. Renata, whose aged mother continues to live in Bangladesh, speaks to her almost every day. She says:

> My mother gives me advice regarding the moral teachings of the Koran. The greatest fear of parents who have children living in foreign countries like America is that these children will give up the identity they grew up with, the identity that unites their people. My mother reminds me to say my prayers, to be upright, and to be truthful. She is constantly reminding

me not to abandon my religion, even though I am in a foreign country where the practices are different. One of her greatest concerns is that I continue to dress as our religion dictates.

People who were forced to migrate face special challenges in communicating with loved ones left behind. In the previous chapter we heard from Camilla, who had to flee Colombia, South America in the dead of night. Her father, who fled with her, returned to his country and was imprisoned for ten years. She describes the challenges in communicating with him during that very difficult period.

My father was given an indeterminate sentence. He didn't know if it would be month, a year, or forever. He was forced to get up each morning and go outdoors to take a shower where the temperature in winter was below freezing. He suffered severe frostbite in his toes, which was very painful. He was allowed to call us every day, but we were not allowed to call or visit him. We could not send him letters or pictures because he did not want the authorities in Colombia to know where we are. Once, we didn't hear from him for two weeks because they had suspended his telephone privileges due to a fight in the prison. When we didn't hear from him, we always thought the worst.

When my father completed his sentence in Colombia, he needed to come to the United States to clear his name here. We heard that he was being transferred to Washington with a brief stop at a detention center in Miami. My brothers closed their liquor store and drove to Miami as quickly as possible. When they arrived at the detention center, they asked to see him so they could give him a hug, but their request was denied. They did open the door and they could see that he was handcuffed, but no further contact was allowed.

The U.S. authorities took his entire history and determined that there was no case against him. It took another nine months to complete all his paperwork, after which he was released. When we saw him again for the first time in a decade, he had turned gray and lost a great deal of weight. He looked so old.

Throughout this period, Camilla felt that things were happening to her family that did not happen to a normal family. She felt it was unfair. She deeply regrets that her father was not present for a formative part of her children's lives. She says, "They were without their grandfather and without all the happiness that brings." Camilla compensated for this as best she could by displaying photographs of her father and frequently sharing stories with them about her childhood in Colombia.

Things to Think About in Advance of a Visit

Visiting with family abroad is often the focal point of the year's activities and begins months before the actual visit. It includes planning, traveling, visiting, and departing. Calendars should be cleared early so the timing of the visit offers optimal opportunities for family to reconnect. Early purchase of airline tickets also allows for cheaper rates. If family members abroad want you to bring items that are more readily available where you live, lists should be sent far in advance. Some thought should also be given to accommodations during the visit and how the time will be spent when the family is together. Expectations and plans should be clarified prior to the trip, with an understanding that some flexibility is necessary.

Complaints about ten or more hours of air travel are common. Most people lose their tolerance for the cramped conditions at about the halfway mark. The "Resources" section at the back of this book includes tips on making yourself as comfortable as possible on a long airplane trip. Just briefly, keep yourself well hydrated; move around when you are allowed to; eat lightly; and bring a good book that you have started in advance of the trip, so that you are "into it" when you board the plane. As people age, long trips and the ensuing jet lag become more difficult to endure. As a result, they tend to travel less frequently and plan to stay longer when they get to their destination.

Traveling with children presents numerous challenges. The "Resources" section offers some guidelines to help make this as stress-free as possible. Generally, the golden rule for successfully flying with kids is to plan ahead and expect the unexpected.

Families who make a transoceanic trip one or more times a year have identified this expenditure as a priority in their lives. Most spend their entire travel and vacation budget on these trips. Gary, a retiree, whose married son and four grandchildren live abroad, says:

> It's a tremendous financial burden for us to visit them or to bring them here. But if we didn't do it, we would not see them. Our children live on the edge and could never afford the travel. It represents a significant portion of our annual income. There are things we might want to do with that money, but we have decided that seeing our children is much more important.

Janice, who lives comfortably in London and has a son in Boston, talks about the trade-offs she has made in order to visit her children several times a year:

> Most of our friends go on very elaborate holidays and travel all over the world. We spend all of our travel budget on visiting our children. We take no other holidays.

> Whenever I look at a pretty jacket or something I might want for our home, my mind quickly transfers the cost of the item into the price of an airfare to see the children. Many things that other people would value, I don't value any longer, compared to the opportunity to see my children.

Thought should to be given to where visiting family will stay and the implications of the various accommodations. Those coming to visit usually stay in the home of their hosts. This works best if the host has a guestroom and guest bath. However, many families do not have this extra space. In that case, one family member becomes displaced for the duration of the visit. If it's a short visit, that's usually endurable. Nonetheless, most people prefer their own space, where they can retreat for a while from the intensity of the visit.

During our last two visits to Israel, our daughter-in-law found us a comfortable furnished apartment to rent just a few doors from their home. It met our needs on every score. It was totally accessible to all the members of the family. Our children and grandchildren could wander over at any time. It also had amenities that they don't have, like cable TV, so it drew them. In addition, it had a great kitchen, so I could make dinner featuring things they loved. So again they came. It was almost like living next door and having the children and grandchildren dropping in at all times of the day. For a week, we could assume the "normal" role of a parent and a grandparent—a loving refuge for the tired and hungry.

The Importance of Visiting

Visits to children living abroad put us in touch with their day-to-day routine and offer us a greater appreciation for the way in which they function in their new environments. Visiting revitalizes relationships and updates our knowledge of their living space, current interests, and current concerns. In *A Guest in God's World: Memories of Madagascar,* Patricia McGregor describes the anticipation, joy, and sense of discovery that family visits brought with them:

> For one who lives overseas, there must be no other enjoyment greater than to have people come and visit your new home. I know it was so for our family. Everything being so different, a visit from family members brought excitement, some sense of security. It gave us the opportunity to share our new experiences, making them real. We were able to share our adventures of going to the market, learning the language, finding new shops, and bargaining at the market. Since we now became "translators" for my parents, it was an encouragement to realize how much of the language (Malagasy) we really understood![1]

Visits reassure parents that the choice their children made is working for them. One young woman reports on the importance of a visit by her mother three months after she moved overseas. Her mother said, "I feel better now that I can see where you are living and I can see what you are doing. I can picture where you are and I feel connected to your new life." It can also enhance a sense of pride. Simon, who moved from the Middle East to establish his own business, says, "My father was initially very unhappy about my move, but now that he has visited me, he can see for himself all of my accomplishments. I have a very nice house, a boat, and two cars. He is impressed that I was able to do all this on my own without any outside help."

When parents come to visit, it is not uncommon for mothers to stay longer than fathers. Mothers generally meld into the routine of the family more easily, becoming involved in household chores and minding grandchildren. After a week or two, many fathers usually long to return to their own environments. Several adult children spoke about the special treat of having their mothers around. Due to visa restrictions in Venezuela, Keyla's mother had to wait three years to make the trip to visit her daughter and her family. Keyla talked about the visit and the sadness the family experienced when her mother left:

> My mother was very comfortable in our home and proud of the fact that we live so nicely. I had to go to work when she was here, but when I was off, we went to the beach or to the park. My daughter loved spending time with her grandmother. They played with her dollhouse, read books, and watched movies. In addition, my mother cooked all our meals and we ate many things that we have not eaten for a long time. I no longer cook traditional Venezuelan dishes because they take too long to prepare. Eating her cooking was a real treat.

> When she left, we were very sad. Shortly after, I took my daughter to the library and the book she selected was about going to visit in Grandma's house. My daughter asked if one day she would be able to visit Grandma in her house. I told her that's not possible now, but perhaps one day it will be.

Keyla has a visa that permits her to travel back and forth. If, however, she took her children to Venezuela, she would have to ask the government's permission to take them out of the country again. Because visits are difficult to arrange, Keyla and her family value and treasure them all the more.

One-on-One Visits

Long-distance relationships need to be reinvigorated during visits. The most effective way to do this is to plan one-on-one time with the people with whom you wish to reconnect. Several of those I interviewed chose to travel alone to visit with family so that they could more easily fulfill this expectation.

Toby, who came from Australia to marry her American fiancé, decided to return to Australia without her family to attend her father's sixty-fifth birthday. In addition to reconnecting with individual family members, it was an opportunity for her to revisit the world of her childhood. She recalls the trip with great excitement:

> Last year I made a trip to Australia alone, without my husband and children. It's very expensive to fly to Australia, so we decided that I would go alone. It was amazing! It was great because I didn't have to make plans for anybody else, and I wasn't responsible for anyone else's comfort level. I felt like a teenager again. I had my dad's car and I could meet up with my friends for breakfast, lunch, and dinner. I went shopping with my mom, my sister, and my niece, and had a wonderful visit with my ninety-five-year-old grandmother. I felt like a child again at home!

Janice, who lives in London, prefers to visit her son and his family in Boston alone rather than with her husband. She says that if her husband is there he monopolizes their son with endless technical and computer talk. If she goes alone, she has more one-on-one time with her son, with whom she shares an interest in photography and cooking.

Ecaterina, who came from a rural area of Romania, was very eager for her family to see the new life she and her husband had established in the United States. She recounts how they arranged to do this on their meager income:

> After we were here for a year, instead of paying for summer camp for our daughter or a vacation for us, we arranged for one member of our family to come to visit us. Since we can't afford to bring more than one person at a time, each summer somebody else comes from Romania. The first person we brought was my husband's eighty-year-old grandfather. Each person who has come has stayed for two months. At first, when we didn't have much room, we gave our visitor my daughter's room and she slept with us. As time passed and we have became more established and have more space, we have set aside a room for visiting family members.

Ecaterina feels that one of the best by-products of a visit is for her Romanian family to be witness to their newfound success in the United States. She says, "It's so nice for them to see how we live and to feel relaxed about the decision we made to move to the United States. It makes them worry less when they return home."

Tension and Conflict

Since visits are infrequent, our hope is that everyone will be on their best behavior and that the time together will be tension-free. This rarely happens, however, because visits place people in much closer contact than they are accustomed to. This proximity, as well as the intensity of the interaction, can be the breeding ground for conflict. It's important to try to isolate the tension, deal with it, if possible, or simply set it aside and get on with enjoying the visit. Generally, people are more accepting of the behavior of their biological relatives and less so of those who are new to the family. In this section we will hear about how three people dealt with tension during phone calls and visits with distant family.

Simon, who is newly married and was the last to "leave the nest," describes visits by his parents to his home as well as visits he and his new bride have made to his parents' home:

> When my folks come, my mother stays a month and my father only a
> week or ten days. He misses his grandchildren, and the newspapers and
> TV that he's accustomed to. When they are here, I can't take off from
> work to be with them, except weekends. That's very frustrating, because
> Irene, my wife, has to be with them alone. My mother wanders around
> mumbling in Spanish, which Irene does not understand, and therefore
> thinks that the mumbling is a result of some dissatisfaction with her. I
> asked my mother to stop doing this, but she can't because she does this
> all the time at home. After they left, Irene was so stressed out that it led
> to a big fight between us.

> We travel to see them once or twice a year. I use all my vacation time
> to visit them. We are expected to stay with my parents. However, my
> parents don't get along very well and there is constant bickering between
> the two of them. I'm used to it, but it is very hard on Irene, who comes
> from a home with much less discord.

> My parents give us the largest bedroom to stay in, but they have only
> one bathroom. My mother expects us for every meal. She is a very good
> cook and I used to love the food she prepared. But my taste has changed.
> Since we are on vacation, we would like to explore new places and eat
> out. One day when my mother went to work, she left us stuffed peppers
> for lunch. But we were away at lunchtime. I ended up hiding the stuffed
> peppers in the back of the refrigerator so we could eat them the next day.

> My mother doesn't drive, so when I come she always wants us to drive
> her to visit relatives. I'm not so interested in seeing relatives. I would
> rather go sightseeing to explore places in the country that I haven't seen
> since I was on high school field trips. When I visit them, I try to make
> everybody else happy, but then I don't make myself happy.

> Irene would like to stay in a hotel, but my mother would be insulted if
> we did that. I have thought that in the future I might go five days before

Irene and stay with my parents. By then they will, hopefully, have had their fill of me so that Irene and I can stay in a hotel for the rest of the visit.

Simon seems to have come up with a reasonable solution to his dilemma, but there is an underlying issue that has not been addressed here. Relationships are not frozen in time. Simon is no longer the young, single adult who lived at home and catered to all his parents' needs. In addition to having married, he has matured and become independent. His expectations of himself, as well as his parents' viewpoint, need to be adjusted to the current reality. Some discussion in advance of a trip should take place so that limitations can be set before the visit begins.

***

Leah talks about the tension she experiences when her father comes to visit her with his girlfriend. Leah moved to Israel from Great Britain prior to her mother's death.

> My mother died five years ago. She was my main connection to the family. Since her death, I've transferred that connection to my father, who now has a girlfriend. I'm happy he has someone in his life because it takes a lot of the pressure off me. He and his girlfriend divide their time between France and America. I would prefer that he would live in Israel and America, rather than in France and America. However, his girlfriend hasn't the least interest in living in Israel. She thinks that it's old-fashioned and primitive, whereas France is quaint and pretty. That creates tension for us. They are not married, but they provide caring companionship for each other.
>
> When my father visits with his girlfriend for a couple of weeks, we try to find them a furnished apartment near us, because there are no hotels in our town. My father is not the easiest person in the world to live with. He might lie down on the sofa and take a nap midday and then there is

nowhere for anybody to sit. My husband finds that difficult. My father's girlfriend is pleasant and she does help out in the kitchen, but it's not like having my mother with me. Sometimes there is tension between my father and his girlfriend. I find that very hard. I like to think of them as happy and when I hear that they are not, I'm upset and tense.

I would like them to have an apartment here so I don't have to worry about whether or not I have found them adequate accommodations when they come. If I had to look for a place for my mother, I wouldn't worry as much. But I want everything to be nice for them, especially since I know his girlfriend doesn't really like to come to Israel.

In Leah's narrative we can still hear her sadness and mourning for her mother. She is, however, realistic about her father's needs and has made every effort to accommodate his new relationship.

***

Pearl has an exceptionally close relationship with her son, who lives abroad, but is not happy about communications with her daughter-in-law.

I speak to my son very frequently, sometimes several times a week or more often. I rarely talk to my daughter-in-law because she never wants to get on the phone. I feel very bad about that and I am trying to change that.

I have never made any demands on her, but I did tell her that I would like to hear from her once in a while. Whenever we do have a conversation, it's been wonderful. Due to the time difference and our personal schedules, it's very difficult for me to reach her at a time when she can speak to me. If I call and leave a message, she does not return the call.

There are several obstacles that stand in the way of our relationship. Her mother died when she was very young. In all the years I've known her, she has been moody and unable to reach out to be hospitable or warm. I'm pleased that she makes my son happy and that she is a good mother. Having seven children is not easy. I compliment her constantly, but we have no real connection.

My husband and I have recently given them a major financial boost—an investment that will go on for many years. I was hoping that this might be a little bit of a bribe and that this would be an incentive for her to have more contact with us. But so far it has not.

There has only been one occasion when I felt there was a breakthrough in our relationship. Our daughter-in-law was in the United States and came to stay with us for three days. We wined her and dined her and made our car available so she could go shopping. I also went out of my way to invite people I thought she would enjoy. One of the people who came to dinner was a former classmate of our daughter-in-law's late mother. Our guest brought with her their high school yearbook and gave it to our daughter-in-law, who has no memorabilia from her mother. It was very touching and moving.

Our daughter-in-law was absolutely floored at our generosity and hospitality. She felt that she had been treated like royalty and that she had never had such a wonderful vacation.

The relationship Pearl describes is truly problematic. Her daughter-in-law's resistance to becoming more friendly cannot be easily penetrated or resolved. Still, Pearl's continuing efforts to reach out are important and commendable. While she is not often successful in connecting with her daughter-in-law, overall Pearl's endeavors do serve to strengthen ties with her son and the grandchildren.

Fear of Facing Illness at a Distance

In Chapter 4, "Getting Through Rough Times," there will be an extensive discussion on how people who are separated by huge distances cope with the illness and death of a loved one. Still, this is a topic that is on the minds of people living oceans apart long before they have to deal with it directly. We hear from four people who expressed concern and fear. Keyla feels the need to be there to offer emotional support; Simon feels he will need to provide financial support; Ecaterina, with tears in her eyes, tells of the plan she has developed with her parents; and Michelle talks about her frustration, following a visit to her aging parents, knowing that she might not be able to travel from Israel to the United States again for another year or two.

Keyla: I am very concerned about the time my parents will become frail and old. It frightens me to think that I will not be there for them. They took care of me and I won't be able to take care of them. I know that my brothers and sisters will help them. Still, that will be something that I am going to miss. And I don't want to because I know that when people are very sick, they take comfort in seeing the whole family gather around them.

Simon: I worry a lot about my parents now that they are getting older. Even though they have some savings, I still worry. I am concerned about their becoming frail and needing assistance in the tasks of everyday living. My siblings are all struggling and won't be able to help much. I'm trying to establish myself financially just in case they will need my help one day. I see it as my responsibility. I am very worried about that. I sometimes ruin my present by thinking about the future.

Ecaterina: It is hard for me to talk about what will happen when they get sick and pass on. My husband and I are only children so we have thought about it and even talked to our parents. We have decided that when one of them is left alone—either my parents or my in-laws—the remaining spouse will come live with us in the United States. This is the hardest part about being so far away.

Michelle: It's important for me to know how my parents are doing and to help to the extent possible. When I visit, I can talk at length with my father. I can have a fulfilling conversation, be brought up-to-date on my mother's status and on my father's state of mind in dealing with her disability. I can offer support and suggestions. I can bring them joy by my presence and the presence of my children. This doesn't work well for us on the phone. A week has passed since my visit and I already miss the closeness and the accessibility of connection and information. How can I keep in touch, keep informed, and contribute from such a distance?

It might help Michelle to tell her father how frustrated she feels by the situation and how much she wants to be more connected, even at a distance. Doing so would let her father know that she cares deeply about both of her parents, and would enlist his help in improving the long-distance communication. They could perhaps agree on the best time of day for her to call and to increase the number of phone calls each week. It is much easier to cope with someone's illness and disability one day at a time than to confront the cumulative effects of an illness over an entire week. Installing quality Skype equipment in both households would enable Michelle's children to talk and be seen by their grandparents as well, strengthening the bond between them.

When Parents Are Separated from Young Children

Young parents sometimes find themselves in situations that lead them to temporarily live apart from their young children so that they can more easily achieve a specific goal. We hear about two young mothers who exercised this option, never anticipating that it would be such a devastating and heartbreaking experience.

Sonya, a Brazilian woman in her mid-forties, trained as a lawyer, was unable to find adequate work to support her two children. Early in her marriage, her husband left her for a much younger woman. At that point, her life was marked by poverty, an addiction to alcohol, and hopelessness. When her children—both boys—were eight and ten, she decided to leave them with her mother, so she could come to the United States to work. She describes her struggle and her journey over the past ten years:

When I came to the United States, I got a job with an agency that provided domestic help. At first, I thought I would bring the children here, but I couldn't get them the necessary passports. I could not go back to visit them because if I did, I would have to remain in Brazil.

When I got here, I felt completely lost. Whenever I thought of my children, I would cry. I spoke to them every Sunday and would constantly tell them that I would bring them here. But I soon found out that even if I received the necessary documentation, I would not be able to have them join me because their father would not permit them to leave. When they reached their mid-teens, my mother lost control of them and both became involved in drugs and alcohol.

At this point, the children went to live with their father. But that didn't work out, so they came back to live with my mother. Even though they are now eighteen and twenty, they still beg me to come back. With the money I have made in the United States, I have built a house in Brazil and am planning to return within a year.

In the years that Sonya has been in the United States she has become a devout Christian. She feels that this has given her life direction and that when she returns to Brazil, she will be a better person, a better mother, and a better daughter as a result. She movingly says, "God has changed my heart, my vision, and my life. I can't undo the past for my children, but I would still like to do what I can for them. I especially feel a big responsibility to my mother. She took care of me and my children. Now I want to take care of her."

***

Nicole is an elegant woman in her early seventies who is an eminent historian. She was born and raised in Tunisia. She married in her early twenties, and she and her husband moved to Paris to do graduate work. When she became pregnant, her in-laws, a prominent, well-off family, offered to take care of the baby in Tunisia while the young couple continued to study in Paris. Grandparents sharing in the care of grandchildren is customary in Mideastern culture. Yet Nicole was not prepared for what followed, and recalls that confusing and harrowing time:

> The baby, a girl, was born in June. From June until September, I took care of her in my in-laws' house. The summer gave my mother-in-law an opportunity to become accustomed to the baby, for whom she would be responsible starting in September.
>
> My husband and I resumed our studies in Paris in the fall, leaving our daughter with my in-laws. When I got to Paris, I cried every night. It was terrible. I lost ten pounds and my hair fell out in a period of a few months. I was depressed by the fact that I was separated from my daughter. At age twenty-two, I don't think my husband had defined any specific role for himself as a father. He simply accepted that his parents were his child's caregiver.
>
> Other than a single letter once a week, there was no communication with the family. My in-laws were very nice about taking pictures and sending them so I could see my daughter growing up. When the pictures arrived, I became even sadder. She didn't look unhappy, so I tried not to worry about her.
>
> During the Easter vacation, we were reunited. My in-laws rented a house in the south of France and we all vacationed together. I was shocked to find that my daughter didn't recognize me and that she was totally attached to her grandmother and not to me. I had to seduce her and attract her attention in order to show her how much I cared about her. I was totally devastated! It took several days for her to get used to me. While it was only a few days, for me it seemed like an eternity.
>
> Following the Easter vacation, I wanted to take my daughter back with us to Paris until the end of July, when my studies would be completed. But my mother-in-law insisted that my daughter was so happy with them. My mother-in-law spent all her time with the baby, relegating the

running of her household to the servants. From her perspective, it was working out very well and she said, "You go take your exam, and when you are finished you come back." And that's what I did. From Easter until the end of July I again did not see my daughter.

It normally takes three years to complete the work for the final exam in history. I worked extremely hard because I wanted to get it done and end the separation from my daughter. I finally completed the work in one year.

In reviewing this period through the lens of time and experience, Nicole said, "I grew up in a society, both in Tunisia and in France, that did not encourage us to present any opposition to parental control. We had neither the will nor the personal skills to reject their offer." Nicole's in-laws projected the feeling that "We know better. We will help you." While they showed a great deal of generosity in their actions, it was the kind that overwhelmed the young couple and stifled any possibility of their participation in the decision-making affecting their own family.

It is interesting to note that separation of this kind is mediated by culture. In Chapter 1, we heard from an Indian father who left his infant son with extended family in India for four years while he and his wife came to seek their fortune in the United States. Since separation of parents and young children is common practice in India, he spoke with pride about the advantages to the child of being reared in his native culture during his formative years.

How Distance Affects Relationships

Loving relationships continue to radiate warmth and affection, even at a distance. Being oceans apart does not change how we feel about those far away, but it does change the frequency with which we might be able to do things together. Then again, when we are able to be together, we tend to have greater appreciation of the experience. Ecaterina says, "One might think that the distance would make us less close, but I think that my relationship with my parents is even stronger. The distance has made me feel that I should not take them for granted, so I value them even more than before."

Ecaterina's sentiments were echoed by my daughter-in-law, Michal, who summed up her feelings about the past twenty years of visits with us:

> I get the "warm fuzzies" just thinking about our visits together. Because they were so infrequent, I think we all tried to squeeze the most out of them that we could. But that didn't mean doing anything special. It meant doing all the things we couldn't do together the rest of the time, and if we could, we might take for granted. Ordinary things, like sharing breakfast, joining you for a trip to the grocery store, having a backyard barbecue for the family, planning the menu for a Sabbath meal, or just sitting and watching the kids play became extraordinary because we were together.

Among the things people missed most was the lack of spontaneity in relationships. You can't pick up the phone and say, "Let's go for lunch," or drop by for a cup of coffee. Others talked about missing birthdays, anniversaries, and school events that bring joy to extended family. Toby, whose parents live in Australia, says, "It's difficult when my children are in a school play that my parents cannot attend. At times like this I do feel there is something missing."

Parents always hope that children who live at a distance and in another culture will nevertheless perpetuate values and traditions taught at home. My husband experiences a sense of parental fulfillment at having successfully transmitted important values to our son. He says, "Josh's love of nature, of hiking, his intellectual curiosity, his interest in writing, his social skills are all things he learned from growing up in our home. I am pleased that he is passing these on to his children."

Realizing that what is significant to us is also central to the lives of our children and grandchildren living seven thousand miles away is an affirmation of our connectedness—it is something we hope will be perpetuated for generations to come.

Lessons from Life: Keeping in Touch—Problems and Opportunities

- Distance puts relationships in sharper focus. It causes people to filter out the irrelevancies and to highlight what they want to remember.

- Recognize that in distant living there are trade-offs. While it might fulfill a career or ideological goal, it also means that families cannot be part of each other's day-to-day lives. We must adjust to this and make the most of the new living arrangements.

- Connections are easier to preserve if we work at maintaining cordial relationships. Avoid conflict by limiting unrealistic expectations.

- Long-distance phone calls in which problems are shared tend to cast a dark shadow, making distant relatives worry about the well-being of far-off family members. This, in turn, causes us to be overly concerned. Remember that many problems are transitory and are frequently resolved in the next hour or by the next day without our knowledge.

- If you are unable to take a vacation when distant family visit, try to take off a day or two from work to be with them. It will alleviate your guilt and make your visiting family very happy.

- There are bound to be some points of conflict during visits. Keep in mind that this is a short-term situation. Try not to let those conflicts override the pleasure of being together.

- Children and grandchildren who live in foreign countries where there is unrest and terrorism need support and sympathy from their distant parents and grandparents. Nagging them to "come home" will only alienate them.

- Although we may be hesitant to do so, parents and distant adult children should discuss how the need for additional assistance during illness will be handled. This is best done before an emergency arises.

- Following a period of separation, the reunion of parents with young children requires a reentry strategy that allows the relationship to be reestablished slowly and comfortably.

- Visits are often bittersweet. As we are enjoying being together, we are lamenting how rare a treat the visit is. Be prepared for possible postvisit sadness and guilt, and develop strategies in advance for dealing with it.

- Lifestyles and value systems vary from country to country. It is important for those who move to absorb some of these in order to adjust to their new environment. Family members from abroad should respect cultural differences and be understanding and accepting of these changes.

- If children marry while they are abroad, you will be faced with getting to know their spouses from a distance. Remember that your son or daughter chose a mate for themselves and not a friend for you. Patience, kindness, and acceptance will go a long way toward developing trust, friendship, and love.

Chapter 2 Note

1.   Patricia McGregor, *A Guest in God's World: Memories of Madagascar* (Eldoret, Kenya: Zapf Chancery, 2004) p.24.

3

GRANDPARENTING AT A DISTANCE

For the first few weeks following my grandchildren's departure, the precious moments we shared were etched in my mind. They were like a series of videos that I mentally played whenever I had the need to feel close to them.
—A long-distance grandmother

My first challenge as a long-distance grandmother came when our son and daughter-in-law, who live seven thousand miles away, came to visit us with their infant son. Preparation for the prospective visit began shortly after the baby's birth. I immediately set about borrowing equipment from neighbors and friends—a crib, a stroller, a car seat, a baby bath, a diaper pail. As each item was put in place, my bond with the new arrival tightened.

I mentally adopted every three-month-old I met on the street, at the supermarket, or in a restaurant. Often I engaged the infant's mother in conversation, inquiring about the child's eating and sleeping habits, where to shop for baby clothes, and what baby detergent to use, plus gathering important data on the latest in child care. Of course, each of these innocent moms had to hear about my newborn grandson who was about to grace the American scene.

Plagued by uncertainty, I wondered if my new daughter-in-law would feel comfortable in my home. Would she trust me with the baby? And would my son, now a married man and a father, still seek me out for long, rambling conversations about personal relationships, his work, my work, our family?

The big day finally arrived. I quickly observed that the baby was a handsome, robust, and responsive child, and that parenthood made my son more mature and my daughter-in-law more confident. Holding my grandson's firm, sturdy body in my arms filled me with an indescribable sense of well-being. And, yes, my daughter-in-law trusted me with the baby and felt totally comfortable in our home. And, yes, my son still welcomed an uninterrupted hour or two to talk to his mother about his new status in life.

On the last day of their visit, I was the designated babysitter. It had been more than a quarter of a century since I had cared for an infant, but I found that it's much like knitting—you never quite forget. I was out of practice, but, on the whole, the baby and I did fine. When I rocked my grandson in the same chair I had rocked his father in three decades earlier, I shed tears of gratitude and joy.

In this chapter, grandparents, adult children, and grandchildren share their thoughts and concerns and the tools they use to stay connected. Topics include:

- Staying connected between visits
- Telephone and other means of communication
- Preplanning visits with grandchildren
- Grandchildren visiting alone
- As grandparents age
- The effect of distance on relationships

Staying Connected Between Visits

When you see grandchildren only once a year, there is a desperate need to make the experience last beyond the few weeks of the actual visit. My attempts to keep visits alive in the mind of my first grandchild prompted me to write a short book about the events that took place during his visit in America when he was two. Since this book was well-received, I put together another one following my visit to see him in Israel, when he turned three. The books, designed for an audience of one, were simple, homemade labors of love that were packaged in slim three-ring binders, with each page containing a photograph and some text inserted in a clear glassine sleeve that protected the contents from sticky little fingers.

Amichai in America was in three parts and included captioned photos of places we went, books we read, and foods he ate during his visit. The next volume, *Bubbe in Beit Shemesh,* chronicled craft projects we did together with materials I brought from America and the celebration of his third birthday at nursery school. For several years, these were among Amichai's favorite books, dutifully read to him by his mother. In subsequent years he read the books to his little brothers, who now sometimes pick them up and read them on their own. While most children's books have a shelf life of a few months, these two books have been paged through for about a dozen years and may very well be read to and by future generations.

To stay connected between visits, it is helpful if the grandchildren's parents are active participants in achieving this goal. Michal, my daughter-in-law, is the mother of four children ranging in age from two to sixteen. All of them were born and raised an ocean apart from both sets of grandparents. Because visits with grandparents are infrequent, she is vigilant about taking every opportunity to include grandparents in the lives of the children. Michal says:

> I think it's important to try to incorporate the grandparent/grandchild relationship into our daily lives. Yearly, or less frequent, visits are not enough to build and maintain that relationship. We look for little things, little ways to bring the grandparents into our lives, and hopefully, bring the grandchildren into theirs. For example:

> On rainy days, we look through family photos of visits we had together and we review some of the experiences we had.

> - If I'm preparing a recipe passed along by one of the grandparents, I discuss with the kids where and when they first ate this dish.
> - When one of the children asks something about my childhood, I will suggest that we call Granny and ask her what she remembers.

- Preschool- and elementary school–age children love to share pictures they have drawn with grandparents. These can be faxed or e-mailed and are particularly welcome for birthdays and other special occasions
- Sometimes, if one of the children is bored, I might suggest that they call one of their grandparents to discuss ideas of things to do.
- Each of the four grandparents has special interests and skills. The children might have a school project or hobby relating to one of them. When this is the case, I encourage the children to call or e-mail the relevant grandparent. For example, one of the boys became interested in horseback riding. I encouraged him to e-mail his grandfather, who was an equestrian. Papa George sent back a lovely slide show documenting his riding days.
- I try to send a periodic update on who's doing what at school and in their extracurricular activities. Sometimes I add something cute one of the kids said or did.
- Somewhere between the ages of four and six, children get to the point where they understand the concept of family structure and they want to know how everyone fits into theirs. I usually play a question-and-answer game: Who's Mommy's mother? Who's Mommy's father? And so on through the family. Simultaneously, the child can draw a picture of the relative or paste a photo that includes a caption. Before long, you have a simple genealogical chart.

Telephone and Other Communication

Long-distance telephone calls, the primary mode of communication between visits, require some preplanning and thought. If you follow a few basic guidelines, your chances of having a satisfying conversation with your grandchildren will improve. It's wise to establish with their parents what might be a good time to call, taking into account the time difference. In order to assess the mood of children and their availability, it is best to speak briefly with a parent first. For any one of a number of reasons, like a bad day at school or involvement in another project, a child might not wish to talk when you call. This is something you must respect and simply let the parent or child know that you will call back at another time. Since young children are not skilled telephone conversationalists, it is up to the grandparent to be prepared with specific trigger questions in order to keep the conversation moving.

In *The Long-Distance Grandmother,* author Selma Wasserman offers a number of excellent ideas on how to speak on the phone to children of different ages. I was most impressed with her ideas for speaking to very young children—those from about nine months to two years old. She suggests that with the phone to the child's ear, we talk to the child in much the same manner as we would if we were there in person. The conversation should center on concepts and words the child already knows. For example, you might say, "Suzie, where is your head, and where are your eyes, and now show me you nose and how about your toes." One grandmother tried this with her eighteen-month-old granddaughter and the child's mother reports that the child's eyes opened wide as she smiled and followed all the instructions. In attempting this exercise, it's important to speak calmly and clearly, and to use the child's name often. Little children love repetition, so this might be done a few times a week.

In talking to elementary school–age children, avoid open-ended questions. "What did you do today?" will usually produce "Nothing" as the answer. It's best to be specific and to talk about their special interests. You may encounter some misunderstanding because young children think very concretely and sometimes don't grasp what is possible and what is not. A few anecdotes follow from Grandmother Donna who lives in Boca Raton, Florida, and speaks frequently to her long-distance grandchildren.

> During a phone call to five-year-old Matthew, I talked about the story of Noah and the ark, which was being discussed in his class at school. I started out by saying that Noah took many animals into the ark. Matthew said, "No!" So I said, "Well, he took a lot of animals into the ark." Again, he emphatically said, "No!" "So, okay, Matthew. Tell me—how many

animals did Noah take into the ark with him?" He said, "Two! Two elephants, two giraffes, two tigers, only two!"

On another occasion Donna asked her four-year-old granddaughter what she would like as a special present when Grandma comes to visit. The granddaughter replied, "Please bring the swimming pool." This child lives in a very congested area without many of the luxuries available in Boca. A swimming pool certainly seemed like a good idea.

***

When Steven's granddaughters lived within driving distance of their home, he saw them frequently and spoke to them on the phone between visits. Two years ago, his daughter, son-in-law and their three teenage daughters moved to Great Britain. He misses the frequent contact and tells how he uses the phone to stay in touch with his grandchildren.

> Each of the grandchildren has her own cell phone. I call each one separately once a week on her personal phone. I purposely do not use the family line because I want each of the girls to feel that this is an exclusive gesture just for them. I usually start out with something humorous and then ask about school and about their social life. I am interested in both the highs and lows in their lives, so frequent questions include "What wonderful thing happened this week?" and "What disappointing thing happened this week?"

> Conversations last about ten minutes. Speaking to them regularly gives me a kick and bridges the gap between visits. I think it makes them feel loved and cared for.

***

The advent of electronic mail has revolutionized long-distance communication. Grandparents I've spoken to report that children as young as seven are now using e-mail. It's inexpensive, it can be sent at all hours of the day or night, and it can be any length you choose. Janice, an author who lives in London and whom we have heard from in Chapter 2, has developed a unique relationship with her eldest granddaughter via e-mail. The granddaughter lives in Boston.

> My granddaughter, who is fifteen, is very artistic and has a fine design sense. I asked her to create the design for my latest novel. I was able to e-mail her the file of the book, following which we had many discussions about various aspects of the design, including the cover and the chapter openings. She did a splendid job! Working on the project together has brought us both a great deal of pleasure and has served to intensify our bond with one another.

A more extensive exploration of the use of technology appears in Chapter 7. It includes creative applications of video communications, family websites, family blogs, and online photo albums.

Preplanning Visits with Grandchildren

Whether in your home or in theirs, a key to the success of visits, especially if they are short, very much depends on preplanning. My preparations for my grandson's first visit, chronicled at the beginning of this chapter, might have seemed excessive. However, because everything was in place when the children arrived, it enabled them to be comfortable the minute they stepped into the house. It also allowed me to be more relaxed and available to visit with them.

In the stories that follow, four sets of grandparents share their experiences in which planning played a key factor in the success of the visit.

Pearl and her husband, both retired schoolteachers, visit their seven granddaughters who live in Australia once a year. The children range in age from four to twenty years old. For religious reasons, these children do not watch television, go the movies or the mall, and do not go swimming at a public beach unless there is a time set aside for single-sex bathing.

With careful planning, which begins in the United States weeks before their departure, Pearl and her husband spend a wonderful two weeks with the girls. Pearl describes how they meet this challenge with projects that are interesting and fun and serve to bind relationships between generations.

> Given the many restriction on activities, we decided that craft projects are the best solution. Before I leave the United States, I scour the craft shops for appropriate projects and books. The Klutz project books[1] are very good because all the items needed to complete a project are included. Greeting cards, paper flowers, and face-painting are among the activities we undertook. Every day we work on a different project.

> We rent an apartment in our children's neighborhood during our visit so that we have our own space and can still be close to the family. Every afternoon, when the children come home from school, it is project time in our apartment. Because it's difficult to work with all seven at one time, we divide the group in two, according to age. The project usually takes an hour, following which we have a snack. After the snack, we take the younger group home, pick up the older group, and start all over again.

The projects require a great deal of supervision. Both Pearl and her husband work along with the kids, interacting with them during the entire session. As an added bonus, each of the children is invited to dinner at least once during the two-week visit. Pearl prepares their favorite foods and they get undivided personal time with their grandparents. The response of the children is truly heartwarming. Pearl says:

> The grandchildren love the time we spend together and look forward to our coming. Before we arrive, the younger ones call to tell us that they would like to do a project they saw one of their older siblings do the year before. This has become a real connection between us. It permits us to visit with them in a way that's satisfying for all of us. The children are very affectionate. Whenever we are with them, they fight to hold our hands and to sit next to us. We don't see them for very long or very often, so we attempt to make it quality time.

I discussed with Pearl differences she may have noted in her relationships with her American grandchildren, whom she sees much more frequently. She offered this comment:

> My relationship with my American grandchildren is much more casual. When we lived in New Jersey, I would drop in often just to say hello, stay about ten minutes, and then leave. Our relationship with our Australian grandchildren is much more intense, even though it is infrequent. Our American grandchildren take us for granted. When they visit us in Florida, they often don't even say "Good morning" when they get up.

> Our overseas grandchildren have none of the material possessions that their American cousins accept as a matter of course. When we come to Australia, we bring presents, projects, and fun times. They can hardly wait until we get there and each one wants to be first to visit with us. This makes us feel very special.

***

Long-held family traditions that have meaning often determine our expectations when we become grandparents. Ginny, a grandmother in her late sixties, grew up in a very close-knit family that had a Family Circle and a Cousins Club. She continues to look forward to meetings where she sees members of her extended family with whom she enjoys a shared history. As her own grandchildren came along, she was resolute about creating opportunities for the children to know each other and develop bonds with one another.

Each year she and her husband sponsor a Cousins Trip for all their grandchildren over the age of three and, of course, that includes the ones who live abroad. The trip will usually dovetail with a family event that brings the overseas grandchildren to the United States. The Cousins Trip, which does not include their parents, lasts for four days and is held in a rented, furnished apartment in a resort area. Ginny talks about the things they do, the response of the grandchildren, and her own reflections on the importance of the Cousins Trip in the lives of her grandchildren.

We might go bowling, to an amusement park, to the movies, or to the beach. When the opportunity presents itself during these trips, we try to share with them something about our family history from the previous generation. For example, we were all together in Scranton, Pennsylvania for my father in-law's ninetieth birthday. Following the party, my husband took all the grandchildren to the cemetery where his mother, their great-grandmother, is buried. He talked to them about her life and shared several personal anecdotes about her. Over the years, a very close connection has evolved among the two families of grandchildren. Throughout the year, the grandchildren will ask when we are planning the next Cousins Trip.

My feeling is that children who grow up as part of significant groups have a greater sense of security. This is true about being part of a family, part of a religion, and part of a community. The Cousins Trip provides our grandchildren with another layer of security. As a result of these trips, the cousins have developed a shared history with one another that is very binding. We hope it will last a lifetime.

Ginny tells me that planning for the Cousins Trip begins at least nine months in advance. It requires clearing calendars, making travel arrangements, and securing a place to stay. She says, "It's a great deal of effort, but well worth the results!"

***

Adult children who live an ocean apart from family often do not have the opportunity to get away alone without children because there is nobody around with whom they would entrust their young ones. Visiting grandparents may be asked to fulfill this role. Even grandparents who are willing to do this are ambivalent about accepting the responsibility. They have a number of concerns: "Can we manage this physically?" "Will the children be miserable and cry without their parents?" "The grandchildren have not seen us in some time. Will they be comfortable staying with us?"

Donna, a grandmother from whom we heard earlier in this chapter, received a long-distance phone call from her son two weeks before their visit, requesting that she take care of the six kids while she was there so that he and his wife could take a few days off by themselves. Donna was not entirely comfortable with the idea, but she agreed to do it if the three days they were planning to be away could be scheduled during the second week of their visit at a time when the grandchildren would be accustomed to having them around. She describes how careful preplanning enabled her and her husband to handle what she perceived as a daunting task:

> The first thing I did was to seek advice from friends who had babysat several small grandchildren while their adult children took a few days off. They advised me to hire babysitters whom my daughter-in-law recommended and who could assist me during the most pressured times of the day. Since the children were all in school until midafternoon, I hired two girls: One came in from 3 to 5 p.m. to help with after-school snacks and took the children to the park. The next one came from 5 to 7 p.m. to help me with supper, baths, and bedtime. In addition, I asked my daughter-in-law to provide me with a written schedule for each child that included wake-up time, bus pickup for school, bus drop-off, afternoon programs, bath and bedtime rituals, and food preferences. She also left me an emergency phone list with the name of their pediatrician, the closest hospital, and a neighbor's number in case I needed additional assistance.

> While I coordinated this effort, my husband helped me with a variety of tasks. Roughly speaking, I was responsible for the indoor activities— cooking, cleaning, and laundry—while he handled the outdoor activities—bus drop-off and pickup and taking kids to after-school activities. He also read the children their bedtime stories, which they felt was a very special treat.

On the whole, Donna felt that the grandchildren were relaxed and responsive during this three-day experience. Now that she has mastered the responsibility, she thinks that next time she would like to be somewhat more adventurous and take the children on a picnic in the park and perhaps a train ride. Their adult children were thrilled to get away and were, of course, very grateful.

Grandchildren Visiting Alone

Today, it is not uncommon for children to travel the world alone. Due to conflicting agendas or financial constraints, it may not be possible for the entire family to make a major trip across the ocean every year. Yet one or more of the grandchildren may be eager to visit distant grandparents more often.

Major airlines all offer services that allow children between the ages of five and seventeen to travel without a parent or a legal guardian. These children, known as unaccompanied minors, or UMs, are ushered onto the aircraft, introduced to the flight attendant, chaperoned during connections, and turned over to the appropriate person upon arrival at their final destination. Airlines do not permit UMs between the ages of five and seven on trips requiring connecting flights.

Michal, my daughter-in-law and the mother of four whom we heard from early in this chapter, offers advice on how to prepare UMs for a long airline flight:

> I try to prepare the children both physically and emotionally. Together with them, I pack ample amounts of their favorite snack food and activities to see them through the journey. I also discuss the procedural aspects of traveling as an unaccompanied minor, so they know what to expect. If, during this discussion, they raise those "what if" issues, I focus on the responsibility of the uniformed airline attendant in charge of UMs so that they will be assured that they will not have to manage

on their own. Finally, I tell them that I am always available and that the airline attendant can contact me if necessary.

Most airlines require a completed Unaccompanied Minor Request for Carriage form, which remains with the child throughout his flight. The person escorting the child provides details, including the full name, address, and telephone number of the person who will meet the child at the destination airport. The person meeting the child must produce documentation identifying him as the person whose details were submitted at the departure point. (See "Resources" at the back of this book for additional information, including "Tips for Parents of Unaccompanied Minors.")

Ecaterina, a Romanian woman who came to live in South Florida with her husband and young daughter, describes her daughter's annual visits to Romania as an unaccompanied minor to spend the summer with her grandparents and other family members:

> When our daughter was ten years old, we sent her to spend the summer with her grandparents in Romania. She was not the least bit afraid. As a matter of fact, she was excited to be going by herself. There is a travel agent in Hallendale who arranges trips for Romanians. There are about five or six kids who are traveling alone, in addition to a few adults from our area who are unrelated to the children. The agent arranges to have them all on the same plane. Even though I don't usually know the adult travelers, the agent gives me their phone numbers so I can call them in advance and plan to meet them at the airport.

> We speak Romanian at home, so our daughter is fluent in the language. She spends two months with our families. The first time she went I couldn't sleep until I knew she was with my parents and my in-laws. When she arrived, in addition to our parents, there were many cousins and good friends who came to greet her at the airport.

> When she came home she told me she had so much fun hearing from her grandparents stories about when my husband and I were small.

In Romania she had much more freedom than she does at home. She seemed to mature a lot while she was there because she did many things on her own. Our daughter feels very special about traveling to Europe by herself every summer. She is very grateful to us for making this possible for her.

There are two factors that contribute to the success of these trips. The first is that the primary language in the child's home continues to be Romanian and that the daughter is totally comfortable in this language. Without this facility, these trips to be with her grandparents in their native country would have been impossible. The second is Ecaterina's encouragement and willingness to provide this exceptional opportunity for her daughter at the tender age of ten.

***

Clearly, some children are more confident about traveling alone than others. A child who flies several times a year is more likely to be comfortable on a plane than one who has never flown alone before. A twelve-year-old who has a fear of flying might find the thought of being alone on a flight for eight or more hours a daunting prospect. On the other hand, a seven-year-old who has never flown alone before might think of an overseas flight as a huge adventure.

Our grandson, Amichai, was the kind of child who viewed airline travel with a sense of great excitement. When he was seven, as his family was planning their annual trip to the United States, he announced that he would like to precede them alone by a week so he could have more time with his grandparents. He had always been a confident, assertive, independent, and articulate child, so his parents acceded to his request. One of his mother's many instructions to him was that if, at any point—day or night—during his week with us he got homesick and wanted to call home, he was to tell his grandmother.

Amichai made this trip at the end of August, when there are customarily many children traveling to visit family just prior to the beginning of the school year. He quickly got to know the other children and joined in their games and conversation. He arrived happy and smiling and full of details about the kids he'd met on the flight. We filled that first day with a shopping trip to buy him new sneakers, and a visit to the video store, followed by pizza for lunch and ice cream for dessert. He was exhausted at the end of the day and fell asleep before dinner. In the middle of the night, I heard the patter of light feet. I looked up to see Amichai's tear-streaked face. He was feeling homesick and wanted to call his mom. When he got on the phone, he talked very little about missing his parents, but mostly about all the things he'd seen and done since he left home. For the rest of the week, he was happy and content and did not have any additional bouts of homesickness.

During that week, my husband, who is a stickler for table manners, taught Amichai how to eat spaghetti by twirling it on a fork so that it balls up and fits neatly into your mouth rather than slurping it so that it spills back on your chin. When Amichai returned home, he had a friend over for a spaghetti lunch. The friend, who had not had the benefit of this instruction, was making a huge mess and Amichai told him, "If my grandfather was here, you would learn to eat spaghetti properly or you would have to leave the table!"

As grandparents, we have found that visits by one or two of the grandchildren at a time is a wonderful bonding experience. We get to know them and they get to know us in a way that is not possible if their parents are present. When they come alone, we give the grandchildren our full attention and are totally oriented to their needs and interests. This is also an opportunity for us to share our values and lifestyle. For these youngsters this a win/win situation. Traveling alone builds their confidence, and becoming intimate with grandparents builds another layer of love and security in their lives.

As Grandparents Age

As grandparents age and their energy level diminishes, they may find it increasingly difficult to keep up with the activities of small children and with visits in their homes of entire families. They also become more set in their ways, finding it difficult to adjust to the more casual lifestyles of younger generations. Janice, who lives in London, commented on the changes that have taken place in her life over the years:

> When our first granddaughter was a baby, our children would visit us for two weeks every year. I recall getting up with the baby at 6:30 in the morning and bringing her downstairs. I would sit on the floor and play with her happily for several hours. Now, fifteen years later, I no longer have the patience to do that with the younger children.
>
> Having them all in the house at one time is simply too much work. I'm not very good at delegating. When I'm exhausted, I just keep going, instead of suggesting that somebody else prepare dinner, for example. When they visit, it's one meal after the other and it's really tiring. In recent years, if we are expecting a visit from one or more families, we all plan to go away together to some vacation spot.

Differences in housekeeping standards and lifestyles also lead to conflict when families visit. Perhaps the lack of tidiness on the part of children and grandchildren stems from the fact that they are on vacation, so they feel they don't have to pick up after themselves. One grandfather complained about this, saying:

> When they visit, there is total chaos in the house. There are shoes and clothes and toys all over the place. I am both offended and saddened by their personal style. I don't know why they can't open the drawers we provide for them, put their things away, and live like normal people! What kind of examples are the parents setting for their children?

While in many ways this response is justified, it engenders anger and resentment and is destructive to a healthy ongoing relationship. There are a few possible solutions. One grandmother says that she has learned to ignore the mess during the visit. Instead, she just concentrates on having a good time with the grandchildren. When they leave, she spends a few days cleaning up and putting the house in order, and doesn't think about it again until the next visit. Another grandmother told me that she specifies the parameters of what's permitted in her home and what's not before they come. This makes the children more mindful of the mess, but it does not eliminate it completely.

***

Gary and Rhoda, grandparents in their mid-seventies, invited two of their grandsons, ages eight and thirteen, to visit them in South Florida. Above all else, the boys wanted to go to Disney World. This request presented a few problems for Gary and Rhoda. They felt that they weren't up to the trip physically—four hours of driving, followed by a great deal of walking. Gary tells us how he solved the problem.

> I explained to the children that we simply did not have the strength to sustain a trip to Disney World and perhaps this is something they could do on a future visit when their parents accompanied them. I also assured them that there were many interesting things to do as day trips that we were sure they would enjoy. With the help of the Internet and the local paper, I researched eight day trips I thought they would find of interest. The activities were both fun and educational and were within an hour's driving time from our home.

> The evening they arrived, sitting around our living room, each of the boys was handed a ballot that listed a brief description of each activity and a place to rank their interest with number one indicating the greatest interest. I kept the master ballot on which I totaled the boys' combined score. We had time for five trips, so we planned to do the five with the lowest combined rank. I then gave them a planning sheet with all the days of the week, so that together we could decide on a schedule with alternatives in case of bad weather. In addition to eliciting their participation in activities, they were given food menu options that were dutifully prepared for them by their grandmother.

Gary reports that even though the boys did not fulfill their fantasy of going to Disney World, they did have a lot of fun deciding how they would spend their time. Including them in the decision-making process gave them a sense of joint ownership of each activity.

Effect of Distance on the Grandparent/Grandchild Relationship

Despite the reality of living in a global world, most grandparents and many parents continue to harbor the fantasy of having their families close by, either within walking distance or a short drive away. Keyla, who moved from Venezuela with her young family, feels that the distance between her children and their grandmother has deprived the children of emotional sustenance that only a grandmother can provide. It is difficult for her mother to obtain a visa, so visits are infrequent. With sadness and regret, Keyla says:

> My kids are missing their grandmother's hugs and kisses and having someone always willing to read to them. They are also missing the family stories about my mother's childhood and my childhood. I remember my mother telling me about my grandmother, who grew up on a farm where she planted and harvested her own vegetables. Grandmothers are for giving kids what mothers don't have time for.

I was surprised to find that grandchildren who were born and raised an ocean apart from their extended family have a very different view. The absence of grandparents in their daily lives is the norm. They have never experienced anything different and have learned to maximize the time they spend together, developing truly meaningful relationships. Corbin McGregor, who grew up in Madagascar, is the seventeen-year-old daughter of missionaries Patricia and Todd McGregor. She says:

> I think the distance has made us closer. Because I don't see my grandparents very often, the times we have together are more meaningful. We seem to appreciate each other more. The experience is more intense and memorable. I am used to celebrating Christmas and marking milestones, such as graduations, without my grandparents, so it's okay.

My grandchildren welcome visits in their home, but prefer the travel experience. They look forward to the excitement and revitalization that comes with being in a new environment. Three of them shared the following with me:

Amichai (age fifteen): I like it best when I come to visit you. I like new places and new people because that makes life interesting. The thing I like best about visiting you is sitting around the dinner table and talking. You are always very interested in what I'm doing and thinking.

I don't wish you lived closer because then it wouldn't be as special seeing you. Now, because we see you about once a year, we look forward to it a lot. Because we talk on the phone often, I feel that I can speak freely with you and I don't think the fact that you are Americans and I'm Israeli is a problem. If I had something that was bothering me, I would talk to you as easily as I would to close friends.

I would like to come to Florida by myself more often, maybe for a month in the summer and maybe I could work and visit.

Binyamin (age nine): Would I like you to live closer? Well, that's a "maybe" answer. If you lived closer, occasionally we would do something fun together. But when you come from far away we do fun things together every day.

I like visiting with you in Boca better than when you come here. I like being in your house because you have nice furniture and a lot of the floor is carpeted. And most of all you have a real cool DVD player and a pool.

The last time I was in Florida, we went to Wannado City (an indoor role-playing theme park for children) and the attendant wouldn't let me go rock climbing because I was wearing sandals instead of sneakers and you said, "My grandson came seven thousand miles from Israel to do this. You have to let him go rock climbing!" And she let me do it. I was so happy, I won't ever forget it. I am so, so proud of having a grandmother who when she wants something, nothing can beat her. I would like to be like that, but I'm not yet. I shouldn't let everything beat me when at first it doesn't work.

Yakir (age seven): I think it would be good and also not so good if you lived closer. It would not be good because then we couldn't do fun things in Florida. It would be good because we could see you a lot of times. I miss you a lot of times, and even if I didn't miss you, I would still want to see you. I think about you a lot, especially when I hear that you are coming.

***

As the above testimonials indicate, it is entirely possible to develop significant and lasting bonds with grandparents who live thousands of miles away. Ethan and Sheila, both teenagers who were raised in the United States, had an exceptionally close relationship with their grandmother who lived in Belgium and visited them three times a year. She recently died of cancer. They share their memories and the lifelong lessons they learned from her.

Ethan (age seventeen): When we were small, every time my grandmother came to visit she would bring us several French children's books. My sister and I would go to her room in the morning and wake her up. We would crawl into bed with her and she would read to us in French from the books that she brought us as gifts. My mother spoke to us in French from the time we were small, so we could understand everything our grandmother said.

If she lived closer, maybe I wouldn't have appreciated her as much. She loved nature and liked to sit outside. I used to sit with her. Sometimes we talked about her childhood and about my childhood. She told me many things about my mother's childhood and the wonderful times they had with their uncles, aunts, and cousins. I liked those stories because it was interesting to hear about my family history. It gave me a past as well as a present.

My grandmother knew how to appreciate the little things in life, like the trees and the birds. When I saw her appreciating these things, I too began to listen more carefully to the birds and the little things in nature.

***

Sheila (age fourteen): When my grandmother came to visit I would go bike riding with her and to the beach. She had several gauzy cover-ups that she used at the beach. When we weren't at the beach, I would play "fashion show" with them. I still have those.

I once interviewed her for a school project and I learned about her experience during the war. She was hidden in a convent by herself without her mother or her siblings. She was treated nicely, but it was hard for her to be away from her family. I learned about the importance of family from her. She made a special effort to come to be with us often, even though she lived far away.

It was hard to see her when she was sick. There were so many things she couldn't do and she really couldn't eat very much. When I said good-bye to her five days before she died, I told her that I loved her and that I will always remember her.

I think about her whenever I pick up one of the French books she brought and read to us. I miss her most during the times of the year she would traditionally spend time with us.

Lessons from Life: Grandparenting at a Distance

- Satisfying and loving relationships are possible even at a distance. They do, however, take more thought and planning.

- Adult children and grandparents should share the responsibility of being proactive in keeping the grandparent/grandchild relationship alive between visits.

- Visits from faraway grandparents tend to be more intense and therefore more memorable than from grandparents who live close by.

- When visiting grandchildren, it is important to respect the lifestyle that their parents have chosen for them and to plan activities that fall within the parameters established by the parents. Acceptance and respect of this kind enhances the quality of the relationship and makes the grandparents more welcome visitors.

- Grandparents are the custodians of family history. Grandchildren who grow up far away from extended family rarely learn about their family's past. A conscious effort to include some aspect of the past should be made during every visit.

- Start planning activities via telephone and e-mail prior to a trip. This enables grandchildren to begin anticipating the visit. Try to set aside some time alone for each child during every visit.

- Gifts of time, whether it is something you do together or make together, are as important as material gifts. All gifts should be acknowledged by children in writing. This is a life skill that should be taught as soon as the youngster learns to write.

- Grandparents should end every phone conversation with grandchildren with some words of approval and love.

⚓ Language is the key to communication. If children are to have a meaningful relationship with grandparents from a foreign country, parents should make sure that children are taught the language their grandparents are most comfortable speaking.

⚓ Prospective unaccompanied minors might need some peer assurance. Ask an older sibling or a friend who is experienced in traveling to talk to the child who is about to do this for the first time.

⚓ Visits are precious and every effort should be made to make them as tension-free as possible. If grandchildren are very messy, simply look the other way and focus on enjoying the kids!

Chapter 3 Note

1. How-to books from Klutz come packaged with the tools of their trade and include a wide variety of projects from juggling cubes to face-paints to yo-yos. They are designed for doing and not just reading. Klutz products are available in toy stores, bookstores, and craft shops. A Klutz catalog is available free of charge and can be ordered from the Klutz website (www. klutz.com).

4

GETTING THROUGH THE ROUGH TIMES

The minute I heard that my father was in the hospital, I wanted to hop on a plane and fly to Venezuela.
—Rebecca, a Venezuelan woman living in the United States

Rebecca's pained words reflect a major concern among people who have moved thousands of miles away from home. Being unable to provide care or emotional support for an ailing loved one arouses feelings of guilt and helplessness. It is also difficult to assess the severity of an illness and determine what action, if any, should be taken when you receive doctor's reports secondhand from siblings or other relatives.

When word comes from afar that a loved one is ill, there is an immediate feeling of insurmountability—"I can't possibly deal with this!" However, once you have the opportunity to digest the information, to speak to family members and doctors about what action has been taken, what is planned for the future, and how you fit into the picture, the initial shock wave does wear off and some sense of relief sets in. The process usually involves the development of new family connections and the realization that "Together we can handle this."

In the last stages of life, people often lose the ability to communicate verbally. Increasingly, we maintain our ties with them through nonverbal communication—a smile, a touch, a hug, or a kiss. Because these nonverbal cues are unavailable across an ocean, our isolation and frustration may grow. If this is the case, you may wish to make the trip so that you can be there in person one last time.

In this chapter, you will hear how eight people learned of their crisis, how they coped with it, and how, through family ties, they were able to maintain their relationships with the stricken relative an ocean away. Various critical life situations are addressed through the poignant testimonials of families who have experienced these rough times:

- Coping with chronic illness from afar
- Sudden death
- Keeping vigil at a distance
- Family strength and unity in the face of life-threatening illness

The people whose stories are recounted in this chapter demonstrate that we can make a meaningful contribution to a family crisis, even at a distance. In the process, we affirm the power and value of family cohesion.

Coping with Chronic Illness from Afar

An illness that extends over a long period places a special burden on those family members who live far away. Frequent trips both impose a financial hardship and interfere with work and home commitments. In making decisions on when to visit, we must be sensitive to the needs of the person who is ill as well as to caregivers.

Difficulties notwithstanding, adult children involved in managing their own lives can rise to the challenge of providing care for ailing parents who live far away. Each of the three people who tell their stories here had specific concerns to tackle. Rebecca has a special-needs child whom she is reluctant to leave. Leah has four teenage children and became her grandmother's caregiver when her mother took ill. And, due to visa restrictions, Vicky could not travel back to her native country when her father had a stroke.

Rebecca was single when she left Venezuela to come to South Florida on a student visa. Shortly after she arrived, she met and married an American and decided to stay in the States. They have one child, a ten-year-old son who suffers from thoracic dystrophy and a compression of the spinal cord.

He lives at home with round-the-clock nursing care. Rebecca talks about the support her parents offered when her child was born:

> My mother and father came when our son was born. It was clear that
> he had special needs from the time of his birth. My mother stayed for
> four months to help me, but my father returned to Venezuela after a few
> weeks because he missed his own environment. My mother treated the
> baby with so much love and compassion. Her support was unconditional.
> When she left, I really felt lost.

Rebecca reciprocated this care and concern when her father became seriously ill five years later. She responded to the needs of her parents in Venezuela even though she had a major responsibility to her son at home:

> My sister called to tell me that my father had had a massive heart attack.
> My mother didn't want me to come immediately. He seemed fine when
> he came out of the intensive care unit. However, shortly after he was
> moved to a regular room he had a stroke. My mother called then and told
> me I should come.

> My son's condition seemed stable and he had the nurses with him all
> the time. Still, it was a nightmare for me to leave him. While I trust the
> nurses, I feel that I need to be there to oversee his care. But I knew I had
> to go, so I prepared his meals for a week and left for Venezuela.

> When I arrived at the hospital, I found that the stroke had left my father's
> left side paralyzed. Mentally he was intact and his speech was okay.
> When I saw him I thought, "Oh my God, this is all happening in a third
> world country! He needs intensive physical therapy." He did, in fact, get
> some therapy, but it was too late and very painful. In the end, he was
> bedridden.

> At that point I became very concerned about the strain on my mother of
> being his primary caregiver. She had to hire people to lift him into the
> wheelchair, bathe him, and take him to the toilet. This was really tough

for my mom, because there was no income following my father's illness. It was very hard for me to leave them. I had the fear that I would never see my father again.

When I came back to the States, I found out that my son had developed pneumonia and had to be hospitalized while I was away. My husband did not want to tell me on the phone while I was with my parents. But I figured out something was wrong because I kept calling during times that they were supposed to be home.

Despite her responsibilities at home, once every year, Rebecca left her son in the care of her husband and nurses and traveled to Venezuela to be with her parents. Because she felt that her mother also needed periodic respite from her caregiving duties, she twice paid from her own modest income for her mother's travel expenses to South Florida. It was during one of these visits that Rebecca received a call from her brother that her father had died:

When the call came, my mother almost fainted. She felt terrible and blamed herself for not being there when it happened. We were planning to take my mother to New York for Christmas to see a Broadway play. We had to cancel our plans and instead fly to Venezuela to make funeral arrangements. I stayed for four days. Following the funeral, I went back to our house and cleaned out my father's things. This was a big help to my mother. It would have been so hard for her to do this alone.

It is interesting to note that while there were two other siblings in Venezuela who could have provided the primary support for their parents, it was Rebecca, the one who lives at a distance, who coordinated their care. She speaks about this matter-of-factly, without any trace of anger or accusation because, as she says, "I was always the one who helped out the most." Now that her mother is widowed, Rebecca is attempting to secure the proper papers so that her mother can maintain a home in Venezuela and also spend six months of the year with her in South Florida.

***

Like Rebecca, Leah, a native of England who now lives in Israel, maintained close family ties during her mother's long battle with cancer. A mother of four teenagers, Leah holds a doctorate in classics and teaches part-time. We met in her active, sun-filled home in Bet Shemesh, Israel.

My mother was diagnosed with cancer before my husband and I decided to move to Israel. She was treated and seemed to be fine, so we never thought it would come back.

Four years later it did recur and it metastasized to her bones. She had surgery and continued to carry on as best she could. When I got my doctorate, she came for the ceremony in a wheelchair just three weeks after surgery. When she went into hospice, my husband and I went to England for four days, leaving our children with my in-laws, who live in Israel. During this visit we brought my grandmother back to live with us because without my mother to look out for her, she was all alone.

A few months later, my father called to tell us that my mother's condition had worsened. The whole family went to England, including my grandmother. We stayed for three weeks and were all there when she died. She was only fifty-six years old. I was at her beside and continued to talk to her, even though she could not respond. I said to her, "It's okay, you can go now." She died shortly thereafter.

Leah shared with me a Jewish ritual she had performed just prior to her mother's burial. It had very special meaning for her because it was part of a family tradition and it was another way to dignify her mother's death, as I recount in my book *Dignity Beyond Death:*

After my mother had been prepared for burial and dressed in white shrouds with her face covered, I was invited to sprinkle earth from Israel in her casket. I accepted the invitation because this was something my father did for his father and now I was being offered the opportunity to do it for my mother. I sprinkled the earth all around her shrouded body and finally on her head and on her heart. As I did this, the ladies of the burial society were kind and reassuring. Finally, I said my last good-bye and the lid was placed on the casket and sealed. A memorial candle was lit and we left.[1]

The sprinkling of the earth from Israel was a concrete connection with the Jewish homeland and an affirmation of the choice Leah made to live there. Her mother was initially buried in England, but two years later, she was reinterred in the cemetery in Bet Shemesh where Leah's father has purchased a family plot next to his wife. While the family was oceans apart during the later part of her mother's life, they will be reunited in death.

Leah reflected on the aftermath of her mother's death and the ways in which it has affected family ties:

> If there is one good thing that has come of all this, it is that my grandmother has a new lease on life in Israel. She has a great social life and does volunteer work in the local library. My children love having her with us.
>
> Before she came to live with us, I think my children were missing a certain depth of experience. Grandparents are the family historians. It's also important for young people to learn to appreciate someone who does not have the physical agility they do, but carries with them the wisdom of a lifetime. I think grandparents provide continuity and security.

***

Vicky, the pharmacist from Romania, talked about feeling uneasy and sensing that something was amiss with her family. She had troubling dreams that were undoubtedly a premonition of the bad news.

> When I left Romania, my father was in good health. But six months ago he suffered a stroke. At first they didn't want to tell me. He was hospitalized for five days and whenever I called during that time, there was nobody home, which was unusual. I had the feeling that something

wasn't right and I had bad dreams. Finally, when they brought him home, my sister called and told me what happened. She said he is okay, but that he doesn't speak anymore and uses a walker to get around. She also told me that there are many things he can't do, and that my mother needs to take care of him.

When I heard, I wanted to get on a plane and go back. If I did that, I couldn't reenter the United States again because I don't have the proper visa. So I didn't go. I was so upset that I took a few days of vacation from my job and called my sister every day.

While distressed about her father's condition, Vicky keeps in close touch with her family in Romania. This is a source of reassurance and comfort for both her and her family. When she talks to her father on the phone, she is mindful of the fact that he cannot respond with words but that he still has the ability to hear and to react emotionally.

When I call, my father recognizes my voice, but he can't speak clearly and he gets upset. I still continue to talk to him and to tell him about my life in the United States and all about my children. I also keep in close contact with my sister, who comes to visit them every Saturday. In the winter, when it's very cold, she takes my parents to her house. I would like to be there to help. Since I can't, I send them money every two months so that they can hire transportation to go to the doctor.

✝✝✝

Notwithstanding other problems in their lives, Rebecca, Leah and Vicky each marshaled their unique strengths and resources to meet the needs of their respective families living far away.

A Sudden Death in the Family

News of the sudden death of a family member tends to magnify the grief. There is little opportunity to prepare for the loss, to say a final good-bye, or to prepare for bereavement, as there is in anticipated deaths from long-term illness or disability. The distress is compounded by distance, especially if the person far away is alone.

Kim and Rajan are people we encountered in earlier chapters. Each of them tells about their response to hearing of the sudden death of a parent. Because communications with Malaysia were very limited forty years ago, Kim did not find out about her mother's death until three weeks after she had passed away. This led to a series of upsetting experiences, which she recounts here. Rajan's response to his father's death was considerably more pragmatic. His immediate concern was his widowed mother's well-being. In his account, we learn a great deal about the nature of his relationship with his father and the role that distance played in Rajan's growth and development.

Kim, the Malaysian woman who left the plantation to marry a Swiss engineer, recalls the trauma of receiving news of her mother's death. At that time, Kim was living with her in-laws in Switzerland while her husband was in England on a project. News of the death was preceded by an ominous dream, prompted most likely by Kim's knowledge that her mother had cancer, but her unwillingness to admit to herself just how severe the illness was. The experience is so indelibly inscribed in Kim's memory that she still remembers it in great detail, despite the passage of four decades.

> The night before I got the news of my mother's death, I had a dream about her. In the dream, I was about five years old and playing on the roadside. There was a truck passing by and my mother was on top of the truck. She was dressed in white with her hair down and blowing in the wind. She was holding a bundle of clothes and I couldn't make out her features. I looked up and called to her but she didn't turn to look at me and the truck kept moving. I began to run after it but I couldn't catch up to it and finally it disappeared into a tunnel.
>
> When I woke up, I was perspiring, as if I had actually been running. Since my husband wasn't there, I woke my mother-in-law and told her

about my dream and that I was scared. She was very kind and she came to my bed and slept next to me.

The following day, I was breast-feeding my infant son when my mother-in-law brought me the folded blue air-letter containing the news of my mother's death. The letter had traveled three weeks from Malaysia to Switzerland. It was written by my brother-in-law and contained only a few sentences. I still keep it in the top drawer of my desk. It said,

> *I am very sorry to inform you that our beloved mother has given us her last breath today. She has left us all behind. I am writing this letter with tears flowing and I cannot write any more. The funeral will take place at the Salem burial ground in accordance with the Chinese customs. That is all I can say. Please do not worry.*

I read the letter and immediately began to cry. I crumpled it in my hand because I could not bear to read this dreadful news. My breast milk stopped immediately. I knew that my mother had cancer, but she was a very tough lady and I thought she would never die. Because my son had recently been ill, I was unable to make the long trip to Malaysia. I don't think that I have ever recovered from this loss. When I told my husband about the death, I asked him to come to Switzerland and drive me and our son to England so that we could be together.

Adult children frequently call attention to the difficulties they face grieving for family members far away and alone. One theme involves the recognition that grieving is collective as well as individual, a family matter as well as a personal one. Distant children feel a special kind of loss and abandonment when their grief is postponed beyond the grief of their families because of distance, or when the grief is completely individual without the proximity and support of family and friends.[2] Kim describes her response to being unable to participate in the communal grieving in the absence of family and friends:

When we got to England, I was still very sad about my mother's death. My husband was at work all day and I was alone with the baby. Every afternoon I put the baby in his carriage and took a walk to the local cemetery. I spent about an hour there, strolling past the gravestones and looking at the sky. I continued to do this for four months until we moved to Scotland.

A few years after her mother's death, Kim went to visit her family in Malaysia. Her sister told her that on their mother's deathbed she had requested that she be dressed in white for burial, just as Kim had envisioned in her dream. The family accompanied Kim to her mother's gravesite, where she was very comforted to find that, in accordance with the Chinese custom, her name and her sister's name were engraved on the headstone just below her mother's name.

Kim's account reinforces the need for all of us to mourn. Ideally, this is done together with family who are similarly grieving. But even if an ocean apart and alone, the mourning process must still take place. For Kim, seeing her name inscribed on her mother's headstone was an affirmation that she continued to matter in the life of her family, even at a distance.

***

Rajan, the physicist from India who holds a faculty position at a major university in the United States, experienced the sudden death of his father shortly after his first child was born. In a pragmatic and realistic fashion, he discusses his decision to forgo his father's funeral and the culturally defined role of the eldest son, choosing instead to travel to India to be with his mother at a later date:

> My father's death at age seventy happened fairly quickly. He had blood clots on the brain that had slowly been getting worse. He did not take care of himself and when he had a car accident, he was gone in three days. My mother called me when the accident happened and I immediately called my brother, who flew from London to be with her.

He stayed for ten days and then I arrived, along with my wife and baby. I was on parenting leave at the time. This made it possible for us to be with my mother for a couple of months.

The funeral pyre should be lit by the eldest son. Since I was not there, my brother lit it in my absence. While I did not attend the funeral, I did accompany my mother when she took my father's ashes to be immersed in the Ganges River, a traditional Indian custom.

I was really okay with myself about not being there to light the first fire. When one lives halfway across the globe, this kind of thing is part of the cost of doing business. You can't have everything. My priority at that point was to maximize the time that somebody was there to help my mother.

As the eldest son, Rajan's bond with his father was complex. Although it was defined by love and respect, it also included a fair amount of ambivalence. Rajan's decision to remain in the United States after graduate school may have been colored by the fact that he needed to carve out his own space. His father's death "half a world away" became an opportunity for a life review that underscored the importance of distance in the relationship.

The tension between me and my father came about because he didn't know how to build a team. He was unable to see other people that clearly. I did many interesting things with him in his political life, but somehow he couldn't share it and he didn't know how to include me on his team.

Toward the end of his life, he really mismanaged his medical condition. I was very angry about that. My mother and brother were more shocked at his death than I was. Despite the distance, I was the one most aware of the deterioration in his health and I knew that the end was near.

In retrospect, my mother and I share a similar perspective on his death. For someone like my father, who lived life at 120 percent, it was best that he went while he was still in the saddle.

My father was a man of considerable ambitions and great accomplishments. My grandfather used to read to him from the poem "Footprints on the Sands of Time," which became my father's credo in life:

> *Lives of great men all remind us*
> *We can make our lives sublime*
> *And, departing leave behind us*
> *Footprints on the sands of time.*[3]

While many mourn the distance from family, Rajan realized that living abroad was important to his personal development. His father was a larger-than-life kind of person, who was a very dominant presence in his son's life. Living at such a distance helped Rajan mature. He says, "Because I was so far away, I was able to make my way in a place and in a field that was outside my father's realm. My success did not depend on his associations in India. That's a good feeling for me." In the end, Rajan paid appropriate respect to his father in death and was totally supportive of his mother during her period of mourning.

Keeping Vigil at a Distance

I spotted Renata's family as I was waiting for an appointment in a doctor's office. I noticed that the women were clad in traditional Muslim dress with face coverings that exposed only a narrow slit for their eyes. Although a little hesitant at first, I decided to approach them and told them that I was working on a book about people who were living oceans apart from their families. I was pleasantly surprised at their interest in and enthusiasm for the topic. Several days later, I met with them in their small, neat apartment.

Renata, whom we first heard from in Chapter 2, is a forty-five-year-old woman from Bangladesh. When her husband got a job in the United States nine years ago, she accompanied him, leaving behind parents and a large extended family. Renata told me that her father, who was ninety-two when he died, had been ill for a long time with a lung disease. She knew when she came to this country that she might never see him again:

> In our religion it is considered a blessing to be able to care for one's parents in their old age. I felt deprived of that blessing because I live so far away. That was very hurtful. In the last stages of his life, I was on the phone with my sisters many times a day.
>
> When I heard from my sisters that he was very ill I booked a ticket a month in advance of when I planned to travel so that I could take advantage of a cheaper airfare. As it turned out, I missed his death by only a few days. It is our custom to bury the deceased the same day, so by the time I arrived in Bangladesh he was already buried.
>
> As a woman, I would not have been permitted to be at the actual burial site. The emotion that women tend to exhibit at this time should not be seen by men, therefore the women must remain at a distance from the men.
>
> It is a custom to mourn for the dead for three days. However, the sadness reverberates for some time. Even though the official three days were over when I arrived, the family was still thinking about the death.
>
> My father was buried in the village in which he was born, about an hour away from the city where my family lives. A few days after I arrived, my brother took me, my sister, and my mother to the burial site. One of the most important things one can leave behind when one dies is a righteous child who will pray for the deceased. Prayer can take many forms. We can engage in ritual worship and we also can choose to perform acts of kindness toward the less fortunate. When I went to the village, I brought food and fed all the poor people who live there.

It is difficult to maintain culturally defined customs at a distance and in a foreign environment. Returning to one's country of origin enables the bereaved to perform these rites in their proper setting. Even though Renata was unable to fulfill all the filial obligations required by her tradition, the ritual of providing for the poor from her father's village was a way for her to reconnect with her religion and her family.

Family Strength and Unity
in the Face of Life-threatening Illness

Learning about the terminal illness of a loved one can throw a family into turmoil, especially if decisions for care must be made at a distance. This is a time to build on the strength of existing relationships and to reorganize roles, responsibilities, and expectations in order to reestablish stability. Personal and family growth opportunities are available if communications are honest and sincere, and if each family member is included as a significant partner in dealing with the crisis.

The stories of Hannah and Ben exemplify the vigor and courage that families muster in facing a crisis together. Especially noteworthy is the fact that their spouses and children were active participants in handling the crisis in their lives. Hannah had the financial resources to sustain frequent travel back and forth across the ocean, while Ben could afford far less. Still, he was mindful of keeping his wife and children involved, even though they were unable to travel to Australia to be with their extended family.

Hannah is a forty-six-year-old physician who was born in Belgium. She is married to an American physician whom she met while they were both studying at the same university in Israel. They now live in the United States with their two teenage children in a comfortable home whose focal point is a gallery of family photographs. She works with her husband in their joint medical practice.

Hannah is independent, energetic, and very good-humored. She has lived oceans apart from her family since she was seventeen. During this time she has experienced the sudden death of her father and, years later, the death of her mother following a long battle with cancer. She spoke about how her family members joined forces to respond to her father's unexpected death.

My father died shortly after I was married and at a time when both my brother and I were living in Israel. My father had gone from Belgium to Zaire, Africa on a business trip, where he had a stroke. When it became clear that he was not doing well, my mother asked us all to return from Israel to Belgium. When we arrived there, my husband and my uncle immediately flew to Zaire, while my brother and I stayed behind with my mother.

My father was unconscious and there was nothing that could be done. He died in Zaire and my husband and uncle accompanied the body back to Belgium for burial. The customs of the Belgian Jewish community did not allow women to attend an actual burial. I was not aware of this custom and was deeply traumatized by being excluded. This experience enabled me to be better prepared when my mother died fifteen years later.

Hannah had an exceptionally close bond with her mother. They enjoyed each other's company and did many things together—including shopping, bike riding, and taking long walks on the seashore. Her mother visited Hannah's family in the United States three times a year and was an integral part of their family life. Even though the distance created complexity, Hannah was determined to be personally involved in the care and management of her mother's illness:

My mother was diagnosed with stage IV colon cancer in Belgium. When she came to visit us, she brought us all her medical reports and x-rays. I felt it was important for me to establish contact with her primary physician in Belgium. Fortunately, there was no language barrier between us because we could both speak comfortably about her condition in French. We decided to have him manage all her care and to select an oncologist who would administer her chemotherapy. During this period, my brother and I took turns taking care of my mother, each of us traveling from our respective homes to be with her.

It was clear from our first discussion that she had a large mass that required surgery. I went back with her to Belgium for the surgery. My brother, who lives in Israel, joined us there. I stayed with her in her room during her hospitalization, while my brother took advantage of the hospital's nearby accommodations for family.

When she came home, my children were on school vacation, so my husband brought them to Belgium and we all stayed in my mother's apartment. She recovered nicely from the surgery and she still looked like herself. The visit was really good for her and for us. Every day our son would take his grandmother down to the courtyard for a little walk. I returned to the United States after a month and caught up with my work and my household chores.

Watching their mother and grandmother suffer was difficult for the entire family. But the burden was eased because everyone felt they were part of this heroic effort. Unlike previous generations, when bad news was rarely discussed, Hannah and her husband were very open with the children about the severity of their grandmother's illness. Every time Hannah went to Belgium, she would inform the children's school principal, so that he would be prepared for any unusual behavior on the part of the children.

Hannah talked about her mother's death and burial:

Her last visit with us was in the summer when we had planned a family cruise. However, she was too weak to travel, so we canceled the trip. She died in Belgium the following spring, right after we had all marked Passover together. Each of the children had an opportunity to be alone with my mother at the end so that they could say goodbye.

Having learned from her father's burial about the prohibition against the attendance of women, Hannah prepared a separate ceremony for her aunts and her female cousins. When the men left the burial site, the women arrived. Hannah spoke about her mother, recited passages from Psalms, and concluded with *kaddish,* the traditional prayer of mourning. Along with her brother, she observed *shiva*, the week of mourning, in her mother's apartment, where they were surrounded by extended family. Finally, Hannah reflected on the courageous and selfless role her family played during this ordeal and how the experience strengthened them as a family unit:

> During the period of my mother's illness, I must have been back and forth to Belgium about twenty times. It was expensive, but we made it a priority and, thank God, we could afford it. Without complaint, my husband shouldered all my responsibilities while I was away. He shopped, he cooked, he took the kids to their sports activities and to their music lessons. In addition, of course, he tended to our medical practice. It was exhausting! However, there was never any question that he would do what he did. It has given all of us a greater appreciation of one another. It was a blessing that we were able to do this as a family.

***

Ben, an Australian in his fifties, moved to Israel with his family about a decade ago. He and his American wife, have five children. Theirs is a close-knit family, all of whom care very deeply about their extended family in Australia. Financial and time constraints do not permit them to travel as frequently as they would like. Ben speaks about the challenges he faced during his mother's illness and death. He points with pride to his efforts to bridge the gap of distance for his nuclear family living so far away:

> Several months before my mother's death, my brother called to tell me that she was really not doing well and I should come as quickly as possible. When I arrived, she was, indeed, in very poor condition. She knew I was there, but she couldn't see me because her eyesight was almost completely gone. I spent most of the time in the hospital, happy to be able to relieve my brother. In a few days, she rallied once again and I returned home.

> Three months later, my brother called me to say that the doctors were not optimistic. She died that night. It is customary for Jews to be buried as soon after death as possible, but my mother left instructions with my aunt that when she died the funeral should not take place until I arrived.

Ben attended the funeral and observed the week of mourning with his family in Australia. It was a comfort to be with them, but at the same time, it was very difficult for him to be away from his wife and children who also mourned his mother. Ben's wife, sensing his need as well as her own to be part of this family gathering, sent an e-mail message to be read to the mourners:

> It is so hard to be so far away at a time like this, when all I want to do is be there with you and for you. I will try to put into words some thoughts and feelings to share with you. I feel privileged to have been her daughter-in-law. What a wonderful relationship we had—as close as mother and daughter. I never understood friends who complained about their mothers-in-law. Frieda was unique. She welcomed me into the family with open arms!
>
> Her home was always open to all. She was a terrific hostess and never let anyone go hungry or thirsty. A cup of tea was offered within minutes of arriving. And, of course, there was always something to nibble on!
>
> All we can do is cherish the memories we have. I learned so much from this wonderful lady.

Ben and his family had previously lived in Australia, so his wife and children knew many of the people who made condolence calls. He therefore kept a little notebook at his side and recorded the names of the people who came and any significant comments they made. He also wrote down the names of friends who called from their community in Israel. Each day, when he spoke on the phone, he shared this information with his wife and children.

Since friends and neighbors from Israel could not be with him, Ben planned a memorial service for them thirty days after his mother's death.[4] He shares his motives for doing this:

> I wanted to do this primarily for my wife and children. I wanted them to be able to grieve with the community. About eighty people gathered to

hear me, my wife, and my children share our memories. This bridged the gap and in some way made up for the fact that my family could not be at the actual funeral and burial.

When I asked Ben if he had any advice or tips for others in his life situation, he offered this testimonial:

> Make every effort to keep in touch. We are not a rich family. We live in a modest house, we don't own a car, but we have made it a priority in our lives to keep in touch with our family abroad. And we have reaped the benefits of that effort. We do not have many material possessions, but we are blessed with a wonderful and loving family. My parents, both Holocaust survivors, were role models for the significance of survival and for preserving these special relationships.

> I hope that we have shown our children the importance of kinship so that they will build it into their own lives as they mature and create their own families.

Gail Sheehy said in her best-selling book, *Passages,* "It is a paradox that as death becomes personalized, a life force becomes energized. In the very jaws of this danger is opportunity."[5] Families living halfway around the world from loved ones who become ill and die have demonstrated that they can cope with the emotional and social adjustment of this life-cycle transition. They are even able to realize that the transition carries with it the potential for growth and development.[6]

Lessons from Life: Getting Through Rough Times

- When parents who are at a distance become ill, establish your own relationships with their doctors and caregivers, so you don't have to rely on secondhand information from siblings or other relatives whose reports might be colored by emotion.

- If you are unable to travel to see your family, due to visa, financial, or time constraints, establish a schedule of phone calls with the person who is ill (if they can still speak on the phone), the person's spouse, siblings, and other caregivers. Each of these people will have a different perspective on what's happening and each will welcome your interest and support.

- In advance of a crisis, develop some guidelines for how responsibility will be shared among siblings and other family members in the event of an emergency or a long-term chronic condition. This discussion might be hard to initiate, but it will provide you and the others with a sense of relief and the security that no one has to shoulder the burden alone.

- Insist that your oceans apart family be open and honest with you. Even when information about illness is withheld by protective, well-intentioned family members, you will probably sense that something is wrong. If you decide to visit, having the information in a timely fashion is critical.

- Plan to have a final conversation with your terminally ill loved one while he or she can still speak. We all imagine doing this in person at the bedside of the dying person, yet it can be done at a distance, either on the phone or in a letter. This is a time to set aside lifelong hurts; to reinforce how much the dying person has meant to you; to say you love him or her; and to say "good-bye."

- If your loved one can no longer communicate verbally, you may wish to make periodic trips. It may be wise to accumulate the financial reserves in advance for this purpose. Involve your family in these plans so they will be prepared to cope without you during your visit, which might end up being protracted.

- Every religion and culture has its own rituals with regard to death. Participating in these at the time of the passing of a loved one provides a strong tie to family and historical roots.

- Discuss with siblings the support that will be needed for the widowed spouse. Carve out a role that you can comfortably fulfill at a distance.

- When the going gets rough, make every effort for your entire family to play some role in responding to the crisis. Do not exclude children. Share with them as much as you think they can understand.

- It's possible to be an important part of the support system, even at a distance. Feel positive about what you can do, rather than guilty about what you can't do.

- A shared crisis, even at a distance, strengthens each individual involved, as well as the family as a whole.

Chapter 4 Notes

1.   Rochel U. Berman, *Dignity Beyond Death* (Jerusalem: Urim Publications, 2005), p. 120.
2.   Jacob Climo, *Distant Parents* (New Brunswick, N.J.: Rutgers University Press, 1992), p. 214.
3.   Henry Wadsworth Longfellow, 1807–1882.
4.   This custom, known as *Sheloshim,* is the Hebrew word for the number *thirty.* The thirty-day period constitutes the full mourning for all relatives other than a father and a mother.
5.   Gail Sheehy, *Passages* (New York: P. Dutton, 1974), p. 246.

6. Froma Walsh & Monica McGoldrick, *Living Beyond Loss: Death in the Family* (New York: W.W. Norton & Company, 1991).

5

MAINTAINING TIES
WITH THE REST OF THE FAMILY

Distant Sisters and Brothers

Of all family relationships, we are likely to share a connection with our siblings for more years than with any other relative. Our shared history includes a lifetime of stories and memories that become more meaningful and luminous as we age. Siblings represent our first testing ground for social activities. They are our playmates, our mentors, our advisors and often our worst rivals.

With the advent of adulthood, siblings generally go their own way and there may be a period of little contact and emotional connection. A need to re-establish this tie usually comes somewhere during our middle years, often prompted by significant life-events within the family such as marriage, divorce, births or illness and death of a parent. At this point in the life cycle, conflict and rivalries are usually set aside in favor of increased communication. Those we hear from in this section are at this stage of their lives.

Geographic distance can create a barrier to reconnecting to distant brothers and sisters, even when there is a will to do so. Maintaining contact is facilitated by the emergence of a catalyst within the family who assumes the responsibility of rekindling and maintaining contact. It is usually the eldest sibling in the family or the one who has moved away and has the greatest need to share lifestyle changes as well as to reconnect with the past.

Staying Connected Between Visits

Telephone calls and e-mail messages are the primary means of communication today. E-mail is generally used for day-to-day contacts, with the phone reserved for special occasions like birthdays, anniversaries, and holiday greetings.

For siblings who have lived apart for many years, certain rituals become symbolic of the ties that bind, and there is great disappointment when the ritual is not fulfilled. One person who has lived an ocean apart from his brother for more than two decades says, "In our family there is not a lot of gift-giving. The way in which you show you care is to call on a milestone. My brother and I always speak to each other on birthdays. Sometimes I am a day late in getting in touch with him on his birthday. When this happens, I feel that I have let him down and also let myself down. I can never recall his missing my birthday. If he ever forgot, it would really bother me."

Sharing details of a new lifestyle is also an important link among those living in different cultures. Rashida who moved from India to the United States, e-mails her two sisters daily—one lives in India, the other in Dubai. She is the focal point of communication in her family because she generally takes the initiative. At the time of our interview, Rashida was pregnant and her friends were preparing a baby shower in her honor. Since this is a custom unknown to her sisters, they were eager for details and each report from Rashida generated requests for more clarification and more contact.

***

Naomi, a research psychologist living in the United States, has recently begun to collaborate professionally with her younger sister, a certified sex therapist, who lives abroad. As they were growing up, Naomi often felt that her "little" sister was invading her space. Now, in their middle years, their relationship is one of mutual respect and appreciation. Naomi says:

I would not have thought that I needed someone with my sister's expertise on my current project. But from just talking to her, I came to realize that she is a fount of very valuable insights and information. I trusted what she said more because of our biological and historical connection. Because we are sisters, I could be far more candid with her than with someone with whom I did not have this connection. It has provided a depth to our work that would not be there otherwise.

We communicate mostly by e-mail and occasionally on the phone. Because we are collaborating, we try to be at the same conferences so that we can see each other at these events. In recent years, we have worked together on professional studies, written papers, and presented at conferences. My sister is a good collaborator and I really enjoy working with her.

The discovery of an adult sibling with distinctive skills has enhanced Naomi's personal and professional lives. The distance notwithstanding, it has added depth and meaning to their relationship.

***

Large families tend to be dependent on one person taking the initiative to keep people in touch. We hear about Monique and Sophia, each of whom has assumed this role in their respective families.

Monique, who lives in the United States, is one of twelve siblings in a Jamaican family. The family is now scattered, some still living in Jamaica, others in the United States, Canada, and Great Britain. She has established a "round robin" telephone system for keeping the family in touch. Every Sunday a different sibling takes responsibility for calling all the other siblings. The person making the calls accumulates information about others and shares it as she moves along her phone list.

Sophia, a physicist, is the eldest of seven Italian siblings and the only one who left home to pursue an academic career in the United States. Every weekend she calls the sister who lives in their parents' home. She offers the following rationale for selecting this particular sister as her main contact:

> When my sister was married, she continued to live in my parents' home. She is a medical doctor and took care of my parents as they became elderly and frail. Calling her is like an extension of the customary phone calls to my parents when they were alive. I feel like I am calling "home."

> I initiate all the contacts. When I talk to my sister, she tells me first about her immediate family and then keeps me informed about each one of our other siblings and their families. We also talk about the friends and relatives who still live in the small town in which we grew up. Every week, my sister then shares this information with our other siblings.

***

A shared commitment to a religious belief is especially binding for siblings who live at a distance. Betsy, who is the elder sister of Rev. Patricia McGregor, reflected on the evolution of her relationship with her sister, who does missionary work in Madagascar:

> When Patsy got married, she knew that Todd had a special calling in his life and she felt called to follow him. When they said that they were going to go off and be missionaries, I didn't even know what missionaries do.

> When they left, I felt bad. But I thought that it would be something they would do for a while and then come back. I did not think it would be long term. Now I'm much more at peace with it because I know how much good they are doing and how much of a difference they are making in people's lives. And also my own spirituality is at a different level so I am able to understand their commitment on a much deeper plane. I know they are in God's hands.

Betsy and Patsy's ability to communicate, as well as the content of their communication, has changed over the seventeen years that Patsy has been in Africa. At the beginning it was very difficult. There was no Internet and it was very expensive to call. One could never be sure that letters would be received. Skype and e-mail have enabled them to be in touch about twice a week. Betsy says:

> We talk about anything that's in our hearts, mostly about what God is teaching us. Patsy and I tend to talk about deeper issues and deeper relationships. We rarely talk about simple facts and do talk more about feelings. This has been a function of the growth in our faith.

Visiting Distant Siblings

The frequency of visits among siblings is predicated on financial issues. For families separated by vast distances, visits to siblings occur once a year or less often, unless there are opportunities to include them in work-related trips. Even if face-to-face contact is limited, it does not necessarily affect the emotional aspects of the bond.

Visits among distant siblings occur more naturally and more frequently when the sibling who has moved away goes "back home" to the place the family lived as they were growing up. We hear from two people for whom this has had lifelong meaning.

Beatrice, an artist married to an American, visits her three older siblings once or twice a year in the small town in Switzerland where she was born and raised. She reflects on the family dynamics as they were growing up and her role as the catalyst in the years since her parents have died.

> We were a very close family, who relied on each other. We were taught to love and respect nature. Hiking was a very prominent activity, one that taught us to tread lightly on the world. The sense of feeling comfortable and wonderful outdoors unites us to this day as a family.

When my parents were alive, their home was like Grand Central Station. They were the source of both incoming and outgoing information. I have since taken over that role because it's my way of staying connected despite the distance. Perhaps if I lived in Switzerland, I would get totally absorbed in other things. But since I am so far away I am absolutely on task to keep the relationships and connections intact and current.

My father predeceased my mother, and when she died I experienced a tremendous crisis of identity. Following her funeral, I asked my siblings to take off several days so we could go hiking together because I knew that this would be a uniting and bonding experience that would bring us comfort. I asked that they not bring their partners or their children so that the four of us could be alone to mourn together.

My brother called it Mother's Memorial March. During the two-day hike in a very remote part of Switzerland, we laughed a lot and cried a lot. We shared a number of childhood memories and found out, to everybody's surprise, that each of us had a different perception of what transpired during any given event.

This family hike was so meaningful that the siblings decided to do this periodically. Since their mother grew up in Berlin, Beatrice suggested that a future trip should be to that city, where they could walk in their mother's footsteps.

Like Beatrice, Kim, whom we heard from in Chapter 4, maintained contact with her Malaysian family following her parents' death. She describes the mutual support during visits to the plantation with her sister, brother-in law, and their nine children.

I was pregnant with my second child when I went to visit my sister and her family in Malaysia. I was supposed to stay just a month, but my husband got a six-month assignment in Australia so I decided to remain and have the baby in Malaysia. My husband was there for the birth of our daughter, but then took off for his assignment.

We all lived together in the huge plantation house, which had support staff for cleaning and maintenance. My brother-in-law, who managed the plantation after my father's death, was very kind to me and my children, and made sure that we were the first to be fed at mealtimes.

It is the Chinese custom that a woman who has given birth does not lift a finger other than breast-feed her baby for one month. I stayed in bed for thirty days, during which time my sister brought my meals to me and took care of my son. When the month passed, I helped my sister with the gardening and the cooking. There was a wonderful feeling of togetherness as we all gathered around a big table at mealtimes.

Sadly, several years later, my brother-in-law, who was the sole provider for his large family, died suddenly at the age of forty-eight. When I got the news, I booked the next flight to Malaysia. My husband was away on an assignment, so I dropped my children off with my in-laws in Switzerland en route to Malaysia.

I took care of my sister and the children. It became necessary for them to give up living on the plantation because my brother-in-law was no longer the manager. I moved them into the city in a house I bought together with them. I painted it and bought furniture with money my husband and my in-laws gave me.

Because it takes thirty hours to travel to Malaysia, Kim manages to see her family only once every few years. However, she continues to provide support for them and has helped to educate her nieces and nephews, all of whom have college degrees. She expresses her continuing emotional attachment when she says, "My Malaysian family is always with me."

***

Connecting with a distant sibling without the emotional draw of "going home" requires considerably more commitment, thought, and planning. Jeb, who is in his early forties and lives in New York, had not had significant contact with his older brother, Jason, in about twenty-five years, except for a few hours during Jason's brief visits from Israel to the United States. With their parents' retirement and move to Florida, there was no longer a central meeting place in New York. Jeb reflects on how much his relationship with Jason has changed over the years, culminating recently in a three-day retreat centered about a mutual interest:

> My brother and I attended the same religious day school. He left for Israel when he graduated at age eighteen. I was then fifteen. His departure had some very positive effects for me. It was not so much a relief, but an opening of space. I felt I no longer had to follow in his footsteps. It also meant that those around me would no longer make assumptions about me.

> While Jason was in Israel and then in college, we lived in two different worlds and had very little contact. I don't recall writing to him and only spoke to him on the phone at the tail end of my parents' conversations if I happened to be at home.

> With the passage of time, we have both matured and I find with each visit in recent years, we have started to reconnect. From my perspective, I am finding Jason less and less judgmental. I think he is more comfortable in his own skin and I think I have grown more spiritual. I enjoy talking to him about my spiritual awakening. Our conversations are much more substantive than they used to be.

Recently, Jeb established some life goals, which included attempting to bridge the emotional distance between himself and his brother. This coincided with each of them becoming interested in recreational diving. Jason extended an invitation to Jeb to join him for a few days of diving in Eilat at the southern tip of Israel. Jeb's thoughts and response follow:

> I have to give Jason credit for having extended the invitation to me to join him in Eilat. In the first moment that he asked me, I immediately began to give voice to reasons why I couldn't do it—"I'm busy," "I have clients

to see," etc. But, after thinking about it, I decided that I should accept because this is exactly what I want to be doing with my personal life—building meaningful relationships. In making my plans, I was encouraged by my wife. At one point, when I thought I would cancel the trip due to business commitments, she insisted that I schedule my work around the planned visit with my brother, rather than the other way around.

It's not surprising that both Jason and I have become passionate about diving. For me it is an extension of my love of nature, which was inspired by the family hiking we did when we were younger. I don't view as circumstantial that my brother found his way to the same place; we are, after all, cut from the same cloth.

In talking to Jason about his attitude toward diving, I discovered that we have the same approach. We both dive slowly, observationally, and reverentially. Diving is by its nature somewhat isolating. Because you have an air hose in your mouth, there is an assumed silence. Yet, there is nonverbal communication which is important.

You dive with a buddy, and at the beginning of every dive there is a body check. Jason and I did it for each other. The series of things that you check are critical functions that ensure that your buddy will stay alive underwater. Doing this with my brother was different than doing it with a stranger. I was mindful of the fact that in checking his hose, I'm making sure that my brother can breathe under water.

The checking procedure involves a great deal of physical contact. I became aware that we have not had this kind of physical contact since we were in elementary school. It made me think back to the time we shared a room as kids. On this trip, for the first time in about thirty years, we once again shared a room. It gave me a sense of comfort and security, just as it did when we were so much younger.

In advance of the trip, Jeb had suggested that they spend some time while they were together exploring topics of mutual interest. Since studying the biblical texts is a skill they both honed in the religious day school they attended, Jeb thought that this would be an opportunity for them to utilize those skills. In the evening, after diving and before dinner, they spent an hour studying various texts over cocktails. It afforded them an hour of relaxed contemplation. Jeb said, "It was pleasurable and I was delighted to participate in some intellectual interaction with my brother."

Jeb summed up his feelings about the trip by talking about how appreciative he was that his brother not only took the initiative to make this experience possible, he also made all the arrangements with Jeb's interests and comfort in mind. Jeb poignantly comments, "What I like best is that I've repaired my relationship with him. It's a great sense of accomplishment in my life. I see it as a work in progress with some challenges still to be met."

Effect of Distance on Sibling Relationships

Positive childhood experiences and shared history go a long way toward sustaining distant sibling relationships, even when visits are infrequent. One person gave this testimonial: "No matter how long we haven't seen each other, when we do, it just clicks back in. It is quite remarkable! I think this happens because we grew up sharing the same values and traditions. When we talk on the phone, it's just like being together—there is no distance. There is a depth of understanding that provides me with a form of communication that I don't have with anybody else. I like having a brother."

People have offered a range of responses regarding the effect of distance on sibling relationships. For Toby, who came to live in the United States from Australia, there is regret. She says, "My sister and I are very different and we don't know each other very well as adults. I think the distance has prevented us from becoming closer. This makes me sad."

Toby shared with me the fact that family trips to Australia are understandably hectic, leaving little time for a one-on-one visit with her sister. From the experiences of others, it is clear that unless this becomes a priority and a block of time is set aside, important relationships do not receive the attention they need to become more meaningful.

Earlier in this chapter we heard from Naomi, who discovered the joys of sisterhood during her adult years, only after her sister moved abroad. She now longingly expresses a desire to spend more time with her sister.

> I really wish we could see each other more often. She is a pleasure to be around. She is honest, she is smart and capable, and she is good company. I look forward to spending time with her.
>
> When I go to Israel, I don't schedule very much else because I just want to be with her. Living in Israel is hard and I know she has a lot of burdens. But she manages her life well and she is someone I truly admire. I would love to have her presence in my life more often.

Ben, who moved from Australia, experienced both guilt and gratitude about his brother's role in caring for their mother in Australia when she was dying. In Chapter 4, we heard about how Ben dealt with the death and the funeral. Here he expresses profound gratitude to his older brother for his efforts during this trying time:

> Whenever I spoke to my brother and heard that my mother was not well, I'd feel guilty. Over the many years that my mother was not well, my brother shouldered the entire burden. In six years, my mother was hospitalized fifty times. My brother had to deal with that himself. In addition, he had to deal with his own family and his own work. Whenever I talked to him, although he didn't complain, I could hear how stressed he was. And then I would ask myself, "What am I doing here?" I felt so guilty. When everyone in my house went to sleep, I would sit on the couch and cry. My mother was very accepting of the fact that I couldn't do much because I was so far away. Not once did she say that she wanted us to come back to Australia.

I often had long discussions about this with my brother. And he said to me, "Look, guilt is a wasted emotion. The situation could easily have been the other way around, with you here and me in Israel." Yet I could hear how overburdened he was. He came every morning to feed her breakfast, he monitored her medication, and he spoke daily—sometimes many times a day—to the doctors and the nurses. He was such a devoted son and brother. He assured me that everything I did was helpful, even if it was just a phone call. He was spectacular!

Finally, we hear from Beatrice, who feels that the distance has brought her closer to her siblings and has enabled her to be more accepting of their partners. She says,

I am the only one who is so far away and as a result I have become the vehicle for reuniting the family. When I come to Switzerland, the whole family comes together.

After the death of Beatrice's parents, her brother and sister-in-law moved into their childhood home. Her sister-in-law immediately remodeled everything. Beatrice felt terrible because the house had been designed by a famous architect and she thought at the time that she would never be able to go home. However, she has learned over the years that she must let go of things over which she has no control, especially since she no longer lives there. She comments reflectively, "Instead of concentrating on material things, like the décor of my parents' house, I've come to appreciate my sister-in-law as a person who is warm, kind, and considerate."

Lessons from Life: Distant Sisters and Brothers

- Distance often makes siblings appreciate each other more. It tends to make coming together a very special experience.

- It is important for at least one sibling to take the initiative to bring the family together.

- Be sensitive to your sibling's reaching out to you. Try not to reject an extended hand.

- In planning a visit, set aside a block of time to reconnect with each of your siblings.

- Siblings planning a reunion following a long separation should be prepared to temper excitement with the knowledge and expectation that unresolved sensitivities and hurts from the past may arise. These should be dealt with or set aside and should not leave siblings feeling that the visit was a letdown.

- When visiting, if possible, try to do something outside of your sibling's home environment.

- If a long time has passed between visits, build in structure in advance that will ease the burden of just engaging in casual conversation.

- If you have developed newfound respect and admiration for your sibling, be sure to share these thoughts.

- Make an effort to establish good relationships with your siblings' partners.

- If time permits when visiting, try to get to know the people who populate your sibling's current life. It will be a point of connection going forward.

♨ On an ongoing basis, be sure to communicate if there is a family problem.

Distant Nieces, Nephews, and Cousins

Whenever our son, Josh, and his family came from Israel to visit us in Westchester, our younger son, Jonathan, would join us for the weekend. He saw his nephew only once a year and had no contact with him in between. Therefore, he tried to do meaningful things with him when they visited so that they would bond. Jonathan shares two recollections of the time he spent with his oldest nephew, Amichai:

> One morning when he was four years old, I sat at the kitchen table reading the *New York Times*. Amichai was peering over my shoulder and gazing at the paper. I decided to include him in looking at the paper with me. We examined pictures from different parts of the world and I told him in terms he could understand why these pictures appeared in the paper. We then went to the atlas, and found each of the places we read about on the map.
>
> Next, we went to the globe of the world, which had been gathering dust in our library for more than a decade, and traced the distance of each of these places in relation to Israel. The following day, I asked Amichai where each of the places we talked about the previous day was located.

This interaction, which is fondly remembered by all the members of our family, is very much in the mode of my husband's theory of how to best relate to children: "You need to find the adult in each child." And what four-year-old wouldn't feel good about having been included in such an exciting adult activity—one that made him feel like a world traveler! Jonathan recalls another visit:

> When Amichai was five, I taught him to ride a bike. We actually planned this in advance because I knew he was getting a bike. We had borrowed a bike with training wheels. I said to him, "I think you can probably ride

this without the training wheels." He agreed to try it. As we walked to a quiet, flat street without traffic, I talked to him about what we were going to do. I told him that part of succeeding is failing and that he would fall several times. And, sure enough, he did fall, but he took it all in stride. He did learn to ride that afternoon.

Perhaps as important as teaching his nephew how to ride, Jonathan taught him another critical life lesson—that we all experience failures in pursuing the road to success.

For Jonathan and Amichai, there were no language barriers as a result of the distance: Both are fluent in English and Hebrew. This was not the case for Ingrid's American-born children when they went back to their mother's native Sweden to visit their uncles, aunts, and cousins. Ingrid describes visits that took place over the years:

At first my children could not speak to their cousins because my nieces and nephews had not yet learned English in school. Even though they didn't share a common language, they had a lot of fun together. The Swedish cousins would bring out toys and my children would immediately join in playing with them. They didn't seem to need to speak. They interacted through the toys. Lego blocks served as a very good vehicle for them to communicate. When they finished playing, they came and told their parents what they had done. The adults had great satisfaction watching them because they got along so well.

When the children visited as teenagers, their Swedish cousins had already learned English in school and they were able to communicate verbally. They shared stories about their different lifestyles and talked about what their parents allowed them to do and didn't allow them to do. In addition, much of the music they listen to and the movies they watch are the same, so this served as another common bond.

Ingrid feels that her strong bond with her Swedish family has been transmitted to her children. As adults, her children have traveled on their own to Sweden to study and visit with family. Over the years they have developed a connection with the culture and the country.

Sophia, the physicist we heard from earlier in this chapter, took a proactive stance on language issues so that her American-born children and their Italian cousins could communicate. She spoke to her children in Italian from the time they were born so that they were comfortable when they spent summers in Italy. In addition, she arranged for her nieces and nephews to come to the United States for extended periods so that they could take courses in English. As a result, the cousins are all able to communicate and have developed a strong family bond. Sophia describes the impact of her deliberate and purposeful actions:

> Had I not taken the initiative to have my nieces and nephews come here to learn English, I probably would not have continued to be close to them. Also, my children's lives would have been bereft of the wonderful bond they have developed with their cousins. They recognize that I have taken this initiative and as a result I am much more part of their lives than I would have been had I not been so proactive.
>
> I feel that I have really impacted their lives significantly. One of my sisters-in-law, who is not a particularly warm person, told me that she feels that she really owes me a lot because her children are what they are now because of the wonderful exposure they have had during their visits to the United States. One of my nephews was able to get an excellent job in Copenhagen because he was fluent in English which he, of course, learned while visiting me.

By bringing her nieces and nephews to the United States, Sophia broadened their horizons in a way that makes them feel comfortable about other travel elsewhere in the world. In all, it has expanded their lives and cemented relationships within the family.

Lessons from Life: Distant Nieces, Nephews, and Cousins

- Nieces and nephews who have moved abroad with their parents lack the input of extended family members who can serve as other adult role models in their lives. A caring uncle or aunt can fulfill that function.

- Teaching a life skill, such as riding a bike or swimming, to a distant niece or nephew is a significant bonding experience. The same is true about sharing a hobby or interest.

- Fostering a common language enables cousins from foreign countries to communicate and develop lasting relationships with one another.

Distant Husbands and Wives

Married couples who live apart due to career choices, professional commitments, or the educational needs of children lead lifestyles that vary from the norm. Greater accessibility of worldwide air travel, plus phone, e-mail, and other telecommunications, make contact much easier to maintain under these circumstances. While increased globalization is producing family models that may be different, they still have the potential for healthy functioning. New models require new road maps.

As an emerging trend, these models are not well understood. Well-intentioned family and friends might tell you that "This is no way to live" and that your relationship is in danger if you continue. It will be your task to educate them that it is, in fact, working for you. Regardless of what people tell you, studies show that long-distance relationships are as stable as others, with similar survival rates.

On June 8, 2008 *The New York Times* reported on a trend in which South Korean husbands and wives live apart for the sake of their children's education. Driven by their dissatisfaction with the rigidity of the South Korean schools, mothers are moving with their children to Auckland, New Zealand, where the educational system is more wide-ranging and includes teaching English, considered a critical skill in the global economy.

Living apart does strain families, with some spouses having extramarital affairs and some marriages ending in divorce. Kim, the Malaysian woman who married the Swiss engineer who traveled extensively, divorced him following a long separation. Others, however, claim that their marriages have benefited from the separation and have grown stronger despite the four- or five-year separation. One couple confessed that every reunion that took place about three times a year was like a honeymoon.

Nicole, whom we heard from in Chapter 2, has the same feeling about reunions. For twenty years, she lived apart from her second husband, an American academic whom she married after she was widowed. During this time she retained her academic position in France while her husband continued as a tenured professor at a prestigious university in the United States. She recalls this period with enthusiasm:

> Living apart from my husband worked out rather well. The academic calendar allows for many vacations and breaks. We traveled back and forth across the ocean whenever there was an opportunity. We also spoke on the phone every day and sometimes several times a day.

> At this time, my children were living on their own. I could be totally involved in my work without feeling guilty. Because all the years that I was raising my children, I always felt guilty that I didn't spend enough time with them. I felt the pressure to do research, to publish, and so on. Now my time was my own. Since my husband and I are in the same field, we often went to conferences together and were invited to travel to Israel, to Egypt, to Turkey, etc. We also share friends and colleagues in common. It was interesting to come to America and meet new friends and to have guests and to entertain. Similarly, when he came to France,

we entertained and were entertained. It was great fun! In addition, I managed to get invited to the States to spend a semester and, in turn, my husband is invited to France to lecture.

We continue to be independent in terms of taxes and separate bank accounts. In terms of my work, it's been very productive. When I came to the States, he was busy with his work, so I would go to the library and work on my projects. We saw each other at the end of the day. The time we spend together was exciting and rich. It was like a continuous honeymoon!

The success described in this narrative was made possible by several factors. Neither Nicole nor her husband bore any primary responsibility for children, all of whom were grown and living on their own. The second factor was that both had senior faculty positions, which allowed them a great deal of flexibility in scheduling their time. Additionally, their financial resources enabled them to visit each other many times during the year.

* * *

In the past decade, a new pattern has emerged among young professionals wishing to make *aliyah*—moving to Israel for ideological reasons. It involves relocating the family to Israel with the breadwinner, usually the husband, commuting to the United States to work for some portion of each month. It is estimated that about 30 percent of the young people currently moving to Israel have a family member who returns to the United States to work.

I met with Jeremy and Lynn separately in their newly renovated home in Bet Shemesh, Israel, two years after they had made *aliyah*. Jeremy, a dentist who maintains his American practice, shared his experience first:

We always had a strong desire to live in Israel. I feel that this is where all Jews belong. Originally, we thought we would not do it until we retired. But then we saw that lots of our friends who thought they would do it, did not because, for one reason or another, their plans got short-circuited.

So, we rethought our plans and decided that it would be best for us to make *aliyah* at a time when our children's lives could be impacted by living in Israel. We have four children. Our oldest son, who is nineteen, did not make *aliyah* with us. He is a student at Yeshiva University in New York. It was a mutual decision that he remain in the States to complete college.

It was always our plan that I would continue to maintain my practice in the States. We moved a year after we made the decision and used that time to put our plans in place.

I have an established dental practice in New Jersey that functions full-time with the help of an associate and an office manager. My associate works more time when I'm not there and less when I am there. The twelve days a month that I'm in the office, I work twelve hours a day, five and a half days a week. When I'm in the States, I stay with friends in Teaneck, New Jersey, about half hour from my office. I have a small basement apartment.

It's all working out quite well. The plan I implemented for my practice has pretty much stayed on course. From a business perspective, this arrangement is much more lucrative than if I worked in Israel full-time.

My wife and I are on the phone multiple times during the course of the day. I call her on my way to the office which is midday in Israel. If something comes up overnight while I'm sleeping she will e-mail me and I can respond first thing in the morning.

I might speak with the boys maybe only once or twice a week. We don't seem to have the patience for talking on the phone. It's not a conducive medium for us to communicate. I've come to accept the commute and it doesn't bother me at all. I'm on a tight schedule with my practice, so I'm concerned about airline delays. In the two years I've been doing this, fortunately, I've not been late for any appointments with my patients.

When I am at home, I'm really totally available to my family. I coach baseball and spend more time with my kids than the average father does who is home, but works full-time.

I think my wife has become more accustomed to my being away. It's a big challenge, much more for her than for me. She has to be both mother and father when I'm not here. During that time she is responsible for all the discipline of the boys, which is difficult. She also has to deal with the school issues. There's no question that the situation is much harder for her than it is for me.

At this point, Jeremy feels that his commuting to work in the States is working for them. Assuming that there are no major upsets with the children, he plans to continue this pattern for an indefinite period.

Originally, I had not planned to interview his wife, Lynn, however, Jeremy thought she would be interested in sharing her viewpoint. I was very pleased that I had the opportunity to speak to both of them, because there is a difference in Lynn's perspective:

The idea of moving to Israel originated with Jeremy. I was working for a large accounting firm at the time. The job involved a great deal of travel, which took me away from the family. I always had work on my mind. Jeremy came home one night from a class at the synagogue and he said, "What do you think about making *aliyah*?" I said, "Will I have to work?" and he said, "No." In the States we really needed the two six-figure salaries to support the lifestyle we had, what with private schools, three cars, the big house, vacations, and so on.

I thought it would be wonderful to give up work. But I feel now that part of my identity is gone. At this point I don't yet have the facility with Hebrew to work in my field. I have a good Judaic background, but one that did not include much in the way of Hebrew language skills. Living in Bet Shemesh, where everyone speaks English, makes it difficult to improve my conversational Hebrew.

Jeremy's commuting half a month is hard on both of us. I have two lives—one when he is gone, and one when he is home. He also has two lives. When he is in the States, all he does is work. When I call him, he frequently can't talk because he's with a patient or between patients and he has only a minute or so and he'll tell me to send him an e-mail. We might speak anywhere from three to six times a day, but the phone calls are not real conversations, they are information exchanges.

Life is very different. The experience is what I expected and more, but not without its challenges. Our personal relationship is harder than it was. In the States, when I was working, we would take turns coming home early to prepare dinner and then we would have Shabbat and Sunday together. Now, during the two weeks he is gone, I'm doing everything. But the two weeks he's home, we often do things together, just the two of us. We might go to a museum, on a hike, or some other outing.

The hardest thing about the two weeks that Jeremy is gone is that everyone is depending totally on me. It's more a mental pressure than a physical pressure.

I don't have any regrets. And I would do this again. I feel that this is the Jewish State and this where we should be as Jews. I immediately developed an emotional attachment to the country. And I knew when we came that I was not going back.

Lynn feels that couples contemplating this relocation must have a strong marriage and a strong foundation in which they are mutually invested. Because Jeremy continues to work in his established practice in the States and they were able to sell their large house, they don't have the financial burdens most Israelis experience. Their home in Israel is mortgage-free and they are able to travel to the United States as a family at least once a year. Her advice to others is this: "On the whole, I would say you have to learn to roll with the punches. And you have to have a core group of friends you can rely on."

While the experience has affected Jeremy and Lynn differently, the arrangement is working because they are both deeply committed to its original premise—that living in Israel is the fulfillment of a dream.

Lessons from Life: Distant Husbands and Wives

- For husbands and wives who have senior positions in different parts of the world, transnational commutation ensures the continuation of a good salary and sidesteps the stress of professionally "starting over."

- Living apart from your spouse requires more independence. Each of the partners needs to have the skills to run their own affairs.

- Share your concerns and fears about the separation. Trust and commitment to the partnership are essential.

- If there are young children involved, develop a plan for ongoing communications with the absent parent. Also, keep the presence of the other parent alive through pictures and stories.

- Keep a diary of activities—your own as well as your children's—so that you can easily share information during phone calls, e-mails, etc.

- In the absence of your spouse, set up a support system you can turn to in case of an emergency.

- Good friends want to help. Be open to both emotional and physical support from people you like and trust.

- In planning reunions, allow time for the returning spouse to become reacquainted and readjusted.

- During reunions, socialize as a couple with friends. This will reinforce their perception of you as a couple.

6

WHAT'S HAPPENING TO MY TRADITIONS?

I love this country, but Christmas is not Christmas for me here. In Venezuela everybody comes to my parents' home where the food is special, the music is exhilarating, and the entire ambience radiates happiness and togetherness.
　　　　　　　　　—Rebecca, who moved to the United States from Venezuela

Participation in family rituals and milestones strengthens family unity, encourages contact among generations, and provides stability for its members. Studies indicate that family rituals contribute to marital satisfaction, to an adolescent's sense of personal identity, and to children's health and academic achievements.[1]

Family rituals often undergo a transformation when people move to other countries. In some instances, practices are lost; in others, they are only experienced during visits back home; and in still others, they are re-created and adapted.

This chapter will explore the ways in which people cope with a variety of cultural changes they have confronted as a result of moving far away from home and family. Topics include:

- The importance of family traditions and rituals
- Celebrations shared and missed
- Coping with the cultural divide
- Hopes for future generations

The Importance of Family Traditions and Rituals

Camilla, who came from Colombia a decade ago, recalls with warmth and longing the family ritual of visiting her grandmother every day after work

There were usually about twenty people representing three generations who came to say "hello" to Grandma and partake in coffee and *arepas,* a Colombian pastry. In this country, Camilla can no longer participate in this daily ritual. However, she has transmitted the essence of it to her children. Several times a week, Camilla bakes *arepas* and other traditional foods and together with her children delivers them to her father who is ill with cancer. She proudly reports that "When it's time to go to my dad's, the kids are first in the car."

Because she fled Colombia in middle of the night, Camilla had to leave behind many prized mementos. She shares the story about the dress her son wore the day he was baptized:

> When my son was baptized he wore a beautiful hand embroidered dress which I kept for my daughter, who also wore it when she was baptized. It was my hope that I would pass it on to future generations, but it was one of many precious things I had to leave behind in Colombia. Just recently, my daughter had her first communion and I bought her a special dress. My cousin in Colombia has a daughter a little younger than mine who is about to take her first communion. I will send her my daughter's dress and this dress will now become the family heirloom in place of the baptismal dress that was lost.

A few years after Camilla and her family moved to the United States, a cousin came to visit, bearing a very special gift—Camilla's wedding album, which the cousin had miraculously found. Camilla was thrilled to have it because it showed the family during happier times. But looking at the photos was a reminder of the many losses, not only in terms of material things, but more importantly in terms of family relationships. Yet, despite dislocation and many adjustments, Camilla has managed to adapt and to create new family customs that will be passed on to future generations.

***

Several people interviewed for this book spoke about weekly family rituals that they miss since moving abroad and now only experience when they go back to visit. Hannah, whom we heard from in previous chapters, grew up in Belgium. She talked about how she misses the weekly get-togethers with extended family:

> I have many cousins in Belgium who go out for coffee every week. I miss getting together with family on the weekends. It is not part of the American culture to simply meet a family member or friend for a cup of tea or coffee and visit for a couple of hours. I found these informal visits very meaningful and enjoyable. I really miss that kind of socializing and that kind of casual relaxation with family.

Even though Hannah's parents are now deceased, she plans to return annually to Belgium to visit their gravesites and to attend the weekly cousins' get-together. Like Hannah, Mariangela, from Brazil, misses the traditional Sunday gathering of family in her mother's home.

> The best part about going home is Sundays when we all get together. On Sundays the whole family comes over to my mother's house for lunch. We cook together and clean up together. And, of course, we all sit at the table together. My nieces and nephews are now teenagers and sometimes they would rather be with their friends, but the rule is that everybody must come. After lunch we play games, talk, and watch TV together. They all end up having a good time, especially when I'm visiting.

Mariangela feels that there is a cultural divide between Brazilians and Americans. She says, "Brazilians are by nature into each others' lives—we tell each other everything." Being far away has denied her opportunities to share details of her personal life with her brothers and sisters. Therefore, going home and participating in the Sunday family lunch ritual reinvigorates her connections with her siblings and their offspring.

Family reunions are another ritual that provide a chance to visit with seldom-seen family members, to meet new ones, and to celebrate common roots. Keyla, whose visa does not permit her to visit Venezuela and return again to the United States, was very disappointed that she could not attend her family reunion there. She describes how she compensated for the fact that she could not be there in person:

> On the evening of the reunion, I called and stayed on the phone for two hours so that I could speak to each person who came. When they said it was very expensive, I said that this was more important to me than anything else. My mother was asked to make a toast. When they sent me the pictures, I saw that my mom had the cell phone to her ear while I was speaking to her. When I saw the picture I felt that I was present in spirit, if not in person.

Kim, who has shared many stories about her life in previous chapters, returned to her native Malaysia for a family reunion. She talked about the reunion, which was a very emotional experience:

> My sister and all my nieces, nephews, and their children were at the reunion. I made a speech in which I told them how happy I was to see each of them. I told them that even though I have been gone for forty years, I will always consider Malaysia home and I will always miss the closeness, the caring and the warmth of my family.

Sharing this event with her family was especially important to Kim because over the years she missed all the births, weddings, and funerals. She is saddened by the fact that her nieces and nephews grew up without her. They are now married and have children of their own, and she was not part of any of this.

For emissaries in the Chabad movement who serve in a hundred countries around the world, their annual international convention serves as an extended family reunion. In addition to attending sessions relating to their work, this yearly gathering is a time for attendees to be reunited with family. Devorah has three children who are emissaries in various parts of the world. She talked about the importance of this event in cementing family relations:

> This is an amazing opportunity for us not only to see our children, but siblings, nieces, nephews, and cousins. Because of this convention, we see each other at least once a year. The homes in Crown Heights, New York, where the convention is held, just open up and anybody who comes from anywhere in the world is offered home hospitality. It's unbelievably wonderful—it compensates for the difficulties everybody may be experiencing all year long.

***

In some cultures, family members from abroad follow a ritual that specifies the order in which they visit with relatives. Touhid is a young man in his mid-twenties who was born in Bangladesh and came to the United States to pursue graduate work. He describes his one trip back to visit family in Bangladesh:

> It's an honor for the family to receive a relative who has come to visit. When I came, the entire extended family met me at the airport. There is a preferred order for visiting. My dad's side takes precedence over my mom's side and within each side of the family, you start visiting with the oldest person first and work your way down. There were so many people to see, I felt like I was diving into an ocean of love.

In Touhid's Muslim faith, ritual prayer also establishes an important sense of connection. Even though he lives thousands of miles away, the fact that his distant family members are in his prayers and he in theirs creates a significant bond.

Celebrations Shared and Missed

Holidays, such as Christmas and Passover, and life-cycle events—births, bar/bat mitzvahs, and weddings—are culturally defined and deeply embedded in the family's shared history. Observing them in a foreign country, with the glaring absence of parents, uncles, aunts, and cousins, presents enormous challenges.

Christmas conjures up a panoply of sights, sounds, and smells that are associated with the comfort and good cheer that come with being home for the holidays. The longing new immigrants experience is palpable. This wanes but continues to linger even as they become acculturated and develop a cadre of friends who serve as surrogate family.

Vicky, the pharmacist from Romania, recalls Christmas at home and shares the loneliness she feels since she left:

> On Christmas in Romania we go house to house, singing Christmas carols and wishing neighbors "Merry Christmas." We always spent Christmas with our parents. In the morning we would go to church and gather for a big buffet that my mother cooked with our help. She made stuffed cabbage, stuffed grape leaves, a special dish of meat and potatoes, and lots of salads. We sit around a large table and eat family style. It's so nice to look around the table and feel connected to each one.
>
> Christmas is a very difficult holiday because I miss celebrating with my family. When it comes, my children ask me, "When are we going back to Romania?" I am so sad that I volunteer to work on Christmas so that I don't have to stay home.

Camilla, like Vicky, misses the celebration of Christmas she remembers in Colombia, but has made an effort to create a holiday atmosphere in her new home, except for one very difficult year.

The holidays in Colombia were very festive. Christmas was celebrated for a whole week. The highlights of the week were a huge parade and the bullfights. We exchanged gifts, and every day we would end up at Grandma's house.

I now make Christmas in my house and my whole family comes. My husband's family is still in Colombia, so this is a very hard time for him. We attempt to re-create some of the atmosphere of home. I prepare the traditional food and the men wear sombreros and listen to the bullfights. One year, after my father had been in jail in Colombia for five years, they promised to let him out so he could be with us for the holidays. But they didn't keep their promise. That year, we didn't celebrate at all. We didn't have company and we didn't get dressed up.

***

One of the major holidays in our family is the celebration of Passover—a weeklong commemoration of the Jewish Exodus from Egypt. The holiday is launched with a Seder that includes the retelling of the story of the Exodus and a festive meal. For many years I hosted our extended family in our home for the Passover Seder. For a few years after our son, Josh, moved to Israel, he and his family continued to join us. As his family has grown, the cost of bringing all of them to the United States has become prohibitive. I find that this is the time of the year when I miss them the most. The need to be connected with family during this festival is paramount. The following stories describe how four people responded to this need.

Ben, who moved with his wife and five children from Australia to Israel, wanted to spend one last Passover with his ailing, aged mother. He describes how he made the trip to Australia possible and the impact on his family:

I told my wife that we should make this trip before our oldest son goes into the army, because once he goes, it will be more difficult for us to leave. We had a little money set aside and we supplemented it with a loan. We went for two and half weeks.

My mother was unable to clean the house for the holiday, or shop and cook. So my wife and I organized and did it all. The seder was at my mother's house with our whole extended family, about thirty-five people. When I look back now, I realize what a wonderful decision it was to go at that time, because after that she started to go downhill.

While we were there, she was able to enjoy the grandchildren and my wife and me. Our children became very attached to her. Every night, the children would play cards with my mother, talk, hug, and kiss. It was a joy to see how beautifully my mother interacted with my children.

Because it is very costly to travel, I usually visit Australia without my family. The best part of this visit was that we were all together and that I didn't have to worry about my wife and kids because they were with me. What I enjoyed most was just sitting around the table and schmoozing with the family.

Ben, who lives on a very limited income, feels that the expenditure for the trip was worth every penny. Now, years later, his children continue to watch the videos they made during that visit with enormous pleasure.

Simon, whom we have heard from in Chapter 2, moved from Israel to the United States as a single man. He is not an observant Jew, but the Sephardic Jewish traditions mean a great deal to him. He talked about his valiant attempt to celebrate Passover on his own and the disappointing and frustrating aftermath:

About three years after I came to the United States, my mom's friend invited me for the Passover seder. She is Sephardic, so she grew up with the same customs. I asked if I could buy something or make something, so that it would be authentic. She told me that her husband doesn't like to bother and so they have abandoned many of the customs. I ended up declining the invitation.

I decided instead to prepare the meal myself. I told my Israeli roommate that since it's Passover, I am going to take off from work. I told him that I was going to cook a holiday dinner and asked him to sit with me so I would not be alone. He said that he didn't observe too much, but agreed to sit with me. He was a "pothead." He'd smoke his joint every day and just fall asleep. That's the way a lot of the foreigners deal with their loneliness.

I made the holiday dinner. My roommate came home, smoked his joint, and promptly fell asleep. I ended up marking the holiday by myself. I made the blessings, I lit the candles, I drank the wine, and ate by myself. I was very sad and very lonely. The experience left me scarred and devastated.

I'm not very religious, but marking the holidays is more about tradition. Since then, I care less for holidays. It's probably a defense mechanism. I don't ever want to feel that way again.

What might Simon have done differently to avoid this disaster? The South Florida community in which he lives does have a Sephardic synagogue, which is hospitable to all Sephardic Jews even if they are not members of the congregation. If he had called the synagogue, in the spirit of "Let all those that are hungry come and eat; all who are needy, come celebrate the Passover with us," they would have been delighted to have him join them in celebrating the holiday.

So ingrained are these traditions that even after more than a dozen years, Toby, who moved from Australia, misses being with her family.

I especially miss Passover. I miss sitting around the seder table with my family and singing the tunes that my grandfather taught us. And I miss the special family dynamics that we all enjoyed. A few days leading up to the holiday I will be very emotional. We celebrate Passover with my in-laws, who are really very warm and loving. I sit at my in-laws' table and participate because it's twelve years now and their traditions are now mine as well, but I cannot help recalling the memories of my family's traditions in Australia.

As families spread out over the world, it is difficult for entire clans to gather for the holidays. Naomi, a research psychologist whom we heard from in Chapter 5, has a warm, caring relationship with her younger sister who lives in Israel. Naomi decided that it would be nice for the two families to celebrate Passover together. There are a total of seven cousins who maintain e-mail contact with each other throughout the year. They range in age from their early teens to their early twenties and are all comfortable with each other. Because the children all have strong Jewish backgrounds, the seder was run by the cousins. They were all very engaged and had a great deal to contribute.

The experience was very fulfilling for both families and might even be the beginning of a new tradition for the two sisters. Naomi's comment about the week the two families spent together is indicative of its success: "Even though my sister's house is small, we all felt very comfortable. You can tell when a host is burdened by company. I distinctly felt that we were not a burden. We were good guests and chipped in with the work. It all felt very good. There was a lot of sharing and a lot of love."

Time and financial constraints often limit family attendance at major milestone events. Miriam and her husband have four sons, two of whom live with their wives and children in Israel. In the first chapter, Miriam described her response to her sons' moving far away. She and her husband recently celebrated their fiftieth wedding anniversary. It was not possible for all the wives and grandchildren to be present, so the four boys decided to mark the milestone alone with their parents. Miriam recalls the momentous weekend:

> About two months in advance of our anniversary, the four boys arranged a conference call with us to ask if we were going to be home the weekend of June 23rd. They know that we are frequently invited out for

the Sabbath. We told them that we didn't have plans. They said, "Good, because we have decided that we are all going to come in to celebrate your fiftieth anniversary." At first I tried to talk them out of it, because it's so expensive. But they insisted that all four of them could be free that weekend and they wanted to come. They arrived on Thursday and they left Sunday night. Three of the four came without family. Our son from New Jersey came with his wife and his son. They all wanted to be together, so we put them up in our house. It was great! They wanted to play golf because in Israel there are few opportunities to do that. We made reservations and my husband, four sons, and grandson went golfing on Friday.

They surprised us with a huge anniversary cake and flowers. We were just family for the Sabbath. I didn't invite anyone else, because I felt the time was precious. On Saturday night we went to the movies and on Sunday we went bowling and ended the weekend with a steak dinner.

We had all our meals at home. I prepared most of the food in advance so I could be with them and did not have to spend excessive time in the kitchen. It was fun just talking and reminiscing. The two families that live in Israel put together an album about things that they remembered when they were growing up. Each of the grandchildren also wrote something on a page that included their photographs, and the younger children drew pictures.

Now that it's over, I am so glad that we did it. Life is full of surprises, some not pleasant. And you never know what the future will bring. Now we will always have special memories of this one occasion. Right after they went back, we called to tell them how grateful we were that they came to celebrate with us. We had such a good time!

These stories underscore the acute need for family during major holidays and family milestones. The familiarity, the camaraderie, the common roots and customs are almost impossible to replace. The marking of these occasions with family reminds us that the repetition of traditions promotes harmony and connects the present to the past.

Coping with the Cultural Divide

For some people the cultural divide represents loss and painful discontinuity. Others find themselves in a perpetual state of transition, and still others celebrate the opportunity to broaden their horizons and embrace their new countries and new cultures, while at the same time maintaining allegiance to their place of origin.

Camilla, who was forced to flee Colombia with her family, says, "My roots are Colombian and I will always feel that is my country." Like Camilla, most of the immigrants I spoke with referred to their country of origin as "my country." This was true for people who had emigrated recently as well as for those who had done so decades ago. The reference to "my country" suggests a sense of ownership, comfort, and pride in their past. It also reveals contrasting feelings of being out of context and estrangement from their new environment.

Toby, who emigrated from Australia twelve years ago, finds it hard to partake in her American-born children's expressions of patriotism. She described her feelings of ambivalence, alienation, and longing:

> At a Fourth of July celebration my children's patriotism was so obvious. They sang songs and waved American flags. It's the kind of patriotism for America that I will never share. That saddens me. In some ways I'm moving away from my old friends. But still when I ride down the streets of Melbourne, I miss the city and I miss the culture.

Corbin McGregor is a college student who grew up in Madagascar where her parents are missionaries and life is devoid of many institutions we take for granted. Visits to her grandparents in the United States provide a variety of new cultural experiences. On one such visit, when she was nine years old, for the first time in her life she visited an American post office. She wrote the following in her mother's book on their life in Madagascar.[2]

> One day while in Florida, I went to the post office with my grandmother and sister. It was very different for me. Even though I am now nine years old, I had never been in an American post office. It was very clean and crowded. The workers at the office had many computers and machines. We bought some stamps for the letters and GG [her grandmother], Charese, and I put on the stamps. GG taught us where to place the stamps. I suggested that we put them on the back to help keep the envelope closed (in Madagascar, the envelopes do not have glue on them), but GG told us that the postal service required that we put the stamps on the right upper corner. When we finished putting the stamps on the letters, we slid the letters in an oblong slot. And do you know what the lady at the counter gave us? A coloring activity book! What a fun trip going to the post office can be!

Now that she is in college in the United States, Corbin says, "I've lived in two cultures and I'm different in each of them. Sometimes it's a hardship not to fit in. I sometimes feel that now." However, she does admit that having had a broad range of experiences has enabled her to adapt more easily to new situations.

Rajan, an academic born in India, has found a way to integrate the Indian and American cultures:

> I find it very difficult to cease being an Indian altogether. On the other hand, I feel I am at home in both places. I feel very comfortable in the United States. I think it's a great country. I tend to be more sentimental about aspects of Indian culture, especially Indian music. It's very fortunate that in my lifetime large-scale forces have driven the United States toward convergence in terms of their interest in other nations as opposed to when I first came here. India and the United States are similar in that they are multiethnic, complex societies. I actually tend to find it

complementary. There was a certain coexistence that I learned in India when I was young. I have learned an American model of coexistence here that is different but that I'm comfortable with.

Touhid, the young man born in Bangladesh, shares many of the thoughts Rajan has expressed about the values of living in a global society and its potential for broadening a person's horizons.

My identity is a bit confused. I have a varied background. I have lived in Bangladesh, Dubai, and the United States. I do have love for the American culture and the American identity. But can I say, "I am a true American"? The answer is "No." I value the American culture. There is a lot of good in it and there is much that is in congruence with our native culture. I believe in the freedom that America provides and I believe in upholding the law. In that way I am very American.

My faith is very much intertwined with my identity as an American. I don't find that it is a contradiction in any way. I have been a student in America and I work in corporate America, and that does not conflict with my faith as a Muslim. I am also able to cultivate my background and the language of my culture.

For both Rajan and Touhid, the idea of globalization and living oceans apart is far less daunting than it was for previous generations. Their observations suggest that we might consider it an opportunity to better our lives. Living apart can generate a yearning for and a vehicle to explore other aspects of human emotions and feelings as well as other aspects of human civilization. These opportunities would not exist if we did not live oceans apart. Distance from loved ones, then, provides a very powerful opportunity for personal growth.

Hopes for Future Generations

Those who have moved oceans apart from family to pursue a faith-based ideology draw strength from their life of service and see similar futures for their children. Rev. Patricia McGregor, whose family has spent the past seventeen years in Africa, says, "My daughters have American skin, but African hearts. They think like Africans." She would like her children to use the gifts and passions that God has given them to make a difference in the world. She is totally prepared for them to choose to live half a world away.

Devorah, who is a member of Chabad and whose family includes five generations of emissaries, expressed a similar view about future generations. She says, "We gain so much from our children being emissaries all around the world. We learn about life in other countries and about the needs and customs of Jewish people all over the world. Our children and grandchildren feel the support of family, even though they may be vast distances from each other. They consider it an honor to follow in their parents' footsteps."

In earlier chapters we read about the important role language can play in communications among generations who live oceans apart. Beatrice, born and raised in Switzerland, has been very mindful of this. She says:

> I am very committed to keeping myself fluent in my native dialect and I have taught it to my children so that they can be comfortable and communicate with my family in Bern. My oldest daughter is very careful about keeping up relationships with my family in Switzerland and has taught her daughter the dialect as well. As a result, when they visit Switzerland, my granddaughter can talk and play comfortably with the cousins her age. This has been very important in cementing ties.

The continuation of customs and traditions by the next generation establishes a significant connection even if they live at a distance. When this does not happen, there is a sense of disappointment and regret. Pearl talks about the cultural divide that exists between her and her son since he has moved far away:

> Our son and his family have abandoned all our religious traditions and have instead adopted the Hasidic traditions of their rabbi. This is hurtful. When we go there for the Sabbath, our son's religious customs

in no way resemble what he saw at home. This makes us feel alien. In addition, he does not name his children after our deceased relatives, only after his rabbi's relatives. This is especially painful for my husband, a Holocaust survivor who would have wanted his murdered relatives to be memorialized in future generations.

For many young adults who have moved far away, there is a desire to share with their children the culture, traditions, and lifestyle of their countries of origin. Kim, who grew up in Malaysia, would have wanted her children to maintain some of her Asian values. She particularly regrets that she has not transmitted the Asian custom of respect for one's elders. She says with sorrow, "My kids have become completely Americanized. They are not bad—they are nice kids—but they don't have the same feeling I did about my parents. Because of this I often feel disconnected from them."

Immigrants who do not have visas permitting them to travel back and forth experience a special frustration about not being able to take their children "back home." Keyla had a dream in which she took her son to Venezuela to visit. She said she was so happy to be there. In the dream, before she left she decided to take her son to the museum to learn about the history of the country. While at the museum, he got lost and she could not find him. When she awoke she was very agitated—a feeling that did not leave her for the rest of the day. She decided that the dream was a message from God that she should not attempt to take her son back to her country.

Keyla uses photographs and family stories to share her cultural past with her children. In addition, Spanish is the primary language in her home, so that the children can communicate easily with visiting relatives.

Some immigrants are truly proud of their multiculturalism and are eager to have their children grow up comfortable in more than one culture. Rajan, an academic, would like his children to know the Hindu customs he grew up with, but finds that there is a certain disconnect because the children do not see these practices reinforced in their communities. He shares his struggle and his thoughts for his children's future growth and development:

> We would like our children to know at least one Indian language. We failed to teach our first child Hindi and are trying very hard to speak Hindi with our second child. We have told our eldest daughter that we don't celebrate Christmas. She is not very happy about that. We are also vegetarians. Once, in the supermarket, our daughter asked if she could be a beef vegetarian.

> No matter where we live, my children's lives are going to be defined in different ways. We live in a global society and I suspect that they will grow up as citizens of the world. So I say to my daughter, "You should learn Hindi, not only because it is part of your heritage, but it is the language of a country of a billion plus people that is a major player in the world economy."

Touhid projects a very optimistic view for his children as citizens of the world:

> I want my children to be tolerant of other people's religion and differences. I want them to continue to know and appreciate their own background as well. One of the things I would love to do in the future is travel, because that's the way my children will learn to intertwine their religion and culture with the American culture. I will do everything to maintain both cultures.

Lessons from Life: What's Happening to My Traditions?

Shared culture is the foundation of many family relationships and connects families who live vast distances apart.

♪ Transmitting traditions and stories of your native country to children and grandchildren creates an important link with the past.

♪ It is important to plan periodic trips back home for holidays or milestone events. They produce important and lasting memories.

♪ If you have been invited to share a holiday celebration with someone in your new country, ask your host if you can bring a traditional food from your country of origin or share one custom representing your tradition. This will make you feel more at home and your host will undoubtedly be pleased to taste or learn something new.

♪ Cultural heritage can be a work in progress with each generation modifying or adding to practices that have been handed down from the past.

♪ Maintain your own foreign language skills and try to pass them on to the next generation. In addition to helping your children forge a connection to the family's cultural identity, it is key to communicating with relatives from abroad.

♪ Learn to appreciate the traditions and rituals of your new country. Adding them to those of your country of origin broadens your cultural horizons and enhances the quality of your life.

Chapter 6 Notes

1. Barbara H. Fiese, Thomas J. Tomcho, Michael Douglas, Kimberly Josephs, Scott Poltrock, and Tim Baker, "A Review of 50 Years of Research on Naturally Occurring Family Routines and Rituals: Cause for Celebration?," *Journal of Family Psychology* 16, no. 4 (2002): pp 445-6.
2. Patricia McGregor, *A Guest in God's House: Memories of Madagascar* (Eldoret, Kenya: Zapf Chancery, 2004), p. 173.

7

CREATIVE USES OF TECHNOLOGY

by George Berman

Our ten-year-old grandson, Binyamin, who lives in Israel, recently visited us for two weeks. As recommended in earlier chapters, we planned his activities in some detail. Having assembled a list of possible trips and projects, we wanted to know his preferences. We sent him an e-mail (at his own e-mail address), asking him to rank the events. So that he could fully evaluate them, we included a hyperlink to the website for each event.

This was so much easier and more informative than describing each opportunity, even in detail. Binyamin could see photos of the actual destination, such as the Miami Seaquarium, read about all the options available, and begin to make his own plans. He responded the next day—designating most sites as top priority!

Upon his arrival in Florida, we presented Binyamin with a camera, so that he could record the highlights of his visit. He quickly caught on to the mechanics of using the camera, and we spent some time talking about composition and other techniques. After Binyamin returned to Israel, the camera dialog continued. Using a program called LogMeIn, I was able to enter his computer, seven thousand miles away, and show him how to use the software that came with the camera to improve and catalog his pictures. During these sessions, we chatted using Skype. It was almost as if I were sitting next to him at his computer.

Maintaining family ties at a distance is largely about communication. Technology has evolved—and continues to evolve—in a variety of ways to help us stay in touch and convey a rich array of information and emotions.

In this chapter, we will examine several of these pathways. You may be unfamiliar with some of them, but the learning curve is not steep. Give each one a serious try, and determine which best meet your needs. Given the pace of innovation, I advise you to remain alert for the latest advances.

Many of these forms of communication require a computer and access to the Internet. At the time this book was written, it was possible to buy a small computer designed specifically for use with the Internet—called a NetBook—for about $350. If this is beyond your budget, throughout the United States you can use a free computer at your local library.

Telephone

A telephone call has much to offer. It is, of course, the easiest way to initiate contact. The content is rich in meaning because the inflection of our voice conveys as much information as our words. With extensions on either end, several people can join in the conversation. We frequently gather around a speakerphone, which seems to stimulate more group interaction than a telephone handset.

Telephone service overseas can get expensive. Here are two ways to minimize the cost:

- Choose a long-distance service that offers the best rates to the country you'll be calling. Our long-distance service, for example, charges eight cents a minute to Israel.
- Another alternative is a prepaid calling card. Because they get your money upfront, the card companies can compete favorably with long-distance services.

Conference calls bring several family members together on the same call. For example, the website Free Conference (http://www.freeconference. com/Reservationless.aspx) offers just that: A free phone number that all participants call at the same time. Each of the participants pays for the call on their own phone bill. Alternatively, you can get a toll-free number to call, so that no one on the call is charged for it. Instead, the conference organizer pays ten cents a minute for each participant.

Voice over Internet Phone (VOIP)

Why pay for long-distance calls if you don't have to? The technology for placing phone calls over the Internet has improved rapidly, and now is virtually as clear and problem-free as Ma Bell. For example, VOIP service Packet 8 provides toll-free calls throughout the United States and Canada. For a reasonable premium, toll-free international service is also available.

VOIP service can be your only telephone service, costing about half as much as wired service. At one time, a subscriber could not be located by 911 emergency services, but that issue has been addressed. The principal disadvantage remaining is that your computer must be running to use VOIP. If the computer fails or if the power fails, the phone cannot be used. If you have a cell phone, there is no reason to worry about these contingencies, as you can use that for emergencies.

The lcast expensive VOIP service is the recently introduced MagicJack (www.magicjack.com). This is a device, about the size of a small calculator, that plugs into your computer at one end, and your telephone at the other. The unit costs less than $40. The service fee of $20 allows you to make unlimited free calls anywhere in the United States and Canada for an entire year. Overseas calls are much less expensive than competing services; for example, 2.5 cents a minute to Israel. The only drawback we have found is that every time the device is used, a window pops up on the computer monitor, announcing the number being called or calling you. On the other hand, this window also provides a record of recent calls, which you can click to redial a call, and a contact list, which also permits one-click dialing. And the intrusive window can be minimized, or stored out of sight at the edge of the monitor.

Internet Video

Once found only in science fiction, the videophone is now a reality. Through a service called Skype, we can now call our family in Israel and see them as they see us. We don't even have to hold a telephone handset. A small camera-microphone combination sits on top of our computer monitor. It adjusts to changing light conditions; it can zoom in on one of us, or out to include the entire room; and it can follow my face as I move around, keeping me centered on the screen!

Don't scrimp on the equipment. Sound quality is very important for successful use of this technology. An integrated camera and microphone costs only a bit over $100, and can be a valuable long-term investment.

Ayelet, our baby granddaughter, is learning to crawl. Once, we would have said, "Hold Baby up to the camera," thus missing the real action. Now, we say, "Turn the camera on her," and we see her making her way across the living room.

Once both parties have cameras and have signed up with Skype, there is no further cost. Audio and video calls are free!

Internet video provides the richest communication content. Voice inflections, as well as facial expressions, now add to our communication. Has a grandson created a sculpture, or a construction project? We can see it onscreen, or even rotate or walk around it. We can show our daughter-in-law the dress Rochel has made for the baby. Opportunities are endless.

Tal, a thirty-two-year-old mother of four living in South Florida, talks about maintaining daily contact with her Israeli grandmother via Skype:

> My grandparents shared a home with my parents in Ivory Coast, Africa. From the time I was very small, my grandmother looked after me while my mother worked. My grandparents also had a home in Israel, and I

would go to live with them for three months every summer. I was so close to my grandmother, I called her Mama.

My grandparents moved back to Israel twelve years ago. At first, I called my grandmother a couple of times a week. It was expensive then, about $2 or $3 a minute. My grandfather passed away three years ago, leaving my grandmother alone because all five of her children live abroad— four in Florida and one in Canada. At that point, I decided that my grandmother had to receive a daily phone call from each family member. I felt that it was very important that she not feel alone and abandoned. Each of us is assigned a different time of the day to call.

When Skype became available about two and a half years ago, all of us began to communicate with her via Skype. My grandmother is a very modern woman, open to learning new things. One of my cousins in Israel set up the necessary equipment for her and taught her how to use it. She has a webcam that has a microphone built into it. She has all our names programmed in, so it's easy for her to contact us.

Skype makes an incredible difference. First of all, I get to see her every single day and she gets to see me. If she doesn't look good, I can immediately ask her, "What's wrong? What's going on?" I can see the expression on her face as she talks to me. The fact that we can have eye contact makes all the difference in the world. I talk to her from my bedroom, and I feel like she is in the room with me. I feel like I'm having a face-to-face visit with her.

When we were only able to talk on the phone, I would be surprised about how she looked when she came for her annual visit. Now when she comes to visit, I know exactly what she looks like because I see her every day. If she buys a new shirt, she will say, "I just bought this shirt. How do you like it on me?" It makes her so happy and it gives her so much pleasure. It's the closest thing to having her right next to me and being able to touch her.

Skype gives me a more accurate reading of her well-being. If things are not right and she's depressed, I can more easily comfort her. Because she can see my facial expressions, it enhances what I say to her. She is a diabetic and if I see that she is pale, I tell her to go have a piece of fruit.

My grandmother recently broke an arm and her hand is in a cast. The fact that I can see the cast gives her injury a greater sense of reality. I feel that I'm part of things that are happening to her, and that lessens my sense of anxiety. I feel that there is a much deeper connection and a much deeper understanding because we can see each other.

It's a wonderful experience for my grandmother to be able to see her great-grandchildren growing up right before her eyes, even though she is seven thousand miles away. She can see when the children have haircuts and comment on the way they look. They will tell her about their day or show her something new that they got.

My grandmother is my closest confidant. Our conversations can be brief if she has guests or if she is tired. Other times, they can be well over an hour. Skype really helps the fact that I can't see her often. I still miss her, but it has transformed my long-distance relationship with her.

***

Skype can be used as a telephone, too. Dialing is as simple as entering the telephone number into the Skype dialog box and pressing Enter. On any website that displays a telephone number, a small Skype logo appears. Click the logo, and you are instantly connected to the telephone number.

There is a small charge for the telephone service, currently $2.95 per month for the United States and Canada; $9.95 worldwide. But there is no charge, and no monthly fee, to connect with any other Skype subscriber via computer.

Conference calls can be easily arranged with other Skype subscribers: Just add each participant by clicking on his or her Skype name.

The principal disadvantage of using Skype as your only telephone service is the inability to put it on a real telephone, with extensions throughout the house. And, like VOIP, it is subject to your computer's availability.

E-mail

E-mail has largely replaced postal ("snail") mail, and for good reasons. There are no formal requirements, such as mailing address or complimentary close. No envelope to address, no postage. It's also immediate: Just open your e-mail program and start typing.

But there are other advantages, too. Time differences are no longer an obstacle: Your e-mail will be there when your addressee wakes up. There are far fewer barriers to replying—time, stationery, postage—so responses are prompt. In fact, they're almost obligatory.

Of course, you can send more than words. You can attach pictures. You can reference a website you like with a hyperlink—right in the text. In fact, on major e-mail browsers, such as Microsoft Outlook Express, you can send the entire web page in the message area. Just click on Message/New Message Using/Web Page and insert the web page address.

Create a "family forum." Open your address book, and click on New/Group. Then, group your entire family under one name, such as FAMILY. Anytime you want to include the whole family in an e-mail, just send it to the group. When you receive such a message, instead of Reply click on Reply All.

One disadvantage of e-mail is that it is basically a verbal communication. Writers often get into trouble because the lack of nonverbal cues, such as a smile or a wink, leads to misunderstanding. You can partly compensate for this through the use of emoticons, little punctuation mark–pictures.

Here are some of the most common emoticons:

(Rotate your head to the left if you can't see the point.)

:-) smile, happy	:-(sad, depressed	:-((very sad
:-D big grin or laugh	:-P tongue out, silly	:-* kiss
:-O surprised	:-/ uncertain	:-| waiting, indifferent
:-? confused	:'-(crying	;-) wink

Another way to add content is through e-mail acronyms. After someone sends you a funny e-mail, your reply might begin "LOL" (Laughing Out Loud). Other common e-mail acronyms:

- BTW: By the way
- IMHO: In my humble opinion
- OTOH: On the other hand
- IANAL: I am not a lawyer (but . . .)

If you receive an acronym that you don't understand, you can find it at www.loganact.com/tips/afaik.html. Or, just try typing the acronym into Google.

The most important difference between e-mail and instant forms of communication like a telephone or videophone is that you have the opportunity to review your words. Anytime you are addressing a complex or contentious topic, anytime you have a nagging feeling about what you have written, don't send it. Save it to your Drafts folder, and let a day go by before sending it. If a more prompt reply is required, hold off for at least an hour. You will find a better way to say what you want to, and prevent unnecessary bitterness or misunderstanding.

Instant Messaging (IM)

You're sitting at your computer when your IM program tells you that Dad is using the Internet (see Figure 1). Click, and a chat box opens on your screen. You begin to type.

> You: Hi, Dad. How are you feeling?
>
> Dad: Hi, Honey. I'm fine.
>
> You: How's Mom today?
>
> Dad: Oh, she's had a bit of a setback.

Figure 1: Start of a chat

Now you see that your sister, Susan, has come online, so you invite her to join the chat. The three of you discuss Mom's health, all in real time. Susan displays a photo of her youngest, sort of walking. Dad goes to get Mom.

This is the wonder of instant messaging. You can begin to chat, live, with any number of "buddies" you have designated. The buddy list tells you who's available to chat. You can send computer files, photos, music, or audio. With a microphone on your computer, you can talk to the group.

According to the Pew Research Center's Internet and American Life Project, over 53 million adults use instant messaging; a quarter of them use IM more frequently than e-mail. And you can see why. Even if both parties to the chat above were watching their e-mail, it could take as long as fifteen minutes to exchange the four messages. The spontaneity is gone, and you've taken a step back toward the time when letters could take a month to reach their destination by sailing ship.

One of the objections to IM in the workplace is that it encourages gossip. But in your personal communications, that's a plus!

Who uses instant messaging? Women use it as often as men, but for significantly longer chats. Of course, the younger generations use it more, too: Among people eighteen to twenty-seven years of age, 62 percent are IM users, while only 25 percent of people over sixty use it.

Family Website

For many years, Internet users were exhorted to create private websites, where they could post news and photos of the family. Many Internet Service Providers offered simplified software for building such websites.

The principal objection to these websites is that they tend to be the "property" of the family member who creates one. It is his or her family that is featured. Communication is basically in one direction. And the website is open to the world.

Family Blog

The family blog has come to the rescue. *Blog* stands for "web log," a format often used to report the blogger's daily activity, like an online diary. Other blogs are journalistic in nature, reporting on events, companies, or political trends.

What makes a blog an ideal form of communication for the wired family is that, unlike a website, it is fully interactive. Anyone can add to the messages that have been posted. Messages are archived, so that latecomers can catch up with any discussion they have missed. Like e-mail, the blog is independent of time differences.

Anyone who uses the Internet can create and contribute to a blog. Blog hosts such as www.blogspot.com offer simple templates with which you can set up your blog. Put a photo here, a text description there, and the vessel is ready to fill up. At any time, the blog owner can start a discussion (a "thread") and invite others to join in by simply clicking the Reply button. The structure of these discussions is entirely up to the participants. One might, for example, have a thread about the grandchildren, or a thread just for siblings.

If Aunt Betty is traveling in the United States, for example, she can post her itinerary for everyone to see. Throughout her visit, she can use a friend's computer, or even find one in a public library, to talk about where she has been, whom she has seen, and the like. Other family members might choose to join her at one of her stops, or recommend a restaurant or museum, for example.

Most blog sites offer an RSS feed (*RSS* stands for "real simple syndication"), a means of letting participants know when something new has been posted, so family members don't even have to check in regularly. And, while many blogs are open to the public, access can be limited to any group, such as family members.

In the world of the global family, a blog offers rich content, time independence, privacy, and easy interaction.

Photo Sharing

There are several free websites where you can place your photos and videos in a private album for your friends or family to see. This is a way to share a large number of photos—more than you could send easily via e-mail—or videos, which may be too large to be attached to an e-mail. It also means you can direct a new viewer to the site, rather than compiling the photos once more as e-mail attachments.

The most popular website for photo sharing is Flickr (www.flickr.com). There you can set up a private group, open to a list of friends, just limited to your family, or open to all of them. In any case, you can restrict any photo on the site to just those visitors you want to see it.

Other such sites include

- Bubble Share (www.bubbleshare.com)
- Kodak Gallery (www.kodakgallery.com)\
- Shutterfly (www.shutterfly.com)

Community Forums

One of the key messages of this book is that you are not alone. There are so many issues surrounding living oceans apart, and so many people dealing with these issues that you have plenty of company. One way to communicate with others who may have faced the same problems as you is to join a discussion group on the Internet.

Yahoo! offers free access to a vast array of interest groups. If you find one that suits you, just sign up. Anytime someone submits a question or comment to the group, all the members receive it via e-mail. You can reply, or just wait to see what others have to say. Figures 2 and 3 show examples of such groups.

Expat-Moms-in-Switzerland
1104 Members, Archives: Membership required

This group is for those Expat moms living in or moving to Switzerland who want to converse with others in a similar situation. Hopefully, you will find this to be a place of support for parenting and personal adjustment issues. Moms-to-be, dads, and grandparents are also welcome! This list was started as a support place for families living in or moving in to Switzerland. Everyone is welcome on this list as long as they treat the others here respectfully :-)

Figure 2: Mothers' Group in Switzerland

BharatUK
1173 Members, Archives: Membership required

This is a nonresident Indian forum to discuss and share information regarding everything and anything. From "Where can I find Indian Pulses in the UK?" to "Could anyone please help me with accommodations at Anytown, UK," from "Where can I find information about the UK Small Business Forum?" to various issues relating to information technology, careers, immigration, education, religion festivals, national international political and nonpolitical issues, terrorism, investments in India and abroad, real estate in India, laws, insurance, stocks, bonds, policies, retirement, NRI banking, NGOs, volunteer organisations, and anything else. Discussions can be started or can take any route to promote information exchange and mutual benefits.

Figure 3: Indian Support Group in the UK

You can search for groups of interest to you at http://groups.yahoo.com. There you will also find instructions on how to create your own group. If you don't find a group that meets your needs, why not start one? If you have a need for community, so do thousands of people like you. Tell others about your group, and start building membership.

"Ambient Awareness" Websites

A new term has been created by sociologists to describe a rapidly growing kind of Internet communication. Instead of whole messages, people are posting little tidbits of their thoughts, as one might write in a diary. These tidbits can be open to the public, or confined to friends and family. No one thought has meaning by itself, but the stream of thoughts forms a picture of what is happening in a person's life.

One website providing this kind of "ambient awareness" is Twitter (www. twitter.com). Entries into the stream, called "tweets," are limited to 140 characters. One woman, for example, posts a "tweet" every day telling the world what kind of sandwich she made for lunch. Who cares? No one, but another subscriber says the stream of sandwich talk is very calming to him.

More realistically, the free-form stream of tweets from friends or relatives can bring you into their lives, and them into yours, in a unique way. One person says, of a complete stranger, "After following Judy's Twitter stream for a year, I'm more knowledgeable about the details of her life than I am about the lives of my two sisters in Canada, whom I talk to only once a month or so." One wonders why he doesn't urge his sisters to begin using Twitter! It is said that the ultimate effect of the new awareness is bringing back the dynamics of small-town life, where everyone knows your business.

It takes a new mind-set to engage in ambient awareness, but it's worth giving it a month or two to see whether it works for you.

The modern global family has been made possible by advances in technology: air transportation, international banking, credit cards, and the like. In the process, the loss of face-to-face communications has been a casualty of this increased mobility. So it is only fitting that we employ advanced communications technology to repair the breach. We can still write, talk, see each other—in short, we can overcome the barriers to communication that threaten to disrupt family ties at a distance.

Lessons from Life: Creative Use of Technology

- Communicate as often as possible with as many family members as possible.

- Sign up for, and use an array of communication media to suit your various needs.

  - Use telephone, VOIP, and instant messaging for instant communication with instant feedback.

  - Use conference calls to bring family members together in conversation.

  - Use e-mail or an Internet forum for communication that is time-independent

  - Share photos and videos using e-mail, instant messaging, or a file-sharing site.

- Write e-mail with care. Review a draft before sending.

- Join or create an online community of people from your own country, or people facing similar challenges.

Epilogue

A Big Victory for All of Us!

When we visit with someone we see frequently, we exchange verbal and nonverbal cues that allow us continual access to each other's state of mind. When we next see them, we don't expect a greeting of "What's new?" to produce a torrent of new likes and dislikes, problems and opportunities. By contrast, when we visit with people who live oceans apart, we find that we sometimes need to get to know each other all over again. This holds true as much for a distant child who is growing up as it does for a distant parent who is growing old.

As I was completing work on this book, our second grandson, Binyamin, announced that he was ready for a solo trip from Israel to visit with us in Florida. Since his birth ten years ago, we have never attended any of his birthday parties, school plays, or sporting events. We have visited back and forth, but we have rarely spent a holiday together. We have not been a physical presence in his life, yet Binyamin has a strong sense of family. While I was in Israel, he once confided in me, saying, "I like when my world and my grandparents' world combine. I really wish you could be here for Passover. I can just picture all of us sitting around the table together."

Most grandparents feel that the sole purpose of a visit from grandchildren is to entertain them. This translates into parading the kids to a series of spectator events—at least one or two a day that end up exhausting aging grandparents and are met with mixed reviews by the kids. In thinking about our visit with Binyamin, we certainly did want to expose him to places and events unique to South Florida, but we also wanted to use this time to share our interests and passions with him. We wanted him to get to know us as we were getting to know him.

As soon as dates were set and his ticket was purchased, we began planning for the two-week trip with Binyamin via e-mail and telephone. From a list we prepared for him (see Chapter 7, "Creative Uses of Technology") he made choices for both outings and projects. With regard to the latter, he chose to learn about photography and swimming techniques from his grandfather and about sewing from me. We tried to include one session of each every day. In addition, we decided to write a book about the visit. This is part of a family tradition I describe in Chapter 3, "Grandparenting at a Distance." I previously wrote two about his brother, Amichai, when he was a toddler. Binyamin told me he wanted his book to be geared to kids his age. I suggested that he should be the author. The result is *Binyamin in Boca*—a twenty-eight-page record of his visit, in his own words, with accompanying photos, some of which he took with a digital camera we gave him (see "Resources"). During the first week he was here, he wrote the following in *Binyamin in Boca:*

> Today there was a hurricane warning so we took the day off. We finished sewing my pajamas and I wore them to bed. I learned electronics with Papa George and I made a cream-cheese pie with Bubbe. It rained all day and I watched tons of TV that I don't see in Israel. A BIG VICTORY FOR ME!

The photography and swimming lessons were a big hit. He was keenly interested, hung on every word, and gave the ultimate positive feedback to his grandfather by repeatedly telling him, "That's cool!" The sewing was okay, but I don't see a budding tailor. However, he did learn how to cut a garment using a pattern, how to thread the machine, and how to sew a straight seam. Outings included a visit to the Miami Seaquarium; a water park; a trip to see the latest Batman movie, not yet playing in Israel; snorkeling in the ocean; and a photo outing to the Loxahatchee Wildlife Preserve.

This visit created bonds and developed mutual understanding that would not have been possible in any other setting. It took place in our home and he was our only guest so we could focus our full attention on him. There were a number of surprises and discoveries that were truly heartwarming: His reactions and demeanor were far more adult than we expected; he talked respectfully and lovingly about his siblings; he was eager and excited about learning new things; and he was not homesick until a few days before he was scheduled to leave. We dealt with this by taking him to Walmart to buy gifts for all the members of his family.

The morning he returned home, our daughter-in-law sent us this e-mail:

> Good morning! Binyamin arrived right on time and received a very warm, excited welcome! I can't tell you how much I appreciated all you did. All the thought and planning and doing that went into this "experience." What a special time, perfectly suited to Binyamin. It was such a comfort to know that he was happy, and busy, and learning and growing and enjoying.
>
> Much love,
>
> Michal

And my response to Michal:

> Both Dad and I so miss Binyamin. He really made a place for himself in our hearts and our home. We especially miss him at mealtimes. He was such good company! I hope we impacted his life as much as he impacted ours. It was truly a privilege for us to interact with a young child who was so eager and so responsive. It made us feel like young parents once again. Give him a big hug and kiss from us.
>
> Love to all of you.
>
> Mom

To use Binyamin's expression of exuberance, this visit was indeed

A BIG VICTORY FOR ALL OF US!

Resources

Suggested Reading

Climo, Jacob. *Distant Parents*. New Brunswick, N.J.: Rutgers University Press, 1992.

Fishkoff, Sue. *The Rebbe's Army: Inside the World of Chabad-Lubavitch*. New York: Schocken Books, 2003.

Guildner, Gregory. *Long Distance Relationships*. Corona, Calif.: JF Milne Publications, 2003. (about adult couple relationships)

Isay, Jane. *Walking on Eggshells: Navigating the Delicate Relationship Between Adult Children and Parents*. New York: Flying Dolphin Press/ Broadway Books, 2007.

Karraker, Meg Wilkes. *Global Families*. Boston: Pearson/Allyn and Bacon, 2008.

Keeley, Maureen P., and Julie M. Yingling. *Final Conversations: Helping the Living and the Dying Talk to Each Other*. Acton, Mass.: Vander Wyk & Burnham, 2007.

Lahiri, Jhumpa. *The Namesake*. New York: Houghton Mifflin Company, 2003.

McGregor, Patricia. *A Guest in God's House: Memories of Madagascar*. Eldoret, Kenya: Zapf Chancery, 2004.

Stafford, Laura. *Maintaining Long-Distance and Cross-Residential Relationships*. Mahwah, N.J.: Lawrence Erlbaum Associates, 2005. (about adult couple relationships)

Wassermann, Selma. *The Long-Distance Grandmother: How to Stay Close to Distant Grandchildren.* Point Roberts, Wash.: Hartley & Marks, Inc., 1990.

Waxman, Chaim I. *American Aliya: Portrait of an Innovative Migration Movement.* Detroit: Wayne State University Press, 1989.

Tips for Parents or Guardians of Unaccompanied Minors

Children between the ages of five and fourteen, who are traveling alone, are designated as *unaccompanied minors* (UMs). The service is optional for children fifteen to seventeen as well. However, airlines will provide it when requested. Unaccompanied minor service ensures that your child will be under the constant supervision of the airline's ground and cabin staff. They will provide assistance to children from the point of departure to their final destination. With this service you can rest assured that your child will receive special care and attention throughout the journey, even in the event of delays. When a child is traveling alone, you must purchase an adult fare when using the airline's unaccompanied minor program. There is usually a fee associated with purchasing an unaccompanied minor ticket. Fees are usually about $100 one way.

Some points to keep in mind if you're considering sending a child abroad as an unaccompanied minor:

- Guidelines for children flying alone vary from one airline to the next. Check your carrier for its specific policies.
- Make sure that your child is mature enough to travel alone and is prepared to undertake this adventure.
- Those between the ages of five and seven can only fly on direct flights with no changes of planes.
- An unaccompanied minor should not be booked on the last flight of the day. This is to prevent the need for an overnight stay in a hotel if the flight is delayed.
- Children need the same documentation as adults. This includes passports, visas, or other official paperwork. You may wish to contact

the consulate of the country being visited to determine whether there are any special requirements for children traveling alone.

- On the day of the flight, it is a good idea to confirm departure time before you leave for the airport.

- When you arrive at the airport, you will be required to complete an Unaccompanied Minor Request for Carriage form, which will remain with the child throughout the flight. This form includes the child's name, age, address, phone number, the name and contact information of a parent or guardian, the name of the person seeing the child off at departure and the name of the person meeting the child on arrival. It may also include information on the child's diet, medication, and language(s) spoken.

- Airlines provide children with some identification—buttons, badges, or around-the-neck lanyards with small hanging pouches—indicating that they are unaccompanied minors. Children should have this identification visible on the outside of their clothes throughout the trip.

- Should there be a flight delay, the airline will notify the adult in the originating city as well as the adult who is designated to meet the child.

- Prepare your child for what to expect on the flight. If this is the child's first time in the air, you may wish to visit the airport in advance. Children should know to whom they may direct questions and concerns. Children flying alone will be introduced to the flight attendant responsible for unaccompanied minors.

- Carry-on luggage should include things to keep the child entertained during the flight. Books, puzzles, simple craft projects, and possibly a DVD player as well as favorite snacks will help your child avoid becoming bored and restless.

- Airlines are not responsible for administering medication. If medication is required, be sure that your child can administer it on his or her own.

- The adult accompanying the child is required to remain at the airport until the plane takes off.

- The responsible adult who meets your child at the destination airport must show a government-issue identification and sign the Acceptance of Responsibility form.
- Airlines are committed to providing children with exciting and safe travel experiences. Under no circumstances will airline personnel turn a child over to a waiting adult without seeing definitive identification and matching that carefully to the information filled out on the pre-departure form.

Tips for Families Flying with Children

- Check with your airline to find out what services are provided for children.
- Smaller crowds mean less stress. If possible, try to book your flight Monday through Wednesday, preferably in the evening.
- In making reservations, ask to be seated next to your children so you can easily keep track of them. It's best if the adult sits on the aisle.
- If meals are served on the flight, ask for the special children's meal. In addition, pack children's favorite snacks.
- If your children are older than three or four, tell them what they may expect at the airport regarding security procedures, takeoff and landing, baggage check-in, and baggage claim. It is also helpful to tell them how they should behave in each situation. Try to generate excitement by telling them how much fun it will be.
- Two or three weeks in advance of the trip, post a countdown calendar on the refrigerator. This builds excitement and interest in the trip.
- Children who are old enough to carry a small backpack should be allowed to pack their own bag with adult supervision.
- Pack an entertainment kit for each child. Toys, puzzles, and books should be dispensed one at a time. Some suggestions: An MP3 player, plus music and audio book; Etch-a-sketch; coloring books; activity books; and blank drawing paper with pencils and crayons. Avoid toys with little pieces. Fetching little pieces that get lost is impractical on an airplane. Don't forget the child's favorite blanket or stuffed animal.

- Bring an umbrella stroller for your toddler and check it as you are getting on the plane. If you plan to bring a car seat on the plane, tell t agent when you are booking your flight.
- If you are traveling with an infant, reserve the bulkhead seats and ask for a baby bassinet.
- Both adults and children should dress for comfort on the flight. Don't forget to pack an extra set of clothes in case of an emergency and good-for-Grandma clothes in a carry-on. Airplanes are usually cold, so pick up extra blankets as you board.
- To a small child, an airport looks like an inviting playground that cries out for exploration. Children must be told that they are not to wander off alone or talk to strangers. If two adults are traveling with a child, one might take the child for a walk to see the sites.
- Talk your children through what you expect them to do if they become separated from you. Even if you don't ordinarily use a child tether, consider using one just in the airport. For safety purposes, attach a card with complete information on the child's shirt.
- Allow extra time at the airport. Everything takes longer when you have children with you.
- The rapid change in air pressure is hard on children's ears. Bring a pacifier or a bottle for an infant and chewing gum or snacks for older children.
- If you are traveling with multiple children, and need to take one to the bathroom, feel free to ask the airline attendant to keep an eye on the other(s).
- If your children are fussy on the flight, expend your energy on trying to make them more comfortable rather than worrying about what other people are thinking.

Jeanne Muchnick, former editor of *Baby Magazine,* says, "Planning ahead and expecting the unexpected are the golden rules of flying with kids." For more tips on flying with kids, search the following phrases on the Internet:

- Plane Sense Checklist
- Plane Tips with Babies
- Flying with Toddlers
- Flying with School-Age Children

Making Your Trip as Comfortable as Possible

Cunard Lines had a slogan: "Getting there is half the fun." That may be true for a cruise ship, but no airline would try to tell you that. Next to the cost, the discomfort of flying for many hours is a major obstacle for many people. Visiting family abroad is a highly anticipated event. Here are some tips to make the trip more comfortable.

Where You Sit

More than any other single factor, the quality of your seat will determine the quality of your trip. Choose and reserve your seats early. Even within the same class and fare, some seats are far superior to others. Consider an aisle or exit row seat for legroom, or a window if you want to sleep. To help you in choosing a seat, go to www.seatguru.com for a fully annotated chart of the seats on your aircraft.

- Choose a window seat if you're planning to sleep a lot. The extra room between the seat and the window allows you to rest your head on the window and to store small items.
- Choose an aisle seat for the convenience of leaving your seat easily. The aisle also provides a bit of extra room.
- Avoid middle seats, where you are often in contention with your seatmates for armrest territory. We consider this so important that my husband and I always opt for two aisle seats, rather than sitting side by side.
- Avoid the last row. The seats usually do not recline, so you would have to sit upright for the entire trip.

- Before making a seat selection, ask if the flight will have a section of "sleeper seats," where the lights are turned off most of the time in flight.
- As the aircraft fills up, watch for two or three adjacent seats. As soon as the flight attendant closes the hatch, jump for the middle seat of the three. Once airborne, you can flip up the armrests and perhaps even lie down. Even reserving two adjacent seats ensures that you won't be squished in.
- For the maximum legroom, request a seat in the emergency exit aisle. You and those accompanying you must be healthy adults capable of assisting others in case of an emergency.
- You may be tempted to request a bulkhead seat—the first row in your section of the cabin. There will be more legroom, but be aware, this is where mothers with tiny, squalling babies are seated, too. This is less likely if the bulkhead is right behind the first class cabin.
- If the airline has overbooked a flight, the attendants may ask for volunteers to be "bumped" to another flight. If your plans permit this, you can demand an upgrade to first class as your reward.

What You Eat

Some people fear flying; others just fear airline food. Here are some suggestions for upgrading the cuisine:

- Consider bringing supplemental food. A large sandwich from a delicatessen will likely trump the main course offered by the flight attendant. When the staff is not serving meals, you can ask them to warm yours in a microwave oven. Coffee, milk, beer, wine, or sodas purchased on board can round out the meal.
- Special diets can be ordered with your ticket: vegetarian, kosher, halal, etc. Provided by third-party vendors, these are often better than the standard fare. You don't have to eat this diet at home to order it on an airline.

- Carry a plastic bag of snacks, such as dried fruit, nuts, or popcorn, for each of your passengers. Seedless grapes are an excellent source of water as well. Pack them loose, not on the stem.

How You Spend Your Time

On a transcontinental flight, time is what you have too much of. Try not to think about it. Don't keep checking your watch. Don't keep staring at the flight map on the TV screen, showing how little progress has actually been made. This will only make the time pass more slowly.

By departing in the evening, you can sleep through much of the flight. Come prepared to entertain yourself and your family during the waking hours.

- Bring a book or a couple of magazines.
- Ask whether movies on demand will be available—a selection you can watch at your seat.
- Rent a DVD player and a movie in the airport. The onboard movie will likely not be one you want to watch, and it will have been edited for an audience of eight-year-olds.
- Bring your own headphones. Best choice: the noise-canceling kind, to shut out the background noise. You can sleep better with them on, and with an adaptor they can connect to the aircraft audio system.
- Bring your MP3 player if you have one, loaded with new music selections.

Take Care of Yourself

The interior of an airplane looks something like a car or a train; in fact, it is different in significant ways that can affect both your health and your comfort. In particular, the cabin air is extremely dry. Drawn from outside the plane, where the temperature is way below zero, the air is then heated to cabin temperature, leaving almost no relative humidity. This can affect your eyes, nose, and throat directly, and your body through dehydration. Don't let that happen. Here's how to avoid it:

- Bring a bottle of water, purchased after you pass through security, or fill a bottle from an airport water fountain. Do not drink unbottled airline water, especially from the restroom. If necessary, purchase bottled water or seltzer on the plane. Keep drinking.
- Carry lip balm, e.g., Chapstick, and use it on your nose as well. Apply it half an inch up your nose with a cotton swab. Or carry a saline nasal spray.
- Pack a travel-size bottle of skin lotion to prevent skin dryness.
- Carry eye drops in case your eyes suffer from dryness.
- Check out what you may bring on board at the TSA website, www.tsa.gov/travelers/airtravel/prohibited/permitted-prohibited-items.shtm.
- If the flight attendant brings a hot towel, just blot with it. Rubbing your face or hands with a hot cloth can painfully dry out your skin.
- Bring a toothbrush and toothpaste. It will help you freshen up after a long night. A Listerine Pocket Pack contains strips of gel that will both freshen and deodorize your mouth. Dental floss and an antiperspirant stick will also come in handy.
- A pack of WetOnes, moistened antibacterial towelettes, is like a bath in a bag.
- If you have a head cold or stuffy sinuses, bring a decongestant, such as Sudafed, to help relieve the pressure in your ears during ascent and descent. Special earplugs, called EarPlanes, are designed to slow the change in pressure to a more tolerable rate. If necessary, buy them on the Internet at, for example, www.drugstore.com.
- Often, you can equalize the pressure in your ears by pinching your nose and blowing into it or swallowing.
- Dress comfortably, and bring something warm to wear. Many experienced travelers wear sweat suits.
- Don't just sit there. Periodically, get up and walk the length of the plane. If you go to the toilet, use the opportunity to get your circulation going again by taking a hike. Find an open area, usually near the back, and do some stretching exercises and calisthenics.

- When you get to the toilet, double check to be sure there is enough toilet paper.
- If you have short legs, letting them hang from the seat will cause circulatory problems. Either rest your feet on your carry-on, or bring a folding foot rest, available from Magellan's (www.magellans.com) and www.amazon.com, as well as local stores like Target.
- Armrests can also restrict circulation. Ask for a pillow, place it on your lap and rest your arms on it.
- If you tend to get a little airsick, drink a bottle of ginger ale before boarding.

Get Some Sleep

As noted, your best bet is to sleep as much as you can. Here are some suggestions:

- Bring earplugs, an eyeshade, and either a filled or inflatable neck pillow. If you forget the earplugs, use tissue.
- A NadaChair S'portBacker is a harness that allows you to sleep while sitting up (www.nadachair.com). It folds into a small packet, and has many other uses.

Fight Jet Lag

Jet lag occurs because you have an internal clock set to your local time. It knows when it's time to go to bed and when it's time to get up. But if you fly from New York to London, your clock is still on New York time when you arrive. After a few days, your clock resets to London time—just in time to cause jet lag on your return. Some strategies for overcoming jet lag:

- Get a good night's sleep just prior to departure.
- When you get on the plane, immediately set your watch to the time at your destination. Start living on that timetable.
- Take No-Jet-Lag pills, available from Magellan's and other travel stores.

- The most powerful factor in resetting your internal clock is light. When you arrive at your destination, try to get a few hours of strong daylight, especially if this would be nighttime at home.

Organize What You Need

Flying requires juggling a large number of items in a small space. Organization is the key to success.

- Put everything you won't need on the flight into your luggage.
- Place a photocopy of your main passport page into every piece of luggage and carry-on bag. If your passport is lost, it will be much easier to straighten out if you have a copy, and easier to retrieve misplaced luggage.
- Pack only one carry-on bag, or two if traveling with children. It's much easier to maneuver and stow a backpack than a bag with a frame and wheels.
- Pack a cloth tote bag in your carry-on. If security personnel decide you'll have to check your carry-on, you will be able to bring absolutely essential items with you in the bag.
- Inside your carry-on, use zipped freezer bags to pack items according to when and where they will be needed:
  - An in-seat hygiene bag: Everything you'll need to stay clean and healthy.
  - An in-seat comfort bag: Everything needed to be comfortable.
  - An in-seat snack bag—one for each child.
  - An in-flight toilet bag: Everything to freshen up in the lavatory. Include several feet of toilet paper, rolled up in a small plastic bag.
- On your person, or in an outer pocket of your carry-on bag, keep an accordion-type document wallet with your passport, ticket, boarding pass, and other travel documents.

Creating a Visit Memory Book

When you see grandchildren only once a year, there is a desperate need to make the experience stretch beyond the few weeks of the actual visit. A simple scrapbook, assembled manually, with photographs and some text can serve as a memory book. For those who are computer literate, a more streamlined volume can be created. So that all generations can continue to enjoy the memory book, two copies should be compiled—one for the grandchildren and their parents, and one for the grandparents. Don't forget to include the date! As the years pass, this becomes increasingly important.

In Chaper 3, "Grandparenting at a Distance," I talked about two books I had created following visits with our first grandson, Amichai, when he was a toddler. A third book was created during a visit with our ten-year-old grandson, Binyamin, who authored the text of *Binyamin in Boca*. A fourth book was compiled the following summer when Yakir, age nine, came to visit, along with Binyamin. It was decided in advance that this would primarily record Yakir's experiences in his own words and would be called *Yakir Is Here.* Binyamin agreed to serve as "chief photographer." Each evening during the two-week visit, Yakir and I sat at the computer and recorded what had transpired during the day as well as his thoughts and impressions. Children who have graphic skills might add a few sketches as well.

The person responsible for photography should carry a pocket camera at all times. Images should include:

People: You capture the true flavor of an activity if you take sequence shots of people engaged in that activity. For example when you meet your grandchildren at the airport you might consider the following sequence:

- A shot of the children with the flight attendant responsible for their care during the trip, if they traveling as unaccompanied minors

- Children hugging and kissing relatives. If you are meeting children alone, ask someone at the airport to take the picture
- Picking up luggage at the carousel

Places: Children will want to share with family and friends memories of sightseeing outings and shopping trips. For example, it is a good idea to take one image of the store, museum, park or movie house you are visiting with the sign clearly in sight. This could then be followed by several activity shots and conclude with an image of the snack they had at the end of the trip.

Objects: Be on the lookout for objects your visitors have never seen before. For example, our grandchildren had never eaten corn on the cob with plastic corn holders plugged into the ends. The kids were delighted with this, so we photographed it for one of the books. You may also include pictures of foods you cooked that they especially enjoyed.

What makes *Binyamin in Boca* and *Yakir Is Here* more than a diary is the photographs and features that appear in "regular" books, such as a title page, the title printed on the spine of the book, a dedication page, and a credits page. On the back page of each book, you can insert one or two testimonials and information about the book and the author.

These twenty-eight-page books were created entirely on the computer and then assembled in one-inch three-ring binders, with each page inserted in a protective sleeve. All four books are assembled in the same manner so that they appear as a series. It usually takes several weeks following the visit to compile the book. We either mail the book or wait until some member of the family visits, and send it back with him or her. There is huge excitement on the part of the entire family on both sides of the ocean when the volume finally arrives.

These books have kept precious visits alive for us as grandparents as well as for our children and grandchildren who live an ocean apart.